Circus of Shadows

Esta Barton

Contents

Prologue

The heat from the spot light seared my skin, though it was set up on the ground at least thirty feet below where I hung upside down from my knees on the swaying swing. The trapeze act came just as naturally to me as my own acrobatic and contortionist acts, which boded well- extremely well- for Ellie, who normally took to the high flying swings and tightrope I would be adding to my performance set that night. Angry with her fire eating lover, she'd taken to the bottle without a care in the world for the duty she held to the show, and for the third time that summer, I'd been assigned her part as well as my own.

"Ladies and gentlemen!" Robbie cried from the center ring to my left, his black velvet top hat and sequined red coat catching every stray beam of light that bounced around under the big tent, and sending them flying off in every direction as he paced before the crowd with perfected, exaggerated movements, "If you'll direct your attention to our furthest ring, you'll see our magnificent! Wonderful! Outstanding! AMAZING! KATE the GREAT swing from a terrifying height- with no safety net- and fly through the air as if she had her own set of beautiful feathered wings! Please, bring a thunderous round of applause! For the BEST performance you'll see of such an otherworldly and beautiful routine! I present to you, as is my greatest honor! KATE THE GREAT!"

I didn't look to the crowd that screamed and cheered my name in an excited and deafening burst of clapping hands and stomping feet. Instead, my gaze focused solely on the tight, taut fabric of the ceiling on the big top. The air rushed through the few shorter strands of my hair that had escaped the severe bun I had gathered my dishwater colored locks into at the beginning of the night, causing them to whip against my cheeks as I moved, still upside down, high the air. In one smooth, fluid moment, I grasped the bar attached to the ropes and dropped my legs out into the splits before using that momentum to swing back up into the seat.

That tiny move, which was really only a basic maneuver, caused yet another wave of applause, and I couldn't help but feel somewhat cynical. These people weren't really excited. They were all caught up in the magic and the grandeur that Robbie had created throughout the night, pumping them up and raising their expectations to near ethereal heights so than any tiny movement swelled the happiness inside them so much, they nearly burst from it. It didn't matter that I was just another human who had trained for countless hours, putting my body to it's most insane limits to be able to perform. To them, I was an otherworldly creature born with this amazing ability; a freak for their entertainment.

Just as Robbie wanted it to be.

With a deep, shuddering breath, I banished the demeaning thoughts, shoving them over the stone and mortar wall I'd built in my mind for the things and ideas I didn't want escaping. I had no time to dwell on any of it. My own act- or rather, Ellie's act- waited for me.

I only barely caught sight of my ringmaster's wide, Cheshire Cat grin before I dropped down from the bar completely, catching my swinging body with just one hand on the smooth wooden bar, the momentum of the flying swing jarring my body for the briefest moment. With all the instinct of a seasoned circus performer, I allowed my muscles to mold themselves into the movement, gaining more and more force as I hung on, knowing that to fall would be to die.

The crowd gasped collectively, echoing my thoughts in an almost comical manner.

I grasped the bar again with my other hand and twisted myself around to face the center ring. Gregory, Ellie's partner, watched me with cold cerulean eyes as I swung through the air, his black hair swishing against itself from his own upside down perch on the swing opposite me. Were it not for the sake of the performance itself, I had no doubts he would let me fall, if only to see my eyes widen in fear before I ceased to exist. Luckily for me, the act meant everything to them. More than even my torture would mean.

The drum roll began just as I hit the peak of my backward swing, the top of my head nearly brushing the faded yellow and red fabric of the tent ceiling. The anticipation was nearly tangible as each member of the audience shifted forward in their seat, entranced by the elaborate show.

Gregory and I both locked gazes as we flew through the air, his arms outstretched as I came rushing forward.

The timing isn't right for this one, I whispered to myself inside my head, as the swing reached its opposite peak and dropped into the back swing again, the spotlight coupled with the sticky summer air feeling as though it would boil me alive.

Three more swings, with the drum roll growing louder and quicker with each height peak the swing hit, and the fates finally gave me my opportunity. An eerie quiet nearly suffocated the entire mammoth of a tent as my fingers left behind their grasp on the now naked bar. With a hint of my own amusement, I took the time to flick the smooth wood with middle finger, relishing the feeling of pure adrenaline and weightlessness as I hung, suspended, in the air.

Time slowed to a near stand still while I maneuvered my body into the forceful momentum my jump had gifted me. The rust colored sand of the ground flooded my vision as my body flipped upside down, my legs snapped open in a vertical split and my arms straight above my head.

Or maybe they were straight below my head, because of the mid-air flip. Funny how I managed time to ponder such a thought as I careened through the open air, liberated and powerful.

Powerful.

Robbie stood below me, turning to watch my flight as I got closer to ending my upside down journey toward Gregory's grip. His midnight colored top hat slid back on his head, revealing his equally dark hair that matched the masculine stubble peppering his jawline. Even his mouth was slightly open with awe, though he had been the one to train me for so many years.

This is where I have control. This is where no one can touch me. I am powerful here. I am the only one with any say here.

A child-like giggle burst from my throat, escaping my lips before I could stop it. I felt a startling, solid crack in my mental wall that served as protection from all the evil things in the world.

No.

With a forceful shake of my head, I brought myself back from that dangerous perch of insanity and chastised myself for allowing it to happen. Letting my guard down was bad. Dangerous.

Gregory's strong, giant hands gripped mine hard, shattering any semblance of madness that could have possibly escaped through the crack in the wall I had been weak enough to let appear. My chest rumbled with the impossibly loud roar of the crowd as the entire tent shook with their enthusiasm. With his hands gripping my wrist, I fell back into normalcy, away from the frightening freedom flying through the air had given me. With that freedom came the hope of Power, and Power only destroyed everything around me, acting like my own personal savior, though I knew she was dangerous and wrong.

"And, there we have it, folks! The amazing KATE the GREAT!" Robbie cried out below us as Gregory brought us back to the tall podium, from which I would climb down and begin signing autographs and chatting with bright and happy members of the audience. Something I had absolutely no interest in doing, but that Robbie had required of all his performers.

After all, we were magic and wonder, and what the crowd wanted was to get just a touch of that. To go home feeling excited and joyous, brimming with awe at our amazing feats. The closer they could get to us, the happier they were.

Except, if any of them knew about how close they'd been to being witnesses of something incoherently horrible, I had no doubts they would have only wanted to run as far away as possible, never looking back, lest the madness behind the magic catch up with them as well.

Chapter 1

"So, you don't remember killing Robert Jensen?"

"No." Lie.

"Were you under any undue stress last month?"

"No." Another lie.

"Do you remember killing any of your other co-performers?"

"No." A third lie.

Dr. Shilling sat back in his chair, appraising me with a careful eye. I couldn't blame his doubt, really. At five feet, two inches and with the lithe and petite body of a wood nymph, it was hard for me to believe I'd been capable of taking out an entire cast of circus members as well as their ringmaster in one night. Though, I suppose I should have known it wasn't really me, but the madness-Power- that had taken over and done it. Otherwise I wouldn't have been sentenced to life in a home for the criminally insane. The jury couldn't bear to put such a timid, shy creature such as myself in a dirty jail cell with burly men who might hurt me. The fifties had brought more and more gangs to rise up and get arrested because of the end of the war. I wouldn't stand a chance, despite the horrendous mass murder I'd committed just a month before.

The good doctor heaved a great, weighted sigh and bounced his pen against his clipboard, producing a rather irritating tap, tap, tapping sound that had my foot twitching in growing aggravation.

"Katherine, you're going to be here for a long time, so I'm not going to put any pressure on you. But, the sooner we can tap-"

Tap, tap, tap... Tap!

A giggle fell from my lips, to my horror.

"-into what caused this to happen, the sooner you can get better. Maybe we can even get you out on parole so that you can find a nice husband and put this all behind you."

He had no idea that he should have been worried about the errant laughter I'd burst out with, no matter how short and chopped off it had been. Girls giggled all the time. And, as a psychiatric doctor over an entire section of wards in Rosenton Home for the Criminally Insane, he was more than likely used to out of place actions produced by inmates- or rather, residents, as they preferred to call us.

"I don't want to put it behind me," I whispered, fighting the slow crack in my mental wall from proceeding any further with every ounce of self control I had in me.

Dr. Shilling raised a thick, brown eyebrow at that, his wrinkled mouth forming a straight line across his face. My left eye twitched against my will as I fought off the smile pressing its way into my mouth. Knuckles white, my fingers gripped the arms of the plush, velvet chair I sat in as my eyes trained themselves obsessively on the burlap sack of apples the doctor kept next to his desk.

The rough texture of the sack brushed over my nose as I moved, leaving the very tip of it a little raw while I slipped soundlessly through Ellie and Fredrick's window. My breath came out smooth and confident, crashing against the burlap bag over my head and bouncing back against my chin and cheeks. I could still smell the peaches I'd emptied out of the sack before taking it.

"Are you hungry? Would you like an apple?" the doctor asked, following my hard gaze. He was testing me and it had Power scoffing at his lame attempt to sound nonchalant. Dr. Shilling knew I didn't care about the apples. Just the bag.

I glared up at him, struggling against Power. Had he put the bag there on purpose? To see my madness first hand? Did he not have a lick of sense? I'd murdered an entire fleet of circus performers in one night. He was just one man. A middle aged, thin, wisp of a man with overly thick eyebrows and large, round, gold framed glasses.

We can take him.

No! He hasn't hurt me. He has done nothing!

He's testing us.

Movement in the window behind his salt and pepper hair caught my eye, but I had no time to study it before he was speaking again, snapping my attention back to him.

"What do you mean, you don't want to put it behind you?" he asked, golden, engraved pen poised to write as he watched me.

I shook my head, hoping to dislodge my insanity somehow so I could focus. That cursed burlap sack just sat there in the corner of my vision, calling to me and taunting me at the same time. My hands curled up into trembling fists.

"I did something horrible. I don't have the right to put it behind me," I stammered with a shake in my voice, slamming my eyes shut to rid myself of the offending sight.

"You did something bad because you're ill, not because you're a bad person. It wasn't your fault. You didn't exactly have a stable environment to thrive in," he replied with far too much ease, excusing my actions as if their lives had meant nothing. As if the fact that I was even capable of mass murder was acceptable and excusable. My stomach turned at his words, making bitter bile shoot up my throat.

"Don't you worry, Ms. Thornton. I know you feel badly and you're having a hard time, but we'll get you fixed up and back to a normal life," he assured me, his voice light and what I supposed was meant to be encouraging.

Unable to form words for fear that another giggle would fly out, furthering the crack in my mind, I nodded sharply, doing whatever I needed to do to just get out of there. The need to escape overpowered everything else in my mind, and my foot vibrated up and down on the tiled floor, itching to run.

"Our time's up for today. Every Tuesday, alright? Three o'clock. You'll have group therapy twice a week also. An orderly will give you the schedule for that."

Again, my head bobbed up and down, refusing to open my eyes until I was able to leave and escape the sight of that stupid burlap sack.

The good doctor excused me, and I shot out of my seat like a bat out of hell. I'd seen bullets eject from guns slower than it took me to leap from that velvet chair and slam the door closed behind me.

I leaned against the wooden door, my grey eyes trained on the ceiling as I steadied my breathing. The corner of my lips twitched up, begging to grin and let Power take control. The fact that a simple item could trigger her appearance terrified me. Before, it had always been being beaten and attacked that spurred her on and had her itching to crash through my mental wall. She offered justice and salvation, always cooing in my ear that I deserved retribution, and that no one would mess with me if I let her out. Now, the very mention of the word, 'burlap' seemed to get her into an excited frenzy, reminding her of the freedom she'd been given for one night and making her ache for more.

I really am insane, I thought with a certain sense of despair crawling around my brain, frowning as my body vibrated with trembles.

"He's a real jerk, that one."

The surprise of another deep and drawling voice was just enough to let Power get a single giggle through. Cursing my own weakened mind, I clamped my mouth shut and swung my eyes up to the owner of the rich southern accent.

"I don't know what he plays at, but he does everything he can to set us all off. Seems to enjoy it. Sicko," the very tall, muscled man in front of me continued, offering me a small, sympathetic smile with pearly white teeth and warm, hot chocolate brown eyes. I couldn't help but stare, not because he was incredibly handsome (which he undoubtedly was), but because at first glance he didn't seem to belong in this horrible place. In fact, his presence was so strange to me that I risked a glance down to see if he wore an orderlies white uniform, but he didn't. Just a pair of clearly faded and worn jeans and a red flannel button up with a white shirt underneath.

Clean, white socks were all that adorned his feet, which sealed it in. This perfectly normal looking man was a resident here, just like me. I wiggled my own socked toes and looked back up at his face.

"First day?" he asked, his chocolate eyes gleaming absolute comfort. One large, tanned hand reached up and pushed his long sand colored hair out of his eyes, his genuine smile still holding up on his sharply angled face.

Still not trusting that I had Power under control and afraid to speak just yet, I nodded.

"Well, you're here on a Tuesday, so that makes you Ward F, right?" he asked, shoving his hands in his pockets and leaning back up against the wall beside me.

He's so... normal. Maybe he's almost done here. Maybe they can fix me like that. Maybe I'll be, or at least seem, normal like him one day.

I granted him another nod in answer to his question, entranced by his entire demeanor. How was he so... easygoing? It was as if he belonged here, like an angel sent for the sole purpose of giving out friendly smiles to all the scared little residents like me.

The amicable smile gracing his olive toned face widened just a bit, enough to show he was pleased. "Good. I'm Ward F, too. You'll probably be roommates with Esther. Hers just got released last week and she's been on the orderlies case like a tick on a dog for a new one. She can't stand to be alone for more than a few minutes without going crazy."

I was all but required to raise an eyebrow at his choice of words, to which he chuckled. He glanced up at a young man walking by with dark circles under his eyes despite his cheery stride and raised his hand in a small wave of familiar acknowledgment. All I could do was stare and imagine a stalk of wheat sticking out from the corner of his smiling mouth. Everything about him screamed, 'farm boy!', from his golden tan, to his hard muscles, to the deep southern drawl his music-like voice held, to the stereotypical red flannel shirt. I'd never tried my hand at reading people, but I would have put the risk of shaving my head bald if I was wrong on the line about it.

"Not, 'what we're all here for' crazy," he assured me with a humored grin after the other resident had passed by. "Just, 'starts warting everyone in a five mile radius to entertain her' crazy."

"Thank you for clarifying," I replied with my own hesitant smile, risking giving Power a sliver of hope to talk to him. I sent up a silent prayer of thanks when she remained silent.

A sudden light danced in his eyes and his posture perked up a bit. "So, you do speak."

Heat flushed my cheeks and I looked away, never having liked being teased.

"I didn't know, is all. We have some like that, you know? Who don't speak," he tried to explain in an attempt to rectify the situation. "I'm glad you do. Conversation's a big time passer around here."

That only served to send more liquid lava to my face. "Th-thanks? I do speak, but I'm afraid I'm not a great conversationalist."

Well, aside from the mindless chatter and praises audience members rang with after each show. I'd become an expert at putting on for that. But, normal, everyday conversation? I wasn't even sure I'd ever had one, to be honest. Being the other performers' scapegoat had ensured a life of solitude, so the skill hadn't exactly been honed.

"That's alright. I'm John, by the way. John Kingwood," he replied with ease, extending his large hand out to me for a handshake. I sneaked another glance up to his face and was rewarded with yet another warm smile that all but welcomed me into the family. I wiped my palm on my skirt and placed my hand in his as he shook heartily, nearly making me stumble.

"Kate the Gr-" I stopped, shaking my head at my stupidity.

He's not here after a show. Get it together, Kate. You no longer even have a show.

"Kate Thornton," I corrected myself, offering him an apologetic look for the awkward slip up. He didn't seem fazed at all, just grinning at me like an old friend.

"Nice to meet you. We'll see a lot of each other, being in the same Ward and all. Want me to introduce you to the others?"

Are they as scary as me?

I ignored Power's sarcastic quip and nodded my head. "Sure."

Meeting the other 'residents' in my Ward left me dizzy and my memory spotty. There were five others, but they'd each been so vastly different and incredibly welcoming that I had to wonder if I'd been sent to the right establishment. These people couldn't be criminally insane. They were too... nice.

"Okay, Kate, we have to do it! Everyone knows it about everyone else here. What'd you do?" a bubbly girl who I was fairly certain had told me her name was Marcie gushed, her small hands gripping my upper arm as she bounced up and down.

My heart sank in my chest like an old gangster had tied a cinder block to it and thrown it in the Hudson River.

"You don't have to answer that if you don't want to. Ed and Lottie never did, and it's perfectly okay," John piped up from somewhere over my shoulder. He'd been surprisingly quiet throughout the whole welcome committee ordeal since everyone had basically flocked to my side as soon as I'd stepped through the heavy double doors and introduced themselves. I'd even somehow gotten Marcie's pant size by the time I'd been allowed to sit down on one of the scratchy orange armchairs surrounding the old radio in a semi-circle.

"It's alright," I replied, turning my head to offer a small smile. I'd have to give them something or they'd get too curious and push for me to tell them more anyway. A watered down version would have to do, especially since I didn't want them to think badly of me. "I'm here because I'm... ah... I'm prone to violence under certain circumstances."

Each word came out precise and calculated, and I took the opportunity to steal fleeting glances over each of their faces from where they sat and stood, scattered over Ward F's lounge room.

"Is that all? Oh, you'll be out of here within a week, I bet," Marcie whined, sounding entirely too displeased with the situation. My eyes averted from her face, uncomfortable with the omission of truth, but deeming it necessary.

"You don't have to worry about that. I'll definitely be here a while," I assured her, trailing off a bit at the end, hoping I hadn't piqued too much interest.

"Good! My room mates always get shipped off too soon, and I'm here for life, so I'm looking forward to it."

I spun around to see the owner of the new, overly confident voice. An older woman, most likely in her fifties, stood proudly in the doorway, long arms perched against her hands on her curvy hips, bust pushed out blatantly against the deep V she had cut into her blouse. She studied me for a moment before breaking out in a wide grin and striding toward me with her hand outstretched for a handshake. "I'm Esther. You must be Kate. Welcome to Rosenton Home for the Criminally Insane. What'd you do?"

"Esther," John warned in a quiet voice from behind us. She barely spared him a look before turning back to me with an expression that clearly stated she expected an answer.

"Prone to violence," I repeated with meekness, shaking her hand and taking an unsteady step back. Leaving the room with the burlap sack in sight had calmed Power down considerably, but Esther's air of confrontation had her on edge, ready to beg to be let free again.

No. Don't even think about it.

She could hurt you.

She's not.

She could.

Choosing the path of least resistance by blatantly ignoring Power altogether since she was weak, I looked back at the Hispanic beauty in front of me.

"What about you? You said you're in here for a while?"

Her ruby red lips spread into a smile as her eyes glazed over, almost as if she were looking back on a fond memory. "Murder. Found my husband of thirty years in bed with another woman. Killed them both. Still don't regret it," she beamed, and I couldn't help the way my eyes widened at her blatant and positive attitude toward what she'd told me. Although, I had to admit, knowing I wasn't the only murderer in my ward gave me the tiniest bit of relief.

"Esther, that's enough for now," John's deep voice commanded. Her dark, almost black, eyes rolled, but she obeyed and didn't elaborate, choosing instead to drape herself down in the chair closest to her, looking every bit like an old 20's film star in a plush photo shoot.

"Honey, we're all prone to violence here. That's why we're criminally insane. What did you do?" she asked again, rolling to look at me, her face upside down on the arm of the chair. For a split second, I saw Gregory, swinging upside down on the trapeze toward me, reaching out to grab me mid-air as I flew toward him from my own swing.

But, no, it wasn't a memory. Her face...

Esther's face!

I could do nothing but watch, my jaw slack and shaking, as her beautiful features morphed into Gregory's. Her black eyes turning bright blue and her long hair shrinking to the short length his had been. My heart slammed itself against my sternum like it wanted to jump out and run away, and that wall...

That stupid wall!

Craaaaaack!

"No!"

My eyes wouldn't- couldn't- tear away from Gregory's face as he watched me, anger written across his features as a thin red line drew itself out across his exposed neck.

"No!"

Scarlet, thick, liquid oozed from the line, dripping down- or was it up?- his neck until it reached his chin, where it pooled until it could hold no more, spilling over onto his cheeks and up- or down?- into his eyes and hair line. I couldn't escape his glare as he grimaced at me.

Or maybe it was a smile since it was upside down. Perhaps he was happy I was caught. Happy I was here, as a prisoner. Happy he could reappear and terrify me, even after he died by my own hand.

Let me take care of it. He shouldn't be here, scaring you like this. Let me take care of him, Power hissed in my ear. I felt her hot breath on my neck, and dozens of arms on my body, pressing me down, down, down.

"No!"

"Kate, you've got to hush. You can't do this here. Come on. Come back, now. You can't let them see you like this," another voice whispered in my other ear with urgency, though not nearly as loud as Power's voice.

"What the heck? John, do something!" Another voice.

Come on, Sane... Please? He's there, already dead. Just let me make sure he's gone forever. I'll protect you.

"What's going on? Is she giggling?"

Gregory glared still as his mouth twisted into a sadistic grin, the edges reaching the lobes of his ears as teeth- many more teeth than any human should have, glistened pink with his own smeared blood at me.

"She's fine. She's fine! She was with Shilling before this. Something's probably been triggered or something."

See? He's scaring you, Sane. Just like he and all of them used to do for fun. Let me break the wall. I'll make sure he can't hurt you anymore.

"Should I go get an orderly?"

Gregory's eyes rolled up, the still flowing blood dripping into the whites, staining them just as red as the rest of him. His body swung too close to me on the trapeze, waiting for me to grab his arms. Instinctively, my hands jerked back to my chest, tears running down my face as I put my all into focusing on closing the crack in the wall.

"No! They'll keep an extra tight eye on her."

Don't shut me back in, Sane! I'm the only one who can help you! Don't trap me back in there! Don't you do it, you little moron!

"What do we do?! Make her stop laughing!"

I squeezed my eyes shut, pulling stone after stone from the wreckage of the cracked wall in my mind and trying, with all I had, to repair it.

"Just shut up and go get some water! Walk, don't run! Don't pull any attention to yourself!"

No, Sane! Don't you do this to me!

"I'll go make a distraction in the dorms. I'll buy as much time as I can."

Stones rubbing against stones. Grinding against themselves as they push each other to fit, like puzzle pieces, to repair the wall.

"No, wait! She's coming to! Keep an eye out for any orderlies. She's coming to..."

NOOOOOOO!

Oxygen flooded my lungs, painful and full to bursting as my body shot forward, nearly colliding with another head. Deep, gasping breaths struggled to consume the air around me, making choking sounds as my throat fought for it. The way my cheeks and lips ached from prolonged strain didn't escape my attention, but I chose to ignore it in favor of stabilizing myself instead.

"Kate! Kate, you're good now! But you can't do that here!" John whispered in front of me, his warm eyes wide with fear as his hands grasped my shoulders with a firm touch, forcing me to look at him. "You can't have episodes like that here! They'll-"

"They're coming down the hall! Get her in a chair and turn on the radio!" Lottie stage whispered from the doorway, her youthful green eyes flicking from me and back to the hallway she stood guard at.

John cursed under his breath and hooked his elbows under my arms, hauling me up and into the nearest chair as if I weighed nothing. George leapt for the radio and turned it on, filling the room with the excited sounds of a radio show about a lone cowboy in a gunfight. Loud, jarring, popping sounds echoed around the small room, bouncing off the walls and into my ear over and over as the gunfight went on and on, the lone cowboy calling for his friend to take cover.

"I need you to listen to me, Katie. You need to lay your face down into your arms and pretend to be asleep. If they see you like this, it'll be bad, okay?" John instructed in my ear with conviction, folding my arms on top of the arm of the chair for me. "Do you understand? You have to hide your face. Pretend you're asleep."

Swallowing the lump in my throat as the realization that I was in trouble washed over me, I dropped my head into my arms and became as still as I could, forcing my breathing to slow down to a steady pace, causing my lungs to cry out in protest.

"Everything alright in here, guys? How's the new resident fitting in?" The casual, overly bright voice appeared frighteningly soon after my head dropped down, making me fear they'd seen... whatever it was John hadn't wanted them to see.

"She's great. Tuckered out after the big first day. I'll escort her to her room before lights out," he answered, his tone light and cordial despite having just used so much urgency in his voice when he spoke to me only seconds before. My heart rammed against my chest, feeling angry and confused.

"Thanks, John. Glad she's doing well. Stop her by the station for her medicine, too. Hers is important."

"No problem. See you in a bit."

My breathing sounded thunderously loud in my ears as I remained still while their footsteps shuffled past us and down another hallway, until they disappeared altogether.

A hand fell on my shoulder, spreading warmth and comfort throughout my shaking form with its weight. "They're gone. You're okay now."

I pushed myself up on shaky arms, feeling the wetness of my salty tears all over my cheeks. The pounding in my chest made my entire torso ache as my lip trembled beneath the hold my teeth held on it. The scent of copper sprang to my nostrils at the same time my tongue tasted the blood my lip had produced from biting down too hard.

John sat, crouched down, in front of me, holding my gaze hostage with his warm, earthy eyes. He took both my hands in his, rubbing small circles on the little spot between my thumbs and pointer fingers. "You're okay, alright? You're fine. But you can't have episodes like that, okay? You've gotta keep it together, Katie," he implored, nearly begging me as he spoke softly.

For a moment, red hot anger encompassed me. Did he think I wanted to be crazy? That I wanted Power to take control of me so easily? I didn't choose madness or insanity!

But, then, another look at his grim expression and the obvious worried looks the rest of the lot were giving me, and I realized there was something deeper at stake. Something no one had told me, and something sinister, judging by the urgent pleading expressions their faces held. Even Esther's brow furrowed in deep concern from where she hovered over me, smoothing my hair from my face and flicking the tears from my cheeks as they fell.

Like my heart had done only minutes before, my stomach began to sink. Only this time the descent was slow and filled with lead, producing a lingering nauseous feeling in its wake.

As my ward-mates stood around me in a semicircle, watching me as if I'd disappear into thin air at any moment, a familiar phrase flitted into my tired and overly tensed mind while I took long, shuddering breaths, doing all I could to calm myself.

Out of the frying pan. Into the fire.

Chapter 2

"So, that's all you need to know, honey. John keeps everyone in our Ward basically stable and sane, so you can let your guard down a bit with us lot, but be careful around the other wards. A petite little thing like you would be just snapped in half if one of them gotcha," Esther babbled, brushing the curls out of her long, black hair from her seat at the small desk-turned-makeshift-vanity in the corner of our shared dorm. Her dark eyes shifted to meet mine through the mirror propped up against the wall on top of the painted metal surface. Neat little rows of various lipsticks, rouges, hair sprays, and other assorted cosmetics lined either side of the reflective plate.

It was so painfully normal.

"John keeps everyone stable? Isn't he a patient, himself?" I asked, knowing she caught the trepidation in my tone when her eyes narrowed after I spoke.

"Oh, don't get me wrong, honey. He's got his own host of issues. They're not any prettier than the little scene you gave us back there. But, he has a way with others, like me and you. Those doctors and orderlies might as well put him on the payroll for all the good he does with our ward that they all have nothing to do with. You know Marcie was in solitary for three years for trying to off herself so many times before John got admitted here? The girl hasn't even shown a hint of violence since. I expect she'll be released a lot sooner than they originally planned."

Even I saw my eyes widen in shock in the mirror as Esther went about using a small rag with lotion to remove the thick layer of makeup she wore. As she cleaned away the cosmetics with steady, practiced hands, her true age began to show. Thin wrinkles revealed themselves alongside the dark circles beneath her eyes. Small crows feet crinkled at the corners of her waterline. All expertly hidden behind layer after layer of expensive makeup.

Looking at her reminded me somewhat of a side show. Robbie's extravagant voice filled my head, crying to the audience, 'Come see the AMAZING woman with no age! Touch her beautiful skin! Feel her silky youthful hair! No one will be able to believe that she's a spry FIFTY-FOUR YEARS OLD!'

"You should get some rest. If you pretend to be asleep before the orderlies get to our dorm, they'll most likely sign off that you got your meds without giving them to you," she told me, her entire body shifting and softening with a sympathetic warmth in her eyes as she smiled at me, her aged face sad for some reason.

My head cocked to the side in confusion. "Shouldn't I take my meds? I'm here because I'm crazy and need to be fixed, right?"

I found that the only time I heard any hint of a Mexican accent in her voice was when she laughed, which she did whole heartedly as she swiveled in the rolling chair to face me. "Oh, honey. It's better to be crazy than to become a mindless drone. With as tiny as you are, sweetheart, you'd be a zombie for days!"

My eyebrows furrowed, not quite following anything she was talking about anymore. When I didn't join her laughter or even smile in acknowledgment, she paused and gave me a hard, but concerned look, crossing her arms over her ample chest. "You don't really think they'll fix you, do you? We're all just dumped here so we're not out there with the rest of society, shooting them up like we did before. They don't want to help us or fix us here. They just want us out of the way. The meds just make you easier for them to deal with and command around. That's all," she told me in a hushed, but soothing voice. My small bed sank down as she moved to sit beside me, taking my small pale hands into her larger tanned ones.

"But, Dr. Shilling said-"

"Dr. Shilling is the worst one of them all. Nobody in this ward is ever quite right after seeing him on Tuesdays. The only reason we're all our normal, chipper selves today is because he was out going to get you and our sessions were all skipped for it. Tuesdays around here are just our own personal funerals of ourselves. It's usually John who pulls us all out of it," she interrupted, her hands tightening around mine, as if to stress the importance of her words.

I could do nothing but stare into her dark eyes as her words began to sink in. I wouldn't be getting help here. Instead, I'd been dumped in the equivalent of a human waste bin, to be stored and forgotten. Panic began to set in, my breathing hitching as I gasped for air.

It couldn't be true. Esther had to be paranoid. It was an entirely plausible scenario. We were in an asylum, after all.

"No, no, honey, don't get upset. You'll get used to it. There's nothing to be upset about, so just calm down. You needed to know this, okay? It wouldn't be fair to let you think anything other than the truth, yeah? Don't cry, honey," Esther cooed, wiping my tears with her thumbs as she pulled me into an embrace that felt as if she thought I'd break with much more pressure. "Our ward's like a family, honey. Even if you're here forever, like me, we always take care of each other. That's why we couldn't let the orderlies see your episode earlier. You're one of our own now, and we take care of our own."

Her soft words did little to comfort me while I sobbed against the white cotton of her nightgown. Her gentle hands rubbed small circles on my back as she whispered encouragements in my ear, repeating over and over that everything would be okay.

But how could it be okay? I'd come here with hope that Power could be defeated. That my stone wall would be reinforced with steel or some other unbreakable material so I could live normally, without fear of doing what I did to my fellow performers ever again.

And Esther was sitting here, telling me it would never happen. I'd live like this, in Rosenton Home for the Criminally Insane, for the rest of my life, constantly battling Power's never ending attack on my willpower and my sanity.

The thought only brought on a whole new barrage of tears as I fell into a black hole inside myself, spiraling down into the darkness with no chance of ever being redeemed.

I can get us out, you know. I can save you from this place and the hopelessness. We can go on the road, find a new act to join. I promise I'll be good as long as no one tries to hurt us.

With Power's soft voice, she sent a childish giggle up my throat and past my lips before I could do anything to stop it.

No!

Knowing she was weak, I cemented up the tiny crack in that wall with a strong vigor, desperation lacing each movement. She couldn't be released. Not here. The whole world knew about my murders. No other act would take me for suspicion of being my next victim, much less any other ordinary job. My only chance for a roof over my head and food in my belly was to stay here - at least for now.

Must think logically. Must keep myself healthy and taken care of.

"Don't cry, honey. Just lay your pretty little head down and get some sleep. Everything's always better in the morning," Esther soothed, standing and pressing me down into my bed, draping the thin white blanket over me and tucking it around me.

I watched her as the tears slowly came to a halt, finding the feeling of being taken care of completely foreign, but nice nonetheless as it sent yet another wave of calming warmth through my body. Had Esther been a mother before being sentenced here? Was I to take the place of whatever children she'd left behind, I wondered? Studying her movements, I shifted to lie on my side to get more comfortable, wiping away the wetness left on my cheeks with the back of my hand.

She smiled down at me, though the expression was hollow, smoothing the hair from my face like she had been doing when I'd come back from Power's attack in the lounge. The sensation was soft and calming, something I'd never experienced before. With a deep breath and a physical resolve to cry no more that night,

I closed my eyes and nestled into the small but soft pillow she fluffed for me.

"Good night, honey. Sweet dreams. We have physical activity tomorrow, so look forward to the positive, alright?"

I walked with Esther down several long corridors the next morning, my stomach demanding food without mercy, making Esther laugh. Every hallway looked the exact same to me, the way back to our ward becoming more and more diluted in my mind as we turned down one hall, then the other, over and over.

"The food here isn't great, but sometimes they'll let our entire ward go on supervised trips to town, and we usually get a good cooked meal at this diner we all love," she told me, her Mexican accent more prominent than it had been the day before. "It's something to look forward to anyway."

I nodded, my head beginning to ache with the absence of food in my belly. "So, they let the entire ward go?" I asked, trying in vain to distract my hunger pangs.

"Well, it's only our ward where every member gets to go. They base it on your behavior and if you're a troublemaker or not. Can't have the crazies going wild in the middle of a small town, you know?" she replied, taking my arm and pulling me down another long corridor. Our socked feet skidded on the polished tile floors, but she seemed to be used to it as the unexpected sliding barely even slowed her confident stride.

"How often do they take everyone to town?"

"Usually once a month or so. It should be coming up soon, actually. Hopefully you can come with us," she answered, her accent growing thicker and thicker. How did she turn it off and on so easily?

Finally, after what seemed like forever, Esther paused in front of a set of heavy double doors and pushed them open, her long black curls bouncing animatedly as she moved with all the self-assuredness of a queen. The heavy scent of burnt toast and undercooked oatmeal assaulted my nose, but I appeased my distaste with the determined thought that sustenance was sustenance. I'd eaten worse for years under the employment of the Jensen and Sons Three Ring Circus. The need to complain existed nowhere in my mind as my gaze flitted over the hundreds of residents sitting at long tables, the air of hopelessness within them thick and choking.

Esther tugged on my sleeve, urging me to follow her to a cafeteria style bar on the wall closest to us. Dozens of pairs of eyes followed me as I walked, their glares piercing me with emotions ranging from curiosity to pure fury. I shuddered, trying to ignore them all. Being the small, weak one with Jensen and Sons left me no stranger to being seen as fresh, new meat to beat into submission, and I prayed that my fellow ward-mates would be able to shield me from them. If no one else, I was certain John and Esther would, and fortunately, they seemed to be the two people with the most influence and sanity in the entire establishment.

A lukewarm bowl of oatmeal crashed into my hands, making me jump as I looked up to meet the cold blue eyes of an overweight orderly who very obviously was none too pleased with her station as cafeteria lady. Her heavy jowls swayed as her mouth set itself into a grim line at my slowed movements. With an efficient and quiet word of thanks, I steadied the bowl in my arms and moved to follow Esther again, who placed a hand on my shoulder for reassurance and steered me toward a table at the back of the dining hall.

At one of the few circular tables in the daunting, sterile room, all of Ward F's members sat talking amongst themselves with small smiles on each of their painfully normal faces. As we approached, John looked up and met my gaze with a soft, heart warming grin. With a wave of his hand, he ushered us over to sit, standing to take my small hand in his large one and pulling out the seat on his left for me to take. His touch sent a comforting wave of heat all the way up my entire arm, making me sigh in contentment for a moment.

"Did you sleep well?" he asked after I sat, his honey colored eyes searching mine with so much genuine care it nearly hurt.

"I did," I answered with a small nod, glancing up to offer what I hoped was a friendly smile to each of my other ward-mates before I made quick work of the bland food in front of me. My ward mates chattered in hushed tones around me, but I made no effort to listen in. The hunger in my belly demanded all my attention, and I afforded it that gladly.

"How can you eat that stuff?" Marcie asked, her feminine nose wrinkling up in disgust as she eyed my empty bowl. She sat at John's other side, her own breakfast untouched. A glance around the table revealed to me that no one had eaten more than a few bites of their food either, while my bowl was picked clean.

I bowed my head, my cheeks heating up in embarrassment. "I haven't eaten in a while," I admitted, pulling my bottom lip between my teeth as my nerves began to quiver at the thought of anyone else's attention focused on me.

John's warm hand covered my shoulder, startling me. "You do eat regularly, don't you? You don't... make yourself sick, right?" he asked, his voice deep and his lips brushing my ear at the question meant for only me to hear.

Shock filled my system like a bucket of ice cold water being poured over my head. I'd heard of girls doing that. Even Charlotte, one of the other trapeze artists had been known for eating herself sick to make herself lighter and leaner. The idea that John or any of the others would possibly think that about me left me horrified and flailing for words, my mouth flapping open and closed like a goldfish.

"No! Like I said, I'm just hungry," I exclaimed, bright red blood painted across my face as my jaw hung open.

Across the table, George cleared his throat, shooting John a pointed look as he rubbed Lottie's back, who had started shaking. John nodded, some silent understanding passing between the man and teen. Or was George a teen? He certainly appeared young, with his face still holding on to a bit of round youth and his messy mahogany colored hair swept up off his head in a style I'd seen on many younger men in the audiences I'd performed for. And yet, the coldness in his icy hazel eyes and the way his thick eyebrows slashed straight across his face belied a much more mature and nearly sinister air about him, despite the way his hand rubbed circles on young Lottie's back in a seemingly comforting, albeit detached, manner.

Lottie's shaking began to lessen a bit at his touch, and it was then I realized how incredibly small she appeared. She couldn't have been more than fourteen, judging by her height and the shape of her face, but her body was thin. Much too thin. The young girl's arms were no larger around than my own wrist, and her plain clothes hung from her frame, making her look like a child playing dress up. Every visible inch of her body sunk in itself in an alarmingly gaunt manner, though her huge green eyes nearly protruded from her head beneath the short, boy-like cut of her dull, light brown hair. Seeing a girl her age with such a short, unfeminine haircut surprised me, but I knew better than to mention anything with the curious exchange that had just transpired.

John gave a quick squeeze to my shoulder and leaned back in his chair, the blue plastic backing groaning in protest of the strain. I couldn't deny the want growing in my stomach for him to stay near and keep touching me. He exuded safety and stability. And maybe something else that I couldn't place, but still yearned for.

My gaze swung over to Marcie as I opened my mouth to ask her where the bathroom was, but the question died in my tongue as I took in the flash of pain in her brown eyes, which were trained on John's hand still placed on my shoulder, the tips of his fingers pressed with only the tiniest bit more pressure than the rest of his hand.

Oh, no. No, I couldn't make enemies here. I looked up at John, hoping to see some kind of guidance, but he only sat there, chatting with George about whatever we'd be doing in Physical Activity in a few minutes. He paid no attention to Marcie, who had turned her bright blond head down to stare at the table, her plump pink lips caught between her teeth as a layer of tears veiled her gorgeous eyes.

I shrugged John's hand from my shoulder, disguising the movement by turning to face Esther on my other side. She offered me a warm smile, sending a knowing look to me before staring at the beautiful girl on John's other side.

"She'll be fine," she mouthed to me as my eyes widened in alarm at the single tear that rolled down Marcie's sweet face. John didn't seem to notice, though Ed, seated on her other side, glanced fleetingly at her, as if to check on her state and nothing more.

Ed's gaze turned to me, making me jump in my seat. His lime green eyes were cold also, except unlike George, his expression seemed much more aloof and dangerous, making my breath catch in my throat for a split moment. Maybe it was the way his eyes seemed much too large and bright for his face, or the way his black hair fell, long and disheveled, around his chin and jaw. Or how pale and otherworldly he seemed with his unusually tall stature and his quiet nature. Whatever it was, something sent off warning bells in my head, all but screaming, "Dangerous! Stay away!"

The irony didn't escape me, that I, a mass murderer, was trembling in the hard stare of a man whose only logical claim to danger was the air of mystery about him. But, I knew that it wasn't me - Sane - who used the strength and talents I possessed to kill. That honor fell completely and totally in the hands of Power. Not the real me.

Not who I hoped was the real me, anyway.

John walked by my side the entire way to the gymnasium type area we'd be in for Physical Activity. Marcie walked behind us, her clear and feminine voice tinkling as she laughed and chatted with Esther, but I still shied away from John's touch as long as she could see it. As much as I craved his nearness and comfort, I knew I'd be here for the rest of my life, and I didn't need to make enemies my second day. Women were catty, evil creatures in reality- a fact I'd learned the hard way over the years as I watched my fellow performers vie for mens attention and destroy each other over what they considered theirs. I wanted no part in that, despite how much I wanted to let John tuck me under his arm and lead me around. So, instead, I pulled myself away from his touch and offered him a smile, hoping he wouldn't be offended.

Thankfully, he smiled back and allowed my body a foot or so space from him as we moved. I didn't hesitate to let out the breath of relief waiting in my lungs for his reaction.

"So, where are you originally from?" he asked, nodding his head to one of the female nurses as we passed by her in the hallway. She grinned, her ruby lips stretching wide before she chuckled and moved on.

My teeth pressed into my lip, something I'd noticed was becoming a new, annoying habit, as I thought of an acceptable way to answer that. "Ah-er... Nowhere, really. And everywhere. I never stayed in one place for more than a week or two."

His eyebrow raised as his interest piqued. "You're a traveler? What all places have you seen?"

Honestly, just the inside of my cabin in the caravan. I'd never been one to hit the town after performances like my coworkers. But, saying that wouldn't do me any favors, I knew. So I kept my answers truthful, but short and vague.

"All over the United States."

"With family?"

A grimace spread itself over my mouth. "Ah... Of sorts."

Marcie's pretty voice startled me as she spoke from close behind me. "Your husband?" she asked, her tone high with hope.

I winced, knowing my answer would only cause more strife for her emotional state. "I don't have one."

"Did you kill him? Is that why you're here?" she asked then, as if her question were as simple and light as asking about the weather.

I choked at her boldness, stumbling over my feet in surprise. John's strong, warm hand wrapped itself around my upper arm, keeping me from catapulting onto the hard tile floor below.

"Marce!" John snapped, but even as he chastised her, a small satisfied grin worked at the corners of his mouth and he looked directly at me.

I thanked him for curing my sudden bout of balance inferiority brought on by cardiac arrest causing inquisitions, my heart hammering against my chest as I righted myself and continued walking. His thumb rubbed a small circle on my arm before he let go and gave me my foot or so of space again.

"She's only asking because that's why she's here," Lottie spoke up from in front of us, George's hand resting on the small of her back as he propelled her forward.

"It's alright. I-I don't need to know," I assured her, but Marcie interrupted.

"No, it's okay. Everyone knows it's why I got sent here. You don't have to be polite about it. I mean, who are all we to judge each other, you know?" she supplied, the sincere smile on her face, directed at me, surprising me. Shouldn't she have been giving me nasty looks and trying to make me uncomfortable? Every bit of experience with my fellow women and their love interests told me as much, anyway.

"Give her a little time to get used to this all, Marce. I know we all talk pretty freely about it all, but she's gonna need some time to adjust. This isn't like the real world, you know?" John told her, turning his head toward her and flashing his pearly white teeth.

"Of course," she submitted, a faint pink blush tinging her olive toned cheeks. He ruffled her golden hair a bit and continued on to the large set of double doors a few yards away.

George and Lottie entered first, followed by John and I, then Marcie and Esther, with Ed bringing up the rear by himself. I'd yet to hear Ed speak much, still, and he seemed to prefer to be alone, only furthering my private thoughts of him being aloof and dangerous.

"What about you?" I asked, turning my attention back to the tall column of tanned skin and muscles beside me. "Where are you from, originally?"

I wasn't prepared for the way my voice echoed around the large, metal room, and my body jumped when the sound came back to me, jarring my eardrums and sending shooting pain through my head. He chuckled at my reaction, taking in how ridiculous I appeared, and replied in a tone laced with absolute wistfulness and longing, making my heart hurt a bit for him.

"A small farm in Texas, originally. After I got back from the war, I found out my ma and sisters had moved to New York, so I followed to take care of them."

"Which place did you like better? I've been to both states. They both have their own charms," I admitted, memories of the hustle and bustle of New York and the humid heat and hospitality of east Texas filling my mind as I waited for his answer.

"Texas, without a single doubt. It was my home home, you know?"

His eyes bore into mine, waiting for me to sympathize, but I couldn't. My home had been a traveling circus, after all. The only stable home I knew was the inside of my cabin. Could a tiny five by five area really be considered a proper home?

It was at that moment another jarring, loud noise boomed across the gym, my unprepared ears feeling like they would begin bleeding any moment at the obnoxious volume.

"I see we have a new member added to Ward F! What's your name, honey?" the source of the ear-splitting blaring nearly shouted, every sound bouncing off the four walls surrounding us. I winced, fighting the urge to muffle the noise by putting my hands to my ears.

A male orderly with a grin too big for his very thin face strode forward, causing me to take a cautious step back behind John so that I was sandwiched between him and Esther.

"Ernie, this is Kate. She just got here yesterday," Marcie supplied, her teeth beaming a bright smile at the man as she combed a strand of her sunny hair with her fingers, her dainty hip cocked to one side.

Ernie's thick black eyebrow shot up. "Kate Thornton? The girl who-"

"Yes!" I cried out, my heart racing as I rushed to step in front of the orderly, holding my hand out for him to shake. My ward-mates couldn't know what I'd done. What Power had done. "Kate Thornton. Nice to meet you."

The thin man studied me for a moment, taking my hand in his and shaking limply. I begged him with my eyes, with everything in my soul, to not mention anything about my crime to everyone else. Another wide, scary grin spread across his face, his beady eyes hiding a malicious intent behind them. But, it didn't matter. I'd let him blackmail me til the day I died as long as he didn't tell my ward-mates about the murders.

“Nice to meet you, too, Kate. I’m Ernie. We’re going to be good buddies, aren’t we?” he pressed, and I shivered at the hidden meaning.

“Of course,” I replied, hoping my voice wasn’t shaking too badly. When I turned back to the rest of Ward F, I met five pairs of curious eyes and one pair of intense, chocolate colored eyes that watched my every movement like a sniper. Guilt crept up my throat, keeping me from being able to meet his gaze as I made my way to stand beside him again, my steps slow and deliberate. I swallowed the lump in my throat as my racing heart began to slow itself.

“Well!” Ernie exclaimed, clapping his large hands together and rubbing them together with renewed vigor. “We’re going to play some baseball today. But you all need to stretch first. Spread out!”

The shuffling sounds of seven pairs of socked feet filled the air as we all moved around, and I made sure to take a spot behind everyone else so that I could stretch like I wanted, without any of them seeing. Ernie’s beady eyes followed my form as I moved to stand behind Ed, the tallest and largest of my ward-mates. Marcie bounced her cheerful body up to the very front, trying to be clever as she made herself closer to John than anyone else. Lottie offered me a small smile from beside George, and Esther came to stand just a few feet from me in the back.

Aching to push my body to its limits, I removed my socks so I wouldn’t slide all over the lacquered wooden floor and shoved them in the pocket of the yellow dress Esther had loaned me. I’d come to Rosenton with nothing but the clothes on my back, and though her dress was a few sizes to big for me, I didn’t dare complain. Especially when she offered to help me choose new clothes at the next trip into town.

"Alright!" Ernie called out, his voice echoing as he stood facing all of us, a self satisfied grin attached to his face. "Arms up!"

Everyone half heartedly reached their hands up, mimicking his actions. But, me... I reached up high into the air, relishing the sensation of my muscles stretching and waking up from their month-long slumber. Somewhere in my mind, I knew the warmth and tingles spreading from my shoulders all the way up to the tips of my fingers was all in my head, but I didn't care. My body wanted and needed to be reawakened after so long, and it grew excited at the prospect, sending energy throughout itself.

A breathy sigh of contentedness had barely escaped my lips when he instructed us all to reach down to touch our toes. Simple, elementary stretches, but satisfying nonetheless. I folded myself in half, spreading my legs to make my feet parallel with my shoulders like everyone else, and placed my palms flat on the floor, knowing I could do so much more and wanting to desperately. My muscles begged and ached for the familiarity of a performance. Even Power, safely trapped behind the brick wall in my mind, seemed at ease and stopped trying to convince me to let her out as I enjoyed the feeling of the stretch.

We continued stretching for twenty minutes or so, none of my ward-mates taking it very seriously, though I basked in the sensation of muscles moving and awakening. I tried to keep myself in check, not stretching to my limits, but rather to the point a particularly limber young woman would be able to stretch. The fewer clues I gave to any of them about my identity, the better.

I stood straight with a small sigh and smile as we finished up, and soon Ernie had walked over to us all with a soft children's baseball bat and a baseball. I guess giving mental asylum inmates items they could potentially use as weapons was a little too much, even for the famously tame and mild Ward F.

Or maybe he'd just chosen them because of my presence, judging by the furrowed, confused eyebrows a few of my ward-mates wore above their eyes.

"John and George! Team captains! Pick your sides!" he shouted out, grinning as he tossed the two items to the men. He blew the whistle around his neck, for no discernible reason other than to rupture our eardrums, and settled down into a plastic chair by the wall, keeping a lazy eye on us.

George picked Lottie first thing, I noticed, and briefly had time to wonder about their relationship before John chose Ed, and George chose me. My bare feet carried me over to my team and I waited as the two teams filled out.

To my delight, as the game was explained to me and we played, I enjoyed myself. For once, the laughter that erupted from my mouth wasn't a result of Power trying to break free. John pitched from the center of the room, throwing underhanded as I got used to the foam bat, studying the way the ball flew toward me and swinging with all my might, just the way George had demonstrated when our team went up to bat. After a few rounds, the two teams switched positions, and Lottie told me where to stand, and to just try to catch the ball if it came my way.

The game went on for a long time, the gymnasium echoing the constant joyous shrieks and laughter coming from all of us as we played. Several times, I caught John looking at me, a bright grin plastered across his face, as if he couldn't help but have it there. I grinned back at him, giggling and feeling two twin heated pink spots bloom across my cheeks.

"Kate, watch out!"

My head snapped around toward the voice. Ed stared at me, his large eyes so wide and full of fear that it shocked me for a minute. He stood, frozen at the batters box, the foam bat hanging from the tips of his fingers.

"Duck!" he yelled, his voice deep and throaty, belying his older age and fitting with his constantly bedraggled appearance.

My eyes shot to the white ball flying through the air, toward my face at an alarming speed. Without a single second to think, my body bent completely backwards, the ball whizzing over my torso just as my palms touched the floor. The heat from the rocketing tiny sphere left its imprint across my stomach before continuing its path past me to hit the wall and bounce off its surface, hard. My legs, of their own habit, pushed themselves up and over my head, swiftly enough that my dress wouldn't ride up and show anything indecent. As my feet landed back on the ground out of the easy flip, one before the other, the gravity of what I'd just done began to sink in like a lead weight in my stomach.

The gymnasium fell silent as I stood straight, unable to bare looking into any of my ward-mate's eyes.

My teeth sank into my trembling bottom lip - again - as my eyes moved everywhere but at the others. I'm so stupid! Stupid, stupid, stupid! The air became hot and suffocating, the tension so thick I thought I'd drown in it before long. Even Ernie remained silent, furthering my mental chastisement for allowing myself to make such a monumental mistake.

"Whoa," a male voice finally breathed, breaking the tense silence that had enveloped the lot of us. I glanced up as my hands began to shake, meeting John's huge earthy brown eyes from where he stood frozen at the pitcher's spot. "How did you do that?" he asked, his voice thick with admiration and shock.

"I... I'm not really sure," I lied, my own voice no louder than a whisper. John studied my face for several minutes, his eyes narrowed as a curious light danced within them. The fact that he was so suspicious made my gut sink in dread. Someone as pure as him couldn't know my horrible secret. I couldn't- just couldn't-taint his soul like that.

And yet, that simple flip had felt so incredibly good and refreshing. Like before, my body pleaded for more than just that tiny taste, and I wanted, more than anything, to indulge and twist and turn and flip and contort and balance and swing and everything else I'd fed my entire being into for so many years.

"That was the coolest thing I've ever seen in my life," Lottie said, no wavering present in the words she spoke, from where she stood beside George. My anxious gaze flicked from her wide, excited emerald eyes to his cold hazel ones.

And he knew. His eyes, cold and eerily intelligent, told me that he knew who I was and what I'd done. Two days, barely, and the one thing I'd hoped to guard with my life was exposed to at least one of my ward mates. Self-loathing tears gathered at the corners of my eyes, but I held them there as he stared me down, no emotion - good or bad - shining through. If anything, he seemed amused, the tiniest hint of an arrogant smirk forming at the outermost corner of his lips.

It was that moment that let me know my hope of starting over had been crushed before I could even barely nurture it.

Chapter 3

"I'm so sorry, Kate. I had no idea it was going to go right for you," Ed apologized again to me as we all walked down the corridors leading back to Ward F's lounge. His already pale face was a shade even lighter than normal, and I could see the whites all around his lime green irises as he watched me, no doubt looking for any sign that I might be angry with him.

I offered him a smile, waving my hand around in what I hoped was a dismissive manner. "Don't worry about it, Ed. No harm, no foul, yeah?" Honestly, I just wanted him to drop the subject so I could put more effort into listening to John and Esther, who walked several yards behind the rest of us, their voices low and hushed. Each time I turned back to glance at them, one of them would catch my eye and pass me a weak smile that didn't reach their eyes before speaking again to the other. My heart pounded in my chest, terrified that they knew and hated me now.

Ed let out a loud, relieved breath and smiled shakily back at me before walking further ahead, probably just as anxious to be away from that conversation as me.

As we all made our way back to the comfort of our familiar and relaxing lounge, Lottie took a detour into the ladies room and George stopped across the hall from the restroom door, leaning against the wall, his muscled arms folded across his narrow chest. As my feet carried me past him, he reached out and stopped me, holding my elbow with a gentle grip to keep me beside him. I stopped and stared at him, positive that my fear and turmoil announced themselves loud and clear in my eyes. He waited, neither of us speaking, until John and Esther moved past us, so deep in a whispered conversation I wasn't sure if they even knew they'd passed us by.

I only just caught the quietest snippet from Esther as they floated by, both with studious, concerned expressions adorning their faces.

"The radio broadcast said the woman slit their throats, John. All twenty of them in one night."

The lump in my throat doubled in size as my breath caught in my lungs behind it. I forced myself to calm down and not panic as I watched their backs while they walked farther and farther away. Dread coursed through my veins alongside the blood that was making my head dizzy with the speed at which my heart pumped it through my veins.

It's over. I'll be isolated. Again...

"Kate the Great, huh?"

I jumped, startled out of my pity party at the sound of George's smooth, oily voice. His eyes, still cold, studied me, his lips still perched into a self-satisfied smirk.

"Come a little closer. I don't want anyone to hear our conversation," he instructed, and I obeyed without hesitation, desperate to beg him not to tell anyone about me. Leaning against the wall on one shoulder in front of him, I stared up at him and watched as he turned to face me also, bringing his face so close to mine that I could smell the spearmint on his breath.

"You know," I blurted, my racing heart unable to bear the tension.

He smirked full on, chuckling a bit beneath his breath. "I do. I see Ernie did as well, though I expect all the orderlies do. And John and Esther will figure it out on their own soon enough, I suspect. If they haven't already."

A very unladylike curse fell from my lips before I could stop it, causing him to raise a single amused eyebrow.

"Why do you want to keep it secret? You know we're all here for things society deems criminally insane."

I scoffed, my heart plummeting to the bottoms of my toes. "What I did... I hate myself for it. And, I like you all. I don't want anyone to hate me like I do. I just wanted an escape, you know? So, I gave into Power, and-"

"Power?" he asked, leaning even closer as I took an involuntary step back.

My head hung low, forgetting that even if the whole world knew what my body had done to my fellow circus performers, only I knew that I'd let Power emerge and take control to do it. "It's nothing. Don't worry about it. Look, this place, as stupid as it sounds, is my escape, okay? My chance at some sort of normalcy." He laughed out loud at that, but I ignored it as I continued on. "I'd hoped I could escape the insanity here, and I can't do that if everyone knows and hates me..."

His hazel eyes rolled in their sockets, as if I were a small child who knew nothing. "That's the most idiotic thing I've ever heard.

You're in an asylum, in case you haven't noticed. Your crazy will always find you here. There's nothing you can do about that. But, if you're so desperate to keep your secret, I can promise you I won't tell anyone. For a price."

"What kind of price?" I asked, my guard up and wary as Power began to knock her way onto the mental wall keeping her out. She hated being threatened, and I couldn't say I was too fond of the idea either.

He grinned at me, looking past me with a thoughtful expression on his young face. "I haven't decided yet. Nothing indecent. I'm not interested in that. We'll just say you owe me, alright?"

No, not alright. Nothing about it sounded safe or acceptable, but I had been left with no other choice. So, backed into the proverbial corner and my teeth grinding in frustration, I nodded my head in grim acceptance.

"Good girl," he replied and patted my upper arm, like I imagined an older brother might do. Angry fire raced through my veins and Power screamed at me for being so weak, but I held her back and stepped away from George just as the ladies room door swung back open and Lottie emerged, walking to George to wrap her willowy arm in the crook of his elbow. She gave me a small, friendly wave as the two of them walked forward again, George resembling something like an official escort as they moved. He spared me not so much as a glance, making it clear that he also had no intentions of letting Lottie know of our arrangement.

With a deep, sorrow filled sigh, I followed behind them back into the large double doors of Ward F's lounge, the loud bang of them swinging closed behind me feeling like a bullet straight through my soul.

“Old maid!” Marcie cried out, tossing her hands up and throwing her head back to let her tinkling giggles float up into the air. I grinned and let a few chuckles slip, myself. I’d always been a good loser with a competitive streak that could only be described as, ‘non-existent’. The happiness of simply playing a game with someone who smiled at me and having fun doing it had always been more than enough to satisfy me.

“Is it really already four o’clock?” Esther asked the room at large, the words muffled through the yawn she produced as she spoke. Neither she nor John had made any move to confront me about their suspicions, though I figured it was really only a matter of time. By no means were the two nonofficial leaders of our ward stupid, and the only way to squelch my overwhelming fear of the inevitable had been to immerse myself in the endless card games Marcie had begged me to play with her.

I leaned back in my chair, away from the coffee table. Esther shot a glance at my sudden movement, trying to appear inconspicuous while doing so. Dread coursed through my body at her cautiousness. I didn’t want any of them to be wary of me. I just wanted, with my entire soul, to be as painfully dull and boring as I possibly could be.

With a great, lengthening stretch, I arched my spine away from the back of the chair, fighting my body’s constant begging to push its limits after the small taste it had been gifted earlier in the day. For the past several hours in the lounge, through every single hand of Old Maid, I’d subdued the urges and fought against my pleading muscles, but I didn’t know how much longer I’d be able to continue limiting myself.

I stretched my arms out above my head and faked a theatric yawn, desperate for any excuse to go be alone.

"I think I'll go take a nap," I mumbled to no one in particular as I stood and made my way toward the dorm rooms. Marcie smiled and leapt out of her seat, pulling me into a tight and surprising embrace. She bounced up and down on her toes as she giggled, forcing my body to jerk up and down along with her movements.

Both Esther and John's strict gazes were locked on me the instant I'd been taken off guard, no doubt watching for signs that I'd become dangerous. George, of course, witnessed it all, causing one side of his mouth to lift up, amused by the situation. With a weak, courteous smile, I awkwardly patted Marcie's shoulder as she squealed on and on about what great friends she and I would be. John and Esther seemed to relax at the action, but still kept an eye on me until I disengaged myself from Marcie's arms and disappeared from sight into the corridor that housed my room.

My mind frustrated with the leak of my guarded secret, my body frustrated with being denied its want to challenge itself, and my soul frustrated with the fact that I was in an asylum for the criminally insane at all, I entered my room and closed the door behind me, careful to make as little sound as possible. I studied the room for a moment before deciding that moving my bed to the opposite wall would give me the space I'd need to sate my muscles need to perform. The legs of my small single bed squealed in protest as it slid across the linoleum, but I waited until I'd accomplished my goal before changing into an old leotard and checking to make sure no one would come and investigate the loud, jarring noise from my room.

Satisfied that I wouldn't be disturbed, my lungs took a great, heaping breath of cool, fresh air, and I began stretching, pushing my body to limits that audience members had called extraordinary after every show. As I warmed my muscles up and prepared them for my own private performance, I closed my eyes and basked in the feeling of being so limber and maneuverable. My body did things few other humans could. It molded and twisted in ways only years and years of practice could possibly produce, and I relished it.

I made once last glance over my room to be sure I had enough space, and began my routine. Again, my eyelids slid down, drowning me in black darkness as I moved with grace and flexibility. Visions of being in the center of the middle ring filled my mind. Robbie to the front right as he announced my entrance, his velvet hat tall and proud on his head. The roar of the crowd filled my ears and the wide grin on my face couldn't have been stopped for anything in the world.

What I'd give for a trapeze swing, high in the air. Or a partner to practice the entire acrobatic routine. But, oh, how amazing it feels to at least be able to release the contortionist performance!

I relived and performed every bit of every routine I could for close to two hours inside my room, pretending the yellow and red big top surrounded me and the rust colored dirt laid beneath my feet, instead of stark white walls and even whiter cold linoleum tile. And for those few moments I'd spared, I felt alive again with the high each performance always gifted me.

As the very last of the routines I could remember came to a close, I unfolded my body and pulled myself back into the standing position, holding my arms up in a high V, picturing the thunderous applause of the audience so vividly I swore I could actually hear it.

Grinning so wide my cheeks burned and ached, my eyes finally opened, greeted by the lackluster view of my room's sterile white walls. Unable to feign my disappointment, I dropped my arms and let the performance smile fade from my lips as the adrenaline pumping through my body slowed to an almost unbearable stand-still. There was no applause. No audience. No big top tent. No Robbie. No trapeze. No… nothing. The let down brought frustrated tears to my eyes, but I didn't let them fall.

Instead, I rolled my head around on my neck a bit and turned to drag my bed back to its original position.

And then froze.

My breath stopped and my eyes widened so large I could feel the skin around them strain. Each and every beat of my heart slammed a deafening beat in my ears as I stood there, unsure what to do or say. Warm, chocolate eyes stared back at me, glazed over with something akin to mesmerism. We stood there for several minutes in our silent standoff. My body wouldn't move, wouldn't breathe as his eyes never once left my form. For the first time in my life, humiliation and a dreadful feeling of being exposed rose in my throat like bile, knowing my routines had been watched without my consent.

I swallowed, my lips trembling. His gaze flicked to the movement of my throat for the briefest moment before moving back up to my eyes, which I knew were wide and terrified.

Without a word, John pushed himself away from the wall he'd been leaning on and moved my bed back where it belonged, no strain from the beds weight evident in his arms as he placed it back in its original spot. I stayed completely still as he maneuvered around me, neither of us breaking the electric silence suffocating the room around us. As his hand touched the door handle, preparing himself to leave my room, I shook myself out of it.

"Wait!" I cried, my arm outstretched toward him, the position begging him to stay and hear what I had to say. He stopped and looked over his shoulder at me, waiting for whatever I had to say to him. "Please. Please don't tell anyone what you saw. Please?" I begged.

His features gave away nothing as he replied, an expert of a blank mask. But I knew he would keep his word, whatever it may be.

"I won't tell anyone."

I sat on my bed, alone, for the rest of the evening, pondering my situation and wondering what would become of me once my secret was out to my ward-mates. Because it was inevitable at that point. George knew for sure, and I was almost certain John and Esther knew... How long until Marcie, Ed, and Lottie were enlightened? What would become of me? Would they hate me like I hated myself for what I'd allowed my body to do under Power's influence?

The door to my room opened, the hinges creaking as the opener took their time, and I watched with careful eyes as Esther slid in, closing the door behind her. Unlike before, no hint of motherly care of concern flitted around her dark eyes and my pitiful little heart sank, not realizing how much I'd wanted her to like me and treat me like a daughter, showing me what a mother's affection felt like for the first time in my life.

"Hello, Kate," she greeted, her smile hollow as she lowered herself into the chair before her makeshift vanity. Her sinewy hand caressed the lids of several jars of her lotions and facial creams, her fingers circling the smooth plastic of each container.

"Hi," I replied, feeling timid and unsure as I pulled my knees to my chest and wrapped my arms around them.

"Are you alright? You never came back to the lounge."

"I just needed to be alone for a little while."

She sighed, picking up one of the smaller jars and inspecting it in her hands. "You know, you have gorgeous skin. How old are you?"

"Twenty-four," I answered, my minds wheels hitching in confusion at her tone.

A ghost of a pained smile lifted the corners of her lips. "You should use this every night, so your skin stays as perfect as it is now. No man wants a wrinkly old hag."

"I'm hardly in the position to be worried about romance, but thank you."

This time she laughed, the sound full and genuine, and her eyes lifted to look at my baffled expression. "There's always the chance of attracting a member of the opposite sex, sweetheart. You don't want to get out of here in a few years and go out into the world with no weapons in your arsenal. You have to take care of yourself so you're always looking your best."

Her tone was so certain, making it sound like it was absolute, irrefutable fact.

I shook my head, offering her a humble smile. "Esther, you don't understand. I won't be leaving here. Ever. I'm here for life."

"Where is it you came from, exactly?" she asked then, unfolding herself from the dinky chair and coming to sit beside me, running her fingers through my mousy brown hair. Adrenaline coursed through my veins, feeling like thousands of microscopic bumblebees shooting through me.

"All over and nowhere," I repeated, my answer nearly identical to the one I'd given John earlier that very day.

She pursed her lips and nodded, my long hair slipping through her fingers like fine strands of silk. "I think you should be awake when the orderlies come for lights out," she said, her constant changes in subject alarming every nerve ending in my body and leaving my brain confused and aching.

I swallowed, nervous. "You want me to take the medicines? Why?"

Her hand stopped stroking my hair and everything in the room paused, not even the tiniest molecule of air shifting in the room, as she stared deeply into my pewter eyes with her own nearly black ones. The air in my lungs halted as I waited for her answer, knowing how monumental the moment was and what the end result would do to affect any relationship or friendship we might have had.

"They're good for people who might prove especially dangerous," she told me after several silence filled seconds, her voice not so much as wavering.

Silent tears stung the back of my eyes, but over the years I had become an expert at holding them back. I took a deep breath, trying with everything in me to keep my lips from trembling with emotion.

"How did you know? And who all knows?"

Her fingers resumed their gentle combing through my hair. "The story was all over the radio. They called it The Great Circus Massacre. Said it was done by one petite little acrobat girl the police found shivering in the mud outside her caravan as the rain poured down. Said she was wearing nothing but a nightgown and an old burlap sack over her head. But, only John, George, and I make a habit of listening to the news. The others only listen for the entertainment shows."

I didn't even notice the tears betraying me and pouring down my cheeks in little rivers until Esther began smoothing them away, smearing the salty water all over my face in the process.

"Can you control it?" she whispered, the coldness in her eyes softening into something warm and caring that I clung to for comfort, desperation coursing through my body for it.

"Control what?" I sniffled, rubbing my running nose with my wrist.

"The insanity. The evil. Do you have it under control?"

"I do. It's difficult sometimes, but I do. Please don't let anyone else know. Please?"

You have me under control? Please! Just the sight of that burlap sack in the doctor's office was enough to nearly make you give in to me, Power snapped from behind the stone wall I'd reinforced.

Esther pulled my body into hers, her arms tightening into a strong embrace around me as she let out a pained sigh. The lump in my throat hardened and I waited, trying not to shake, for her to speak.

"I won't tell anyone as long as I don't feel like you're a threat. The others have a right to know if they're in danger. But... as long as I feel like you're not, I won't say anything."

I could have sobbed with the enormous weight that lifted from my shoulders, providing the sweetest relief I'd ever felt in my life. "Thank you," I whispered, hoping and praying the extent of my gratitude shined through my voice, but knowing that was impossible.

Esther pecked my cheek, a small genuine smile gracing her red lips as she pulled back and let me lie down on my bed. Her soft hands tucked the thin blanket in around me, providing more warmth and comfort than any action I'd ever been given.

"Good night, Kate. Sweet dreams, sweetheart," she whispered, tucking a stray strand of hair behind my ear and smiling down at me. Like what I imagined a mother would do. I returned her smile and closed my eyes, left to dream of a childhood I never had, where I was a small girl again, and my mom had dark brown, almost black curled hair and eyes that matched.

Chapter 4

"Group Therapy?" I echoed, my voice high pitched with apprehension as my wary gaze met emotionless hazel irises.

"Yeah. You, me, and Lottie have it together," George replied, standing from his seat at the breakfast table. Lottie cast me a small smile from her chair, pushing her untouched toast away from her.

"Look after her, George. Paul's a jerk," John said, his voice eerily quiet so that no one else in the massive cafeteria would hear.

"Paul?" I asked, raising a questioning eyebrow.

"The almighty therapist. He's got a god complex. Sometimes I think he should be the one locked up in here," Marcie supplied, shooting me a sympathetic look with her pretty doe eyes. I swallowed the ball of nervousness in my throat. Why did all the authority figures in this place seem so... evil?

"You'll be alright. Just don't pull attention to yourself. George will keep it under control," John told me, offering me a small, friendly smile meant to ease my worries. Unfortunately, it didn't alleviate my cautiousness near as much as I would have liked.

George smirked, but said nothing in reply as he waited patiently for Lottie and I to stand and join him. My chest rumbled with fear as I rose from my seat, unable to hide the dread in my soul as the thought of potentially having to admit my crimes in front of an entire group of fellow residents throbbed through my brain. Lottie followed suit, and before long the three of us were walking at a leisurely pace through the confusingly similar corridors.

It amazed me how all my ward-mates seemed to be able to navigate the endless maze of hallways so effortlessly. How long had each of them been here to be so familiar with the building and not get lost in the endless winding, identical corridors? And even more than that, to know which doors led to which destinations?

You'll certainly have all the time in the world to learn, won't you? Power sneered inside my head. I made a point to ignore her, and that rewarded me with the distinct impression of her sulking as she stared at the stone wall before her.

But I would not crack. Not in this place.

It was the moment I stepped into the large room with eleven chairs placed in a wide circle through the center, filled with other various residents from different wards that I realized the stark difference between the members of my ward and every other ward in Rosenton. My feet paused of their own accord at the doorway as my eyes glided over the eight people in the room. Aside from the overly confident man sitting directly across from the doorway wearing a smart suit and a snarky smirk, George, Lottie, and I were the only ones in the room who didn't look like we belonged in a mental institution. Even the tall, bald man John had waved to when I'd first met him in the hallway outside Dr. Shilling's office still had dark circles under his eyes despite his hollow smile.

My hands shook as I forced my feet to continue their path to the chair beside George, where Lottie sat on his other side. The young girl slumped low in the seat, trying to make herself look as small and unnoticeable as possible. Was that what I needed to be doing? John had told me to not call attention to myself, after all.

George's dead eyes held no answers to my silent question when I looked to him for guidance. Did his opinion of me change when he found out about my crimes? Would he do as John had requested and look out for me, or would he leave me for the metaphorical wolves in this terrifyingly intimidating 'group therapy' session?

Of course he will, stupid. Look at you! You couldn't even keep what you let me do secret for three days before half of your ward-mates figured it out! Power snapped at me. You're weak and a disappointment at this point. I'm strong, and you know it. You should just let me take over so you can sit prettily behind this blasted wall instead of me. I'll take care of us so much better than you ever could!

"No," I whispered under my breath, squeezing my eyes shut against her furious tirade. George turned his head to look at me, his eyebrows furrowed in question.

Oh, please! You can't hold me back forever, Sane. You're too weak. I'm strong!

"Stop it." I tried my best to keep my voice quiet, my trembling hands balled into tightly coiled fists as she taunted me, threatening to take me to that dark place again. My breaths came in harsh, quick pants as I fought her away.

Open your eyes, stupid. Look at me!

As if I had no willpower over my own body, my eyelids lifted and every bit of air in my lungs exploded into horrified star bursts.

A version of me stood in the doorway, but she was not me. My dull grey eyes were bright and charismatic on her ivory face. The mousy brown hair that fell limply to my waist was wild and curly, with hints of golden hues sparkling as it fell away from her head, grazing the floor from her upside down perch on the top of the door frame. She grinned wide, her stark white teeth filed to razor sharp points that poked her bottom lip, causing blood to drip down her deranged face and into her gorgeous hair.The crimson liquid trailed from her bottom lip, through the middle of her sharp teeth, down the left side of her delicate nose until it reached her bright eyes, where it pooled in the corner of her tear duct before overflowing and making a tiny red river down her forehead and into her thick curls. The leotard she wore was mine- the one I'd performed in countless times over the years. Navy blue sequins caught the light and ricocheted it off in thousands of directions, making her seem to glow as she stood there, arms loosely crossed over her small chest.

My mouth parted in a sick mixture of awe and terror. Power had never showed herself to me before, and to see her, an insane version of me, for the first time, hanging upside down from where her feet planted themselves on the top portion of the wooden door frame… I barely held back the scream that lodged in my throat as her sadistic grin widened even further at my distress.

My awestruck gaze stuck to her like glue, unable to tear myself away from the sight of her for fear she'd move. With a patronizing wink, she put her hand to her lips and blew me a sarcastic kiss, laughing silently at me as I shook in my chair.

A cold grip on my upper arm snapped my gaze away from her, and I was lifted from my seat by brute force, my feet stumbling beneath me.

"Bathroom," George's emotionless voice snapped before the therapist could inquire, and he steadied me roughly as my legs buckled from the force of his grip. He squeezed Lottie's shoulder before directing me from the room. I slammed my eyes shut as we walked, praying I wouldn't run into Power's sentient body as I passed through the doorway. George's grip on my arm never loosened or allowed for any misstep, and I took a chance by trusting in that so I didn't have to open my eyes and witness anything I didn't want to see.

Scared of me, Sane? Scared you won't like what you see again? Scared you'll realize I'm the better of the two of us, she taunted. I could nearly feel her warm, humid breath in my ear and shivers wracked my body as a result.

When I dared to open my eyes and brace myself for whatever I might see, I found myself sitting in the corner of a small wash room, my arms and legs sprawled out around me as if I were a marionette whose strings had been snipped. Two hazel, emotionless orbs hovered in front of me, which was the last thing I saw before I felt my eyes roll up into my head and the visions overcame me again.

Saney, Sane, Sane! Power sang out, giggling. Or maybe it was me giggling. I could never be sure when I fell away like this. Power and Sane meshed together, forming one twisted and fluid being instead of two conflicted, constantly battling souls. Where one began and the other ended no longer mattered or even existed in this state. We were one, and we were no longer part of the real world, choosing instead to frolic together, as a single being, in our mind.

"You can't have me," I giggled, the sound echoing around the cold bathroom as it all melted away like a badly done watercolor painting. Everything melded and shifted until I was in my tiny cabin again, running my fingers over the rough burlap sack in my hands. Dozens of sweet, supple smelling peaches floated in the air around me as I rubbed the sack to my cheek, savoring the scratchy texture and what it stood for.

Maybe not now, but it won't be long until I'm more than you, sweetheart. Then, nothing will stand before us that we can't crush. We'll never be hurt again once I'm in control. Just like those pathetic comrades who abused you at Jensen and Sons.

I shook my head, the cabin tipping sideways as all my belongings and my bed began to also float around the small space.

"They didn't deserve to die, Power. I could have ran," I argued, but the emphasis died away on my lips as laughter punctuated the end of the sentence.

You always run. Together, we are survival. Fight or flight. You are flight. I am fight.

Laughter shook my body at her clever analogy, but as I doubled over and wiggled my toes in delight, my lungs stopped working. Panicked, I began to gasp for breath, but none came. My eyes shot from corner to corner of my little cabin at lightning speed, searching for a cause. Power's bright, smiling face watched me from the small window in my cabin, her hard stare glinting like steel at my struggle. Her pointed, needle-like teeth grew as her mouth opened wider and wider, until the entire top half of her head unhinged, falling against the back of her neck. Her vibrant hair bounced around her shoulders as she began throwing her body against the minuscule window, each impact leaving longer and longer spiderwebs of cracked glass.

Fear took over my being and I frantically floated around my cabin for an escape. Where my door once stood, only smooth wall remained. The only other opening was the window. The window Power's demented form was banging herself against. Cold sweat poured from my brow as I realized I had no way out, and she would soon be on me, having her way with me as I sat there, unable to move or breathe.

Milliseconds later the glass shattered, glinting pieces of jagged edges flying all around, slicing into my skin as they made impact. Power's body froze. I watched, my lungs screaming for air, as the top part of her head lifted to align itself once more with the bottom half, meeting in a literal ear to ear smile that sent more terrified sweat down my spine. Her long fingers pushed themselves onto the windowsill, broken glass cutting the skin and sending blood pouring into the room. I finally found it in me to scream as she began to push herself into the cabin.

Her small, lithe body was halfway through the window, her face never leaving mine, when another voice broke through the barrier.

"Kate, snap out of it. Come back, now," the masculine voice commanded, leaving no room for disobedience.

Power paused, cocking her head sideways like a dog trying to listen for a far off noise.

"You're not there. You're here. Pull yourself out of it," he snapped, and a sharp stinging sensation bloomed across my cheek. I gasped, pulling in an agonizingly fulfilling breath of air.

"Kate!" he snarled, his tone now even more angry. And that was enough to pull me back.

I gasped for more air, the powder blue, sterile bathroom coming back into view as the eerie cabin melted away, alongside Power. George hovered in front of me, his eyes dark as he shook my shoulders. I jolted upright, my head smacking against the tile wall with the sudden movement. Black and white spots exploded in my vision and I gulped for pure oxygen again. He stopped shaking me and brushed the hair out of my face.

"Good now?" he asked, no hint of concern apparent in his tone. I nodded, still quivering from the episode as I struggled to regain my bearings again.

"Splash some water on your face and get it together. I don't like leaving Lottie alone." He didn't even look at me as he spoke.

"Sorry," I whimpered, reaching for the sink above me and pulling myself to stand before it. I obeyed his instructions without question, too shocked that I'd come from the episode unscathed and grateful for his foresight to bring me away from the others to do anything else.

George nodded, his brown hair moving across his forehead with the motion as he waited for me to finish. A weak, nauseous wave crashed over my chest as I took deep, stabilizing breaths, my knuckles white as I held onto the edge of the sink. Cold sweat dripped down my neck, making me shiver yet again.

"Here," he said, offering me a damp paper towel to wipe my face with. I took it with careful fingers and scrubbed, hoping against everything that maybe the furious action could erase my insanity. The mirror above the sink taunted me, begging me to look into my reflection, but fear that I wouldn't see myself there kept me from obliging.

"Let's go," I whispered, straightening my posture and meeting George's unwavering gaze after I could no longer feel the tears on my cheeks. The tremble in my body had reduced to a barely noticeable state, and hopefully by the time we made it back to the Group Therapy room, it would disappear for good. George nodded and took me by the elbow, leading me once again back to the large room we'd just left.

We didn't speak as we walked down the quiet corridor, but the firm grip on my arm made it undeniably clear that I was under his care, and he was to be obeyed. In all honesty, I didn't mind.John had already told me to be under George's care, and although George was a cold, emotionless young man, I trusted John's judgment without prejudice. Plus, I couldn't deny that not having to think, and only being responsible for obeying commands, was a bit of a relief on my part. At least until Rosenton and all its quirks and unspoken rules became more familiar and comfortable.

As we approached the door, we both froze. From inside the room, a broken, heartbreaking sobbing noise emanated through the closed door and into our now very alert ears. I turned toward George, alarmed as I realized I recognized the voice behind the wails.

He cursed under his breath and gripped my wrist like a vice as he slammed the door open with a jarring, resounding BANG! Immediately nine pairs of startled eyes jolted our way, and what I saw twisted my heart within my chest.

"What happened here?!" George snapped, fury coursing through every syllable. I stared, slack jawed at the scarily thin young woman kneeling on the floor in front of her chair, her short hair mussed and her face pale and gaunt as endless tears poured without mercy from her oversized emerald eyes. Without wasting another second, George strode toward her and pulled her to her feet with one hand, the other still holding onto my wrist as he dragged me behind him. Lottie buried her face in his chest and sobbed as everyone else in the room watched on, some with shock, some with interest, some with angry sneers on their disturbed faces.

"We were simply discussing the benefits of growing from a child into adulthood. Miss Holbrook is having a breakthrough. Why don't you three sit back down and we can continue," the therapist stated, his demeanor eerily calm. Goosebumps ran up my spine as his dark eyes turned toward me. The man didn't move as he spoke, appraising the three of us with disinterest written all over his expression as he used his middle finger to push his thick glasses back up his nose.

"Go to hell, Paul. We're taking our leave for the day," George growled, as Lottie all but tried to make herself disappear against his chest.

"That's not a wise decision, Mr. Baker. These group sessions are not an option. They are mandatory." Paul's tone held the promise of a threat and I found myself, like Lottie, trying to hide behind George from him.

"Call it a sick day."

Paul smirked as George dragged the two of us from the room, his lips pursed in a thin, forced line as his jaw clenched and unclenched, as if he were trying to not explode on the creepy therapist.

"We will see you three on Monday!" he called out to us in clear amusement from his relaxed stature in his seat. The other residents watched in shock as we left, the door once again slamming behind us.

I found myself once again in the same bathroom as before moments later, only this time it was Lottie breaking down as George tried to snap her out of it. Acting on pure instinct, I dropped to my knees beside her and pulled the broken girl into my arms, rubbing her back with my hand.

"It's alright, Lottie. Forget everything that happened in there. You're okay," I muttered into her hair, closing my eyes as tears burned behind my eyelids for the poor, hurting soul in my arms. George sat crouched beside us as Lottie sniffled and pulled herself even tighter into me. He began to run his hand along her arm in what I supposed was an act of comfort, though his face remained calculated.

"You're safe, Lottie," he cooed in her ear as he hugged her from behind, sandwiching the frail girl between us. I opened my eyes and looked to him for guidance, hurting for Lottie, though I didn't even know why. His cold gaze held my teary one for a moment as he studied me over her shoulder.

"I hate it here!" she cried out then, jolting my attention back to her shaking form.

"Don't think about it. You can't break down in front of them. You know that," he replied, causing me to shoot him a warning glare. She needed comfort, not cold logic.

"You're alright, sweetheart," I whispered to her, not breaking the glare I held toward George. "We're here. You have us to lean on." Concern that she'd turn me away because we really didn't know each other flitted around like nervous worms in my veins, but that didn't happen. Instead, she seemed to bask in the kind, supportive words, so I uttered more and more of them to her as she trembled and wailed in my arms while George remained quiet and resorted to rubbing her back.

He watched, his expression a mask of curiosity, as I tried my best to calm the small girl. Like he was studying the interaction between us, as if he'd never seen it before. But, that couldn't be right. Even I, having lived with the circus all my years with no family, had known at least small portions of comfort in my short life. As I stared back at him, something seemed to click in his mind, and the change in his visage became evident.

Lottie continued to cry against the two of us, and I continued to soothe her, but I couldn't help but be at least a little scared of the glint that had flashed through George's multicolored eyes. It meant something for me, I was sure of that.

I just didn't know what.

We returned to an empty lounge, save for Ed, who sat on the couch with a game of Solitaire spread out in front of him on the thick wooden coffee table. His hands trembled, sending each card flying a little off course with each toss into whichever pile he aimed for. I watched, wary, as his foot vibrated against the white tiled floor while small droplets of sweat formed along his temples and up to his forehead.

"Go on out," George told him, after a quick glance at the clock overhead. Ed bolted from his seat, sending cards flying in every direction through the air. Within seconds he had all but flown from the room in a blur of black hair and large lime eyes, leaving the heavy double doors to slam shut by their own weight behind him.

"Is he alright?" I asked, turning to look at George.

He smirked, an air of superiority and arrogance seeping from his skin like an aura. "We're all in this nuthouse for a reason, Kate. What do you think?"

My mouth clamped shut and I looked away from him, every nerve ending in my body on high alert in discomfort. "I'm just going to go rest in my room," I muttered, gifting a small warm smile to Lottie, who returned it while still trembling, before leaving the lounge and heading toward mine and Esther's dorm. The orderlies at their station glanced up at me as I walked by, watching me for some kind of crazed killing spree outburst, I suspected. I paid them no mind as I opened my door and slipped inside, letting out a strained breath as the pressure and stress of the past few hours had me cracking a bit.

To my relief, Power made no moves to taunt me like she normally would have in my mentally weakened state.

Trying to distract myself, I hummed as I pushed my bed to the other side of the room and changed into my lone leotard, stretching my limbs to their limits and closing my eyes to focus on anything but Power's ruthless attack and how different and strong she looked, hanging upside down in the group therapy door frame.

My reflection caught my eye when I glanced up and my lips turned down into a frown as I compared the girl standing there with the woman Power portrayed herself as. My dull, straight hair hung limp down to my waist in undignified strings, where hers had been full of life and bounce and curl. She'd had no bags under her eyes like I did, and while my grey eyes just sat in my skull, afraid and wary, hers had been the color of steel with a spark of life flashing through them. She'd even had the rosy, healthy tinge to her cheeks that my pale and colorless cheeks didn't. Her perfect face haunted my mind, teasing me and provoking me to compare the two of us, knowing I could be her.

"I'll never be you," I whispered to her. "Never again."

She didn't answer strangely enough, considering she always used any opportunity she could grasp to argue and talk back to me. She loved it when I acknowledged her, especially out loud. Her absence made my teeth clench, but at the same time, a sense of relief that I felt like a normal girl without murdering psychopath in her head washed over me.

Moving my gaze from the mirror, I closed my eyes again and focused on my routines once more. Every bit of stress and tension left my mind and body as I went through each part, feeling each muscle stretch and move, parts of my skin touching parts no other person could. The acrobatic routine in particular helped me relax, the flips and soft sounds of my feet and hands slapping against the tile floor burning off excess negative energy from the previous hours.

As I wound down and began to move into the last parts of my last routine, I took a deep breath and looked up.

My body jumped in surprise when I saw John standing in silence by Esther's vanity, closer to me than last time. How had I not noticed him come in? Was I really so immersed inside myself that I hadn't sensed another person come into my room and watch? I couldn't really be that oblivious, could I?

"Ah... Hi?" I said, biting my lip as the awkward tension between us threatened to swallow me whole. His face was blank as he studied me, his eyebrows scrunched together and his lips pursed, as if he were trying to figure something out.

After a few moments of silence wherein my heart nearly beat itself out of my chest, he spoke.

"It's time for lunch."

I nodded, eager to move on from the nerve wracking situation that had every muscle in my body twitching. Like last time, he moved to grab my small bed and began to slide it back to its original spot, but this time I snapped out of my shock and grabbed the other end to help him.

"I'll wait for you outside," he said when I looked back up at him, my gaze questioning his actions. He turned and walked back out of my room, his stride long and confident as his opened red flannel shirt billowed behind him.

I swallowed and allowed myself a few quick breaths before rushing to change back into a dress Esther had loaned to me and meeting him back in the hallway. Neither of us spoke as we made our way to the cafeteria. The large doors opened and once again, I was struck by the fact that aside from my ward, none of the other residents looked normal or sane.

A loud clattering sound startled me and I gasped as a thin bald man near the center of the room began rocking himself back and forth in his chair, knocking his and everyone around hims lunch tray to the floor as he moaned into the air. A woman several tables over began to scream obscenities at the man, her matted hair wild as she waved her arms about.

John's hand pressed on my elbow, nudging me to move forward in line. "Come on, Kate. Don't look into it too much. It won't help you," he muttered so only I would hear. My feet took shaky, uneven steps forward as the scene burned into my memory.

"Is that what we're all like?" I asked under my breath, not sure if my voice would even carry to him.

I felt, rather than saw, him shake his blond head from behind me. "No. Those people can be helped, but they won't be. They have no one to look out for them or heal them. Our ward is a family. We're together. We care about each other and we help heal each other. We're not like them."

His voice came out so firm and confident that I had no choice but to believe him. And then, something even deeper than confidence rang through his words. It was conviction. Esther's words about the role he'd played within Ward F rang in my ears as I moved forward in line yet again, closer to the mush disguised as spaghetti, according to the chalkboard menu. He kept us all sane. He cared. He was the head of our messed up little family, and that kept us all a step above what we'd come to Rosenton as.

Comforted by the revelation, my body relaxed as I took the tray of food the same disgruntled cafeteria worker from the day before handed me. I walked alongside John to our table and sat down in the chair beside him again, noting that everyone seemed to take the same seats each meal, save for Ed who still hadn't returned from wherever he'd gone earlier. Had my chair been empty before I'd come along, I wondered passingly as I glanced up at Marcie on his other side. She grinned at me and I returned the expression, though I could tell it was hollow compared to her brightness. Luckily, she didn't seem to notice and began chattering about her approved trip to town for Friday, a full week before the group trip, apparently.

"Will you bring me back a dolly?" Lottie asked, her large and eager eyes lit up in excitement. I frowned in confusion, but one look from Esther shaking her head wiped the expression from my face and I saved my question about a fourteen year old wanting a doll, and asking in such a childlike voice, for later. Instead, I settled for watching the young girl from the corner of my eye, my curiosity piqued.

As lunch wore on I noted that she often poked or twirled her food on her fork, but never took a bite. Beside her, George kept a strict eye on her, though he said nothing. My mind reeled with dozens of questions about the curious pair. Who was George to Lottie? Why didn't she eat? Why was her hair so short and cropped, unlike most girls her age? Why was George so protective over her when he seemed so cold in general? Why were her interests in items from town centered around child's play toys instead of makeup and magazines?

John squeezed my shoulder, jarring me from my thoughts and silent questions. He smiled a warm, closed mouth smile at me, and I returned the gesture. "You ready to head out?" he asked, nodding toward the cafeteria doors where the rest of our ward had already collected themselves as a group, staring at the two of us as they waited.

My eyes widened at the realization that, once again, I'd been so internally focused that I'd not noticed major things happening around me.

Chapter 5

I glanced around the sterile lounge room for Ed, hoping no one would notice my wandering eyes. For whatever reason, asking questions to my other ward-mates intimidated me, and I couldn't bring myself to face them. Maybe it was the fact that I didn't quite trust them yet, or maybe it was the giant plethora of secrets the ward held, despite claiming to be a tight knit "family". Whatever the case, I resolved to keep my inquiries to myself until I was alone with either John or Esther.

The six of us sat in silence, all of our gazes trapped on the large bay window with steel bars running vertically across it. Splatter after splatter of fat, heavy raindrops pounded the glass, sounding like thousands of tiny fists beating against the transparent surface and making it impossible to have conversations without shouting to each other over the noise. The sky loomed over Rosenton, as charcoal colored as the bars making sure we couldn't escape.

Well, escape life anyway, I thought to myself, remembering the portly police officer jamming his sausage finger onto the seventh floor button on the elevator the night I'd been escorted here. Jumping from our particular lounge window meant certain death.

Weak people kill themselves, Power scoffed, and I could all but see her folding her arms across her chest in utter arrogance as she spoke to me. I shook my head and ignored her unwanted input.

"Hey, have you been able to find your way around by yourself yet?" John asked me after several minutes, leaning close so I could hear him over the thunder booming over us. Again, his warm breath on my ear caused a fresh batch of shivers to race from the nape of my neck all the way down my spine, electrifying every nerve ending on the way.

Swallowing the nervousness in my throat, I shook my head and twined my fingers together, unsure what to do with myself and scared to look up and see if Marcie had seen him talking to me. Her evident jealousy and kindness toward me seemed unbalanced and foreign, and the last thing I wanted to do was get on her bad side. The newcomer always lost out in these type situations, and I was certainly not looking for any reason to be involved in an altercation.

Not in this place, and not with these people.

"Come on," he whispered, grabbing my hand and pulling me to my feet from the scratchy orange chair I'd come to familiarize myself with for its position in the back corner, next to the radio. I'd hoped by choosing that seat, I'd become less noticeable and blend with the wall, but the fact that John seemed to fancy sitting in the other scratchy orange chair beside it always caught at least Marcie's attention, making me the target of her intense, but not unfriendly, stares.

I let him lead me from the room while the rest of our ward-mates gathered around the barred window to watch the lightning strike. They all seemed fascinated by the storm, and in a way, so was I. The dark skies, the rolling pewter clouds, the howling winds, and the bruising rain… It held a certain mystery and intrigue. Nothing could stop it. Nothing could touch it. Nothing could contain it. It simply was, and nothing could change that.

I'm like that, Power snipped, the playfulness she used in her tone unusual. I chalked it up to her confidence and the way I admired the storm, then made it a point not to reply to her, just like before.

As the heavy door closed behind us, I caught one last glimpse of Marcie, just as she turned to see us leave the room. Her beautiful face fell and her bottom lip quivered as her eyes moved over to the oblivious John, who kept walking, not bothering to look back. I averted my eyes, my heart aching for this girl who was in love with this man, and I let the door fall closed, blocking us from her sight. My teeth sank into my lip as I tried not to cry for her, all the while Power teased me for being so emotional and weak. Who was I, a mass murderer, to feel things like sympathy for other people?

John stopped at the corner where our hallway met another and waited for me to catch up, his hulking frame seeming almost inhuman as it filled the corridor. The desire to know what he'd done to end up at Rosenton overwhelmed me, but asking that question would open up the conversation for him to ask me the same. And, though I was sure he already knew, I wasn't ready to verbalize it to anyone yet. The other performers had been cruel to me, but they hadn't deserved to die. Especially the way Power had murdered them. And I'd allowed it, making me even more ashamed of myself and my actions.

“How big is this place?” I asked, coming to a stop beside him and admiring the way bright golden strands of his long hair glistened under the fluorescent lights overhead..

“Sixteen floors. It’s the largest asylum in the United States,” he answered, a strange sense of pride swelling in his tone, as if the asylum was his work and he wasn’t an inmate here like the rest of us. He started walking down the corridor toward a staircase- the first staircase I’d seen in the building. I’d come up by elevator, but even that I couldn’t remember the way to. I’d been drugged with enough sedatives to take out a horse when I’d arrived, but even if I hadn’t been, the place was a giant maze of identical hallways and doors, only the occasional nurse’s station or doctor’s office breaking them from being too similar.

“How many wards?” I asked, following him again as he walked toward the staircase. His heavy footsteps were audible, even though he only wore socks. Those footsteps brought his body to walk a little closer to mine, and I accepted that with a tiny wave of excitement bubbling in my belly.

His replies were sure, so confident that I knew again, without a doubt, that his knowledge of the asylum was accurate. Which meant, I gathered, that he’d been here long enough to see all of it, meaning a substantial while. Again, my brain begged me to ask him his story, but I shut it down without entertaining the thought. I couldn’t open myself up like that. Living in mystery of this interesting man I couldn’t help but want to be near was much more appealing than speaking about what I’d done.

“Eleven wards. The first floor is reception and where we go for visitors. Second through twelfth are wards. The fourteenth and fifteenth floors are medical floors, and the sixteenth is a big supply floor. You were lucky to end up in Ward F. We're the only floor in this place that has any hope of not going all the way insane." He muttered the last part, sounding like he was talking more to himself than to me.

I took the information in, grateful for the little bit of light shed on the intimidating establishment. Somehow, knowing the monstrous building wasn't shrouded in mystery sent a floor of stability and maybe even the tiniest amount of trust to slide under my always dangling-for-hope feet. I glanced back up at him as we marched on in silence, nearing the staircase at the end of the hall. His ever-present soft smile stayed trained on his face, as if he knew no other default expression. I basked in it for a little while, wondering if this was how Marcie came to be so infatuated with him. It wasn't unlikely. John held a certain humble, but confident charm that couldn't be missed by the hormones of the opposite sex. His muscled build and tanned skin only added to the effect, making him seem like some sort of angel of masculinity, sent down for the sole purpose of making my heart beat five times its normal speed in his presence.

We began the descent on the tiled staircase, John offering little tidbits of useful information about where to find certain important areas on our ward's floor. I committed each piece to memory, taking special note of his directions to the cafeteria and the fact that the only gymnasium in the entire building was on our floor. I already knew some of his directions, like the way to the showers and to the lounge, but I listened with interest anyway just to keep him talking so I could savor his smooth southern drawl.

"So where are we going that's downstairs?" I asked as we passed down the door to the fourth floor.

He grinned, his teeth seeming to brighten the entire area around him.

Could you be any more of a lovesick teenager? What, you've never seen an attractive guy before? Your inability to be cool around him is embarrassing, Power snapped, her frustration with my timidness clear in the way she pronounced each word with a sharp edge.

"You haven't looked out the window of your room, have you?" he asked, though it came out as more of a confident statement than a question. I shook my head and waited for him to elaborate.

"There's a huge rose garden down there, and a courtyard too. And a vegetable garden in the very back. It's the best fresh air you can get around here. Almost like you can pretend to escape and live out there in the real world again," he explained, his voice giddy with excitement. A smile etched itself across my face at the pure, childlike joy in his expression as he went on and on about the vegetable garden in particular. I ate up every word he spoke about his memories of his family's farm in Texas, and how he'd loved the process of planting and harvesting as a teen, before he'd been drafted to the war.

He spoke with such passion, such happiness, that when we reached the ground floor and he opened the door to go out, I'd forgotten that he'd meant to show it to me in the first place. Every word he spoke created a picture in my mind, and it took me away from the real world and what we were supposed to be doing.

We walked past reception, where, like always, John nodded and smiled a friendly greeting to the pretty receptionist there. She grinned back, no doubt a fellow victim to his charms, and allowed us to pass through into yet another hallway that he told me would lead us to the entrance to the courtyard. I followed, trusting him without hesitation.

John was still talking as he turned a corner a few feet in front of me when he fell silent mid-sentence, turning on his heel with wide eyes, telling me something I couldn't decipher. Before I had the opportunity to question him, he'd grabbed my hand and opened a narrow wooden door that I had just passed. With a firm but still gentle touch, he pushed me into the tiny room and followed behind me, closing the door with his hand on the door frame, preventing it from making a sound when the lock clicked in place.

I raised a questioning eyebrow at him, obeying his silent command to keep quiet as he placed a single tanned finger to my lips. Power stirred behind my mental stronghold, not liking the surprise and questioning his intentions. John pressed his ear to the door, a small grin lifting up the outermost corner of his lip. I took the opportunity to look over our surroundings and found he had pushed us into a minuscule supply closet, shelves with various cleaning products lining the walls dangerously close to our heads and a large bucket with mops and brooms resting in the corner, the rope strands of the mop mussing my hair.

Satisfied we wouldn't be discovered or heard, he leaned back toward me and his grin grew, a mischievous light twinkling in his chocolate eyes.

"Dr. Shilling," he explained, his voice a husky whisper. His warm breath on my face reminded me exactly how close we were in the cramped space. "I had a session with him today, but I skipped out with a sick excuse. If he sees me out and about, I'm in for it."

“But it’s only Thursday. I thought Ward F’s sessions were on Tuesdays?” I whispered back, glancing at the door for any sign of intrusion.

“I have him twice a week. Tuesdays and Thursdays. He took a special liking to me for some reason.” His large hand reached up to rub the back of his neck, as if he was embarrassed by what he’d told me.

“Is he always so…”

“Yeah. He’s always trying to set off whichever unfortunate soul ends up in his office. Don’t fall for it, okay? Ignore everything he says. His life mission seems to be making sure we all hit crazy-town well before our intended arrival time.”

My heart sank, feeling like it had collided with my stomach. “Why? Why would he want to make us worse instead of better? He’s a doctor…”

His next breath hit my face with more pressure than the ones before as he sighed, sending my hair flying backwards a little. He looked away, then back at me, his eyes piercing me with a scary determination that made me wish I hadn’t asked about the doctor.

“I’ll tell you one day, but not here, Katie. Can you just trust me for now?”

My head nodded of its own accord, without permission from the logic side of my brain that screamed, ‘No! I want to know what’s going on! I want to know what I’m in for at this place!’

His face relaxed, relief flooding his entire frame and making his gargantuan presence in the tiny closet seem even bigger somehow. I sent up a chaste and pointed prayer of thanks that I’d never been afraid of small spaces, because the situation was a claustrophobic person’s nightmare. Three inches of open space on both sides separated me from colliding with the shelves surrounding us, and the backs of my heels dug into the lip of the large mop bucket behind us. I didn't even want to think about the fact that John was pressed up against me, my head brushing the collar of his flannel shirt and our hands still clasped together.

John turned around, with difficulty thanks to his stature, and cracked the door open less than an inch. His body leaned forward, pulling me with him, as he squinted to peer out into the hallway. My heartbeat pounded in my ears like an old Indian powwow drum as I waited for him to tell me the coast was clear and we could continue our path to the gardens, despite the raging storm outside.

With a gentle tug, he pulled me from the closet, and despite my intense and thorough training in things like acrobatics and balance, I fell right into John's side, nearly taking him down with me as I stumbled. The two of us went careening to the far side of the hall, simultaneous bursts of laughter sounding from both our mouths at the immaturity of the situation. He reached down to steady me, but I'd recovered within seconds of the initial incident already and was only left standing there, holding my stomach as I tried to keep my laughter from becoming too loud and drawing attention to us.

A throat being cleared a few feet behind us sobered us both up, snapping our mouths shut as we glanced at each other with matching alarmed expressions. John looked up first at the owner of the noise, and the relief in his face granted me the courage to look as well.

Larger than even John, and looming over us with a wicked and amused grin was Ed. I took in his relaxed and easy demeanor, mentally comparing it to his earlier shaky and nervous form. Whatever he'd spent all day doing had brought him back down into the land of sanity, and I found myself much less frightened of him.

Though that didn't help the red hot blush on my cheeks.

"Having fun in there?" he asked, smirking toward the supply closet. John choked beside me and I cast him a sideways glance, unsure what had made him so uncomfortable.

"It was nothing like that," John stammered, his voice a few pitches higher than normal. "Just hiding from Shilling."

This time it was Ed who laughed, his voice deep and magnetic. "Alright, alright. Don't worry. I won't tell any of the other ward members about your little escapade."

It clicked. And if my cheeks hadn't been on fire before, my open jaw and the sensation of lava throbbing under the skin of my cheeks made sure I knew I looked as humiliated as I felt.

"Oh, my goodness! No! I don't-don't do things like that!" I cried, waving my hands around all over the place as my ears began to burn with fire. Once again, Ed laughed at my flustered state and waved it off, shaking his head as if thinking, 'kids these days!' John put a hand on Ed's shoulder, stopping him as he went to walk off, and mumbled something in his ear. My eyes squinted as I tried to hear what he said, but it didn't work. Instead, Ed nodded with a knowing smile and continued on his way, looking every bit like a giant as he lumbered down the hall toward reception.

When he was out of earshot, I threw my hands over my face and groaned. "I think I preferred dark and brooding Ed."

John let out another little chuckle and took my hand again, leading me down the next hallway. "Then you'll need to see him before three in the afternoon every day. His trip down here always livens him up."

"Does he walk the garden too?"

"Who knows? Whatever he does keeps him on the safe side of crazy, so I don't ask questions."

I nodded, gripping his hand tighter and loving the way the tiny contact between our skin warmed up my whole body.

"Why doesn't Lottie eat?" I asked Esther that night as she ran her silver plated brush through my hair, the gentle motion massaging my scalp and nearly lulling me to sleep where I sat.

Esther sighed, her chest rising up higher than normal with the weight of the air leaving her lungs. "She's... She has problems. I can't tell you her story, because that's for her to reveal, but I will tell you that she wants to remain a child as much as she can. Lottie is terrified of growing up and becoming a woman, and in her mind, the way to stop that is to deprive her body of what it needs to grow."

I frowned, my heart producing a dull, throbbing ache for the young woman. "She has to know it doesn't work like that, right? She can't stay a little girl forever."

She put the brush aside and began twining my still damp hair into a loose braid down my back, tying the end with a small elastic. "Deep inside she knows. But, she's here for a reason. In her mind, it does work that way to some degree, and she's hanging on to that hope like a lifeline."

We both sat in silence for a while, the only sound reverberating throughout the room coming from the soft rustling of the sheets on my bed as she moved around to pat some of her special creams and lotions onto the skin of my face and neck. This little routine had become sort of a bedtime ritual for us, and I couldn't say I minded. By the time she finished primping and prodding me every night, I was always exhausted enough to fall right asleep before the orderlies came in with the medicine cart.

"Why does George take such a special liking to her?" I asked, my eyelids dropping as if tiny lead weights were attached to my eyelashes.

"He doesn't like to see weaker people being bullied. Lottie knew nothing but being bullied growing up, and since he found out about it during his first week here, the two have been inseparable."

"That's kind of him."

"No," Esther snapped, stopping her hands from their massage on my cheeks and bending down to look in my eyes, her face stern and her body rigid. "He's not kind. Don't get mixed up with him. He doesn't have friends. Only people he can use."

"Even Lottie?" I whispered, backing my face away from her intimidating glare. What would she say if she knew I was already mixed up with him? That he was helping and blackmailing me at the same time?

She nodded. "Even Lottie."

"Then why haven't any of you put a stop to their relationship?"

Her hands continued rubbing a new lotion onto my face and her body released the tension it had held moments before. "Because he doesn't want to hurt her. Like I said, he doesn't like bullies. He wants to protect her and help her, which is good for her. But he'll want something out of it. We haven't figured out what yet, but as long as it won't hurt her, we won't interfere. And he knows that. Now get in bed. I can hear the nurse's cart coming down the hall," she instructed, her voice brusque and stern, expecting no disobedience.

I obliged and snuggled down into my sheets. Esther, like every night, tucked me in and planted a motherly kiss on my forehead. A satisfied smile lifted the corners of my lips, and I closed my eyes just as she crawled into her own bed and turned out our bedside lamp. A solid, three bump knock sounded at our door, as it had every night so far, and when no lights came on in our room and neither of us answered, the squeaky wheel on the cart signaled the nurse's departure. Feeling safe and confused by Esther's explanation of George in particular, I kept my eyes closed and waited for sleep to overtake me.

Chapter 6

I nearly jumped out of my skin the next morning after I stepped out of the shower room, hair still dripping wet trails down the back of yet another slightly too big dress Esther had let me borrow. I ran right into a pair of cold, hazel eyes. George stood in front of the girls showers, leaned against the opposite wall with his arms crossed over his chest. I glanced down both sides of the hallway to see if anyone saw him waiting there. Surely someone would have questioned him if he had been seen, right? The only rooms down this hallway were the womens showers, bathrooms, and a couple supply closets filled with spare bedding and other odds and ends.

"No one has come down this hallway since you went in. You're a late sleeper this morning," he said, the way he answered my unspoken question sending a wave of goosebumps down my arms. I may have been in an asylum, but I was still level headed enough to know he wasn't psychic. Just unusually observant. And that was even scarier than the possibility he could read minds.

"Why are you here? Won't you get in trouble?" I asked, my nerves feeling as though they'd jump up out of my skin and take off running down the corridor at any moment.

"You missed breakfast, and I need to talk with you. I know what I need you to do for me, if you want me to keep your little secret," he replied, breezing through the sentences as if he weren't talking about something as vile as blackmail. My eyes widened as my stomach sank to my toes and twisted into tight knots.

"What's that?" Caution laced each syllable. Another droplet of water from my wet hair hit the floor below me, making the tiniest plop as it made contact with the cold tile floor and splattered a bit.

George pushed himself off the wall and came to stand close to me. Much too close to me. Alarm bells rang in my head at the sudden breach of personal space, but I held my ground. Not because I was especially brave or courageous, but because fear had frozen all four of my limbs, preventing me from making an escape. All I could do was stand there, stiff as a statue, as visions of past confrontations flitted through my mind at breakneck speeds, leaving me disoriented and terrified.

Hit him! Scream at him! Something, you pathetic swine! You're useless! Let me out! Let me out! Let me OUT! Power screamed over and over as his overbearing demeanor suffocated me from where he stood not even six inches away. Her fists pounded on the stone and mortar wall, threatening to crack it and tear it down if I didn't do something.

George leaned in, his eyes peering into mine as he opened his mouth and spoke, his words quiet enough for only me to hear. "I want you to watch over Lottie when I can't. There are times I can't be with her to keep her safe and sane, and those are the times I need you to be there. You can't let her have a breakdown, and if she does, you can't let any of the doctors or orderlies see it, understand? I won't have her taken to the thirteenth floor, and you're going to help make sure of that," he said, his voice low and barely audible as he spoke into my ear. It was a command, his tone making sure I knew there was no room for negotiation.

"I can do that," I whispered, frustrated with how scared and weak my voice sounded. My hands began to tremble as he stared down at me, studying my face for several seconds, his eyes flicking between mine over and over. Satisfied with whatever he saw there, he broke the terrifying glare and reached for a dripping strand of my mousy brown, limp hair. He curled it between his fingers, ringing out some of the water and both of us watched as a thin stream of water poured onto the floor.

"Dry your hair or you'll get sick. I need you well enough to do your job," he instructed, breaking the small trance the water had held over me. Without another word, George spun around, hands deep in his trouser pockets, and strode back down the hall, toward the lounge.

The breath my lungs had been holding hostage escaped in a great, shuddering heap and my muscles finally relaxed.

What the heck had just happened?

I walked toward the lounge in a daze, my mind still reeling over George's unexpected and suffocating visit. All he wanted from me was to watch out for Lottie? There had to be more than that. Nothing in my life was so simple. I'd expected nothing short of slavery, especially after Esther's divulging of his true character. A user. Someone who only saw other people as tools for his own benefit. What benefit did me helping Lottie give to him? And, not that I was dumb enough to up and say it to him, but I'd have looked out for the young girl and helped her in any way I could regardless of his blackmail over the situation. Something about her pulled at my heartstrings, making Power snicker at my "weakness".

You're pathetic, Sane, you know that, right? You won't stand up for yourself, but you'll watch out for a messed up little crazy girl.

You're a psychotic, controlling, evil, murderer. Leave me alone.

She laughed at my halfhearted retort and shook her head, her voluminous curls brushing the stones of the wall she stood behind always. Even I felt the wall shudder, as if her touch repulsed it.

My entrance into the lounge silenced the chattering the others had been taking part in. Five pairs of eyes turned to appraise me, while George just smirked, his posture lazy from his perch on the arm of Lottie's chair.

"You missed breakfast," John commented from my usual orange chair. Worry laced his tone, making me feel slightly guilty for my overindulgent, extra long shower. I turned toward him, offering a reassuring smile as I strode to sit beside Marcie on the overstuffed couch.

"Just one of those days where the shower felt too good to leave," I tried to deflect, settling down to get more comfortable in the middle seat of the large sofa. His expression made it clear he didn't believe me, which I found ironic since it was technically the truth. George had cornered me after I'd already missed my meal anyway, so I saw no reason to bring him into it.

Marcie turned to face me, excitement and giddiness rolling off her in high strung waves. I broke eye contact with John and faced her, waiting for her to speak. I didn't have to wait long.

"They're letting my mother take me shopping in town tomorrow!" she exclaimed, bouncing in her seat as her grin stretched to impossible widths across her gorgeous face.

"That's great, Marcie," I replied, my tone much more calm and radiating politeness more than anything else. George's weak attempt at blackmail still held my minds full attention, making it difficult to focus on the girl beside me. He had to have a hidden agenda. He had to. He was too intelligent to let me get off so easily.

"I was hoping you'd like to go with me, Kate. If we go talk to them now, the orderlies and Shilling might okay your request."

That succeeded in snapping my attention to her.

"What?" I asked dumbly, biting the inside of my cheek in shock. True enough, Marcie had never acted on her evident jealousy of John's attention to me, but I hardly expected her to want to be buddy-buddy with me either. Was she really that innocent and pure? We'd spoken less than five hundred words to each other in the few days I'd known her, and now, after she'd been hurt by John's attention to me, she was asking me to be her shopping buddy?

No, you idiot. She told you she killed her husband, herself. Make up an excuse. Don't get me killed because you're a gullible moron, Power snapped, and for once, I listened to her.

"Marcie, I don't think they'll let me go. I haven't been here for even a full week yet, and from what I understand approval is based on behavior, isn't it?"

"But, we can ask," she pleaded, not phased by my attempt at logical rejection.

"You should just ask them," George interrupted, causing every head to turn his way in surprise. I bit the inside of my cheek to keep Power from snapping at him. Was he trying to get me killed? Was that his secret motivation?

If he thinks you're a danger to Lottie, that very well may be his intention. For all you know, he put Marcie up to asking.

I swallowed, my nerves dancing beneath my skin. I couldn't help but consider Power's words. I already knew she had a much better sense of evil than I did. She trusted no one, not even her host - me. But, her instincts were on the money more often than not, and that gave me pause to think about the precarious situation.

But why would he ask me to help him protect her if he thought I was a danger to her?

"Come on!" Marcie begged, hopping up from the couch in a whirlwind of childish excitement. She grabbed my hand and pulled me to my feet, hauling me behind her as she literally skipped from the room and down the hall to Ward F's orderlies station. I stumbled over my feet behind her, trying to keep up with her quick pace.

"Can I speak with Martha, please?" she asked a short, bulky male orderly I hadn't met before. He nodded, raking his eyes down Marcie's womanly figure before he seemed to remember she was in a home for the criminally insane for a reason. His disrespectful lingering gaze didn't affect Marcie in the slightest, and in fact, she straightened her spine and pushed her chest out, blasting him with a clear view of her cleavage and a stunning bright smile.

My feet shuffled beneath me, so uncomfortable with the situation that I didn't know how long I could stand there and let a young woman, who obviously had issues, offer herself up to a man who would be taking complete advantage of her if he acted on her presentation.

Thankfully, the male orderly turned before I was forced to watch anything I didn't want to witness. Without a word, he walked back through a set of wooden swinging doors at the far side of the station, and returned a few seconds later with a willow thin red headed woman.

"What is it, Marcie?" the woman, who I presumed to be Martha, asked, her voice naturally husky and sounding like she desperately needed to clear her throat.

Marcie bounced on her heels, beaming up at the older woman. "I want to see if Kate can get approval to come with me tomorrow. Please, please, please, Martha?"

Martha's lazy gaze swung over to me, studying me before she spoke. "Kate? Kate Thornton?"

I nodded, unable to speak past the nervous lump in my throat.

She frowned immediately. "I'm afraid we haven't had enough time to appraise your behavior properly. And if the town citizens found out we let-"

"I understand, completely," I interrupted, drumming my fingers on the laminate surface of the counter I leaned on. "Thank you for your time."

"Oh, please, Martha? Just this once?" Marcie cried, her tone giving me the distinct impression that she didn't not get her way often. I placed my hand on her arm, making her look at me.

"It's alright. Rules are rules, yeah? Maybe next time, Marce," I told her, hoping my soft tone portrayed the calmness and acceptance I wanted it to. She pouted, her bottom lip full and pink with the girlish lipstick she applied every day.

"Oh, fine," she finally whined, throwing her hand in the air in a dramatic show of exasperation. "But, I'm bringing you back some clothes, Kate. Clothes that fit. You're too pretty to be running around in clothes two sizes too big! I can't believe you even came here with nothing to wear!" She spoke as if I'd arrived at a wedding in black or a funeral in red. Or maybe it was more like I'd arrived at senior prom in a garbage bag. Her obvious displeasure with my state of dress made it seem as if I weren't good enough, hadn't tried hard enough, to properly fit into their dysfunctional little family.

My cheeks burned scarlet at her humiliating outburst. "Whatever you want to do, Marcie. I'm just going to get some fresh air in the garden."

I left her standing there before she could add any more insult to my offended ego. I knew she hadn't meant anything by pointing out my clear lack of fashionable and fitted clothing, but I'd hardly had a choice in what I'd brought with me to Rosenton. The police had swept me from the fairground Jensen and Sons' train had stopped in without giving me even the shortest opportunity to gather any of my belongings. The month I'd spent in police custody, they had dressed me in the traditional prison uniform the entire time. I literally owned nothing but the single dress I'd come to Rosenton in and my old practice leotards. No pictures, no jewelry, no makeup, not even a hairbrush. Just a single dress, a couple basic leotards, white stockings, one pair of socks, and my undergarments.

Esther had been kind enough to lend me her own clothing. Even though they were two sizes too big, her kindness had meant more to me than anything in the whole world. In fact, everything the abrasive Mexican woman had said and done for me had been out of pure kindness, and Marcie had all but stomped on how much the act of Esther lending me clothes meant to me. It had hurt my heart, stabbing it and twisting the knife inside.

I just needed a minute outside to gather myself back together and not cry in front of anyone.

The door to the stairwell John had shown me appeared quicker than I thought it would, and I peered around for orderlies or nurses before sprinting for it. Letting the wood door fall shut with a quiet click behind me, I descended the stairs two and three at a time until I reached the ground floor. The same receptionist from before glanced up at me, then back down at her files, as I walked by her, trying to keep my pace calm and normal.

As I walked down the hallway, I couldn't help but blush a bright crimson when I passed by the closet John had pulled me into. Memories of just how close he had been to me heated my skin, making me long for his always comforting presence.

But, I couldn't rely on him all the time. I needed to handle some of these emotional episodes by myself.

The cool blast of fresh air that nearly knocked me back when I opened the door to the courtyard was heavy with a sweet, floral scent. My frazzled nerves began to calm as I made my way past the small fountain and into the rose garden behind it. My mind fell numb, all thoughts encasing themselves in ice, as my socked feet padded down the cobblestone path, deep into the roses. I didn't stop until my unfocused gaze landed on a decorative concrete bench, tucked away into a small alcove surrounded on all but one side by thorned flowers.

My breathing hitched over and over as I lowered myself down onto the bench. I clutched at my chest as every emotion I'd tried to suppress for weeks all boiled over, sending white hot tears to gather across my eyes. Anger at Power for what she'd done. Sadness that I'd allowed her to take over in the first place. Frustration that I'd been naive enough to think I'd get help here.

But most of all, I felt guilt. Overwhelming, overpowering, all encompassing guilt. Whether it had been Sane or Power, both women were me, and that meant that, as much as I hated myself for it, I had killed them all. Twenty-three people in one night. I'd snatched their life breaths away from them when they least expected it, when they'd been most vulnerable. Not all of them were like me, orphaned. Most of them had families. People who cared about them. Friends. Lovers. Children. And I'd taken everything. Everything.

I sobbed, my face resting on my knees as my fingers dug into my chest where my heart should have been.

I had no right to be upset over Marcie's insensitive quips. I didn't deserve fitted or fashionable clothes. I didn't deserve to be in the one ward that wasn't doomed. I didn't deserve to be given this chance - this do over. I should have been sent to prison, let come what may.

A sharp ache shot through my lungs as they struggled to expand and contract through my desperate wails. I don't know how long I sobbed, but when a soft, comforting hand was placed on my arm, I looked up to see that the sun was hiding, cut in half by the horizon.

"Everyone's been worried. What's wrong, chiquita?" Esther asked, her face wrinkled with worry, showing her true age.

I tried to speak, but nothing except the jerky, halting breaths that gave way to a round of unladylike hiccups came out of my mouth. I buried my face in my hands while Power demeaned me over and over again inside my head, trying her hardest to crack the wall while I was weak.

With a sigh that belied her age given wisdom, Esther pulled me into her arms and began to hum a distinctly Mexican sounding tune, letting me continue to cry until it was all used up and I had no more tears to shed. As the last salty droplet fell from my cheek and onto the concrete bench, staining it a darker grey than the rest of the surrounding surface, I pulled out of her loving embrace and looked up at her. She smiled at me, wiping my wet cheeks with the sleeve of her cotton sweater.

"What's wrong, sweetheart?" she asked again, stroking my hair as I laid down on the bench, resting my aching head in her lap. My fingers played with the hem of the dress she'd let me wear, the yellow cotton fabric soft beneath the pads of my fingers. I looked out toward the red, white, and pink roses surrounding us and breathed in their scent before I spoke.

"I just feel so guilty," I managed to whisper, my voice barely audible through its hoarseness.

"For what?"

I looked up at her, shooting her an incredulous expression. "For what I did. For killing all those people. I hate myself for it. It haunts me and kills me inside. How could I have done something so horrible, Esther? What kind of person am I?" My voice broke with the last few words, forcing me to swallow down the painful lump in my throat that seemed to enjoy tormenting me at emotional times.

Yet another wistful sigh fell from Esther's lips, floating into the twilight air around us and hanging there, mingling with the scent of the flowers.

"That's what makes you deserve a second chance, nina."

I frowned.

"You feel remorse. You don't feel righteous about what you did. It means you're still human and not a monster," she explained. "I don't tell anyone else, so don't go repeating it, but I feel guilty every day for killing Horatio and his mistress. I never even knew her name. I ask God every day to forgive me, because the burden is so big."

"Why did you do it? If it's not prying, I mean..."

Her lips curled up into a rueful smile, full of everything but the joy a smile should mean. "I found them in my marriage bed together. It broke my heart, and I lost my temper. I threw things at them, screamed at them, and told them to get out of my home."

I waited, knowing there was more to the story if she'd ended up here.

"And then, when I demanded to know why he'd done it, because we were happy, I'd thought, he answered. I should have never asked for an explanation. I should have just kicked them out and moved on. But I just had to know, so I asked. Horatio told me that he wanted children. I'd been barren for our entire thirty years of marriage, and he couldn't keep shooting a dead horse, he said. So he took matters into his own hands, and brought in a woman who could fulfill her wifely and womanly duties. The duties I'd failed at, even though I kept an immaculate home, held onto my beauty and youth, told wonderful stories to lift him up to all my family and friends, never complained... But, none of my hard work was enough. I wasn't enough until I bore him a child. When he told me that, I lost what little bit of me I had left and grabbed the gun from our bedside. I shot him until every bullet was gone, then bashed his mistresses head in with a lamp. I couldn't stop until she was unrecognizable. And then, because I'm an honorable woman," she said, her tone heavily sarcastic, "I called the police and turned myself in."

"Oh, Esther," I whispered, sitting up and pulling her into a tight hug. No wonder she'd mothered me so much. I was the child she'd needed her whole life. And, coincidentally, she was the mother I'd never had. By some dark twist of fate, we'd been brought together to give each other what we lacked. We needed each other.

"I can't imagine why a mother would abandon her child. Especially you. You're a wonderful young woman, Kate. I wish I'd had a daughter so that she could be like you. And I'd still have my Horatio. And my family. They've all disowned me, you know. Not that I blame them."

I shook my head. "No, I wouldn't want my mother to look at me and know what I've done. What I'm capable of. You're the closest thing to a mother I've ever had, and I'm so happy to know you," I told the older woman, tears of earnestness gathering in the corners of my eyes.

I watched as she sat back, flicking a few stray tears of her own off her grinning face. "Enough with the mushy gushy mess. Let's get back to the ward before they send out a search party," she said and pulled my to my feet. We began the trek back to the building, the night air bringing a familiar chill to my exposed skin. Memories swirled around my thoughts of walking around at night after performances, when the audiences had been long gone and the grounds had been cleaned up. I would go to the train cages with the lion and tigers, just to talk to them when no one else was around and pet their soft muzzles through the iron bars.

The elephants and their gargantuan size had always terrified me, though I was familiar and trained my entire life alongside them. They were just too overpowering and intimidating, even when they rested at night. But the lions and tigers... Something about them had called to me, and I'd lost count of the number of times I'd stayed right outside their cages all night to wake up on the ground before them the next morning.

"Kate?" Esther asked, jarring me from my reverie of times long passed.

"Hmm?"

"Don't ever tell Shilling you feel guilty. Tell no one except your ward mates. Shilling will use it against you and drive you to have episodes and breakdowns so he can send you to the thirteenth floor."

I paused, furrowing my eyebrows and twisting the fabric of my skirt in my hands. "What's on the thirteenth floor?"

She didn't answer as we walked, and I'd resigned myself to think she wouldn't. I'd certainly settle for her gratuitous warning and be thankful for that. But, then, as soon as my hand touched the door handle to go inside, her hand fell over mine, causing me to look up at her.

"The thirteenth floor doesn't exist," she said, her tone slamming down with resolute finality. My lips pulled down into a confused frown, but she gave me no time to ask anything else. She sashayed by me with purpose, opening the door and striding down the hallway just slow enough that I wouldn't fall behind.

Why warn me about something that doesn't exist?

I thought hard about the cryptic message all the way back to the reception room, trying to remember what John had told me about the thirteenth floor. But, then I realized no matter how much I remembered about what he'd told me, I couldn't recall anything about a thirteenth floor. First was reception. Second through twelfth were wards. Fourteenth and fifteenth were medical, and sixteenth was storage. He'd said nothing about the thirteenth, I was sure. How had I overlooked that before? I'd hung on to every word he said like a lifeline, but hadn't noticed a gap in numbers?

"I'm going to the powder room for a moment. Wait for me?" Esther asked once we got to reception. I nodded, my mind still befuddled by the mystery I'd been presented.

She walked into the bathroom a few feet from the reception desk and I took a seat in one of the plastic chairs in the waiting area, still pondering the mystery I'd been presented.

"Rough night?" the receptionist asked, her voice filled with out of place cheer. She looked far too young to have a job, much less one at an insane asylum. But, then again, I was often told I looked fourteen or fifteen, so I couldn't exactly judge.

"Just needed some fresh air," I replied, my smile weak and twitching with the effort it took to keep it up. She nodded in acknowledgment and went back to her paperwork. I turned to look straight ahead again when a large sign by her desk caught my attention.

Directions!

Trying to nonchalant even though my heart pounded against my chest, most likely leaving a bruise, I got up and walked over to the large hand painted sign. Each floor was listed, along with what was on each one. I scanned the list until I saw Floor 12, and my eyes raced down to look for the next consecutive number. Except it wasn't there. Right under Floor 12 and its label read Floor 14.

I wet my lips, my brow furrowed as everything spun around at a million miles a second in my head. For all intents and purposes, Floor 13 didn't exist, even to the staff, apparently. But my ward mates knew about it, and knew - somehow - that it was real. How?

And, more importantly, why?

Chapter 7

"We're going to be painting a nice, peaceful beach scene today, guys," the man at the front of the makeshift classroom said. His voice was monotonous and sleepy, like the painting he wanted to to create. I guess in a room full of insane murderers and psychopaths, you don't want to have them paint anything to get their emotions all riled up. Smart man.

Three wards had combined for craft class on Saturdays in the large gymnasium, and the space was crowded, to be put lightly. Dozens of easels, paintbrushes, stools, canvases, cups, and paints were spread out all over the wood floor, all facing the frazzled looking red headed man up front. His clothes were splattered with blue and white paint from the earlier class he'd instructed already that day.

"Everyone go to a seat, and an orderly will bring by your canvas and brushes," he called out to all fifty or so of us, gesturing to the easels and stools all spread in rows and columns, much too close together for comfort.

"Come on," John murmured in my ear, tugging my hand to follow him as all the residents began to shuffle toward the stations. I followed without question and allowed him to lead me to an easel in the third to last row. I perched on the cold metal stool and placed my hands in my lap, picking at my nails as people I didn't know and didn't trust took up seats around us.

John sat at the easel to my right and grinned at me. I returned it and watched as the rest of Ward F scattered about in the crowd. Besides John and I, only Lottie and George stayed together.

"Have you been to the beach?" he asked, leaning forward to rest his elbows on his knees. My lips quirked up at the odd sight. John's long legs and bulky body didn't look comfortable or even able to fit correctly on the small stool. He reminded me of the part of our show where the elephants would stand on the small platform, precariously perched and balanced, threatening to fall over at any minute.

"I've been to beach towns, but never to the beach," I replied, stifling my chuckles. "Have you?"

He shifted on the tiny stool, grimacing as it teetered about on uneven legs. "These things are shoddy and kid sized," he mumbled under his breath, making me laugh quietly. He stood up and flipped the stool over, bending down and tinkering with the legs of it as he continued to talk. "I went once when I was a kid. Before my dad died, he took my ma, Elsie, and I to Galveston one weekend. The sea wall was still being built up then."

"Is Elsie your little sister?"

"Yeah. She was a toddler back then. She's what? Eighteen, now? Nineteen? I forget sometimes. I was six when she was born. How old am I? Twenty-eight, right, so that makes her..." He paused his breathless chatter, a shocked expression flitting across his face for the slightest moment. "Shoot. That makes her twenty-two now. Where did the time go?" An awkward pause filled the air around us before I broke it, desperate to keep up the light, happy atmosphere.

"You get along, then?" I asked as he twisted one of the legs of the stool tighter, muttering something about shoddy prefabricated furniture being crap quality.

He tipped it right side up again and sat down on it, testing the stability. "Yeah, we do. She's married with a couple kids now. Susan and Johnny. You can guess who she named the boy after," he said, puffing out his chest and winking at me. I felt the blush rise up to my cheeks as I laughed again, shaking my head at his mock arrogance.

John's face lit up as I chuckled, and I only quieted down when an orderly walked over with a canvas and paintbrushes, squirting several colors of paint onto a small plate, then doing the same for John. I glanced at him from the corner of my eye and grinned when I caught him doing the same. Butterflies didn't even begin to describe the wild, Amazonian sizes creatures zinging around my insides, pinging off every wall of my stomach and making me feel flushed and... and squirmy.

We continued to sneak unsuccessfully furtive glaces at each other throughout the class, bringing a sense of childish adventure and mischief to the boring and dull craft instruction. I paid only the barest attention to the instructor as John and I played our little game, a wide smile plastered to my face.

Needless to say, my painting looked like crap. The blended colors of the horizon on everyone else's canvases shifted from color to color seamlessly, while the colors laid across in distinct stripes on mine. In fact, nothing on my canvas looked even remotely like anyone else's.

I licked my lips as I tried, for the first time that entire class, to take in what the instructor was telling us to do. I looked back and forth between his actions and mine, comparing the way I held my brush, how much paint I'd picked up on the bristles, and everything in between. As far as I could tell, I was doing what he said, and the stupid fluffy clouds simply would not translate onto my canvas. Instead, thick white blobs that resembled melted marshmallows plopped at the top of my painting.

I growled in frustration as I only made a bigger mess the more I tried to fix it.

I reached up again with the abused and battered brush, ready to undoubtedly smear more white paint into a formless blob, when warmth enveloped my hand. Startled, I glanced down and saw the welcome sight of John's large hand on top of mine. He grinned at me, looking every bit the presence of comfort and security I'd come to associate him as, and moved our hands up to the canvas. With a feather light touch, he began to make swift strokes in a circular motion over the white mess. The giant melted marshmallow began to transform , albeit slowly, into slightly larger than realistic clouds.

Not that I could pay attention to the warped and unimpressive painting before me when he held my hand in his.

His painting, of course, was perfect.

When the blob was successfully transformed into something vaguely recognizable as a large, overbearing cloud, he moved his hand back down, taking my hand with it. His fingers interlaced with mine, squeezing around the paintbrush as he stared straight ahead at the instructor, pretending to listen.

I loved it. Every single second of it. I basked in it, savoring the joyous tattooing of my heart against my chest at his touch.

Look, I like the guy as much as you do, sweetheart, but can you try not to act like a blushing school girl around him for ten seconds?

Power liked him?

Of course I do. He's tall, confident, and has everything under control around him all the time. He's an alpha male, Sane. How could you expect me not to like the guy? He's my male counterpart.

I chose not to reply to her, still shocked that Power and I agreed on... well, anything.

Was that a good or bad thing?

I shook my head, dislodging my inner turmoil. Enjoying the contact between us was far more important at the moment, and I didn't want to waste a second of it.

The next twenty minutes went by far too quickly, and because my hand and paintbrush were both lodged within his grip, my painting made no more progress. A furious blush warmed up my pale cheeks and stayed there as my insides jumbled up, twisting and turning in every direction and adding to the whole pleasantly squirmy feeling that had overcome me. John didn't look at me again, but I saw the closed lip smile on his face as he continued on with his own painting.

I'd turned to make sure the instructor or orderly hadn't caught us when Marcie's pain filled face cut across my vision. Acting on pure instinct, I pulled my hand away from John's and back into my lap, but it was too late. The damage was done, and more than likely, Marcie now hated me, like I'd expected her to the first time I'd noticed her jealousy.

She stared at the empty space where our hands had been joined for a few more seconds before the orderly from the day before - the one who had eyed her up like a piece of candy before fetching Martha - stopped beside her and asked if she needed assistance. She looked up at him, dragging her longing gaze from the spot between John and I, and swallowed. I barely heard her whisper, "I'm alright, thank you." The orderly nodded and started to walk away, and Marcie's demeanor changed in a instant. The forlorn expression fell from her face to be replaced with a bright and shining grin, and she reached out and tapped his arm. He looked back at her, his eyebrow raised in question.

"Actually, could you help me out? I'm not quite understanding how to paint the crashing waves correctly," she stage whispered, her cheeks rosy and inviting. He crouched down beside her and the two began to flirt without shame.

I took that as my cue to try and catch up on my pathetic looking catastrophe on canvas.

John's fingers found their way to mine later that day in the lounge. I pulled my hand away and offered him an apologetic half smile, my eyes darting to Marcie. He followed my line of sight and frowned. She wasn't even looking our way, but the fact that seeing any sort of familiarity between us hurt her was enough for me to put off any lingering affections between us.

She'd been kind to me, like Esther. I couldn't bring myself to make her feel anything negative toward me. Her marked jealousy was clear as day, and I knew how fortunate I was to not be on the receiving end of menacing glares and catty name callings. Pushing my luck would have been stupid.

With a stiffness to his shoulders that I hadn't seen before in him, he looked back to me and inclined his head toward the doorway leading to the corridor.

Power's hackles rose, remembering the last time we'd been told to meet someone away from a large group of people in a similar fashion. The bruises. The broken bones. The screams as we'd tried, in vain, to punch back at our attacker. My vision blurred as I bit my tongue and fought to push back the looming episode Power was pushing on me.

I won't attack unless he does! I like him! Just let me out, to be sure! She screamed at me from inside my head. I squeezed my eyes shut and forced myself to stay in control, telling her that her reaction was absurd over and over again all the while.

This was John. Not Gregory or Cecilia or Ellie. I'd known him for less than a week, but I knew for a fact John wouldn't hurt me. And by now, Power should have known that, too.

He stood and walked from the room as I gathered my sanity back into one nice, neat little package at the forefront of my brain. Within minutes Power calmed herself down enough for me to trust her - or as close to trusting her as I'd ever get - and I followed after John.

He met me outside the large double doors, a pensive expressive on his chiseled face.

"You're worried about Marcie?" he asked, tucking a stray piece of hair behind my ear and sending those over sized butterflies catapulting at breakneck speeds all over my insides yet again.

I nodded, forcing myself to remember what on earth he'd just asked me. "She likes you, and I don't want to hurt her. I don't want to make enemies here."

His shoulders heaved as he sighed heavily and leaned against the wall, arms crossed over his chest as he looked at the ground in deep thought. "Kate, Marcie is... a difficult and complicated person. She finds something she likes and clings to it for dear life. When I convinced the doctors and orderlies to change her medicine up and get her out of solitary confinement, I became that thing she likes. But, it's not a two way street there, you see what I'm saying? I care about her like I would a sister, and she has to learn that."

"But, I don't want her to hate me, John," I pleaded, not liking how whiny my voice sounded. I cleared my throat and continued, keeping my voice lower so the pitch wouldn't escalate again. "I don't want to hurt her."

John stared at me for a moment, searching my features with a soft, closed mouth smile. "You're a good woman, Kate. If I hadn't seen that episode you had on your first day, myself, I wouldn't be able to believe you even had a reason to be here."

A bright, furious wave of heat bloomed across my cheeks. But, that didn't change the fact that I, in no way, shape, or form, wanted to have a conversation that could have ever in a million years led onto the topic of my reason for being at Rosenton. I was positive he knew. Esther had told me he did. But, it was too nice to pretend he didn't know I'd done something so incomprehensibly horrible, dark, and inhuman.

"Would it be alright for me to ask what brought Marcie here? Or would that be too prying?" I asked, directing the conversation as far away from my own story as possible.

His shoulders lifted up in a nonchalant shrug. "She killed her husband."

"That seems to be a trend in this ward."

That lovely smirk graced his lips again as he laughed silently for a moment at my observation. "Luckily, she and Esther are the only two who can say that. Marcie was a newlywed, though, where Esther had been married for around thirty years, I think."

"Was her husband hurting her?"

"No. She has… moods, I guess you'd say. You'll see before too long. It's like she's two different people."

I sucked in my next breath so hard it caught in my throat, leaving me coughing and gasping for air. Two people, hm? Power cackled, her amusement made loud and clear as the description hit way too close to home for my liking. John patted by back as I regained composure, waving my hand for him to continue.

"She only has two emotions, and they're both extreme. Every couple of weeks or so they'll switch out. You got here while she's overly happy and more hyper than a flea in a pound. Before long, though, she'll wake up and be real depressed. It'll last for a week or so, and it'll go right back to the woman she is now. When she gets sad, she stays in bed for days. Nothing makes her do anything otherwise. But, as bad as it is now, it was a hundred times worse before they switched her meds," he said, his voice low and quiet in case anyone could hear.

"Why did she kill her husband, then?" I asked, curiosity taking over as he filled me in on the beautiful young woman.

He glanced down the hallway on both sides, checking for anyone else, before answering. "She didn't actually succeed, but she doesn't know that. She was going through one of the depressed times, and thought that they both were better off dead, so she poisoned the dinners she cooked. Arsenic. She thought she was doing him a favor."

"So, he's alive and she doesn't know?"

"Exactly. And it's needs to stay that way. He's remarried and three states over now. Barely recovered from her murder attempt."

I bit my lip as I let that sink in. Did she feel guilty? What would she do if she ever found out he'd lived and gone on to start a new family without her? Did he still love her? What would it be like to be so thoroughly depressed and self-loathing that I'd poison my spouse to put him out of his misery of being with me?

Marcie seemed so bubbly and happy, flitting around, laughing, and flirting with everyone. How did she do it? How did she move on and become filled with life again? She made it look so easy...

I bit the inside my of cheek as I pondered the new information. John remained silent, watching my face and waiting for my response.

"She wants you, though," I started, balancing on my tiptoes as my fingers fidgeted with the hem of my dress. "And, if she's bound to turn depressed soon, I don't want to contribute to her feeling that way. It feels cruel. I want to hold your hand, I really do. You have... You have something that draws me in and makes me want to be near to you. But I don't want to hold your hand at the expense of Marcie's feelings. It's just too mean. I can only be with you when she can't see and be hurt by it."

I felt the warmth of his large hand caressing my cheek before I saw his extended arm. His thumb brushed my jaw, and I nuzzled into his touch, closing my eyes and savoring it. Why did I feel this way toward him? I'd known him less than a week, and no one had ever effected me like he did. Were my feelings toward him just a result of him being the first person to ever go out of their way to be kind to me? I'd read novels and poems about love at first sight, but it seemed too far fetched, especially for someone like me. Even if he did seem to be feeling the same things I was.

Just go with it, Sane. Even I want it. Want him. Who cares if Marcie gets hurt? She has to learn. He said it himself. He's the first person to ever want you. And we both want him. Why are you making this so complicated? Power asked, her tone for once calm and collected. Had John's touch and presence subdued even her, the untamable?

When I opened my eyes his gentle smile greeted me, his face filled with something I could only akin to admiration, though I couldn't imagine the cause.

"You're a good woman," he repeated, his voice lower than a whisper. "My ma would love you."

"She would love a mass murderer?" I blurted before I could stop the words from tumbling off my tongue. If I could have slapped myself for that, I would have the second it happened. He quirked an eyebrow, as if he was unsure I'd admitted it out loud himself.

"I know you did it, Kate, but I can't believe it. All I've seen from you is good and hope and humility. The idea of you killing one person, much less an entire fleet of circus performers, seems absurd. Tell me it was a one time thing. Tell me you just snapped. Because I won't believe for a minute that's who you really are."

My lips trembled under the pressure of his gaze. How could he even think anything good of me, especially after hearing the news report for himself? Tears pricked the back of my eyes as my fists clenched into anguished balls at my sides. I couldn't look at him, choosing to study the tiles at my feet instead. The floor had been freshly waxed, shining and reflecting my image back at me.

I stared at my pained face in the watery reflection for a moment, wondering how the girl I was staring at had been capable of taking so much life from others.

She smiled.

My breaths came faster as she continued to smile, mocking my panic and undying guilt.

Give it up, Sane. He's wrong. Our hands killed them. There's no taking it back. I'll never regret protecting us.

"No," I replied. "I'll never be that again."

Chapter 8

Numb.

Dizzy.

Cold.

Dazed.

Gone.

Not even Power's seductive voice could break through the heavy fog enveloping my mind and body. My fingers glided over the silver surface of the bristled object the woman with black hair had given me.

I should know what this object was.

I should know what it's for.

But, how could I figure it out if my eyes wouldn't even focus on it to study it?

What was it she'd said to me when she'd put it in my hands? Oh, yes… "Brush your hair, honey."

I flipped the intricate handle over in my palm. I knew that I knew how to brush my hair - using this object that I still couldn't remember the proper name for - but the individual steps eluded me, shying away from my inquiring mind. It was really quite rude, the way the knowledge pranced away from me, huddling in the deepest portion of my brain so I couldn't access it.

"Oh, Kate," a voice sighed from above me. I looked up, slowly. "Those meds are hitting you harder than they do for most. Maybe because you're so petite, nina. John's going to be worried sick over you all day. You poor darling."

Why did this black haired woman's voice echo so loud inside my head?

Why couldn't I just focus on her? What was wrong with my eyes?

And where was Power? Shouldn't she have had something to say about this whole situation by now?

"Come on, let's get you to the lounge. I suppose it doesn't really matter that you're in those over sized pajamas for today. You most certainly won't care, anyway," the woman babbled on, taking the silver object from my hands and running it down the shafts of my hair over and over again.

That's right. That's how to brush my hair. Silly me.

My head fell forward, suddenly far too heavy for my neck to hold up.

The woman tilted my head back up, two fingers under my chin. "Kate, honey, you get in this room by seven-thirty every night from now on, you hear? You're a walking zombie. You can't let them give you those meds again. We're lucky it's Sunday and you have no classes or appointments today."

She spoke far too much for me to hang on to even a single syllable of it. The words floated up into the air above me, disintegrating into microscopic particles of nothingness. I looked up, squinting my unfocused eyes as I searched for evidence of the sentences that had fallen from the woman's scarlet lips.

Nothing.

What had she said, again? Something about perfume?

No, that's not right.

Medicine. Some.. Kind of...

How was I in the lounge all of a sudden? Why was the radio so loud?

"Kate? Good grief, the meds did this to her? How did this happen, Esther?"

I was drowning in warm, earthy chocolate. How could something so simple be so beautiful?

"She came in from her shower at the same time the nurses came by last night. There wasn't an opportunity for her to fake sleep. I had no idea it would be this bad, though."

Warmth. Safe, comforting warmth caressed my face, and only a few seconds later did I realize that warmth was from two hands smoothing my hair away from my eyes. Hands... Connected to strong, tanned arms. I smiled at them. Safe, safe, safe. That melted chocolate seared into me again. I withered beneath it, wishing I could immerse myself and live there. Safe.

"Katie, come on, now. Can you hear me? Do you know who I am?"

Maybe I would if my eyes would just focus.

"You're... safe...ty," I mumbled, closing my eyes as the room expanded and contracted. A giggle fell from my lips as I realized the room was breathing.

"Should we lay her down on the couch?"

What have you done now, Sane?

"No, we need to get her to try to come back to us. I can't believe the number they did to her. Even Lottie tolerates them better than this."

Stupid girl. You let this happen to us. You took those meds.

Why did Power sound so weak? Like she'd just woken from a thousand year long slumber? Her voice was barely a whisper in my mind, bouncing off the walls of my skull like butterflies landing and taking off again.

"John, Lottie's not a mass murderer. They probably gave Kate a larger dose on purpose."

I can't even see through our eyes. You are such a bloody idiot, Sane. Did you do this on purpose? To weaken me!?

"Don't call her that."

My body swayed side to side as I struggled to remain balanced enough to sit straight. Why was it so difficult? Was I forgetting a step to sitting?

"What?"

Large hands landed on my shoulders and steadied me. I crumpled forward beneath the weight of them, landing on a rock hard, breathing, thumping surface.

"Mass murderer. She's too..."

"But, she is, John. She may not have wanted to let it happen, but it did."

"Just don't call her that, okay? I know she did it. But, I can't... I just can't."

What were they talking about again? Words... There were words... That meant... something.

Get it together, you useless twit!

My lips turned down at the corners. How utterly mean of Power to say such things.

“Let’s sit her upright. Start asking her questions. Get her to focus and get out of the fog.”

Questions? About what?

My back made contact with scratchy material.The thumping surface no longer held me up, but the two large hands on my shoulders remained. I liked them there.

“Kate, honey, look at me,” a woman’s voice commanded. I tried to obey, but each movement was just... so... difficult. By the time my eyes met dark, nearly black ones in front of me, I’d forgotten what I was supposed to be doing anyway.

“Can you tell me who I am?” she asked.

“A... little bit,” I replied, my tongue thick and over sized for my mouth.

“Who am I, Kate?” she persisted.

She’s Esther, you idiot!

“Esther,” I blurted, following Power’s lead. The voice in my head perked up a bit.

Want me to take over, Sane? Give them the answers you can’t? I can help us.

I was sure there was a reason I should tell her no, but for the life of me I couldn’t find that reason anywhere in my foggy, messed up, discombobulated brain. Her grin ate up at the insides of my very soul, but it felt good in some strange way. Good meant it was alright, right? I could trust her. I’d trusted her before for... something...

"Good," the woman named Esther affirmed, reassuring my trust in Power. "Tell me where you are right now? Anything about where you are."

Hell. Some place reserved for scum. Imprisoned. Somewhere we don't deserve to be.

"Hell... Pris... Be?"

God, you're useless.

Esther's face scrunched up in confusion. "Tell me again. Tell me where you are, Kate."

"Am I... yellow?"

"Let me, Esther. Go watch for orderlies. We may just have to let her sleep it off if she can't snap out of it."

Earthy, chocolate, safety again.

"Tell me who I am, Kate."

"Warmth," I whispered, my body leaning forward, yearning to be closer.

"What's my name?"

Have you forgotten even him, Sane?

No! I haven't forgotten him! Just... his name...

I won't help you anymore. Not until you let me take over for a little while.

Faint, barely audible alarm bells rang somewhere in my head, but they faded away. Had I imagined them?

"Alright... Tell me how."

"Tell you how, what?" those earthen brown orbs asked, but I ignored them. Power would take care of us.

Take down the wall. Lower it so I can come through. I'll take care of everything, sweet Sane.

"Okay."

And just like that, with surprisingly little effort, I let the wall crumble down.

Loud, startling giggles erupted from my mouth as my muscles all went rigid. Coldness seeped into every pore, filling my body with its cool, watery sting. From far away, the voice belonging to that brown warmth I'd felt before began to call my name. He sounded panicked, but I soon forgot about it as my vision blacked over, my insanity driven giggles growing in volume and intensity.

I felt myself recede back as Power surged forward. Her strong hands gripped my arms as we crossed paths.

Don't worry, my sweet. I'll reward you for letting me out. Now, rest for a while. Leave it all in my care, she cooed in my ear, giving me a slight push backward. I stumbled over a pile of crumbled stone and fell back, landing on my rear as the smooth rocks began to rebuild themselves into a new wall.

It felt... wrong. But I didn't know why.

I watched through Power's eyes as she surfaced, her smile wide and her eyes glinting silver.

"John," she spoke, rolling her shoulders as if she were stretching pent up muscles.

That's right. The brown warmth was John. How silly of me to forget something so important. He looked up at her face, startled. "Kate?"

"Of sorts. She's safe. Resting. The poor thing."

His grip on my - her - shoulders tightened. "Who are you?"

She laughed, the sound like ringing bells all around. "I'm Kate, silly! And you expect me to tell you your name? When you don't even remember mine?"

I frowned. You're not Kate. I'm Kate. You're Power.

We are who we are, aren't we?

She stood, causing John to take two pronounced steps backward. He kept his gaze locked on her, studying her bright and mischievous face and her limbs as she stretched them. "You're not the Kate I know. Who are you?" he repeated, his tone firm and expectant of answers.

I laid down, closing my eyes. God, I was just so... tired.

Power cocked her head to the side, a pout on her full lips. "Why so rude? I'm the one who should be offended. You couldn't even call me what I am. Poor, poor Sane. She denies it over and over, and she tries so hard. She really does. She locks me away, like a prisoner, when I'm the one who freed us, you know? I stopped the bruises. The broken bones. The slavery. It was me."

There were those warning bells again. Louder this time.

"You're the... the..." He still couldn't say it.

Power walked toward him, her stride confident and slow, a panther stalking her prey, in disguise as a young woman. She reached her hand out, pressing it to his chest as she looked up at him through her eyelashes. "She really adores you. Lucky for her, so do I."

He swatted her hand away and glared at her. "You... You're the one who... You're the..."

Her chuckles were soft as she leaned up on her tiptoes, her balance perfect and unwavering. Hands clasped behind her back, she leaned forward, her lips close to his ear. "Say it, love. Say the word. Say, 'murderer.'"

My stomach turned.

This wasn't right. I'd made a mistake. A horrible mistake.

Please stop this, Power. Please, I begged without shame, not really knowing what I was pleading for, exactly. But this... whatever she was doing... It wasn't right or good.

I saw the change in John's gaze before the tensing of his muscles. The soft, comforting presence was gone, replaced by a hard and commanding machine. My heart dropped, forming a puddle at my toes as the body I watched, my body, become a threat to him. He towered over her as she looked up at him with an amused smirk.

"Would you hurt me? This is her body, too, you know."

Unflinching, he ignored her quip. "Bring her back," he demanded instead.

Fury ignited a wild flame in her belly. I felt it burning beneath my feet as she took another step to him, challenging him. "I am her."

No, no, no, no, no, please don't do this.

Power and John both turned, jumping in their surprise, as the doors to the lounge opened, revealing a distracted and murmuring Ed.

Reality began to slip from Power's mind as her swirling, angry eyes locked in on the seven foot tall giant. I saw, through her eyes, as his black hair moved and transformed around his head until he became a wavering reflection of my deceased ring master.

"Robbie," she whispered as Ed lowered himself into the chair beside the radio, pulling a deck of cards from his coat pocket and shuffling the weathered pieces with expert ease. He gave neither John nor Power a single glance, focused instead on the gentle continuous fwiiiiip of the cards.

"Why aren't you dead?" she murmured to herself and possibly me as well. Her challenging stance toward John withered as she took a sinister step toward Ed. John grabbed her wrist, and I sighed at the small weary victory.

Power snapped her head back to him, teeth bared in an animalistic snarl. "Let me go," she snapped, yanking her arm in his steel grip.

"You're not going near him. Not until you bring her back."

I shivered at the low, threatening tone of his voice. The words rumbled from his chest, making my heart pound in anticipation. Strangely enough, despite the promise of harm between the lines, I felt no fear.

No. I felt confidence. Assuredness. He wouldn't let her hurt anyone. He'd stop her. Another relieved sigh expelled from my aching lungs.

"He's already dead!" she cried, her fury turning wild and dangerous. Fire danced in our veins as her temper erupted all around us.

Finally, Ed's head jerked up, eyes widened toward Power and John, as if he hadn't even realized they were there.

All at once several things happened, producing wild, abandoned chaos within the small Ward F lounge room. Power met Ed's gaze with her own raging glare, only recognizing him as Robbie instead of Ed. She broke from John's hold and lunged for the giant man, becoming a blur of untamed violence the closer she got to him. Ed jumped from the chair, landing against the barred window. The glass shattered around him, the steel bars the only thing keeping him from tumbling from the opening and falling seven stories to his untimely death. John shot toward Power, wrapping his arms around her waist as he took her down to the floor, trapping her angry, clawing, screeching body beneath his weight. Even she couldn't move the rock wall that was John Kingwood.

He clamped his hand over her mouth as she screamed obscenities, muffling the volume of her angry cries. The fog around my mind seemed to clear as the severity of the situation settled in, and I began to panic inside my own mind.

Stop it, Power! He's not Robbie! Stop screaming or you'll get us hurt! Stop it! I begged, telling her over and over that she hadn't seen Robbie. Robbie was gone. Ed had never hurt her, or let others hurt her. Ed was innocent!

As the struggle between Power, John and I went on, I began to feel myself get sucked back to the surface. Power was releasing her control back to me, too weak to fight anymore. She said nothing to me as our bodies brushed each other in the limbo between my mind and my body. Whether she realized her mistake and was embarrassed, or simply had no more in her to continue on, I didn't know. But, I took the opportunity presented and ran for the surface as she walked, head hung down, back behind the wall.

I opened my eyes, breaking through the barrier, gasping for breath against John's thick palm. On instinct, I grabbed for his wrist, pulling at it so I could inhale large gulp-fulls of sweet oxygen.

"Kate?" he whispered, his face dangerously close to mine. He searched my face, trying to confirm my presence and absence of Power. I nodded fervently, clutching at the skin around his muscled arm. "Don't scream," he warned just before obliging me and removing his hand.

I gasped for air, loud, sobbing noises scratching my throat as streams of tears fell down the sides of my face, into my hair. John's heavy body still pinned me down, his reluctance to believe I wouldn't go for Ed again clear in his expression. Tiny shards of glass sliced into the back of my arms and shoulders, slivers scratching at the back of my head through my hair as well. I couldn't see Ed, but I heard the doors to the lounge slam shut, meaning he'd probably already left. More voices infiltrated my ears, eluding to more than John and my presences in the room.

"I'm sorry!" The sobs burst from my lungs, choking me as my wild emotions formed one solid ball in my throat.

With that, John finally relaxed, his tense body going limp above me. "Hey, hey... It's fine... Shh," he whispered in my ear, smoothing my hair from my cheeks. "It's alright. You're okay. You're back."

"What happened?" the third presence in the room asked, and through the still light fog, I recognized it as belonging to George.

"She had an episode and attacked Ed. She became someone else."

"She attacked him?"

"I'm sorry!" I blubbered again, the pain in my chest from my guilt becoming more and more intense.

George's face appeared to my side, glaring at me. "Let me talk to her," he demanded. John's body stiffened above me.

"Not right now, George. It's not the time to-"

"It is the time. Come on, Kate," he cut John off, grabbing my hand and pulling me to my feet. John stumbled up and grabbed my upper arm, pulling me against his chest.

"I don't know what you think you're doing, but you're not going to touch her."

The teen sighed, rolling his eyes in an obvious show of exasperation. "I'm not going to touch your precious girlfriend. I just need to say something to her. In private."

"You don't need to say-"

"It's alright," I interrupted John's growing wrath. "It's just a talk." My voice sounded weak, and I hated it. His chest heaved against my back as he considered it. After a tense and loaded silence, he released my arm and turned away from me. My chest heaved as I took in great, huge lung-fulls of air, my body exhausted from the past hour.

He was hurt. My heart ached as he walked from the room, slamming the door behind him. I had no time to dwell on it, though, because in the next second George had pushed me back to sit on the couch, sending the already embedded shards of glass further into the skin of my shoulders. I winced, but made no sound to show the pain.

"I have a message for that little psycho inside your head," he began, squatting down to look at me at eye level. I squirmed under the intense scrutiny. "I don't know if she can hear me, or if you'll have to relay the message or what, but somehow, some way, I need you to make sure she gets the picture, understand?"

Power raised her head from where she'd collapsed in an exhausted heap, her ears perked to listen.

"Make sure she knows I will find her and rip her out of your head by her throat, then rip that throat from her neck, if she tries to attack or hurt another member of this ward. John may be the golden boy and have reservations about hurting you, but I'm not that good of a guy. I will do worse to her than she could have ever dreamed of doing to your circus friends if she pulls another stunt like that. Whether you share a body or not. I like you, Kate, and I don't want to hurt you because I consider you a part of this ward - this family, so it would be best if you kept that psycho locked away so I don't have to do anything drastic, get it?"

I couldn't move. Couldn't breathe. All I could manage to do was stare, eyes like saucers, at the sinister young man in front of me.

"Nod if you get the picture," he snapped, grabbing my chin in his cold hand. My head bobbed up and down of its own accord, without instruction from my brain. Power remained quiet, mulling over his threat seriously even though she hated being threatened at all. She knew George shouldn't be messed with. She could sense something in him, maybe the same darkness that she lived in.

He let go of my chin and stood straight, pulling a mask of friendliness and smiles over the dark, twisted expression from only seconds before. "Good. Now, when John asks what we talked about, you tell him I gave you some tips for keeping that disgusting thing in your head under control. It's not a lie, is it, Kate?"

I swallowed, shaking my head 'no'. That earned me a smile that sent shivers down my neck. "Good girl. I'll let the others back in. Put a smile on your face. Act happy."

Do it, Power supplied, her voice serious. That was enough for me to make the quick decision to obey. If Power was afraid of him, it was for good reason. With a deep breath, cleansing the fear and shock from my system, I blanked my expression, then placed a gentle smile on my lips just as John, Esther, and Lottie entered the room.

John wouldn't look at me, and it killed me. He took a seat across from me, glanced down at all the broken glass, then stood back up and left the room. Esther sat beside me while Lottie perched herself on the arm of the chair George had taken, like a small child.

"Marcie should be back soon," the young woman chirped, grinning as if she couldn't sense the tension swimming in the air. I smiled a little wider and nodded in acknowledgment.

"She said she'd bring me back a dolly. I hope it has a beautiful dress. Maybe she'll bring some candy back. Her mommy loves to buy her candy and chocolates," she continued on. George rested his cheek on his hand, propped up on the arm of his chair by his elbow. His other hand landed on Lottie's shoulder, pulling the sleeve of the dress that hung from her frame back up on her shoulder from where it had fallen down her bony arm.

John came back into the room holding a broom and dustpan. I stood and went to help as he swept up the glass. Trembling, I placed my hand on his around the handle of the broom. He looked up, meeting my apologetic eyes. With a deep, accepting sigh, he squeezed his own eyes shut then opened them again, nodding his acceptance of my apology. My fingers stroked his for a moment in silent thanks and I took the broom from him to sweep up the mess that was my own fault. He held the dustpan for me, and we walked out of the room to take the two items back to the supply closet together after disposing of the shattered glass in the waste bin.

"Did he threaten you or hurt you?" he asked as soon as we got to the closet in the connecting hallway.

I shook my head. "No. He just told me what to do to keep her under control next time." The ease with which the lie slid off my tongue frightened me, but I swallowed the guilt and muscled through it.

"Don't trust him, Kate. He's not bad, but he's not good either. He-"

"He's a user. I know. Esther told me. Thank you for trying to tell me also, John," I whispered, glancing up at him with a gentle smile.

He stopped short and pulled my hand into his. "I'm sorry I had to tackle you like that. She's... She's volatile."

A smirk lifted on my lips. "Oh, trust me. I know. You have nothing to apologize for. I could see what was happening, but couldn't do anything about it. I was really quite thankful when you kept her from getting to Ed."

"Did I hurt you?" he asked, rubbing his thumb across my knuckles.

"No. I think I fell into some of the glass, though. I'll ask Esther to check and help me get it all sorted."

He leaned over to look at my upper back and shoulder blades. A frown etched across his mouth as he looked back at me. "There's a lot, but nothing deep. I'm so sorry." His lips brushed against the back of my hand, and my heart began to bruise the inside wall of my chest, it pounded so hard. "Go lie down on your bed. I'll send Esther with some bandages and alcohol."

"Alright," I replied, staring at the place his lips had kissed on my hand. He ruffled the hair on top of my head and tried to grin at me, but I could still feel the weight behind them. He knew I was truly dangerous now, and it was a hard enough fact for me to accept, much less someone else I cared about so much already.

With that depressing thought, I turned and headed for my room.

Exhaustion slammed into my body like a freight train as soon as I laid, stomach down, on my bed. Just as my eyes rolled up into my head to welcome much needed sleep, the door to my room pushed open, revealing Esther, Marcie, and Lottie as they filed in.

"John said you needed help," Esther said, moving toward me as I groaned against the waves of sleep fighting for my surrender. "Glass in your shoulders and scratches?"

I nodded, burying my face in my lumpy pillow. One of the three women pulled back my pajama shirt from my back, her touch gentle. All three of them hissed in sympathetic pain less than a second later.

"Oh, Kate. You poor thing," Marcie said, squeezing my hand in hers. I refused to look up, my brain still holding on to some of the fog from the medicine I'd taken the night before.

"Let's get you cleaned up then," Esther interrupted Marcie's pitying comments and I winced as she used her tweezers to pull slivers of glass from my shoulders. The tink, tink, tink of the pieces landing in the glass jar at my bedside nearly lulled me back to sleep as Marcie and Lottie babbled on about the things Marcie brought back from town. Esther, like me, remained quiet, though I didn't know if she was upset about something or just concentrating on the task at hand.

The awful sting of alcohol being poured over the various cuts made my body jerk as a pained hiss shot from between my teeth.

"Shh, now. It's over. I'll bandage it up in a second and you'll be fine," she soothed, brushing her fingers through my hair. At that moment, I knew I would have done anything in my life to experience having Esther as my true mother. I bit the inside of my cheek as the sting dulled and the wounds were covered and wrapped under her careful and soft hands.

"We'll sit with her if you want to go eat lunch," Marcie offered as her chatter with Lottie died down. My brain was still too dazed and dizzy to ask why I needed to be babysat out loud.

"Thanks, girls. I'll bring back your lunches on my way back here," Esther replied. The spot that had sunk under her weight released and sprang back up, signaling her leave of her position on my bed. With one last brush of her fingers through my hair, she placed a gentle kiss to my forehead and left, the door clicking shut behind her.

My aching body bounced clear up a couple of inches from the mattress, shocking my eyes open to see Marcie and Lottie jumping on my tiny bed to sit on either side of me. Both had expressions mirroring each other, light beaming from their smiles and excitement bubbling in their eyes.

"I felt absolutely terrible for upsetting you yesterday, so I bought you new clothes!" Marcie blurted, her voice a high pitched squeal. Somehow, confusing my fragile mind because I hadn't seen evidence of any shopping bags prior, she produced three large bags, all with fancy cursive writing scrawled across the fronts. My jaw dropped as I recognized the expensive brands. Why would she rain such lavish gifts on me?! The idea that she should abhor me still flirted with my thoughts, knowing her feelings for John.

"You shouldn't have!" I cried, pushing myself up on my elbows as I winced against the pain. She took the literal sentence as an exclamation of gratitude, I assumed, because she bounced up and down, a girlish giggle erupting from her lips as she began whipping dresses, blouses, and skirts from the bags, laying them out flat on the only clear area of the bed. Expensive silk, lace, and other fabrics spread like plush ocean waves over my blanketed legs as I took the clothing in with pure awe.

"As soon as I told my mother I had a new friend who had to borrow clothes, she insisted we buy you your own, just like I hoped she would! I hope I bought the right size. I really only guessed. You're only a tad smaller than me, with thinner hips and smaller chest. You're my perfect dress up doll, Kate!" She spat the word 'borrowed' as if it were bile on her tongue, leading me to believe our beautiful Marcie was rather well off, and reinforcing the idea that she got her way more often than not.

Although, who wants to be in an insane asylum, Power mused, her echoing voice thick with amusement.

"Marce, I can't pay you for these things," I said, eyeing the gorgeous fabrics. I couldn't accept them, but that didn't mean I didn't long for them anyway.Not a single piece of the clothing was cheap, and the ripped in half price tags only proved that. Sure, I couldn't see the actual prices since they had been torn from the tags, but the knowledge that they were all from various high end boutiques and stores told me despite that.

Marcie waved her hand around in the air, rolling her eyes at me. "They're gifts, silly. You're my friend, and you were in need. Why shouldn't I help you since I have the tools necessary?"

Because I've never even seen the amount of money one of these pieces alone costs.

Even Power was in awe of the brilliant clothing.

"She won't take no for an answer," Lottie supplied, grinning ear to ear. "Her mom is loaded and insists on spending money everywhere she can. Just accept them, Kate."

My jaw hung open as I finally decided to take the clothing into my hands, running them up and down the sleek, plush fabrics. This had to be a dream. I, Kate the Great, the circus star and mass murderer, couldn't have possibly been given such lavish, wonderful gifts from someone who should hate me. I felt as though I'd been dropped in an alternate universe, where nothing made sense to me, but was perfectly normal to everyone else. Had the doors to Rosenton been the portal?

I shook the suspicious thoughts from my head. I would bask in this happiness, just this once. A lifetime of abuse afforded me at least this small delusion, right? Because I found it much more likely that I was hallucinating under the prior night's medication than actually experiencing this odd kindness.

So, before carefully hanging each piece of expensive clothing in my half of the cheap, plywood armoire beside my old, worn leotards and settling down to sleep off the slight fog still trapping my brain, I thanked Marcie from the bottom of my double sided heart - Power included. Marcie beamed beneath my gratitude and nearly crushed me to death in a hug between her and Lottie.

"Wonderful! Now, just get yourself some sleep, beautiful! Tomorrow is a fresh new day, and you have a ton of beautiful clothes to go with your beautiful face," she commanded, kissing my cheek.

I nodded, unable to speak against the welling positive emotions overwhelming me without bursting into grateful tears. The two girls left my bed to go sit on Esther's bed, and I laid down to oblige my aching eyes plead for sleep.

"You know starving yourself is no way to cope, sweetheart."

"I don't recall asking your opinion, Marcie."

"I know... But I care about you, Lottie. We all care about you. It kills us to see you hurt yourself like this."

"It's none of your business. Drop it."

"Lottie-"

"No! I said drop it. I don't need your lectures. I get enough of that from Shilling."

"I'm sorry. I really am. I just care about you. You can't stop yourself from growing up, whether you eat or not, love. And, you're here with us. You're safe. No one can hurt you. Do you really think George would ever let anything happen to you?"

"I... I know that it won't stop me from aging... I know that... I-I just..."

"Oh, sweetheart, don't cry! Please. I didn't meant to upset you! I only wanted to try to encourage you to eat something. I'm so sorry."

"G-George tells me... all the time! That-that no one can hu...hurt me anymore. But, I'm s-so scared, Marce! M-My cousin will come back f-for me, I know it."

"Shh. He won't come back for you. We will never let any more harm come to you. We want you to be happy and healthy. Please eat? Please?"

"You know I c-can't."

"We love you, though! We hurt when you hurt. Please?"

"I can't... I'm t-too scared. He'll be back f-for me..."

Bile shot up my throat as my eye wrenched open, destroying the haze of that inconclusive state of maybe-asleep-maybe-not. I had just enough time to see the startled expressions on both girls faces before my body heaved over the side of my bed and my stomach evacuated its contents. With not even an ounce of energy remaining within me, I leaned back on my pillow again and let my eyes roll back up in my head, welcoming the black nothingness of a dreamless medicated sleep.

Chapter 9

My eyes opened, greeted by the dull grey of the early morning hour. Groggy and filled with hunger pangs that nearly made me double over in pain, I sat up on my bed and scrubbed the sleep from my eyes with the heels of my hands.

The black rimmed, basic clock on the wall held its stiff hands to reveal that it was barely five-thirty in the morning. Breakfast wouldn't be for another two and a half hours. My stomach screamed in protest at the thought of waiting that long.

I sighed, resigning myself to it, before stopping and grinning like a fool.

Esther, you amazing, beautiful, kind, generous woman! Power squealed my own identical thoughts as the sight of a small plate with two wrapped roast beef sandwiches from the cafeteria filled my vision. They sat, wrapped in shiny foil, on top of my nightstand, waiting for me to devour them.

With a monstrous victory cry, my stomach leapt in excitement as I unwrapped the sandwiches and all but inhaled them both. They were bland and slightly soggy, but my gratitude to Esther for being so kind and leaving them for me overwhelmed any unsavory taste or texture my tongue touched.

As I finished them, licking the tips of my fingers for even the tiniest speck of food left behind, I stood from my bed and walked over to the small, prefabricated armiore. Surely the pile of beautiful clothes Marcie had brought me the night before was a decadent and fleeting figment of my imagination. The fact that she had bought me such nice clothing on a whim had to be a dream.

Silk, crushed velvet, lace and an entire assortment of various lovely fabrics hung from Rosenton's cheap metal hangers on my side of the cheap little armoire. Even some delicate, feminine undergarments were folded into neat little squares below the clothing hanging above them. My cheeks flamed at the thought of another person buying me underwear, but I was too stunned to feel anything more complex than gratitude and slight embarrassment.

Maybe these people really were my friends. Maybe they were my family. Maybe I could stop second guessing them and being suspicious.

Make sure she knows I will find her and rip her out of your head by her throat, then rip that throat from her neck, if she tries to attack or hurt another member of this ward. John may be the golden boy and have reservations about hurting you, but I'm not that good of a guy. I will do worse to her than she could have ever dreamed of doing to your circus friends if she pulls another stunt like that. Whether you share a body or not. I like you, Kate, and I don't want to hurt you because I consider you a part of this ward - this family, so it would be best if you kept that psycho locked away so I don't have to do anything drastic, get it?

George's words of warning echoed in my head, as if to remind me that nothing could be all sunshine and roses. They still considered me a liability - a danger to themselves. Maybe John wouldn't hurt me, but George had told me blatantly that he would, and even Esther had put me below the other ward mates when she had warned me to not let Power get out of control. Of course, having only been at Rosenton for less than a week, when they had all known and been here with each other for years likely had something to do with that mistrust.

Shaking my head to dislodge the wandering thoughts, I pulled a soft silk dress from the hanger and grabbed my meager bag of toiletries.

A shower sounded heavenly.

All during Group Therapy, George deflected each and every question from Lottie and I. His smooth voice manipulated the conversations with such ease that I began to see how he could be dangerous in a way that had nothing to do with any threat he could ever make. He was a master at the craft, often leading the conversation by the reigns and having it go precisely where he wanted. I watched his lips move with wonder, expecting some glittering magic to escape his mouth as he spoke, twirling around the air until it infiltrated and consumed the voice box and mind of the people he interacted with. How else could the young sixteen year old hold such excellent control over an entire room of people, Paul the arrogant doctor excluded.

No, Paul sat and watched George with a trained eye. It was clear he knew just as well as I did that George was in charge of the situation and conversation.

Yet, he said nothing, and I began to wonder if that was normal for the man Marcie had said had a "god-complex". He certainly sat like he thought he was a Greek god. His spine straight against his chair, making himself seem much taller and elegant that he probably was. The leather of his armchair made gentle thud, thud, thud noises as his lazy fingers tapped in quick, staggered succession on its arm. The man looked positively bored.

I swallowed and looked back to the other people around me. Some rocked back and forth in their chairs, not speaking at all, while others participated with what I was astounded to see was excitement. Those hung on George's words, entranced by his glowing charisma. None looked quite right, though. One woman had large chunks of her long, straw-like hair missing and she picked even further at the rest as she bit hard enough into her lip to draw blood. The man I'd seen the first day, who John had waved to outside Shilling's office, sat ramrod stiff in his chair, his sagging skin pale and the dark circles under his eyes nearly black as he stared at the wall, eyes unfocused. Another man glared with so much fire in his stormy blue eyes when our gazes met that I jumped back in my chair, my nerves twitching like crazy at his furious demeanor.

And, on the list went. All people, none fit enough to live out in the freedom of the rest of society.

"Katherine," Paul's voice cooed, dragging me from my observations, "Why don't you tell us why you're here? What... issues do you wish to resolve at your residency at Rosenton?"

I didn't hesitate as the words tumbled from my mouth without prior thought. "I'm prone to violence under certain conditions." It was enough of the truth to not have to elaborate, though I knew

Paul already knew who I was and what I'd done. Nonetheless, the phrase had become a infinitely rehearsed answer to that particular question.

A slow smirk spread across the therapist's face as his fingers formed a steeple in front of him. "Let's study that, shall we? What brought you to Rosenton? We'll start there."

My body froze, fire shooting through my veins. I swallowed, my breath catching in my throat as I wracked my brain for an acceptable, but not revealing, truth.

"I... I hurt my family in a violent outburst. That's why I'm here," I stammered, shooting nervous glances to George, who lounged back in his chair, watching me with a carefree expression and cold eyes telling me he was ready to come to my defense if I needed it.

Clever boy. He's weaning you, Sane. He wants you to take care of yourself, little by little. How cute. You're like a baby bird to him, having to learn to fly by careening from the nest and into the wide open air, where you'll break your neck or be eaten by a stray cat if you don't thrive.

Power's little speech did nothing to calm my anxiousness.

Paul's malicious grin widened and my jaw fell open as he winked at me, making it clear he knew exactly who I was, what I'd done, and that I didn't want anyone else to know it. Another opportunity for me to be blackmailed, surely. George watched the exchange, his demeanor relaxed and studious as he let me take up for myself.

"I see," Paul continued, his voice rippling through the room like the hiss of a deadly snake. "We'll continue this next time, then, Ms. Thornton. We've run out of time for the day. Everyone may retire to their wards for the rest of the afternoon."

Before the opportunity for Paul to corner me alone and blackmail me could come along, I hopped from my seat and beat everyone else out of the room, the weighty burden on my shoulders lifting the moment my feet crossed the threshold.

"Walk with me to the garden?" John asked as I drifted toward him in the hallway outside the lounge. I grinned, happy for the positive turn of events, and jogged toward him, nodding my head in agreement. He returned the smile, his eyes lit up with boyish sparks, and offered his elbow to me. I looped my arm through his, resting my palm on his forearm, and let him lead me to the staircase, a light bounce in my steps.

The cordiality of our actions felt silly to me, but in a good way. As small as the moment was, it was far past time for a little lightheartedness in my stressed life. Between the enigma of the mysterious thirteenth floor, making sure my crimes remained secret, George's curious actions, Marcie's jealous and friendly cocktail, and Lottie's refusal to eat, the weight of the world felt like it rested on my shoulders. Maybe John sensed that, or maybe he needed the airy moment as well. Whatever the case, I was grateful and savored it.

"Having a good day?" he guessed as we bounced down the steps in the stairwell.

I laughed. "Not particularly. Not until you caught me in the hallway, anyway."

He looked at me, his smile wide enough to show most of his sparkling white teeth. "So I've made you happier, then?"

"Your presence always seems to lift my spirits, John. I look forward to seeing you every day," I admitted, feeling the faint blush tinge my cheeks. His other hand came down to pat mine in the crook of his elbow.

"I'm glad. Your happiness means a lot to me." Though he didn't blush like I did, a red, splotchy tint crawled up his neck, giving away his nervousness.

Is this what courting feels like? I wondered, glancing up at him. I no longer held onto any denial that I felt something more than friendship for him, and he had all but outright said he felt the same. It had all come to be so quickly, really. I hadn't even been at Rosenton for a week, and already I felt like I'd known John for months. Almost immediately, he had captured my complete trust, and soon after that my complete respect. Had it happened that quickly for him, too? It had to have been fast seeing how it had only been six days since we'd first met.

I'd heard other performers gushing about their ever changing love interests before. When you know, you know! Charlotte had proclaimed in a loud, cheery voice to Ellie one night outside my cabin. Of course, the man she just knew was The One had been sleeping with Ellie when Charlotte was training, so my knowledge was not only limited, but a little biased and jaded.

But, then, when I looked back up at John again, all the jaded and cynical thoughts melted away. He radiated goodness. All goodness.

We made our way down to the gardens, chatting about frivolous things. John told me a few funny stories from before I'd arrived that had led to jokes I wouldn't have understood otherwise. I told him about various performances and routines that had wowed the audience. As I spoke, I tried not to think about the fact that none of the people I talked about existed anymore, and it was because of my own two hands.

"I wanted to explain myself for... Well, for watching you those two days when you were practicing."

Reminiscing, not practicing, I mentally corrected, but smiled and nodded for him to continue instead.

"I know it probably freaked you out, especially since we're in an asylum and all. It's just that - when I saw you doing those routines, it looked so familiar. I had to stay and watch and try to figure out where I knew those movements from. I finally figured it out earlier today, though," he said, his words rushing from his mouth far faster than normal for him.

"Familiar?" I asked, pausing to sit on the same stone bench in the same alcove I'd sat and talked on with Esther before.

John nodded, lowering his bulky body down to take the seat next to me. "Yeah, familiar. How long have you been in the circus, Kate?"

My lips turned down into a confused frown at his odd question. "Since I was six or so. Maybe younger. Why?"

His expression turned pleasantly wistful as he looked back at me, his earthy eyes nearly glowing with warmth. "I've seen you perform before. Before I was drafted. The night before I was drafted, actually. The circus came to town, and Ma pulled money from her jar of savings to take Elsie and I to see it. I kept telling her I could pay, but she wouldn't have any of it. She's a stubborn woman. Said she wanted to treat her kids in the middle of all the war going on."

My mouth hung open a little as I stared at him, shocked at the revelation. Doing the math quickly in my head, I deduced that I must have been thirteen or fourteen at the time he'd seen my performance, provided he had been drafted at seventeen like most other young men who had gone to war. And that was ten or more years ago! The idea that the sight of my performance sticking with someone, especially with John as that someone, for ten long years shocked me into a stunned, stupid silence.

"H-how can you be sure it was my circus?" I asked, finding my voice again after several seconds, wherein he watched my expression with amusement written all over his tanned face.

"I wondered the same thing. That's why I stopped to watch you the second time. I had to be sure. And I am, especially now. You were with Jensen and Sons back then, right?"

I nodded, too dumbed to work my vocal chords correctly.

"The routine was the same. The only difference was that you weren't a little girl anymore." He shrugged as he said it, as if those two sentences explained everything.

"You remember my routine?! After ten years?!" I cried, my voice cracking as my throat was forced to let the words leave my stomach. My hands flew in the air in dramatic circles, trying to capture some sense in the notion that somehow, my routines stuck in his head for so long! It was impossible! Robbie had wanted me to create magic with my performances, but never in my wildest dreams did this particular scenario enter my head when I imagined that so-called magic.

A deep, throaty laughter rang in my ears as I stared at him, wide eyed and slack jawed. "I imagine every person who has ever seen you perform would remember it for years to come, Kate. You're... you're amazing, to put it lightly. You do things that the human body shouldn't be able to do. It's beautiful, really. Aside from that, it was the last night I had with my family before the war. For that, it's even more engraved into my memories, and will probably be there forever."

"Wow," I muttered in response. Power straightened up behind my mental wall, the pride at his attention and reverence gleaming so brightly I thought it might blind me from the inside, out.

I jumped, startled, as the warmth of his large hand covered mine where it sat, gripping the edge of the bench between us. How strange and eerie that we shared a connection that preceded our meeting in Rosenton by ten years. My eyes lifted to look into his, and I found myself engulfed in the kindness and comfort they provided.

"You seem unreal," I admitted. "Like you don't even have a reason to be here, other than to be the strength the rest of us need."

His eternal smile dimmed and faltered for a moment before he broke eye contact and sighed. "I'm here for a reason," he corrected me, sounding none to thrilled with the admittance. Though, really, who was I to blame him? I was guilty of the same desire to keep my insanity hidden, even in a mental asylum.

"I won't judge you, you know? If you wanted to tell me… If that's not too presumptuous," I whispered, intertwining his fingers in mine and squeezing, hoping that simple action would show him how much I cared for him and wanted to support him as much as he had me.

His thumb stroked mine, the motion absent-minded and gentle at the same time. His face glazed over, the detached, emotionless facade unfamiliar to me on his face.

"I was drafted on my seventeenth birthday, the day after the attack. I tried telling them over and over that I wasn't eighteen yet, but I guess that didn't matter. It wouldn't have bothered me, and I would have gone gladly, if not for the fact that I was the only person who could support my ma and Elsie. They had nothing without me, and it terrified me for them. So, I went off to train, leaving them behind with nothing. God, Kate, it made me feel like a failure. The one thing my pop told me to do before he died was to take care of them, and I wasn't able to do it. All because some Japanese suicide bombers brought us into a war we weren't involved in before."

The bitterness in his tone surprised me. He seemed like he would have been a much more patriotic man. Even I could remember the righteous anger and pride for my county's need for retaliation, and I'd only been a young teen at the time.

"You didn't want to fight for our country?" I asked, not intending to be so blunt, and wincing after I said it. He looked over at me, something akin to anger swirling in his expression, though not directed at me.

"I would gladly die for my country. I love it just as much as I should. But, my family needed me and I knew they couldn't make it without me. The bank nearly shook with anticipation, knowing they'd be able to take a poor widow's home from her once I'd gone. I fought for four years, never once able to come home. I sent all my earnings back to my ma just so they could survive. When I was discharged, with honors even, I came home to an empty farm and a note saying they'd had to give it back to the bank and move to New York. New York, of all places!" he growled, his hatred for the enormous city loud and clear in his tone.

My teeth grinded against the pain in my fingers as he squeezed them, though I knew it was unintentional.

"Everything my pop worked for, and I had worked for right after, gone. My ma and sister had to move to a danged slum in New York just to survive." His grip on my hand hardened even further as his voice turned cold enough to frost glass. "It took me a month, but I finally found them. Their tiny sardine tin of an apartment was situated right smack in the middle of territory being fought over by two rival gangs. That's why it was so cheap, but if I'd have been there, I could have told my ma that before she moved into it. She'd never been away from the farm to a place like New York. She had no idea that she would have to look out for those things."

A pit formed in my stomach, making me feel light headed the more he talked. My heart ached for him and his family, and I wasn't entirely sure I wanted to hear more, but I nodded to have him continue anyway.

"I got there and lived alright enough with them for a couple weeks before one of the gangs caught wind of a war hero living in their midst. I was cornered by the leader and some of his little pets one night on my way home. The deal was that they'd leave my family alone and protect them before anyone else if I joined and helped push the other gang back to their own neighborhood."

"So you joined?" I asked, stroking the back of his clenched fist with my other hand, earning myself a much looser grip on my pained hand as he realized what he'd done.

"Yeah," John confirmed, though his face twisted into an unpleasant grimace. "Everything was alright for my family for a while. I'd go and help intimidate some rival members to leave the neighborhood every now and then, and my ma and sister stayed safe wherever they went. I hated it, but I knew it was the only way."

The image of John, my John, being in a gang in New York wouldn't register in my mind as I tried to picture it. He was too pure, too tanned, too farm boy for such things. And as the pain in his expression intensified beyond what I'd ever hoped for anyone I had ever cared about, my heart broke for this man. Good men like him didn't deserve this. Good men like him deserved a quiet life on his farm, with a wife and kids and a simple, pleasant life. Not this.

"One night Snake, the leader, knocked on my door, telling me there was a tussle going on down the street and they needed me there. So I went. I'd never had to actually fight anyone before. Whatever stories and exaggerations they rumored up about me scared everyone off as soon as they saw me coming. But they were all too angry that night." He paused, his breathing becoming deeper and heavier as he tried to calm himself. I placed my hand on his shoulder and kneaded, hoping he knew I supported him.

Power sat motionless and quiet, enraptured by his memories. The fact that I didn't know why she was so interested bothered me, but I couldn't place too much time on the thought before he continued.

"As soon as the fight started, everyone started yelling and flashing switchblades. Before I knew what was going on, I wasn't there, in that stupid slum, fighting knock-kneed wannabe tough guys anymore. I was back in Normandy, fighting for my life and killing anyone who ran at me. I didn't stop, Kate. I didn't just kill the rival gang members. I killed everyone there. Except I didn't even know I was doing it. I saw that I was back in France, fighting Germans for my right to live and come back to Ma and Elsie. And when I woke up, all I saw where the bodies all over the street. I was covered in their blood. It was everywhere, and I stood there forever, not understanding what had happened."

Tears that I held back stung the back of my eyes at his confession and the way it turned his happy, jovial features sad and haunted.

His darkened eyes turned to me, searching for something, though I had no idea what. It didn't hinder my body throwing itself to his, wrapping my smaller arms around his massive form in some sort of reassuring embrace. I could think of nothing else. He had to be comforted. I had to comfort him and tell him it would all be alright. In that moment, pulled toward him by an unseen force, I knew without a doubt that he needed me and I needed him. The pull was even stronger than the one I felt for Esther or Lottie. Stronger than I'd felt for anyone in my twenty-four years of life, period. My arms were his to be held in, and his alone.

John didn't break down or cry. He didn't even so much as sniffle or tremble with emotion. In my embrace, he just sat there, his eyes unfocused and his own muscled arms wrapped back around me. His touch sent me reeling as the safety, warmth, and comfort of his entire being surrounded mine in a melody of broken pasts and cracked psyches. Neither of us perfect, but both of us whole.

I didn't cry or sob for him as I thought I might have if I had been told this night would come before. Instead, I smiled into his chest and inhaled the crisp scent on his flannel shirt. Tears were for pity, I decided as I stayed there, basking in his trust and openness with me. And, I didn't pity John. If anything, I saw that he was strong. Much stronger than me, or Esther, or George, or anyone else. He'd set himself to helping us, despite his own problems and issues. He looked over his little family in Ward F, and acted as our angel of protection and guidance, even though he was in the same boat as all of us. But in that boat, he was captain, and we all looked to him eagerly for instruction.

No. John was not to be pitied. John was strong. Unbreakable.

Power nodded her agreement inside my head, enjoying his nearness as much as me.

He's ours, Sane.

Chapter 10

Recognition didn't dawn on me as I watched the glowing figure in the mirror until my own dull grey eyes fell into view.

I couldn't stop the small gasp that shot from my mouth like a bullet from a gun at what I saw. Esther's primping had become noticeable, and the fresh, crisp looking woman staring back at me in the mirror exuded far more beauty than little Kate the Great ever could have on her own.

My fingers lifted to my face, pulling at the pink skin on my cheeks and inspecting every smooth and flawless inch to see where this discernible difference had begun. For as many times as I'd glanced at the jars on Esther's vanity and thought them a waste of money and useless, I was now staring at living, breathing proof that they worked, at least to some degree. Even my hair, normally brushed once a day in haste, had begun to curl slightly and get softer and less stringy under Esther's routine of brushing it in slow, gentle rhythms for several minutes at a time every night.

I licked my lips, my nerves jumping all over as I stared back at myself in the mirror.

My reflection smiled, making my heart thud loudly because I knew, without a doubt, that I was not smiling. As my body froze and I watched on in horror, my reflection widened her grin and turned her head toward the door to my room, the motion slow and deliberate. Without moving her head back to face me, she looked at me from the corner of her now sparkling steel eyes and winked, nodding at the door she faced.

I shrieked at the resounding knock that broke the terrified silence I'd sat in. My head snapped toward the door, then back to the mirror only to see the same wide eyed, petrified girl I knew I myself to be.

You're becoming me, Sane. I'm flattered, Power mocked, exceedingly happy with her little parlor trick. I glared at my reflection, sending every ounce of hatred I had for the psychotic beast in my head through my sneer. Her tinkling laughter rang out in my head before the knock on my door came again.

"Come in!" I called, closing my eyes to slow my heart and my breathing. I needed to calm down. I had to calm down.

The gentle creak signaled the entrance of my visitor. I squeezed my eyes shut, took in a deep, cleansing breath, opened my eyes again and looked back up toward whomever had come to my room.

"Are you alright?" John asked, his brow set in a concerned furrow from where he stood inside the door frame.

My body's relaxation was instantaneous at the sight of him and the sound of his deep southern voice. A smile etched itself across my lips, Power's teasing and mind games forgotten in his presence.

"I'm fine," I breathed, more than said. "Is something wrong?"

His lips formed a gentle smile and he shook his head. "Nothing's wrong. I was just wondering if it'd be alright for me to walk you to Shilling's office for your appointment?"

Giddy warmth coursed up and down my veins and my cheeks began to ache with the grin plastered across my face. "I'd love that, John. Is it already that time?"

I watched in amusement as his body visibly puffed up in pride at my acceptance, his face lit up in satisfaction and happiness. Without a doubt, he was a man's man, raised to be an alpha male, and the knowledge that he'd chosen to gift his affections to me made me sigh with my own womanly sense of pride that complimented his.

Was I even good enough for that? Timid, little field mouse Kate?

Don't discredit me. You've got some spark with me in here, Power chipped in, her voice filled with mirth and self-satisfaction.

"It's in fifteen minutes. You don't want to be late or you get the 'it's so important to be prompt in life' speech, and that usually extends your appointment by at least another half an hour." The grimace alone that he pulled when he said the name of the lecture was enough to convince me, and I hopped out of my chair to walk over to him.

Like the day before, he offered his arm out to me, and I took it, looping my arm through like a true normal gentleman and lady couple. The thought was exciting, and the extra bounce in both of our steps attested to that.

We walked in an upbeat, happy silence down the hallways to Shilling's office. I pulled my lip into my teeth to keep from letting Power push out her own girlish giggles about the situation she also found quite pleasing, but I only stopped her out of habit.

My body trembled and hummed with bubbly, excited swirls, and the giggles Power made herself evident by would have been the perfect outlet.

"Can I wait for you?" he asked just before I reached for the doorknob.

I smiled up at him, loving the things his presence did to my entire being. "Of course, but only if you really want to sit out here for an hour."

He smirked, rolling his eyes toward the ceiling. "Darlin', I literally have nothing better to do."

I laughed. Not girly, delicate giggles, either. The laughter that burst from my mouth was loud and boisterous, taking in the harsh truth of his words and the absurdity of there being anything to do at all in this asylum. Sure, we had the weekly classes and therapies, but those things only took up an hour or two of each of our days. The rest of the time, we basically hung out in the ward lounge, talking or playing card games. There was the garden also, but never anything pressing, and never anything to give any of us a sense of purpose.

As Esther had told me from the beginning, we had all been placed in a human waste bin, just dumped in one fenced in area to keep us away from the rest of society. The classes and the therapy worked as nothing more than a false image presented to our loved ones to prove the doctors wanted to "make us better". The whole thing was a win-win situation for everyone except us residents.

But I suppose the world couldn't be a good place for everyone. Especially for us who had committed such heinous crimes as I had.

John gave me a reassuring tap on my shoulder and propelled me back toward the door, shaking his head at my laughter even though his smile was so large I could see the pink fleshy gums framing his white teeth.

On a childish whim, I stuck my tongue out at him and slipped in the doctor's office, schooling my excited expression down to a contented one as I came face to face with the middle aged man who held my fate in his hands.

"Hello, Miss Thornton," he greeted, closing the door behind me with an ominous click that had me on edge. It all but screamed, "trapped!"

Sane... Power warned, her tone laced with caution and readiness to take over, should I let her. I shushed her and took a seat in the large armchair across from his.

"How have you been this week?" he asked, pressing his glasses further up his nose with his middle finger. I watched as he grabbed his pen and clipboard, readying it to write out whatever he needed to, the pen poised about an inch from the paper.

"Good," I replied, swallowing the lump in my throat.

He nodded. "I'm glad. Have you adjusted well to your ward and ward mates?"

"I have."

"Ward F is quite the ward. We put the most dangerous of our residents in your ward. Do you know why they're so dangerous?" Dr. Shilling asked. My breath hitched. My ward mates weren't dangerous. They were far safer and more stable than him and the other staff members who'd given me the heebie jeebies from day one.

But, I played along anyway, not willing to make a spectacle of myself. "Why?" I asked, my voice no louder than a whisper or breathy exhale.

The doctor smirked, tapping his pen against the clipboard. "Because you are all perfectly aware of your capabilities. Your minds work on a level that is conscious and present. And yet, you've still done despicable things. You are very fortunate to not be in prison instead of here."

And just like that, my good, cheerful mood from earlier vanished into thin air, leaving me with a crushing sense of guilt and horror at the good doctor's words. I sucked in a sharp breath, my jaw clenched down so hard I was sure my teeth would crack.

"I understand," I replied, the silence of the room ringing in my ears as his eyes never left my face.

"Don't let it upset you, Katherine. It also means I have high hopes that you will recover from this little fiasco and go on to live normally." Every word left his lips deliberately, with every single letter pronounced with the upmost coldness. What might have been a warm encouragement became nothing more than arrogant mocking, as if the idea of giving me false hope gave him the highest form of pleasure.

But I had been warned by my ward mates about him. I would not fall for it.

"That's good to hear, sir," I replied, challenging him with my eyes as I kept hard eye contact with him. We sat there in something like a Mexican standoff for ages before he cracked a grin and let out a dark, humorless chuckle.

"I might have underestimated you, little mouse. Let's continue. Have you formed any relationships with any of your ward mates?"

The force behind Power's surge to the forefront of my mind had me reeling, my knuckles white against the fabric of the chair as I struggled to stay upright and in control. Dozens of thoughts, all brought to my attention by the shrill shrieking tones they embodied, raced around my head, drowning out everything else around me.

He called you, 'little mouse'! How could he know that?!

He can't know about your closeness with John! We have to protect John!

Don't tell him you've become friends with your ward mates! Protect them!

He knows you're not as timid as you act! He knows I'm here!

Let me kill him, Sane! Let me out!

My head pounded, pain exploding behind my eyes and in my temples at Power's alarmed outburst. Her cries overlapped each other, taking over every bit off space in my brain and leaving room for nothing else except her demand to let her take over.

With more effort than I had ever had to use to push her back before, I slammed my eyes shut and pushed her away, shoving her with every ounce of mental strength I possessed. I felt her screaming, kicking, fighting at me, enraged that Sane, by herself, had overtaken the strong and huge Power.

As her fight quieted and finally diminished completely, I opened my eyes back up and smiled at Dr. Shilling, who met my eyes with a cocky smirk. The florescent light above us bounced off his gold rimmed glasses, hiding his eyes in the bright refraction.

"I mostly stay to myself," I lied, fully aware he knew I wasn't telling the truth. "It's easier to stay calm and at peace that way."

One side of his mouth quirked up, amused at my will to stay strong, as if the notion that I were anything more than a shivering, shy little child made him want to bust out laughing.

"I see. We'll move on, then. Let's talk about your time with Jensen and Sons."

Don't tell him a thing, Sane.

"What do you want to know?" I asked, wary of his intentions, aware that nothing good could possible come of anything he had to say.

"What was your daily routine?" he asked, shifting to rest his lower leg on the opposite knee.

I shrugged, looking away from him to the window behind his desk. "It was just like everyone else's daily routines. Practice, chores, performances... Nothing special."

Power beamed in my head at my easy lie.

"Robbie wants you to wash the elephants? Just have Kate do it. She loves taking on everyone else's chores, don't you, little mouse?"

Charlotte's smile was deceptively friendly as she turned to look at me. Her teeth shined like pearls from her mouth, but her eyes glinted with cold intent. She knew I was the elephants terrified me.

The young man she spoke with turned to give me a curious look. The boy was new, unaware that I was the scapegoat for anything and everything within Jensen and Sons, but he'd learn soon. And that curious, caring, concerned look in his eye would be permanently replaced with the same malicious, disgusted look everyone else wore when they looked at me.

Swallowing the hope that he'd be different, be nice to me, I nodded and hung my head in defeat. Better the terror of the larger than life beasts that haunted my dreams at night than the very real physical beatings I'd be sure to get if I refused.

"If you don't want to-" the boy started, but I put a shook my head to silence him.

"It's fine. I'll do it," I said, already feeling the tears burning the back of my eyes at the thought of being so close to the enormous pachyderms.

"That's right!" Charlotte exclaimed with a grin that was far too wide. "Kate just loves helping us all out. And she just loves those elephants too. So, if you have to change their hay or get them dressed, just go to Kate for all that nonsense too. She'd be glad to do it."

I began to tremble as she shoved me toward the elephants quarters, giggling flirtatiously at the new boy. "Off you go, dear! Remember to keep from under their feet as you wash them! Wouldn't want our little mouse to get trampled to death!"

Charlotte and the boy left me alone, chatting as they strode from the tent. The boy turned to give me one last concerned look over his shoulder, but let Charlotte keep leading him away. As the tent flap closed behind them, I turned m head to look at the gargantuan beasts before me. My heart raced as every nerve in my body fired off terrified electric snaps, and I had to fight my quivering muscles to keep from fleeing completely. The elephant directly in front of me flopped his ears back and forth, shuffling on his feet, big enough to crush me with one solid stomp.

Shaking even harder as the tears fell down my face in salty rivers unbidden, I reached down into the bucket of water with the sponge. The ripple effect of my hand in the water never lessened as I trembled, water sloshing over the brim. My legs were weak with fear as I stumbled over to the animal watching me with wary, beady eyes.

His trunk came forward, prodding my terrified face and chest with the leathery appendage. I froze, sobbing, as he inspected me, my eyes squeezed shut so hard they ached. Tingles swarmed up my legs and arms as my breathing came faster and shallower. My head swam with the excess oxygen and I choked on a loud sob when the elephant wrapped his trunk around my hand, taking the sponge from me and squeezing it, wringing the soapy water out over my head. Water splattered all over me as I fell to my knees, cradling my face in my hands and crying in complete and total terror.

Outside the tent, I heard dozens of different voices laughing at my sobs and quiet begs for mercy.

We'll get them, my sweet, Power assured me, cooing in my ear as I cried. *They won't laugh at you for long.*

My legs were stiff and pent up with unused nervous energy as I walked from Shilling's office and slammed the door behind me. Unladylike obscenities flew from my lips in a constant mumbling string as I thought back to the disastrous appointment. How dare he? How dare he?!

With a little bit of indulgence to Power, who had been begging to stretch her legs in my body the entire hour, I gave her the tiniest bit of control, which she used to turn right around and land a forceful kick to the good doctor's office door.

"Watch your back, old man!" she yelled to him through the thick wood, using my vocal chords. It might not have been the smartest idea to let her out, but my anger was too monstrous, and in the back of my head I knew the only way to be satisfied would be to let her do her thing.

"Kate?"

I shoved Power back behind the wall and closed my eyes to cleanse the fury from my being. Slapping a big, bright smile on my face, I spun around to face John, whose face was a mixture of concern and amusement, somehow. He sat on the floor against the opposite wall, legs outstretched and arms crossed over his bulky torso.

"I'm good," I assured him, though the look in his eye told me I'd done anything but convince him of that.

"He does it on purpose. Brush it off, okay? It's all a giant mind game. Just remember that," he said, his voice low so that only I would hear as I moved to sit beside him. My body was already exhausted from the strain it took to keep Power in check for that full hour. My arms and legs may as well have been cooked noodles and my head felt like it was spinning out of control on top of my neck.

I nodded to him, offering him a tired smile. "I know. It's just hard. Pow-... The other side of myself is really difficult to fend off when things like that happen."

To my surprise, he slung his arm over my shoulder and pulled me into his side, resting his head on top of mine. "Tell me more about her."

My eyebrows rose clear into my hairline, I was sure. I pulled back and looked up at him, incredulous. "You mean my crazy?"

"Yeah. It seems like she's a whole different person." As he spoke, I felt Power's anger dissolve into pride and she grinned inside my head, more than happy with his interest in her.

I sighed and leaned back into him, my lips a thin line across my face. "She is and she isn't. She calls herself Power."

"Is she all bad?"

I shook my head, no. "She's like my opposite, I suppose. Where I'm weak, she's strong. Where I'm timid, she's confrontational. It's like she's my gift and my vice. Without her, I wouldn't have survived at Jensen and Sons, but with her, no one else survived it."

John pondered that for a minute, his hand rubbing my upper arm in absent minded circles. "Has she always been a part of you?"

I shook my head, feeling the tension ease itself from my muscles. "I came to the circus as a kid. Barely six years old. I think I was normal back then. She appeared later."

When the others started beating you and you couldn't take it anymore, Power added in my head, not hesitant to remind me of the good she had done for me.

John said nothing for a little while, and I assumed his questions were over until I felt him swallow and speak again.

"Do you like her?"

The question caught me off guard. My eyes narrowed at nothing in particular as I rolled it around in my mind, trying to find that answer, myself. Power remained silent, her curiosity piqued as well.

"I... I don't know. She saved me from a lot, and I'll always be grateful to her for that. She took over when I couldn't take anymore. It saved my life on more than one occasion. But... I can't trust her. The two times I've given her complete control, she killed an entire crew of circus performers and then attacked Ed just because he looked like someone else. She's too trigger happy, I guess, and she is always trying to get that control. She calls me names and demeans me, but at the same time, she tries to keep me safe and alive. I don't know if it's because she cares about me, or if she just needs my body for herself to survive. Fighting her off is like trying to hold back a stampede of elephants." I shivered at just the mention of the gargantuan beasts.

"It must be hard," he commented, his voice near a whisper.

I paused for a minute, wanting to ask him what had been on my mind for ages, but unsure if it would ruin the rest of the day. The decision ping-ponged back and forth across my thoughts for a while before I set myself to just go for the gold, consequences be danged.

"John, can I ask you something?" I began, and even I could hear the caution in my tone.

"Anything." The warmth in his voice was bittersweet to me as I thought about the possibility of my question putting him in a bad mood.

My hangs wrung against themselves as I steeled myself for an unpleasant answer.

"What's on the thirteenth floor?"

His entire body went stiff as concrete. The hand stroking my arm stopped abruptly and I cringed, knowing I'd messed up.

"It's where they take out of control residents. But, it doesn't exist. You can't go around talking about it. It's dangerous," he replied, all warmth gone and replaced with coldness and clinical efficiency.

My heart pounded as the back of my throat went dry. "What do you mean, it doesn't exist? I don't understand..."

He looked down at me, his face like a statue's. No emotion. No feeling. No warmth. No comfort. "People don't come back, Kate. And the few that do would be better off dead."

My jaw hung open, not helping my dry throat. "They don't help them?"

His eyes pierced me, as if irritated with my question. "Nobody here gets help. We've told you that, Kate. If the outside world knew about the thirteenth floor... Well, heck, they'd probably pretend they didn't hear about it and go on their merry way so they didn't have to think about it. The doctors own us, and the scary thing is, they know it."

"What do they do up there?"

John grimaced before his expression flattened and turned even harder, making me wince back. "It doesn't exist," he said, demanding my cooperation silently between his words.

I swallowed the nervous lump in my throat as fear made a slick and frigid trail down my spine. Recognizing that I would get no more from this conversation, I nodded in compliance and looked forward, toward Shilling's office door. His words mulled over themselves in my head, their vagueness and cryptic meanings trying to coincide with something, anything, that made sense. But, as we sat there for close to an hour in the quiet, sterile hallways, no possibilities I could even begin to fathom felt even remotely logical.

"We should head to the cafeteria," John said, breaking the long silence with his quiet, drawling voice. "It's dinner time."

He stood, dusting his hand off on his jeans before holding it out to me, offering to help me up. I placed my small hand in his larger one and allowed him to pull me to stand, biting my lip as the cool air around us seemed to shift with our movements.

Something bad is coming, Sane. Can you feel that? Power asked, the worry in her tone uncharacteristic, and frankly, terrifying. What would have Power scared?

John and I walked down the corridors, making our way toward the cafeteria to meet with our other ward mates. We were almost there when he grabbed my arm and jerked me back against his chest, startling me from the pensive daze I'd found myself in.

"What are you-"

"Sh!" he snapped, pushing one hand over my mouth to silence me and jerking his thumb over his shoulder toward the hallway we had been just about to turn down.

I heard it then. The sound of anguish and fury, melting together into one ear piercing wail.

"Go get the sedatives!" yelled someone and within half a second John pushed us both flat against the wall just in time to see an orderly and a nurse fly past without seeing us.

"How did he get down here?! He's supposed to be in Ward J!"

"He was running down the emergency stairwell when we saw him!"

"The fire escape?! On the outside of the building?!"

Another animalistic shriek engulfed the area, followed by the grunts and overworked pants of the other orderlies trying to subdue whoever or whatever was causing such a ruckus. Minutes went by as we stood there, unable to move, while the staff wrestled with the being. It screamed and yelled and wailed constantly, making inhuman growls and cries as they struggled.

John must have felt my fear, because his hand reached down and took mine, squeezing it to try to relay some kind of comfort to me. I looked up at him, my lips chapped from breathing so hard. For the first time, I saw my own fear reflected in his chocolate eyes. He wasn't cool and in control of this like he seemed to be with everything else. This was out of even his realm of safety and control. My lip trembled as I stared back at him, hoping for some miracle to happen and sweep us away from the horrors of this demented place.

"John," I whimpered, terrified that we'd still be there if whatever was in the next hallway got loose and came this way.

"It's alright. It'll be alright," he whispered back, but his voice held no conviction to let me know he meant it. The fear and uncertainty I felt was just as evident in him as it was me. His hand squeezed mine again, harder, and he pulled me even closer to him, shielding me from the entrance to the next hallway.

"What are you doing here?"

We snapped out of our trembling embrace, both of us rigid at the new voice directing its stern accusation at us. A woman in a nurse's uniform stood in front of us, her face the picture of irritation and her hands placed on her hips. Without giving either of us the chance to reply, she snatched me by the collar and John by the arm and hauled us into the hallway with the screaming being and struggling staff.

Just as the hallway came into sight, a new scream that didn't belong to the previous beast-like creature erupted into the air, pain and agony shaking the walls as my hands slammed over my mouth in horror. The nurse let us both go as she ran for the scene, a glistening needle in her hand.

Cold, jolting shock filled my system as I stared at the view in front of me. I felt John still beside me, taking it in just as I was.

Three orderlies and two nurses stood in the area, restraining a single man in a hospital robe. The man's eyes were wild, overflowing with fear and anger as he fought against them, thrashing and biting everything he could. Blood dribbled down his chin as he roared like an enraged beast. An orderly snatched the syringe from the new nurse and jammed it into the man's kicking leg.

Across from them, huddled against the wall, another nurse stood, doubled over and sobbing as she held her hands against her face. More blood poured like a waterfall between her violently shaking fingers. Her sobs got louder and louder as she began to scream, crashing to her knees against the shining linoleum.

My eyes shot back to the man as he let out one last, terrifying roar before he, too, fell to the floor in a lifeless heap. He looked up at me as his limbs gave out, making eye contract and keeping it even as his body collapsed onto itself. I watched as his eyes rolled into the back of his head, leaving nothing but the whites of his eyes to stare back at me. The man's mouth fell open and huge fleshy chunks of blood and tissue flopped down with a sickening fwop from his mouth and onto the floor in front of him. The crimson liquid spread around his head, staining the pristine linoleum. Horror overtook me as I realized what had just happened, and what those fleshy chunks were and where they came from.

"Get him to the thirteenth floor before he wakes up!" one of the orderlies yelled, his face splattered with blood that he swiped his hand across, smearing it even further. The other two orderlies obeyed instantly, hauling the man up by his shoulders and dragging his unconscious form past us, not even bothering to look at me or John.

The orderly who instructed the others turned to the screaming woman on the floor, rushing to her and pulling her hands from her face.

My stomach rolled as I looked at the woman, my jaw wide open in absolute terror.

"Oh, my God," John whispered beside me, his expression mirroring mine.

The nurse sat crumpled on the floor, screaming as more and more blood splattered from the gaping hole where her cheek had once been. Vomit rose to my throat as I watched her teeth and tongue move from the side of her face where skin and flesh had covered only minutes before. I leaned against the wall and let my stomach's contents evacuate all over the shining floor, further staining it with even more bodily fluids.

"Who are you?! Why are you here?! Go back to your ward!" that same authoritative orderly yelled at us when my violent vomiting alerted him to our presence. John grabbed my arm to turn me so we could leave, but I didn't make it that far. As soon as his concerned, terrified face fell into view, my world went black.

Chapter 11

"Hello, Katherine Thornton," Ernie greeted as soon as I followed my ward mates into the gymnasium. I threw him a small, chaste smile that I hoped portrayed politeness without interest, and hurried to stay close to John and George. Ernie's creepy grin widened as I rushed past him, and he turned his head to follow my movements.

Betraying my desire to keep Marcie from being uncomfortable, I slipped my hand into John's and stayed as close to his side as I could. My skin prickled in goosebumps all over my body at Ernie's disconcerting attention. Every alarm in my head rang off at an ear splitting volume in his presence. "We're going to stretch and play some soccer today. Everyone spread-"

His slimy voice was cut off as the door to the gym opened, revealing the pretty little receptionist from the first floor. She smiled at us all and waved to Ernie.

"Three of your residents have visitors today," she chirped, cheerful energy seeping from every pore in her body as she bounced on the balls of her feet. I found myself envying her carefree, happy exuberance. But, all too soon I realized what she said, and what it would mean for me. She slipped a pink paper from the pocket of her pleated skirt and scanned it before reading off the names. My breath caught in my throat as I prayed I wouldn't be left alone without John or at least George to buffer me from Ernie's creep factor.

"John Kingwood," she called. My heart sank in my chest as he gave my hand a final squeeze and walked toward the woman.

"George Baker." Fear rose in my throat. My two main protectors were gone, leaving me to fend off Ernie by myself. I glanced over at the Physical Activity director, seeing his smile widen further as he no doubt realized it also.

"Kate Thornton."

I blinked.

"Miss Thornton? Is she present today or is she sick?" the receptionist asked, her delicate features marred with confusion as she looked over each of our faces for recognition.

"I-I'm here!" I cried as I scampered toward her, desperate to leave the gymnasium though I was sure my name being called was a mistake. Everyone I'd known in my entire life I'd killed several months ago. There was literally no one who could even come to visit me.

The three of us followed the young receptionist down to the first floor, none of us speaking as I wracked my brain for someone, anyone, who would possibly come to see me. My lawyer had no reason, seeing how I'd already been sentenced, and the performers were dead. My mother had died when I was just four, and it was sheer luck that had led Robbie's father to me at the orphanage. I had few memories prior to Jensen and Sons. All I knew came directly from my adoption file, which Robbie had given to me after his father's death some years ago. The fact that Mr. Jensen, whose first name I didn't even know, was legally my father was strange and unorthodox for a circus. But, he'd never acted as a fatherly figure. Just the boss. The trainer. The ring master.

We halted outside a large wooden door with a glass cutout. The receptionist inserted a key into the doorknob and shooed us inside, closing and locking the door behind us. Within seconds an orderly approached us and took us, one by one, to three separate tables of the dozen or so scattered around the room. I watched, wringing my hands together as my nerves grew more and more strained with anticipation.

George was taken first. The orderly sat him down at the table farthest from the exit and clicked his wrists into the handcuffs attached to the table. George waited for the orderly to walk away before he slumped down in his chair, obviously not pleased with the situation.

He escorted me to another table in the opposite corner from George, doing the same routine with the handcuffs, making sure I couldn't slide my thin wrists from the shackles before he left and did the same with John at another table close to the door and walking out. John shot me a reassuring smile, trying to comfort me as we waited for the orderly to return.

Neither of us had spoken about the incident from the day before. I don't think we needed to. The image of the screaming, sobbing woman who was most likely dead from her injuries forever burned itself into my memories, haunting me when I closed my eyes. The deranged residents anguished cries and wails echoed in my ears any time I found myself in silence. Blood's familiar, coppery scent filled my nostrils as I fell in that state between sleep and wakefulness, startling me to full awareness. I wondered if it was the same for John, but I found myself content not knowing. I hoped we had made a silent agreement to never speak of it again, to be honest. The memories invading my brain were bad enough without reliving them with someone else, even if that person was my forever warm and comforting John.

The three of us sat in the quiet room, the silence ringing in my ears so loud that I never heard the door open back up. My face heated as I waited for whoever had requested a visit with me. For whoever claimed to be associated with me at all.

An elderly couple walked in the room first. I knew immediately who they came for when I saw the swirling hazel eyes on the older man. Though George's face still held onto some rounded youth, the older man who shared his eyes eluded a confidence that portrayed his age, and his weathered skin stretched over high cheekbones that seemed somewhat European to me. My eyes flicked between the man and George as the couple walked directly toward him, not sparing John or me a single glance.

The door opened again and my gaze drifted over to it, my heart hammering against my chest as blood rushed through my head in anticipation. A woman, likely in her fifties, with another younger woman who seemed only a few years younger than me shuffled in. Both darted their eyes around the room, their postures identically stiff and wary as they huddled close to each other and made their way toward John. The younger woman was easily one of the most beautiful women I'd ever seen. The very picture of the classic American housewife, her presence in a mental asylum aside. The striking resemblance between her and John told me she was his sister- the kind and cheerful Elsie. As soon as she took her seat across from John, her nervous countenance melted away into childlike excitement as she leaned over to wrap her lithe arms around him in a tight hug.

The older woman's tense shoulders relaxed the closer she also got to her son. Her embrace to him was much gentler, as if she were afraid too much strain would break her. Thick silver strands wove themselves into her shining golden hair- the same golden color as both her children. I watched the happy trio, wondering if John's father also bore the same flaxen locks and earthy complexion. They looked like a box set of perfect, beautiful dolls.

A throat cleared in front of me.

Startled, I gasped a little and jumped back, the handcuffs digging into the soft flesh around my wrists. A hiss of pain shot through my lips and I looked up at my visitor, who I hadn't even noticed walk in the door.

Everything around the room began to spin as I took in the onyx colored hair, the dark stubble peppering the familiar masculine jawline, and the uncharacteristically nervous look in the grey eyes I'd come to know so well over the years. He wore clothes I'd never seen on him before. The black velvet top hat fell absent from his head, red waist coat nowhere to be seen, and even his everyday work shirt, suspenders and trousers were more familiar than the black leather jacket and casual jeans adorning his body as he stood, shuffling his feet, in front of me. Were it not for his impossibly black hair and ever present five o'clock shadow, I wouldn't have recognized the man I grew up with.

"Robbie," I breathed, unable to contain my disbelief.

I knew it! Power screamed inside my head, her arms waving wildly as she panicked. I knew he was alive! How?! I killed him!

Robbie nodded, offering me a weak smile that didn't quite reach his anxious eyes. I'd never seen him like this. The Robbie I knew exuded- no, glowed with confidence and exaggeration at all times. Seeing him without his performance smile and without his eyes lit up in passion and wonder made my jaw drop in almost as much shock as the mere sight of him.

"Kate," he whispered, moistness coating his weary eyes. He fell into the chair across from me, taking my cuffed hands in his. "Kate, I'm so sorry."

I frowned in confusion. "What could you possibly be sorry for, Robbie?! I was the one who- I was the one who tried to... I should be the one apologizing, and yet no apology could ever be enough. I'm so glad you're alive! Is anyone else...?" I stammered, my jaw open in shock as my numbed brain tried to process the impossible sight before me.

His eyes cast downward as he shook his head, the motion solemn and pained. "No. No one else made it." Without meaning to, I looked down at his neck, where I remembered clearly how Power had taken her knife across the tender flesh there. Only a gruesome, maroon colored scar remained, jagged and diagonal across his throat. The memory of the bright crimson liquid cascading down his gurgling neck like a waterfall overwhelmed me, and before I knew it, I was sobbing into my hands. Guilt slammed into my chest like a freight train, crushing my heart into pulverized smithereens.

"Hey, hey, don't cry. I didn't come here to make you upset," he said, his voice soft and low as he grabbed my hands from my face and squeezed them. "I just wanted to make things right. I wanted to tell you how sorry I am, and how much I wish I could have been a better ring master for you. I had no idea... I had no idea about what the others were doing to you, Kate. If I'd have known..."

"None of that matters," I replied, hiccuping as the tears poured down my face, unrestrained. "No matter what, I should have never let what happened happen. I'm so sorry."

Robbie said nothing in return. Instead, he held onto my hands, listening to my apologies and muttering his forgiveness while also asking for my forgiveness as well. We sat like that for a while, both of us crying like long lost siblings finally meeting again, holding hands and murmuring incomprehensible things to each other as the pain and guilt flooded over us.

"How did you survive?" I asked, my voice hoarse with sobs as I wiped at my eyes with the heels of my hands. Robbie leaned back in his chair, scrubbing his palms along his stubbled jaw.

"I guess I was just lucky. They said I was the last one you..." He paused as I flinched. "I was the last victim, and I suppose by then you were running out of strength and energy. You didn't use enough force, didn't press down hard enough or something. I was in the hospital for a while, but I got out last week. When they told me what happened, I couldn't believe it. The others mistreated you so badly, right under my nose, and I didn't have a clue."

Another wave of that heavy, pressing guilt crashed into my chest again. "I'm so sorry. I thought..." My teeth gritted as I tried to find a way to explain myself without telling him a whole other person lived inside my head. "I didn't know you were in the dark about all of it. Charlotte and Gregory always made it out like you knew and approved. So, I never thought to say anything or go to you. I'm just... I'm sorry."

"No," he said, shaking his head, his body slumping down into the chair even further. "No, I'm sorry. I failed you. All of you were my responsibility. You, especially. You're my sister, technically. I should have been a better boss. A better ring master. It all came to this because of me. I should have been more involved in your lives outside of the performances. Then, I would have known. I could have done something and you... You wouldn't be here."

A weighted sigh fell from my lips and I copied his poor posture as emotional exhaustion rolled over me. "It's not so bad, really. I miss performing. I miss the circus, period. But, I have friends here. They're good for me, I think."

Robbie looked back up at me, his grey eyes boring into mine with such intensity I shrank back into my seat. "Kate, I came here to see you, but I also need to tell you something. This place isn't what it seems. I'm worried about you."

I felt my brow scrunch in confusion, an emotion that was quickly becoming commonplace in my life.

He leaned in closer, motioning for me to do the same. I obeyed, more out of habit and trust than curiosity. Handling another mysterious secret wasn't something I wanted to handle after the past week's events.

"I had a cousin that was sent here a few years back. He didn't come back right, Kate. Everything about him was worse than when he came in. It took his mom months to get him back to a semi-stable state. I don't like this place for you. I want to get you out of here."

His words swirled around my brain as I tried to take all he said in.

"What do you mean, he didn't come back right?" I asked, my voice trembling and my hands shaking. Images of the day before, and the meager snippets of information I knew about the thirteenth floor raced through my mind, making my heart speed up in something close to fear.

He closed his eyes for a short moment, pulling in a deep, hissing breath. "He came back… almost feral. Like a wild, rabid dog. Then, at other times, it was like he was somewhere else completely. He'd be unfocused, unresponsive, unmovable. Whatever they did to him screwed him up, permanently."

I winced, thinking of the man who'd bitten the nurse's face off. The description was so fitting it was uncanny, and that sent a wild flush of shivers down my spine.

"And that's not all," he continued, opening his eyes to capture my gaze. "There were scars. Dozens of them. Precise little surgery scars, except not. No surgeries I've ever heard of left scars like the ones he had. Some of his fingers and toes were even completely gone, and he had no memories of how or why they were no longer there. There were marks all over him. Even on his head. Whatever they do to the inmates here, it's not for the good and it's definitely not medically acceptable. I have to find a way to get you out of here, Kate. I can't let you end up like that."

My heart beat a steady, slow, but powerful rhythm in my chest. Even Power had no words to describe the fear coursing through both our veins. She sat, stunned, behind the wall, taking in Robbie's secret just as shell shocked as I was. We both knew something wasn't quite right about Rosenton Home for the Criminally Insane, but whatever Robbie was pointing us toward was far more evil and vile than I had ever thought possible.

"I can't leave my ward mates behind," I stuttered, fear for not just my life and wellbeing, but theirs also, sending bolts of alarm through my body. They had protected and looked after me. I would be the worst kind of abysmal if I didn't try to save them with me.

He nodded, surprising me. "I agree. I wish I could get everyone out of here, period. This place is a joke. Or maybe a nightmare. I'm not sure which. But I'll work on it, okay? I'm going to get you and your ward mates out of here. I have to. It's the least I can do after letting the other performers hurt you for so long."

I gifted him a sad smile. "You don't owe me anything, Robbie. I owe you everything, though." My eyes hung onto the sight of the purplish scar gracing his neck. I had done that. I had tried, and almost succeeded, to end his life. With a painful grimace, I swallowed the bile that rose in my throat. He didn't agree, and I could tell. After so many years working with someone day and night, it became second nature to be able to read them, and that didn't exclude Robbie and me. With a shake of his head, he sighed and scanned his eyes up and down my body.

"So, you're alright? Nothing has... They haven't done anything horrible to you?"

"My ward mates have protected me. They've been everything to me," I admitted, choosing not to mention how suspicious I was of them at the same time. Trusting someone with your life but being wary of their intentions was a difficult thing to put into words, and I possessed no desire to try.

"Good. Keep a low profile, alright? Try to stay unnoticed, if you can. I'm going to work day and night to get you guys out of here."

"Thank you," I whispered, much more calm than I should have been. Maybe the gravity hadn't sunk in yet. Maybe the horror of his words still felt minuscule in light of the sight John and I had witnessed the day before. I couldn't pinpoint the reason, but I was well aware of the fact that I was not reacting the way a normal person would react.

You are far from a normal person, my dear, Power cooed, her voice lilting and pleased with that fact. Of course she would be, though. If I were normal, she wouldn't exist.

"Are you going to reinstate Jensen and Sons?" I asked, exhausted of the horror filled talk about Rosenton, desperate for outside news. Something to think about besides my fate in a mental asylum.

"No," he replied, surprising me. My shoulders stiffened as he spoke. "I don't deserve to lead another circus. After what I let happen right under my nose, I think it's best to retire Jensen and Sons."

My jaw fell open. "Robbie! The circus is your passion! You've worked so hard and built up such a name! Please don't let this destroy that."

For the first time, I noticed the dark purple circles under his eyes and the pale color to his normally tanned skin. The man looked tired. No, he looked spent. Exhausted. Sympathy and more guilt formed a hard to swallow cocktail in my throat as I looked at the miserable expression his face wore.

"I've ruined you," I breathed, another round of tears burning the backs of my eyes. His face lifted to look at me, his face hard and his fists clenched.

"No! You didn't ruin me. All the other performers who hurt you... They ruined my circus. You are not to blame," he snapped. I shrank back at the ton of his voice. The tone he used when he found Ellie drinking before her trapeze act or when the lion bared his teeth at Kevin, his co-performer.

"I'm sorry," he repaired after seeing me flinch back. "I just don't want you to blame yourself. I don't blame you for what you did. After everything I was told they did to you, I can only wonder why it never happened sooner. You're a strong girl, and I suspect they knew that and wanted to break you. That's why I blame them, and not you."

A deep, filling breath rushed into my lungs. "Robbie, if you don't reinstate Jensen and Sons... I'll have nowhere to go. I have no skills. No family. No home."

A flash of hurt swam across his expression before he shook his head and bore that penetrating gaze back at me. "You're my sister, Kate. Blood or not, by law you're my sister. You have family. You have a home. I'll teach you whatever you need."

"I can't ask you to do that."

"You're not. I'm telling you that's the way it will be."

A warm hand on my shoulder stopped the next protest I was ready to give against Robbie's unfailing kindness. His eyes flicked up, confusion masking his features.

"Hello," he offered, holding his hand out with a hint of caution. "Robbie Jensen."

"John Kingwood," the owner of the hand supplied and my muscles instantly relaxed. The two men shook hands and John slid into the seat next to me.

"Not locked up anymore?" I asked him, lifting my handcuffed hands into view and grinning as the cold metal clanked against itself.

"I can be persuasive," he replied, winking. His entire demeanor felt light and airy, and I could only attribute his lifted spirit to the visit from his mother and sister.

"I need to learn that trait, then. These things are barbaric," I muttered, ready for them to come off so I could rub the pain from my wrists. "Oh! I'm sorry. John, Robbie was my ring master. Robbie, John is my ward mate," I added, embarrassed by my failure to properly introduce the two men. It seemed the chaos of the past few days muddled my manners.

"I'm also her brother," Robbie added, shooting me a meaningful look. I blushed, unused to any kind of familial connection being attributed to myself. It felt strange and foreign to my perpetual lone wolf status, but at the same time it warmed my heart to know he cared for me still, even after what I had done to him and his beloved circus.

John's face lit up. "You never told me you had a brother, Kate."

"I wasn't exactly aware of the fact either," I answered, grimacing at the explanation I was sure to be asked to give if I didn't go ahead and bite the bullet. "Robbie's father was Jensen of Jensen and Sons. He adopted me from an orphanage, but I didn't know about that until a few years ago. So, technically, legally, Robbie is my brother."

John nodded as he followed my explanation while I marveled at the fact that he took it in like it was no big deal.

"Could I ask you a huge favor, John?" Robbie asked then, eyeing him up and down for a quick second, appraising his worth, or maybe his capabilities, and finding him acceptable.

"Shoot," John replied, an easy smile on his face as he leaned in toward my... my brother.

"Watch out for Kate. Make sure nothing happens to her," Robbie all but pleaded, the lacing of desperation clear in his tone. I felt something strange in my chest, some heavy but pleasant feeling emanating from the bottom of my gut as I realized that he meant it. I wasn't alone. I had family. Someone cared about me.

What a strange twist in fate. Perhaps it's a good thing he didn't die as he was supposed to, Power mused as we watched the two men agree and talk over their plans to keep me well rounded and safe. It felt nice, if not a little degrading that they didn't think I was capable. But, I knew that insulted feeling came from my pride talking more than anything. One trip down memory lane, starting with the murders I selfishly committed and ending with the terrifying scene from the day before, and I was easily ready to admit that I was not enough on my own to keep myself in check. I needed that backup, that reassurance, that safety net. And John had long past proved he was more than capable of keeping Power in line, even when she was a free woman behind the steering wheel of my fleshly body.

Robbie glanced down at the shining gold watch on his wrist. I recognized it as the one his father had left to him, the one he never took off. "I've got to go. But, I'll be back, alright, Kate? Remember what we talked about. I'll see you soon," he said, standing to embrace me in a tight hug, as if he'd grown up with me as a sister instead of an employee.

But, then, the more I thought back, the more I realized that he had always taken me under his wing when I'd been in his circus. Memories of dining in his cabin, listening to the radio shows together, all the extra practice time and attention he gave to me, the encouraging talks and praise I'd always received from him... At the time I'd seen it as pity because I thought he knew about the abuse from the other performers and he felt some kind of guilt. Now, though... Now, I saw it for what it was. Robbie had always tried to foster that sibling relationship with me. I'd just been too blinded by my own fear of the other performers to see it.

Too late, Power hissed, tsking and mocking my startled revelation with malice. Now you're legally insane and he's lost everything because of it. You're a rather silly and naive girl if you think he won't eventually resent and disown you for that.

"It was a pleasure to meet you, Robbie," John said, standing and shaking his hand, the action all masculine and firm with resolution. Robbie inclined his head toward him, returning the acknowledgment, and pressed a quick, brotherly kiss to my cheek.

"Be careful, kiddo. I'll be back to see you again soon."

"Alright," I whispered, my mind reeling with the giant mass of new information and realizations that had pummeled into my brain in just the last hour alone. "I'll see you then."

With one last ruffle to my hair, he tossed me a much more relaxed smile than the one he'd entered the room with, and turned to leave, walking with purpose as he disappeared from sight behind the large wooden door.

"So, your brother, huh?" John asked, turning backward in his chair and leaning his back against the table.

I nodded. "And, I'm just as surprised as you are. I've known for a few years that technically we're siblings, but I just assumed..."

"Did he mistreat you?"

I scoffed. "Robbie? Never. At the time, I thought... Well, I thought he knew what was going on and chose to turn a blind eye to it. It turns out I was wrong, though. Power was wrong."

"I saw the scar. How did he survive?"

My mouth turned down into a deep frown at the reminder. "He was the last one I attacked. Apparently she was tired by then and didn't... didn't press the knife as hard as she did with the others."

"It's funny how that works. I figure God must have known he was innocent and gave you both a break when it was his turn," he mused, his expression thoughtful as his brown eyes turned toward the ceiling.

A great, shuddering sigh left my lips. "Truly, that's the only way he could have survived. Nothing aside from the Lord, Himself, could have saved him from what Power did that night."

He shifted in his seat, leaning forward to straddle the chair as he rested his forearms against the top of the backing. "So what all acts did you do in the circus?"

A grin spread across my face at his change of subject and I turned to look at him full on. "Robbie trained me a little in everything. But I'm best at the contortionist, acrobatic, and trapeze acts. Once I even swallowed a sword. And I helped train most of the lions and tigers," I listed, my beaming face showing my immeasurable pride at my vast experience.

"The lions and tigers, huh? That's amazing. No one would guess by looking at you that you've tamed wild beasts before. What about the elephants? I seem to remember them at your circus the first time I saw you perform," he asked, giddy with excitement.

The color in my face drained at the mention of the horrid gray pachyderms. "No. No elephants. We didn't exactly get along. I'm terrified of them, to be honest."

His eyebrows scrunched together and he tilted his head to the side, incredulity written across his masculine features. "You faced down wild jungle cats and tamed them, but you were scared of the elephants? Aren't they more calm and docile than lions and tigers?"

I pulled my lip between my teeth, a sense of unease coursing through my blood with just the mention of those massive beasts. "We only had female elephants, and I suppose they were gentle enough, if they'd been left alone for a while." John stared blankly at me, waiting for me to continue.

Twisting my mouth into an unappealing grimace, I did just that. "Robbie had this employee who trained only the elephants. And-well, unlike Robbie, who wasn't fond of using physical reprimands to train the lions and tigers, Elton was rather fond of using the bull hook on the elephants. It made them nervous and volatile. They didn't like people, and they're just so large, and..." I glanced up at my ward mate, unable to verbalize any more without crying again, like a weak little fool.

The curious lines around his eyes softened and he reached up, rubbing the course padding of his thumb across my cheekbone. "Hey, it's alright. Everyone's scared of something or other. It just surprised me. You don't have to talk about it if you don't want to."

That odd, squishy feeling returned, making my insides squeal in delight and an unrestrained smile erupt through my quivering lips. I opened my mouth to thank him, but was interrupted by the obnoxiously loud, jarring sound of the large wooden door to the room slamming shut.

George strode over to us after the orderly unlocked his handcuffs, his face red and anger seeping from his pores as his breaths came out in irritated huffs. The orderly came to me, sliding the tiny silver key into the lock of my cuffs, releasing my sore wrists from their confines. I rubbed at the red welts with my hands, trying to relieve the ache in them as we were led from the room and back up to the lounge.

As soon as we entered the room, Lottie hopped from her seat and ran to George, wrapping her thin arms around his neck and hugging him so tight I thought his head might just pop off his tense shoulders. He seemed to relax at the contact, much like I knew I experienced with John whenever I found myself stressed or worried. Their relationship confounded me, knowing he used her though his every action spoke to his possible care and feelings toward the young woman.

Shaking the confusion from my thoughts, I made the decision to rest my aching, whirling mind and not think about any more of the mysteries revolving around Rosenton or its residents for the rest of the day. Instead, I slipped my hand in John's, resting my tired head on his shoulder as he engaged Ed and Esther in a game of poker.

He smiled so warmly at me, my insides melted into a puddle of watery goo, then evaporated into the air just to return to the pit of my stomach again. And when he leaned down and planted a tiny kiss to the top of my head before regaining his blank face for the benefit of the game, I relaxed into him and watched, laughing and chatting with everyone else about nonsensical, trivial things for the rest of the evening.

As if I hadn't just met with my dead ring master and brother, only to hear Rosenton Home for the Criminally Insane was more than a madhouse.

It was a nightmare.

Chapter 12

Six months passed me by in an anticlimactic, even pleasant daze. For all the buildup and stress of everything that came to pass in my first short week at Rosenton, the next half a dozen months felt like a vacation at the spa in comparison. Each week brought the same routine, the same people, the same food, and the same attempts to just get in and get out of my appointments with Shilling and Paul in group therapy.

My relationships with my ward mates became more and more relaxed as I spent all my time with them, day in and day out. My wariness of their intentions shrank down to a small pinprick in the back of my mind the closer I got to them, and only Power ever gave her suspicious thoughts of their kindness. As time went by, my expectations that George would throw some other condition to his blackmail on me were proved wrong when he never so much as gave me a calculating look. Instead, once or twice a week he would pull me aside and nod toward Lottie without a word, expressing that I should stick by her like glue until he returned from either his own appointments with Shilling or wherever else he needed to go. I never asked, and he never pried into what Lottie and I did together while he was gone.

Which, to be fair, was nothing but idle chit chat and sometimes a couple rounds of Old Maid with Marcie.

And Marcie still had yet to act on her still transparent jealousy. Instead, whenever she caught John and I holding hands or smiling those secret smiles we had just for each other, she would jerk her gaze away and throw herself into the nearest activity she could. Sometimes, that activity included flirting with the orderlies, and while John seemed to not notice, I always kept her in my peripherals when it happened. Had something happened to her because of her reaction to me, my heavily burdened conscious might have just cracked and spilled Power out in all her vile glory. Otherwise, Marcie and I had become quite close. Often, I found her waiting for me in my room at he end of the day, giggling and bouncing on her feet to tell me the latest juicy morsel of gossip from her mother about her old friends from her hometown. I felt as though I knew all the people she told me about personally, as much as he chattered endlessly about them.

Esther took over the role of my surrogate mother with gusto, and I basked in it without restraint. I needed her and she needed me. The fact that we had been thrown into such a lucky situation where we had found each other was the best thing that could have happened to either of our sanities, I think. Although, we did have a silent agreement to never speak of our rather mushy feelings toward each other. She didn't fancy herself an emotional, weak woman, and I felt all too happy to go along with that. The fewer weaknesses I showed to Power, the less chance she would pounce.

And, then there was Ed. The enigma. The behemoth. Ed remained the dark, terrifying giant with a nervous tic for the first half of the day, and the demeanor of a cheerful giant with a secret from three o'clock until light's out. I didn't know what he did in the gardens at three in the afternoon, but whatever it was changed him from a timid Chihuahua into a confident, smirking brick wall of a man. The only clue he seemed to leave behind was the slight scent of woodsy smoke lingering on his clothes as he ducked into the lounge upon his return and the occasional trace of black soot on his hands or smudged on his face. He towered over the rest of us. Poor Lottie only reached his midriff, while the top of John's head barely brushed the mans collar bone. His tremendous height and width coupled with the eerie lime color of his large, always wide opened eyes made Ed the scariest of the seven of us, by far, upon first glance at our strange group.

And yet, he was easily the most harmless from what I'd seen and experienced. Ed kept to himself, though in the most friendly way possible. Something about him, despite his shakiness and seven foot tall stature, made all of us comfortable around him. He was the proverbial kitten in a bulldog's body.

Or, more accurately, the David in Goliath's body, inside a mental institution.

"Kate?"

Pulling myself from the thoughtful reminiscence of the past six months, I glanced up at my opened door, smiling at the sight of John's frame leaning against the door frame.

"Hey," I chirped, swinging my legs over the side of the bed and grinning like the lovesick fool I had irrevocably become. The paperback I'd been holding but neglecting to read emitted a soft thud on my nightstand as I dropped it there, letting him know he had my full attention.

"Do you have plans today?" he asked, eyes lit up like candles on Christmas morning. He bounced on his feet as his excitement wafted through the air and to me.

I laughed, the very idea of having made plans in this place preposterous. The only thing to even remotely look forward to at Rosenton was the sporadic visits from Robbie, who I'd become quite close with over the months. It sent a secret thrill down my spine that he and John also got along, acting as though they'd been friends for their entire lives. Their instant friendliness spurned on suspicions that Robbie had come to call for John for some visits on his own in secret, maybe to discuss his ever present request for John to keep an eye on me and make sure I stayed safe and healthy. However, who was I to look a gift horse in the mouth? Everyone got along, life was peaceful and easy, and I didn't own any desire to know the specific details. I just wanted to enjoy the time I had and savor it, because something dreadful in the pit of my stomach told me it wouldn't always be as such.

"You're hilarious," I deadpanned, still smiling as my eyes roamed the room around me, as if looking at a grand party instead of four white walls and a equally boring tile floor.

He chuckled and walked into the room and took my hands in his, pulling me to my feet.

"Come on. Bring that thing you wear when you practice your routines," he instructed, opening the armoire Esther and I shared for our belongings. The happiness slid off my face like a mask and I dug my heels into the floor, alarm spreading through my body.

“Why do I need my leotard? John, I can’t let anyone see it. You know that.” The words babbled from my lips uncensored and I felt the skin around my eyes tighten as they grew wide and fearful.

He turned back to me and placed his hands on my shoulders, bending down to look in my eyes while the light in his own twinkled and danced with excitement. “Hey, stop panicking. You trust me, don’t you?” he asked, then pecked my cheek before spinning back around and rummaging through my wardrobe, courtesy Marcie’s generous mother.

I couldn’t help it. I giggled at the sight of him sifting through countless feminine pieces of clothing, tossing them aside and leaving a muddled, forgotten mess all around us from his search. As always, his touch and drawling voice eased my wariness and left me warm and cheered again.

“Esther will murder you when she finds this mess,” I quipped, then blinked at my choice of words, and quickly added, “No pun intended.”

His shoulders twitched at the laughter he held in. “She’ll live. Things have been too complacent and unexciting for her lately anyways. It’ll give the crazy woman something to do.”

“John!” I cried, though the laughter ringing out of my throat canceled out any reprimand I intended.

“Come on!” he insisted, ignoring my shout and throwing the white sequin leotard I’d hidden in the very back of the armoire at me. I barely caught it as it hit my chest with a sturdy sounding fwop.

“What are you going on about? Have you lost your mind, you crazy man?!”

And then, without warning, he ambushed me, sweeping me up into a tight embrace and swinging me in a speedy circle, my legs dangling as more shrieks of happiness rang out from my lips. My long, slightly curled hair whipped around us, stinging my cheeks and probably his as he spun again and again, making us both dizzy with contagious excitement.

"Stop arguing and come on!" he ordered, pecking my cheeks over and over again through the words. "But, but quiet!" he added in an overly dramatic stage whisper, winking and sending my heart tumbling into my stomach with that odd, yet pleasant, squirmy feeling again. "We can't let anyone see us!"

"Okay, okay! Put me down, you brute!" I jested, tapping at his chest through his flannel shirt with my palms in a false show of obstinacy. His smile brightened, reaching what I was sure had to be several thousand watts, and he set me back to my feet, taking hold of my hand again.

I snatched up the leotard just as he pulled me back through the door and into the hallway. Dinner had started fifteen minutes before, and the long pearly hallway remained empty of any presence except our own. Even the nurses and orderlies had deserted the floor in favor of filling their stomachs. We ran, our socked feet sliding across the waxed floor and sending us careening into walls, but he never slowed down. He led me to his room, where he picked up a small rucksack, then pulled me along back out and to the staircase. He slowed as we bounced down the stairs, peeking over his shoulder at me every few seconds to make sure I hadn't tripped or lost my footing, the mischievous light in his eye never dimming.

"Where are we going?" I asked, struggling to keep up with his quick pace. The scent of roses wafted into the air around us as he led me straight through the sweet smelling flowers and to the vegetable garden behind them. Curiosity and wonder overwhelmed me as he stooped to pick a few tomatoes, pulls some carrots, and snap several squash from their vines. I grinned, holding the rucksack open so he could dump his loot into the bag on top of what I suspected to be a blanket, though I had no time to really check. I watched the muscles of his arms and back stretch and move as he worked to get at the vegetables, their form still visible through his shirt. Vaguely, I wondered if my attraction toward him would ever waver, because after six months I had yet to not feel heat rush to my cheeks when I caught myself staring at him.

He didn't answer my question, and I found that I forgot I'd even asked it as his expert hands worked at a swift and efficient speed to gather the ripest vegetables. I had no idea what to look for when picking them, but he seemed to know on instinct, discerning which ones were acceptable or not by a single glance. Something base and primal in my psyche preened at that, though I struggled to pinpoint why.

It shows he's capable of providing for you. Taking care of you. That's why you're looking at him like you want to eat him alive with chocolate sauce and a cherry on top. I told you before, Sane. He's an alpha male. The top of the top of the food chain, Power supplied, her tone strictly informative, as if she were a teacher explaining a commonly known theory to a foreign student.

I nodded at her explanation, barely having time to close the rucksack before he took it back from me and grasped my hand in his, dragging me off yet again and looking over his shoulder at me with a sly grin that portrayed the giddiness he fought to keep restrained.

"John, where are we going?" I begged, giggling as we tromped through the lawn, keeping close to the barbed fence surrounding the building. He placed a silent finger to my lips and winked again before tugging me behind a particularly overgrown shrub. And by 'shrub', I mean wild looking bush that stood close to four feet tall with branches the size of my arms jutting out at odd, angry looking angles.

The branches pricked and scratched my arms as I stumbled to my knees behind him. His hot breath in my ear sent shivers up my spine and a thrill to my stomach when he whispered a quick apology before crouching down and pressing his back against the fence. A portion of it gave under his weight, revealing a hole in the chain link just large enough for someone to crawl through on their belly.

I gasped, jaw hung open as the implication settled into my mind like a cold, wet blanket on warm skin.

Escape! It's possible to escape! Power cried out, jumping to her feet behind the stone wall and dancing a ridiculous looking jig in her excitement.

My head snapped toward John, my face making an excellent impression of a goldfish as I floundered around for words. Robbie's instructions to find a way out swam through my head in a muddled swarm as I stared at him, unable to believe what I saw. Something... something like hope flared up in my chest, burning me inside out as my lips pulled back into a grin almost identical to the one gracing his face.

"You go through first. I'll hand you the bag. Stay close to the fence so they can't see you," he whispered, guiding me toward the small hole. I nodded, pinching myself as discreetly as I could to make sure I hadn't stumbled into a wildly realistic dream. He held the fence back, widening the hole as much as he could while I crawled on my belly, shimmying along the dying grass to the other side.

We could run.

I looked back at John as he slid the rucksack through, flirting with the notion that I could be free of Rosenton and the thirteenth floor, Paul, Shilling, and... And, my ward mates. The smile on my lips inverted into a pronounced frown. No, I couldn't leave them behind. Not in a million years.

Which begged the question... What exactly were we doing? What had John planned? Surely we weren't leaving, letting the others fend for themselves? The thought left a cold pit in the base of my stomach.

Quit freaking out. He only told you to bring a leotard. Don't you think he would have had you pack clothes at least if he planned on whisking you away?

Of course, level headed Power brought up a valid point. I sent her a silent thanks, which she snatched and gloated upon while I helped John pull his enormous frame through the tiny opening in the fence.

His body uncurled from its crouch as he stood, tugging me up with him and pecking my cheek again. As was the theme for the day apparently, he led me by pulling on my hand, sneaking into the dense woods behind Rosenton. The mammoth skyscraper stood tall and intimidating behind us as we left it behind, like it was warning us to return or else. Maybe it'd box our ears, or bend us over for a good spanking.

Or maybe you'll get sent to the thirteenth floor. Come back with a few less digits on your hands and feet, like Robbie's cousin, Power quipped, studying her nails as she leaned against the wall, only looking up for a fleeting moment. My feet dug into the ground, halting our progress. John turned, ready to admonish me in a playful tone by the look on his face, but he stopped, studying the pale color of my fearful cheeks.

"Kate?"

"If we're caught?" I asked, whispering as my eye flicked between his, begging him to tell me something positive and good. That we wouldn't be sent to whatever lurked on that horrid floor.

His gaze softened upon seeing my terror. "They won't search for us. Robbie requested us for a visit so no one would come looking when we don't show up for dinner or bed check. I've taken care of it, sweetheart. We'll be back around midnight, just as Robbie told the staff, and no one will know the wiser. Do you trust me?"

Some of the tension in my chest released at his calm reassurances and the muscles in my body relaxed.

"Of course," I admitted and offered him a weak smile, though a deep foreboding feeling still dug itself into my chest.

He nodded in acknowledgment and we continued our journey through the thick forest again. John's speed walking slowed, giving me time to follow without stumbling. He seemed to know exactly where he was going, and because when I told him I trusted him I told the absolute truth, I asked no more questions and used the time to think.

So he has been having private visits with Robbie, Power mused, tapping her finger against her chin as her steel eyes looked up into the air in thought.

And, Robbie knew about whatever John had planned for today, as well, judging by the fact that he helped orchestrate it.

Do you really trust them both, Sane? Don't you think you're being rather naive? One is certifiably insane, literally, and the other you tried to murder less than a year ago. Is trusting them like you do really a wise decision?

I frowned at her insistence that it had been me to try to kill Robbie. Power tried to kill him, not me.

Tomato, to-mah-to. We are who we are, aren't we?

Weren't we, though? We shared a body, true enough. But, it became clear to anyone with eyes that Power and I bore completely different personalities and ambitions. Her strong, violent nature was something I could never pull off, and the very idea of Power acting like the scared little field mouse I embodied was just absurd.

The forest floor of dead leaves and broken sticks crunched beneath our feet as we made our way deeper and deeper into its abyss, the sharp edges and broken pieces poking the bottom of my socked feet with each step, though never hard enough to hurt. Rosenton shrank smaller and smaller in the distance until it seemed the same height as the trees around us, no longer towering over us menacingly. Curiosity over our final destination nearly killed me as I fought myself to not hammer John with endless question about it, but I managed to keep quiet as we moved along the forest floor.

Just as the sun began to set, John veered us from the straight path we'd taken all day, tossing a quick smile back at me. I bit my lip to keep from tainting the natural crisp sounds of the woods with a giggle and continued trailing behind him. Neither of us had spoken since my proclamation of complete trust in his intentions hours ago, but I found myself comfortable in that silence. Walking for so long in the forest, letting him lead me as birds and squirrels flitted from tree to tree, leaves falling from their branches and the warm wind caressing my hair around my face. It seemed surreal. Ethereal. I could almost pretend we didn't reside in a mental asylum, and that neither of us had committed murder. Instead, we were two people on a secret voyage, traipsing through the woods on weightless feet, leaving no clues to the outside world of our existence.

My feet only just began to hurt when we topped a rather large hill and John stopped, choosing to change course down a steep embankment. Wincing as my sore feet protested the movement, I tiptoed down behind him, our fingers interlocked as they had been for hours. We reached the bottom and I opened my mouth to ask him if we could take a short break, but his voice broke the silence first.

"We're here. Stand here for a minute and I'll light the way."

I glanced around until I saw what he was talking about. John stooped low, entering the dark, rocky opening in the hill to our right.

A cave?

He disappeared into the pitch black entrance, and seconds later I saw the telltale orange glow of a flame being lit, followed by another and another progressively deeper until no more appeared. He resurfaced shortly after, a wide, messy grin plastered to his face, and led me inside.

The crunching leaves of the woodsy ground beneath me transitioned into a cool, dirt floor. John held onto my hand tightly as we made our way deeper into the cave.

They'll never find your body in here, you know.

I shook Power's tainted implication away, noting the way the ground got smoother and even colder the further down into the cavern we went. Already torn and tattered from the trek, the dampness of the cave floor through my socks coupled with the distinct constant dripping noises encompassing us told me water ran somewhere nearby.

My head swiveled on my neck, taking in all the formations and structures around me. Stalagmites taller than even Ed stood tall and firm, almost regal in their stances surrounding the slick, smooth path we walked down. From the ceiling stalactites hung, the water I heard dripping forming tiny beads at the tips of the cone shaped forms before plummeting down, just to be followed by another and another all around. Each drop echoed in the eerie quietness, while small bats twitched and groomed themselves from their upside down perches along the walls, getting ready to wake and fly out into the night. I ducked as one took off over my head, barely missing my face.

John chuckled at the girlish squeal that I let out. "Afraid of bats, too?" he teased, rubbing his thumb along my palm.

I pulled myself upright, taking on an air of false haughtiness as I scoffed at him. "I think it's more of a fear of getting hit in the face by a small flying rodent than fear of the rodent, itself."

He grinned and tugged me along again. "Fair enough. Come on. There's only a little more to go."

Our path narrowed as we trailed along, until John had to walk sideways and I had to hold my breath to keep from brushing against the wet walls at my front and back. Then, just as I was sure John wouldn't fit another ten feet, the space in front of me exploded open into a monstrous, gaping room with a stream of clear water trickling at a rapid speed along the far wall.

Even as a woman used to seeing the surreal and shocking, I gasped at the beautiful sight. The room radiated beauty and elegance, with a ceiling at least twenty feet tall and easily stretching a hundred feet across. Along the far wall with the stream, a small, modest waterfall poured from an opening from another level of the cavern, the light from the torches John had lit reflecting off the clear water and bouncing in beautiful, otherworldly waves of light on the walls.

Dozens of stalactites littered the ceiling, and as my gaze moved over the enchanting space before me, I saw something that made my heart race with excitement.

"John," I whispered, a lump of shocked and heartfelt emotion taking up residence in my throat. "Did you do all this? For me?"

He squeezed my hand, planting a kiss on my forehead as he took in what I assumed was his handiwork. "It was a collaborative effort, I'd say. I told Robbie where the cave was, and he came and set it all up. He worked on it for a month or two, making sure everything was safe and secure."

My eyes misted over as my hands made their way to my mouth, twitching at the huge smile attached there. "This is amazing! Thank you! I-I don't know what to say!"

"Perform for me. That's thanks enough," he murmured in my ear, and I wasted no time running to the rope ladder attached to the two trapeze swings drilled into the ceiling. Across from it, a tightrope stretched from one stalactite to another, again drilled straight into the formations. There were no safety nets, and I found myself endeared to Robbie that he still had enough confidence in my abilities to know I wouldn't need any.

"Wait!" John called, making me pause and turn to look at him, anxious to fly through the air and feel the rush of the performance again.

"Your-your thing. That sparkly thing you wear when you practice."

I glanced down at the silk dress I wore. Not trapeze material in the slightest. With a sheepish grin I walked back toward him as he bent down to pull the garment from the rucksack. He handed me the leotard and turned his back to me, facing the narrow entrance to the cave as I slid off the dress and shimmied into the leotard and tights.

"You can turn around," I offered, and ran to engulf him in the tightest hug I could muster, hoping that somehow it would portray just how thankful I felt for his kindness and thoughtfulness. He accepted the embrace, hugging me back and laughing at my uncharacteristic show of exuberance.

While he held no reservations about reaching for my hand or kissing my cheeks, I had yet to feel so comfortable, and he never asked me to do so either. I suppose the fact that I accepted and basked in his affections was enough for him to be satisfied, but as I watched his earthen eyes light up with glee at my forwardness, I found the desire to show him how much he meant to me more often. Maybe with more hugs that I initiated, or by taking his hand in mine instead of the other way around occasionally.

Certainly, I had never known a relationship like the one we had. What Ellie and Gregory did behind closed doors was simply physical- I was intelligent enough to know that. What John and I had fostered for six months now was something much more. We held hands. He kissed my cheeks often. We hugged. But without ever having truly kissed or anything further, I'd come to see him as mine, and I knew without a doubt he saw me as his.

The word "love" seemed intimidating to say aloud, but I cared for him, and he cared for me. It felt enough to satisfy both of us until we weren't in such a precarious position, living in a mental asylum.

"Will you perform?" he asked, sweeping his hand out to gesture at the equipment in front of us, his other arm still around my waist, holding me to his side as we stared, taking in the beauty of the room before us. It felt like a dark, haunting ballroom, lit by torches and silent aside from our talking an the rushing water. Fitting for the demons we both kept as tenants in our minds.

"I would love to," I replied, not wasting a single second before answering and running for the rope ladder again. My hands and feet made quick work of each rung, scaling the swaying ropes with practiced ease. Adrenaline burst through my veins like thousands of angry bees as my smile spread so far my cheeks ached.

This is where we belong.

I couldn't agree with Power more on that. Performing held the honor of being my absolute and unwavering passion, the excitement and rush never dying down no matter how many thousands of times I'd done it. I paused at the top rung to look back at John on the ground, my muscles twitching and shaking with giddy anticipation. He had pulled out the blanket from the rucksack and spread it on the ground, sitting with his arms locked around his knees on top of it, all the vegetables he'd picked from the garden spread out beside him in a colorful heap. Our eyes locked for a moment and I swore my heart stopped in my throat as the impact of how much he and Robbie had done for me by setting this up settled in my mind.

Swinging my right leg and right arm out, off the ladder, with a great flourish, I thrusted my chin up high and beamed at him as I tried my best to mimic Robbie's charismatic and exaggerated ringleader tone.

"Ladies and gentlemen! Boys and girls! Children of all ages! Welcome to the Kingwood Thornton Acrobatic and Trapeze Show Extraordinaire! Gather your attention to the ground below, where you'll find the master behind the work, John Kingwood!" I cried out, my lone voice reverberating and echoing off the grand walls around us as I looped my remaining arm through the rung to clap wildly for him as he sat below me, his expression soft and pleased as he watched me with something akin to adoration, though I hesitated to assume it. Dozens of bats stirred from their perches at my loud cry, taking flight through the air and whizzing past my head as I curled into the ladder and giggled. Several pairs of leathery wings caressed my arms and back as the tiny animals fled the room through the narrow opening we entered through, sending an uncharacteristic wave of delightful shivers up my spine.

John's deep rumbling laughter echoed along the cave walls amongst my own giggles as I held tight to the swaying rope ladder, the force from the bats flying past and through it sending it swinging back and forth. As soon as it slowed enough, I climbed the last rung and pulled myself onto the trapeze bar, closing my eyes and grinning as I pictured Robbie there below me, yelling, "Listo! Ready! Hep!"

With that, I pulled my legs into a vertical split and flipped upside down on the bar, hanging by my knees as the trapeze continued to swing, building momentum. For once, my mind didn't transcend me to the big top, where red earth sat below me and the crimson and sunshine colored striped tent hung above me. I saw no roaring audience, nor heard thunderous applause as I let my muscles fall into their practiced, expert motions.

Instead, my eyes snapped open and the world around me shined bright and clear. The cave reality granted me with only blazing torches for light and a crisp, trickling stream and waterfall behind me, pearly white stalactites and stalagmites surrounding my equipment, and only John, my comfort and warmth sitting on a pale blue blanket below me, watching and never taking his eyes away, felt- dare I say- better than the big top performances. There, using the equipment set up just for me, by the two men who cared about me more than anyone ever had, my performance was personal and thousands of times more satisfying and fulfilling than my shows under Jensen and Sons had been. A year ago, being told I'd feel so much more for this simple little act inside a secluded cave than for the show that had become my very life and breath, I would have called them insane- an insult I didn't miss the irony in.

And yet, there I was, smiling like I'd never smiled before. All for the lone man sitting below, with chocolate brown eyes trained solely on me, without the dramatic lights or Robbie's voice to pump him up for the show.

My heart fluttered, actually fluttered, in my chest.

I was enough for him. I, Kate Thornton, orphaned circus performer and mass murderer with an extra, psychotic woman in her head, was enough for John Kingwood, kind to a fault, protective, loving war veteran with demons as deadly as my own.

My gaze met his once more and I smiled at him yet again before grasping the shining chains in my hands and pulling myself to lie with the bar across my lower back, suspended in air stiff as a board, only my perfected sense of balance keeping my body from plummeting down to the ground below. With a deep, gratifying breath, I licked my lips and began the show.

My back arched downward, keeping my legs straight and allowing my body to slide down, as if falling, until my flexed feet caught the tension spot where the bar met the chain, leaving me hanging upside down with only the pressure my ankles held against that spot holding me to the trapeze. John's sharp intake of breath made it to my ears, even from my high perch, but it only served to make my smile wider. My act had flourished, becoming more unbelievable and dangerous, since the time he'd seen my performance ten years ago. Without shame, I planned to show him every bit of it and throw as many tricks as I could possibly muster into the private show.

I reached up for the bar after counting to three, giving him enough time to take in the dangerous perch I so wanted him to be witness to. Crossing my arms, I grabbed onto it and let my legs fall from the chains into a split before slowly, with control over each muscle, letting them come back together below me, leaving me hanging by my crossed arms. Pointing my toes, I bent one knee and pulled it up, resembling a ballerina suspended in the air, before bringing one arm down at a right angle in a gesture of grandeur.

And so my private act went on. I spent close to an hour on the trapeze, flipping over the bar, swinging by single limbs, twirling and swirling through the chains and over and under the wooden bar. My body reveled in the release and Power basked in my confidence, soaking up the easy reliance I felt toward my seasoned abilities. My muscles twitched in excitement to be used and stretched again for the purpose of a performance. And, I used up every last drop of energy I could muster on it, falling into difficult and advanced tricks with ease and comfort. John no longer let out little breaths of nervousness, his own confidence in my abilities now tried and true as I came to a close on the act after nearly an hour.

As the blood vessels in the backs of my knees begged me to rest, as they'd busted, leaving dark purple and blue bruising snaking up and down the backs of my legs, and my raw and blistered hands began to bleed, I made the decision to bring my nirvana to a grudging close. Power groaned in protest, as did my own mind, but I knew when my body was spent, and to keep pushing would risk injury, or worse, a fall to the hard, unforgiving ground below.

So, with a sigh of discontent, I took the whistle from inside my leotard and lifted the necklace over my head and looped it onto the wooden bar above me, tugging on it to make sure it stayed secure. I slipped the whistle into my mouth and let myself down, under the bar, with slow, precise movements until no part of my body touched the trapeze. Suspended only by the necklace of the whistle around my neck, the other side looped tightly around the bar, I took another deep breath and twisted hard. The movement twirled the chains of the trapeze around and as it spun back around, my body straightened like a board. The necklace spun the opposite direction, the ropes twisting around itself and twining around over and over, sending me into a wild and furious spin. My lungs blew on the whistle with all my might as my hands lifted up above my head in a high V.

The world melted into a blur of dark blues swirled with the glistening white of the cavern formations around me as I spun, making my insides tingle with pleasure at the adrenaline high.

This is where we belong, Sane. Forever, you know?

My surprise at the uncharacteristic tenderness in her voice came short lived as everything around us began to come into focus again, signaling the end of the trick and, consequently, the end of my performance.

I sighed, my heart heavy and melancholy as I hoisted myself back up and made my way all the way down the rope ladder. Unless John and Robbie conspired to make our secret outing a regular occurrence, this would be my last performance in my lifetime. My breath hitched in my throat as my heart shattered into a thousand pieces at the very notion. By the time my bare foot touched the cool, damp cavern floor, tears flew down my reddened cheeks unrestrained.

Stop this, Power begged, her own voice crackling with emotion.

For once in our combined existences, she and I moved to the same wavelength, mourning our loss of passion together with our guards down, opened to each other and trusting. We melded together as one somber being, wishing for what we once had and would never have again.

"Kate, that was breathtaking. Why are you crying?" John asked, folding me into his chest as his arms wrapped around me. He let me sob there for a long time, not pressuring me to elaborate or talk about my feelings. Maybe he knew how badly that phrase "talk about it" tasted on the tongue after our shared experiences with Shilling and Paul always pressuring each of us. For that, I found myself grateful, and I pulled myself away from him, wiping my eyes with the backs of my hands. Hiccups jolted my heaving chest as I sniffled, trying to reign in my intense emotions. Power disentangled herself from me again as I came to, folding herself into a tight ball on the floor behind the wall as she sat in silence, too exhausted to speak anything more.

"I'm sorry. This was amazing, John. Just... wonderful. The best thing anyone has ever done for me. Thank you," I whispered, squeezing my arms around his neck and inhaling his scent in order to always connect the time down in the cave with his essence. I wanted to remember it for the rest of my life, and never let go of the sweet memory.

I think my overenthusiastic gratitude made the hulking farm boy uncomfortable, his lips encased in a closed mouth smile and his hand reaching up to scratch the back of his head as a deep red color crawled up his neck.

"Ah, it was nothin'," he stammered, his eyes trained up at the still swaying trapeze swing. "Robbie did all the labor. I just had the idea. He ran with it."

I sighed, smiling at his embarrassment as his humility drilled a hole in my heart and took up residence there. The man wasn't perfect by any means, but he possessed a heart of pure, untarnished gold.

"Let's eat," I said, for once pulling him along toward the blanket. "I'm starving after all that work. The vegetables are here for that purpose, right?"

He snapped out of his awkward stance instantly and laughed. “Yes, they’re here so we have something to eat.”

Chapter 13

"Tell me about the circus."

I smirked, licking the tomato juice from my fingers as I pondered that question. Which side did he want to hear? The good times? Performing, practicing, and dining with Robbie? Or the bad times? Broken bones that kept me out of commission for weeks on end? Bruises stage makeup couldn't disguise? Facing my ultimate fear every night as I was forced to feed and wash the mammoth elephants?

"What do you want to know?" I settled for, instead of taking the guess.

John leaned back on his hands, his bare feet dangling in the frigid water of the trickling stream. "What was it like to travel all the time?"

"I can't say. It's all I ever knew, so I have nothing to compare it to. Every week was a routine of arriving, setting up, practicing, performing, taking it all down, packing up, and hitting the road again," I replied, shrugging my shoulders. The sequins of the leotard I still wore sent tiny beams of light shooting off every surface of the cave with each movement I made, transforming the dark torch lit cavern into a faerie-like wonderland.

"Were the other performers as good as you?"

Heat rose to my cheeks, but I found I couldn't lie to him, even for the sake of humility.

"No," I answered, saving my embarrassment by choosing not to elaborate. Bragging only reaps a temporary reward. Showing you skill and impressing people by making them believe the impossible reaps a permanent reward without ever saying a word, Power had told me over and over throughout the years. Of course, how was I to know she wasn't speaking of just my performance, but my ability to kill and maim as well? She had followed her own advice, never telling me how dangerous she was until after the fact. And then she never once let me forget it. Sure, she'd always defended me and protected me, but the defensive stance and the offensive strike proved to be two vastly different worlds.

His head bobbed up and down in understanding. "That makes sense, I guess. I can't imagine anyone being able to show you up. I've never seen anything like what you just did. You're even better than you were ten years ago."

Another tomato made its way to my mouth and I bit into it, savoring the rich flavor as more juice seeped out and ran down my fingers. I bent over and dipped my hands in the water, letting the stream wash away the juice after I'd finished the whole thing.

"What about you?" I asked, dragging my hand back and forth through the water. I shifted to lay on my stomach on top of the blanket, watching the dancing waves of light on the wall. "Tell me about growing up on the farm."

"Again?"

I grinned back up at him to see his own mirroring mine. "Again," I confirmed.

He shook his head. "I've told you about my childhood dozens of times. If you think baiting me to talk about my life will keep you from talking to me about yours will work, you're sadly mistaken, sweetheart."

I tossed my head back as high pitched laughter rang out from my throat and I folded my arms under me to rest my head on them. "I don't know what to say. Your life is so much better than mine. You have a mother and sister who love you. Nieces and nephews. Memories of your father. You know so much about everything and anything. I like hearing your stories, even if it's over and over again."

The blanket shifted beneath me as he moved to copy my position laying down. We'd long ago given up the idea of returning to Rosenton until morning. Cherishing and savoring the night of freedom we had in the cave tempted us beyond what we could handle for our own goods. Consequences be danged, we would spend the night together in my own private circus arena.

"Tell me about the others. Why Power killed them."

Every muscle in my body froze in place, my eyes widening at his request. Then, as I realized he had said Power killed them, and not me, my insides melted into pleasantly jello-like goo. He believed in me. He believed Kate Thornton to be inherently good, and that meant more to me than he could ever know.

"Are you sure you want to ruin the night like that?" I asked, caution lacing my words.

"I can handle it if you can."

I looked deep into his warm eyes, looking for an ulterior motive, a reason to know me and use me, but found none. Just that familiar warmth and confident comfort he radiated at all times. His skin glowed beneath the torches around us, looking a pale blue instead of its normal tanned olive tone.

A deep, cleansing sigh preceded the words Shilling and Paul had tried to drag from my lips without success.

"They tortured me. They saw I was weak and exploited it as far as they could. I was the scapegoat for anything bad that happened to anyone."

John frowned and reached over, tucking a stray hair behind my ear. "They beat you?"

I nodded, biting my lip as my heart raced at the memory of the excruciating pain. "Often. One of them would tell me to meet them behind the caravan after sundown, and a group of them would be there, waiting for me. I lost the opportunity to perform so many times because of broken bones. That was the worst part, because performing was my escape."

"Why did you go, then?"

"If I didn't go when they told me to, they'd come for me and it would be worse. They'd force me to work with the elephants for nights on end, knowing it broke me. Power was the only reason I lived through it all."

He stared at me, our faces inches away as we both laid on the blanket. "So, Power's the reason you're alive?"

I predicted the flashy peacock dance Power made inside my head at his compliment before she even did it, making me roll my eyes at her arrogance.

"She is. She showed up when my mind was too close to cracking for me to bear, and she's been with me ever since."

His grin lit up and he shuffled even closer, taking my hand in his and intertwining our fingers. "So, she is to thank for something, then. As horrible as she can be, I have to say I'm grateful she's there."

My insides tumbled and twisted at his words as everything in my brain ached at the contradicting thoughts and feelings rushing back and forth. I hated Power, and yet I owed her everything. But, she'd murdered, made my body murder, and landed me in Rosenton. Her presence confused and humiliated me with how wishy-washy my feelings toward her came. Maybe I was the user, instead of George. After all, I pushed and pushed and pushed Power away, never working with her on anything, until I needed her to save me.

Don't flatter yourself, Sane. I'm not some weak little twit and you know it. You using me is exactly what I want. Get yourself together and stop wallowing in self pity. You're giving me a migraine.

Of course. How could I ever forget? How could I overlook the fact that she twisted and manipulated until she got exactly what she wanted- to be used?

"Kate?'

"Hm?"

"What happened that night?"

I opened my eyes, not even realizing I'd dozed off. "What?"

"The night Power killed them. What happened?"

My teeth pressed down onto my bottom lip until blood sprang out with a sharp burst of pain. "John..."

"I won't judge or condemn you. I'm here for multiple murders, myself, in case you forgot," he said, his lips twitching into a sad, melancholy smile.

I sighed, knowing he'd trusted me with that information. He'd told me long ago about his story, and I'd given him nothing of mine. And, while he'd never asked or pressed for the information before, I felt I owed him that little kernel of trust in return, no matter how much I loathed even the thought of repeating what I'd done.

With one more great, heaving breath, I looked at him and spoke of my crime for the first time since I'd been on trial months ago.

I stared into the mirror, my chest twitching and jolting in sporadic and violent spasms as I giggled. Nothing I did stopped the incessant laughter. Not even thinking of the latest set of injuries or the behemoth pachyderms in the next tent over. Gregory liked to pull my trailer next to the elephants, just because he knew how terrified I was of them, and he tended to revel in that.

Don't try to fight it, Kate. I just want to help you. Help us. I'm in here too, you know. When they hurt you, I feel it. Don't you want to give me the chance to fight them for you? For us? Power whispered, her voice seeming to materialize in the air around me, caressing my cheeks and brushing through my limp hair, instead of coming from my head like she normally did. Surely, you're not so cruel to deny me the chance to defend myself?

I gasped for air through the laughter as the idea of keeping her from having to experience the pain I felt horrified me. When I looked back up into the mirror, the tiny trailer I called home seemed to expand and contract with my breaths, as if it inhaled and exhaled the same way I did. Feathers from elaborate costumes ruffled, sequins sparkled as they moved, the wooden walls creaked and groaned with the movement, and the glass window to my right cracked, sending a spiderweb pattern across its surface. Beside me, the burlap sack of peaches seemed to be the only object to stay stationary, unmoving, and firm.

"I didn't know you felt the pain, too, Power. I'm so sorry. You've always seemed too strong to feel what I feel," I wheezed, the giggles abiding for just long enough for me to speak before taking over my body in full force again. Hot tears streamed down my face as my whole body began to turn bright red with the force of the unrelenting laughter.

I had to be strong for you. For us, sweet Kate. But, they're getting meaner. Tougher. I don't know if you can handle the next one, Kate. Why don't you let me out for a while. I'd love to teach them a lesson. They'll never hurt us again, I swear it.

"I envy you. You're so strong. Will you teach me how to be strong like you?"

My own head nodded in the mirror as a sly smile worked its way across my face. My lips parted, mouthing the word, "yes." Another fit of giggles took over and I doubled over across the tiny vanity, scratching my fingernails into the cheap wood as I struggled to control myself.

Just let go, she whispered, cooing in my ear, encouraging the laughter. Let me have it. I'll only be a little while. Truly, Kate. And, then you'll never have these again, she added, my reflection raising her shirt to expose the deep black and purple bruising decorating my abdomen. The last beating three days ago hadn't left any broken bones, but Gregory's steel toed boots had made sure my stomach muscles wouldn't have the strength to perform. The tricks where I laid across the trapeze bar were the ones Robbie wanted me to show off, and even stretching for my contortionist act aggravated the marbled skin and muscles.

But, I'd still done it. I swallowed four pain pills with a glass of water, and had stepped out onto the stage with pride in my eyes and my shoulders back. Gregory's cold eyes as I'd swung toward him haunted me still, but Power had encouraged me to show him I wouldn't be held back this time. Ellie's slaps and punches to my face and chest had stung, but the anger at Freddie for "cheating" on her was mild compared to the worst of the times I'd been taken out behind the caravan. Maybe because she'd been hammered, or maybe because Power had grabbed her wrist after several minutes and shoved her away, startling the tall redhead into stumbling her way back to her own trailer, willing to pass out and sleep off her drunkenness.

Don't you want them to know they can't keep hurting you?

A short, high pitched whimper escaped my lips. God, yes, how I wanted to stop being punched, kicked, slapped, beaten!

Let me have your body for just a little while. Kate. I'll take care of everything. Just sit back and watch. I'll give it back as soon as I've finished.

With those words, I obeyed, closing my eyes and falling back into my own head with surprising ease. Power stroked my arm, a satisfied smile on her lips, as she passed me by to take center stage with my body. The ache in my stomach faded away, making me wonder if Power had lied about feeling the pain I did. I shook the thought away as she took her position, breaking the surface and leaving me as a spectator of my own movements.

I watched, lounging on the plush velvet chaise Power regularly draped herself on. The relief of not having to make my own decisions and face my fellow performers melted me to the spot, making me wish Power could take over forever. Too bad she ran out of steam so quickly. More often than not, she tugged me back to the forefront after a couple hours, exhausted and ready to rest. I had noticed, however, that the times she surfaced were lengthening bit by bit. As if she were building up endurance for the outside world.

Power smiled at the mirror, the motion much more confident and, dare I say, arrogant than anything I could ever pull off outside the circus ring. Our fingers stroked the cheap wood of the small vanity we sat at, though the cool sensation of it under my fingers felt muted. Like I had fallen into a dream.

She twirled our hands and fingers in the air, laughing at the fluttering motion. "Oh, Kate, I do wish I could do this more often," she sighed, the longing in her voice obvious.

With a dramatic flourish, she swept our hand out to caress the burlap sack of peaches beside the vanity. Though muted, I felt the rough texture beneath our hands as the scent of sweet peaches infiltrated our nostrils. Power breathed it in, closing our eyes in ecstasy. "This will do nicely," she said, a slight smile twitching our lips.

She lifted the sack up, letting out a strained breath under the unexpected weight of it, and dumped the peaches on my bed, leaving the sack empty and flat.

What are you doing? I asked, curiosity perking me up to watch with more interest.

"Relax, sweet Kate. Just trust me. I'm taking care of everything.," she replied, her voice smooth and soothing.

With a hesitant nod, I leaned back in the red chaise and allowed myself to do just that- relax. She lifted the bag, using our hands to widen the opening before sliding it over our head and securing it with a small length of crude rope around our neck.

Power? I trembled, a black pit in my stomach forming as my hair stood on end at her strange actions.

"Do you not trust me? Have I ever done you wrong? I have a plan, my sweet. You mustn't question me. Alright?"

But-

"No buts. I'm in control for a while. Just sit back and enjoy the performance. You'll never forget it."

The lump in my throat doubled in size, but I settled back down onto the chaise again, knowing I didn't have a choice in the matter anymore. I'd let her out, given her my trust. She had never wronged me before, so I had no reason to suspect anything bad would transpire under her control.

To my surprise, I could still see through the burlap sack, our eyes able to focus past the scratchy brown surface and through the small holes to the outside world. Everything filtered through in slight sepia colors, though, making it all seem more like a dream and less like reality. Maybe that was her purpose. The knot of anxious tension in my stomach thought so, at least.

She stood from the plush but cheap stool, smoothing down the knee length white nightgown we wore and turning side to side in the mirror, as if making sure our image portrayed what she wanted adequately. I felt her satisfaction coupled with a hint of smugness and excitement as I took in the reflection in awe. The sight left shivers running up and down my arms. I could have been anyone without our face revealed, and the scent of peaches intoxicated my senses as our image twirled in a whimsical circle. The childishness seemed to mock the seriousness of the situation, though I had yet to even know what the situation entailed.

Power took one last, long look in the mirror, admiring the sight, before reaching for the sharp knife I kept under my bed for paranoia's sake. The knife remained untainted, as I'd never been attacked in my trailer before, but it seemed to prelude something sinister as she stroked the cool metal with our fingers, holding the handle with a firm grip. My heart rate doubled as the possibility that I'd made a grave error popped in and out of my head, but I kept my mouth shut, praying my instincts were wrong.

Power's stride was long and graceful, like a ballerina floating across stage, as she made her way out of my trailer. When she crossed the empty fairground in the moonlight, our legs worked as two discreet phantoms, making little to no sound against the crunching, dry and dead grass. The time for after-performance parties had well passed on by at around three a.m, and the clock on my trailer wall had read four-thirty. Experience told me everyone had retired their joyous rounds of beer and moonshine in favor of a hard nights sleep before we packed up and traveled on tomorrow morning. Only Power, in my body, moved around the camp, bouncing like a butterfly floating from flower to flower, eerily silent and light on our feet. She stifled a giggle, jumping and twirling in the air, turning cartwheels and bending in and out of slow flips as she progressed toward the main circle of trailers. Even from my spot inside my head, I felt the rush and satisfaction of our muscles stretching and contorting, bringing a wide smile to my face as I reveled in the sensation.

Her stride slowed, becoming even lighter and cautious as she neared the ring of trailers inhabited by the other performers. I felt the carefree demeanor drop under my feet as she took on a completely different role that I couldn't place, because I'd never experienced it before.

Tucking the blade into our palm, she approached Ellie and Charlotte's trailer, though everyone knew Charlotte passed out regularly in the fire-eater's cabin, leaving Gregory to sneak into the bed with Ellie. Secret romances, backstabbing, and jealousy thrived among my co-performers and to double cross one another meant nothing to them. In fact, it seemed a way of life. We lived the life of the extreme. Of drama. Of shine and sparkle. It seemed only natural for them to pull all of that into their personal lives.

Power sneaked to the window, stroking the cool glass before peering in, our hand tightening around the smooth handle of the butcher's knife. As expected, the two lovers laid intertwined, pieces of the costumes leaving a definite trail from the door to where they lay. A stocking crumpled here, a metallic green unitard slung there. I shuddered at the sight, my virgin eyes uncomfortable with seeing the aftermath and preamble to their carnal acts.

Power, however, smiled, her giddiness overflowing into my own body, making me sweat with anticipation.

She pressed her hand to the glass, applying more and more pressure until the window creaked open with a quiet, but no less startling, sound. She stood motionless, our eyes glued to the two figures on the bed. Neither moved, pleasing the woman in control of my body.

Our hands pressed farther until the three by three window raised completely open, the draft from outside fluttering the discarded clothing all over the plywood floor. She took her time hoisting herself up and into the cabin by the window, making sure she left no sound to alert Ellie or Gregory of their unwelcome intruder. She reached up instead of down as our body slid into the space, grasping the thin wooden rafters and crawling, upside down onto them. Legs wrapped around the beam, feet hooked onto the side to allow mobility without falling, as our hands gripped the rafter, the knife still tucked securely into our palm. One long moment passed, our breath crashing against the burlap sack just to be sent right back onto our face, the scent of peaches exploding all around our head.

She smiled, hiding her thoughts from me as goosebumps erupted like a bucket of ice water all over my skin. The moment she took to steady herself gone, she went on the move, crawling upside down along the rafter until her perched directly above the slumbering lovers.

A sick feeling worked its way up my throat. You're just going to scare them, right? I asked as my breaths came shallower and shallower.

She didn't answer, and I began to panic, standing from my seat and running for the surface. I only took two steps before the white stone wall I recognized as the one I regularly used to keep Power in check rose before me, trapping me behind its barrier.

Power! I cried, banging my fists against the hard stones. Power, you're just going to scare them, right?! Please! Please, tell me that's all!

Silence was the only reply I gained, sending me into full alarm as I watched her release our hands from their grip on the beam, uncurling our body until we hung by our legs, still upside down, above Ellie and Gregory, inches above their sleeping faces. So close that the sound of Gregory's soft snore made its way into my covered ears.

Terror overrode every sense in my mind as she raised the knife, the moonlight glinting off the silver metal, as if it were too excited to do exactly what Power wanted to use it for.

Inside my own head, I screamed as the treacherous knife made quick work of the two performers' throats, slicing through their fragile skin in swift succession so that the gurgling sounds of one wouldn't wake the other. My jaw hung open, horrified as the scarlet liquid gushed from their throats, mingling into one dark stream between them. Their eyes, which had opened the moment the blade pierced flesh, stared up at me with absolute and certain fear etched into their now milky depths. The two lovers died together, in each other's embrace, staring their horrifying killer in the face. Except they weren't even awarded that mercy- to know who ended their lives. Instead, all the man and woman saw before their souls ascended or descended into their destined afterlife was the rough, crude burlap sack over our head.

I felt Power's wide grin as our cheeks ached from the strain of such despicable joy. She paused, soaking in the gruesome scene and storing it in her memory to cherish forever.

I, however, stumbled back onto the chaise, my mind numb and in shock over what just happened. She killed them. Murdered them in cold blood. Slashed their throats, without even the barest hint of mercy.

God, please forgive me, I whispered, my eyes so wide that the white was visible all the way around my grey irises. My heart pounded slow but painfully hard in my chest, bruising the tender flesh there and making me lightheaded. This couldn't possibly be real. It just couldn't.

I sat there, dazed and in shock, as Power slithered back up into the rafters and out the window, our smooth and graceful body moving like a snake in the dark. She repeated the process in every other trailer, sneaking soundlessly through the windows, crawling like some demented demon from my nightmares through the flimsy rafters, and slashing each member's throat, only pausing to watch and bask in the glory she felt as their blood trickled from their necks and onto their bedsheets. No one fought her, even though they saw her figure above them before fading away. Yet, all of them died with the same terrified face as the realization washed over them like the blood that coated their upper bodies, creating a slick and wet sticky film over them. Blood dripped from her precious blade, leaving a morbid trail behind her as she moved from cabin to cabin.

Agony ripped through me as I tried to get back in control over and over to no avail. I was powerless to help them, and by letting Power take over, I caused their untimely deaths. In more ways than one, I knew I had killed them.

Tears poured down my cheeks as I tried to look away from each murder, but my eyes refused to cooperate or even just close as each victim fell prey to the vicious blade in Power's even more vicious grip. Despite all they had done to me- beaten me, tortured me, humiliated me, I never wished this on them. I never wished them dead.

I was a fool to trust Power, but the realization came too late. Too late for me, and too late for them.

Crimson, regal liquid pouring from slashed throats and unfocused, milky, horrified eyes haunted my vision every which way I turned, making the tears pouring down my cheeks come harder and faster with each passing second until I found myself on my knees. I clutched at my own chest and throat, sobbing as I begged Power to stop the madness, the insanity.

Power ignored me, not even sparing a second to mock my weakness or soothe my hysterics. Instead, she strode, toe-to-heel, with the long and quiet prance I used to enter the ring for every show, until she brought us outside the ring of trailers.

My heart sank, hoping it was all some sick dream, but know I would never have the pleasure of being so lucky. For now, though, at least it was over.

Why? I asked her, my voice trembling and hoarse.

She didn't answer me, but twirled around to take in her handiwork, beaming at each bloodied and gruesome trailer as if they were precious to her. She glowed with eager pride, basking in what she'd done while I doubled over inside my head, gagging and trying not to vomit.

"We're not finished, yet, Kate. There's one more, and we have to hurry before I have to let you have control back. So, don't lose sight of the goal now!" she whisper-shouted to me, girlish laughter tinkling from our lips and into the silence around us. With that, she spun around and skipped toward the other side of the caravan.

As we passed the lions and tigers cages, they stood and paced, their movements anxious and agitated, growling and snapping at us when we passed. They knew. Their keen instincts told them something was very wrong with the woman they'd grown up with, and they didn't like it one bit. Ginger, the tiger Robbie had supervised me to train by myself, bared her long ivory teeth at me, hissing and snapping as her hackles stood on end.

I'm sorry! I yelled out at the pacing beasts, the guilt of letting them down by becoming this thing Power wanted crushing my soul as their deep amber eyes watched Power move with a pronounced wariness in their bodies. Of course, I knew they couldn't really hear me, but as Ginger's ear pricked forward, eyes trained on Power and cocking her massive head to the side, I wondered if they could hear what humans couldn't.

Power passed them by, keeping up her bouncing prance, her footsteps falling silent against the snapping dead grass. My head fell into my hands as I wished I could travel back in time and refuse her advances. She walked on, while I closed my eyes and tried to transport myself somewhere else, into another dimension or world, away from her and what she had just done using my body.

The soft creaking of yet another window sliding open jolted my attention to the forefront again. All the performers were dead! What could she possibly hope to destroy now? Was an entire circus fleet not enough? Had she dragged me and my body into the nearest town to get her next sick thrill?

While she hauled herself through the window, I noticed that her breathing seemed heavier and her strong, overbearing presence felt weaker. As if it were diminishing through the effort it had taken. Her movements came less fluid, even clumsy, as she struggled to keep her energy up.

Our hands gripped onto the wooden beam above the window and she heaved herself up onto it, crawling on top of the wooden plank rather than slithering upside down from it like she had done with the other trailers.

But, whose trailer was this?

Her grip around the bloodied butcher knife faltered as fatigue began to siphon her strength, and I prayed she ran out of energy before she could kill again.

Risking even more heartache, I looked below us and my heart stopped.

Please, no, Power! Please, leave him be! Please! I begged, more sobs crashing up my throat, muffling and cracking my voice into some indistinguishable animalistic noise.

I felt her irritation rise up below my feet, snapping at me to shut up without ever saying the words.

You can't do this! He did nothing, and you know it! He never hurt us!

"He approved it. He could have stopped it, but he let it continue. Don't you see, Kate? He is entirely to blame for all of it!" she whispered, her words coming out in hard, labored breaths. Below us, Robbie stirred in his sleep, his black hair falling across his stubbled jaw as his eyes rolled beneath his resting eyelids. Hot, salty tears streamed down my flushed cheeks as I continued to beg and plead with her to not hurt my ringmaster. My only pseudo-friend in the entire world.

Her annoyance grew and festered into indignant fury with every word I spoke, as her waning strength wore on her more and more with each passing second. Hands shaking, she swiped our arm across the top of our forehead, smearing the sweat from our brow as our teeth clenched in solid determination.

And, then, before I could process what happened, much less try to stop it, the blade lashed out, catching his throat and severing the thread of his life.

Robbie's eyes slammed open, shock and horror written across his expression as he caught sight of my body with the burlap sack tied over my head and the blood coated knife in my trembling hand. I watched as his mouth opened, only to allow more scarlet liquid to fall from his lips alongside the rasping noise as he tried to say something to me. Power held on to her hold over my body with the last ounce of her will, eager to watch the life flee from his eyes.

I, on the other hand, couldn't take my eyes away for a different reason.

I'm so sorry, Robbie. Please believe me. I didn't want to do this, I whispered on the off chance that being near death would grant him some kind of sixth sense so he could hear my soundless cries. His dark, almost black, eyes flicked between mine as the alarm gave way to despair, then finally, resignation.

Power let loose her white knuckled grip on her control and fell back under the surface, thereby thrusting me back to the front. Whiplash snapped my body to and fro as I shifted back into control of my being. Hot, lightning white flashes burst in my head while Power collapsed, losing her consciousness and leaving me alone to deal with the terrible crisis she created.

My lip trembled as I took in Robbie's searching gaze and an enormous, overwhelming ball of emotion swelled in my throat. I reached out to him, brushing the stray black strands of hair from his pale face.

"I'm so sorry, Robbie. I tried... I t-tried so hard to stop it," I sobbed, my words stumbling and halting, my apology useless since it couldn't undo Power's despicable actions.

Robbie gave no acknowledgment that he heard or accepted my apology before his eyelids slid down for the last time.

Thunder cracked overhead as a sudden flood of rain pounded against the trailer roof, so eerily fitting with the horrific events that just took place. I walked, utterly spent and numb, out of his cabin, using the door rather than the still opened window where rain poured in without restraint, soaking his beautiful velvet top hat and shining red ringmaster's coat.

My feet carried me a few feet outside his trailer, where I sank to my knees in the forming mud and cried until the police arrived the next morning.

John stared at me, his eyes wide and his fingers clenched around mine as I concluded my retelling of the awful memory.

"I never imagined that it would have happened like that," he finally murmured, letting out a heavy breath. My teeth pressed down onto my bottom lip, waiting for his reaction.

"Thank God Robbie was the last one and she didn't finish the job."

A burst of inappropriate laughter shot from my lips, and for once, it wasn't by Power's doing. "John, that's hardly the appropriate response to what I just told you. Not that I'm not happy he's alive, too."

His teeth beamed from his wide, sloppy grin. "I told you I wouldn't judge you. And, that's really the first thing that ran through my mind, anyway."

I rolled over onto my back, smiling as I shook my head at him. Only he had the ability to make me feel anything other than crushing guilt after speaking of what I'd done.

"Are you at Rosenton for life, too?" I asked, hoping his answer would be "yes", but then chastising myself for being so selfish.

He turned onto his stomach, reaching into the cool stream and splashing the water toward the wall. A gentle smile flirted at the edges of his lips. "I'm here for as long as I feel like I need to be."

I frowned, my brows knotted together in confusion. "That's quite the cryptic answer."

His hand splashed the water back at me, the frigid droplets clinging to my cheeks and arms. "I wasn't sentenced here. I came here by choice, so I'm technically free to go whenever I want. The police never even arrested me for what I did. I think they were just happy the gang members were dead, but I couldn't let myself go without punishment or without getting help for whatever happened to me. Not that I've gotten any help here."

"The why are you still here?" I asked, flicking the droplets off my face with my thumb and forefinger.

John glanced over at me, his face soft and serene, nearly glowing that angelic comfort as he seemed to ponder what to say next. "I found people who needed help, possibly more than I do. Esther was already here, and so was Marcie. When she saw how I convinced the doctors to change Marcie's medicine and help her, Esther begged me to stay and help the others. I've grown too close to all of you to even think about leaving now. What kind of man would I be to abandon my friends in their time of need?"

My heart warmed over, melting like a chocolate bar on a summer day. "You're a good man, John.," I whispered, squeezing the hand I still held onto. A light, sardonic laugh fell from his lips.

"I'm nowhere near as good as I want to be. I'm still a murderer."

Silence permeated the air around us after that as I pondered his words, secretly applying them to myself though I knew he wouldn't have wanted me to. But, I couldn't help but wonder... No matter how much good I did in the world, I'd still killed over twenty people. No amount of good would bring them back.

Maybe, just maybe, John and I were doomed to be damned together.

Chapter 14

The trek back to Rosenton was long and rough on my poor, aching feet and bruised knees. John had roused me an hour before sunrise so we could hopefully be back in our beds by breakfast time, but with so little sleep and being physically exhausted, we didn't make it back inside until an hour after the morning meal.

As soon as I stepped into my room after sneaking past the lounge and several staff members, I collapsed on the bed and fell back to sleep, my eyelids weighted and my body so drained that I never heard Esther come in to wake me for lunch at noon. Three o'clock barely passed on the clock on the wall before my swollen eyes forced themselves open.

The bright light shining above me caused way for a bursting headache to take over my skull, throbbing and shattering any hope of a bright and cheery countenance for the rest of the day. I groaned, sitting up with the utmost care to not jostle my head. My mouth twisted into a grimace as I took note of myself in the mirror across the room. The sight of my disgusting shape made it clear a shower and toothbrush were top priorities.

Still yawning, I swung my feet over the side of the bed and padded my way to the womens showers, clothes and toiletries in hand. The cubicle I chose regularly for my shower welcomed me, the steaming water pelting my skin and scrubbing away the grime and dirt. Sharp jolts of pain radiated from my bloody palms and my legs felt like goo, but I steeled myself and savored the cleansing water, sighing in contentment as it massaged my sore muscles.

Washing my hair and body took less than fifteen minutes, and afterward I stayed under the steady stream, basking in the fresh and clean feeling the hot water left behind. I would cherish our time in the cave until the day I died, but rinsing the dirt from my body seemed almost as satisfying as the night before, altogether.

We can get out now.

My shoulder slumped, wet clumps of hair falling in my face. "And here I thought I'd be free of you for a little while," I murmured, rolling my eyes. Exasperation flooded my veins, and for the first time, I felt like I wanted to fight Power, instead of ignoring or hiding from her. Maybe it stemmed from the confidence John's presence seemed to give me.

Or, maybe I was finally just sick of her.

Feisty today, are we? Look up, Sane.

"Leave me alone. I don't even want to think about you right now," I snapped, the mocking way she called me Sane snapping the last of my patience. It was something she'd picked up only after she'd murdered everyone at Jensen and Sons. I guess to remind me of the distinct differences between her and I while still patronizing me. It had always failed to bother me before, but something about the change from last night and the now made it impossible to hear her call me that without wanting to wring her perfect neck.

Oh, I see. Now who's having murderous thoughts? I wish you could truly fight me, Sane. It would certainly be my pleasure.

"Just shut up!"

My shout echoed around the large room, making her laugh and sway from side to side.

I'll leave you be for today if you just look at me. Come on. A day of freedom. All you have to do is look. Her voice slithered through my head, sly and conniving.

But, to pass up the opportunity to not have to worry about hearing her vile voice in my head would be my biggest regret come morning when I could have pretended to be a normal woman.

That's it, sweet Sane. Just look. C'mon. I'm right in front of you.

Bracing myself against the wall with one arm, I forced myself to obey and raise my eyelashes to meet her evil gaze.

Except, only the slick, wet shower wall greeted my reluctant glare. Anger gave way to confusion and I pushed myself to stand straight.

Boo! Her hot breath tickled my ear, sending shivers up my spine as I whirled around to face her head on. You certainly do look so much more like me than you used to. I like it, Sane. We could be twins. Esther's secret potions stash is doing you well.

My sparking pewter eyes flashed at hers, daring her to say something else. Power stood in my shower cubicle, fully clothed in one of my finer performance leotards, crystals and feathers rustling as she shifted from foot to foot, examining me like a chunk of prize beef. The water from the still rushing shower pelted her, drenching her and her outfit to the core. Even the delicate crystal headdress couldn't hide from the hot droplets spraying down on the two of us.

"I couldn't care less about your approval, Power. I looked at you, now get out." My tone carried a sense of confidence and finality I didn't know I could master, and a wave of pride washed over me, making me feel taller, stronger.

Her head fell back and she laughed, exposing her ivory neck. You're certainly in a terrible mood for having had the best night of your life last night. Is it because he hasn't kissed you yet?

Before I knew what I was doing, my hand curled into a tight fist and flew straight at Power's beautiful face. Her figure vanished into thousands of tiny particles at the contact, taking her awful voice along with it. My palm felt seared as my fingernails dug into the already lacerated and blistered flesh. But, I couldn't relax. Every muscle in my body drew taut and rigid, waiting for her return so I could finish the job of bloodying her stupid, perfect nose. I'd never hit anyone before in my life, but to bestow that honor on her seemed infuriatingly fitting.

"And, stay away, you god awful tart!" I cried out into the empty shower room, the words echoing and bouncing back into my sensitive ears.

I stepped out of the shower room, still towel drying my hair and shivering the coldness of the tiled floor seeped up into my bare feet. I stopped, taking in the white nurses shoes in front of me and trailing my eyes up to meet the gaze of the older woman with far too much makeup on her aging face. And not the good kind of too much makeup, like Esther. More like the clowns from Jensen and Sons. My lips pressed together to hold in my smile, certain she'd take offense.

"You're to come with me," she said, everything about her tone brusque and demanding. My eyebrows raised into my hairline, her demand making me wary.

"Alright," I replied, watching her with a careful eye. "Just let me put my towel away."

Quicker than I thought possible for such a heavy woman, she rolled her milky eyes and snatched the white cloth from my hands, tossing it back in the shower room behind me. "The janitor will take care of it. Dr. Shilling wants to see you, now."

My feet planted to the floor in shock. None of the nurses had ever been anything but cordial. What had I done to warrant such nastiness as well as a visit with Shilling on the ward's craft day? I should have been gluing popsicle sticks together like a third grader, not getting snapped at by a clown nurse with a superiority complex.

"Hurry up, girl," she growled, her jowls bouncing as she moved to shove me in the right direction. I sidestepped her hand with ease, shooting her a nasty look.

"I'll go there, myself. I just ask that you not put your hands on me, ma'am," I returned, adopting my best Power stance and looking down my nose at the beastly ogre of a woman, even though she was at least six inches taller than me. The nurse huffed out an exasperated breath and rolled her eyes again.

"Fine, you deranged lunatic. Start walking."

My jaw dropped. Even if it was my diagnosis, no one had called much such names before at Rosenton, much less the staff. The nurses and orderlies preferred to ignore my existence or smile at me quickly and look away, as if scared of me. Who the devil was this awful woman? Of all the times for me to make a deal with Power for her to vanish…

I practically heard her devious snickering behind the stone wall, soaking up the luck of her excellent timing. Or maybe she knew all along and this was her plan coming to life.

Whatever the case, I straightened my shoulders and speed walked down the stark white hallway, not bothering to check behind me to see if she could keep up with my fast pace. As I made my way to Shilling's office, I turned a corner and nearly got ran over by Ed, my face inches away from colliding with his diaphragm area. We both jerked backward at the same time, flicking our heads toward each other in surprise.

He nodded at me in acknowledgment, a sly grin twitching at the corner of his mouth. "Late for a very important date?" he asked, his deep voice at odds with the teasing tone and Lewis Carroll reference.

I channeled my inner angry nurse and rolled my eyes, my shoulders slumping. "You would get it right on the first guess." I glanced behind me for my prison ward nurse to find her still at the far end of the hallway I'd been in before, huffing and puffing her reddened cheeks as she tried to catch up to me. "I can't talk, though. I've been summoned to Shilling's lair."

Ed's thick, black eyebrows rose up, making his lime eyes stand out even more on his stubbled face. "Shilling? Why?"

Twisting my mouth to the side in an unconfident grimace, I shrugged. "Not a clue. I guess I'll find out when I get there. Maybe he decided I'm getting better and can be released into the natural world again. Like a wounded deer or something."

I expected at laugh, or even just a slight lifting of the corners of his mouth, but not the immediate concern etching its way across his face. Like he knew something I didn't, or suspected something and didn't want to tell me. Bile rose in my throat when I considered why he wouldn't want to tell me something. Ed, although a quiet man, had never lied to me in the few short times we'd held a serious conversation. The man and the phrase, "sugar-coating" didn't even exist in the same realm. The only reason he could have to hide something from me would be to keep from scaring me too badly to function.

All of a sudden, my impromptu trip to the good doctor's office seemed much more menacing than I had originally thought. I gulped down the growing ball in my throat and let out a shaky laugh, trying to calm my nerves and wishing for Power's confident presence.

"I'll see you around, then," I stammered, running one hand through my still damp hair.

Again, he nodded in acknowledgment and offered me a small, nervous smile before heading on his way. I watched as he passed the furious nurse, turning around to study her for a moment before shaking his head and walking down an adjacent hallway.

"What are you waiting for, girl? Go!" Nurse Angry shouted, spittle launching through the air from her puckered lips. My lip curled in disgust, but I spun around and all but sprinted for Shilling's office, hoping I'd find refuge from her nastiness behind his wooden door.

To my immense negative fortune, stepping into Shilling's office revealed and even more hostile atmosphere than Nurse Grumpy had put off, if possible. The good doctor stood, leaned against his desk, arms folded tightly against his chest as his mouth pursed into an angry expression. Even his gold rimmed glasses seemed furious with the way the light from the window behind his desk gleamed off their shining surface, the reflection hiding his eyes from me.

I took a hesitant step in the room, my earlier flippancy long forgotten as the seriousness of the situation began to sink in. Ed's austere demeanor suddenly seemed less of an overreaction as I took note of Dr. Shilling's tense stance across from me. Choosing to cut off any chance of my unpleasant chaperone joining us in the room, I closed the door behind me, but stayed where I stood, hating how I couldn't read his eyes.

"You sent for me, Doctor?" I asked, gripping my skirt in my hands and twisting the material in nervous circles.

He gave a curt nod, showing no other sign of movement as I stood there, averting my eyes from his terse form. It was obvious he was displeased with me, and I could only think of one reason why.

John and I hadn't returned from our "visit" with Robbie at midnight at planned. We'd both known there would be consequences, but as I began to shake in front of the fuming doctor, I realized we may have underestimated those consequences. Somehow, I didn't see Shilling giving me a slap on the wrist, like I'd tried to convince myself would happen.

"So, the prodigal couple has returned. Where were the two of you last night, Ms. Thornton? And, don't give me any lies about being with Robert Jensen. I know better," he sneered, his voice like the low growl of a territorial wild dog. My body shrank back into the door of its own accord, making me wish for the company of the unpleasant nurse rather than the furious doctor now that I heard him speak.

Now, more than ever, I wished I hadn't made that stupid deal with Power. If her presence was beneficial anywhere, I had a sinking feeling this exact scenario was tailor made for her.

My mind raced to come up with an explanation. Anything to keep his fury from unleashing on my defenseless body.

He moved to walk closer to me, the reflection on his glasses receding enough to allow me to see the rage boiling over in his cold, pale blue eyes. "Did you try to escape, Ms. Thornton? To find the nearest town and run for it? No, I don't think you did. Otherwise you wouldn't have come back. Have I ever told you what happens to residents who misbehave to the extraordinary level you and Mr. Kingwood have? You and Mr. Kingwood... You've been close, haven't you? My staff has told me as much. Did you take a lovers rendez-vous? Romantic relationships between residents, especially residents in Ward F, are not allowed, Ms. Thornton. Have I never told you that?"

The man ranted on and on, taking small, pronounced steps toward me as he spit the words of his daunting lecture in my face. I flattened my trembling body against the door, my hands fumbling for the doorknob so I could make a run for it.

"I-w-we aren't romantic-romantically involved... sir," I stuttered, missing the feeling of Power's rising hackles when she felt threatened. Until now, I'd never noticed how accustomed I'd become to her protective tendencies. To a level, despite how much I hated her, I wanted her protection. I felt safe physically, if not mentally, with her presence mucking around in my head.

"Is that so? I suppose friends hold hands now? Adult friends who are no longer of the age for such actions to pertain to innocent companionship?"

I flinched as each syllable pounded at me with more volume than the last. What could I say to him? The knowledge that Dr. Shilling was a monster was nothing new, but experiencing his awful personification of said monster was new. This type of thing seemed to be John's forte, as he always had the skill set to handle Shilling's evil ways.

"We spent the night in the garden. Star-s-stargazing. I'm sorry. We fell asleep," I lied, praying with everything in me it fell sweet on his ears.

He froze, glaring at me with such intense hatred bubbling in his eyes that I felt tears prick at the back of my own as real, true fear rose up from my toes to the top of my head. A light chuckle filled the air as his lips twitched into a humorless, cruel grin that reminded me all too much of the hallucination I'd had of Power in my old trailer so many months ago. It seemed as though his smile would stretch and stretch, not stopping until it reached his ears.

"Is that they story you want to stick with, Ms. Thornton?" he asked, his tone holding a distinct threat, loud and clear.

I nodded, squeezing the cold brass doorknob in my sweating palm.

"You know how I can tell you're lying, you disgusting little miscreant? I've had six months worth of sessions with you. Six months worth of opportunities to study you and figure you out. When you lie, Ms. Thornton, your eyes widen just a fraction of an inch beforehand. Nothing anyone would ordinarily notice, of course," he said, waving one hand in the air, as if to let the world know exactly how much more important and intelligent he was than the rest of us. "But I notice. I see it all. Aside from that little tidbit, there's another way I know you're lying. Would you like me to elaborate?"

No, I certainly did not want him to elaborate. I wanted out of that office. I wanted as far away from him as I could get. I wanted to run as fast as I could and never return. The last thing I wanted was to spend one more second in that enclosed room with a man who seemed on the verge of a murderous rage in his own institute.

Nonetheless, he didn't give me a chance to answer. Instead, he began to pace the width of the room, sweat seeping through and staining the underarms of his crisp, tailored shirt. I tried turning the knob in my hand, hoping to escape, but the dampness of my palm coupled with the smooth metal of the small sphere rendered the task impossible.

"I know you're lying because two members of my staff saw Robert Jensen drunk out of his mind at nine o'clock at night, alone, in town. With neither John Kingwood nor Katherine Thornton in sight. Were you not signed out by Mr. Jensen yesterday afternoon, to be returned at midnight?" he led, as dread encompassed my stomach like a steel weight.

"W-we came back earlier than th-that, and John and I-"

"Lies! Do not take me for a fool, Katherine Thornton!" he screamed, storming toward me with with a glint in his eye and twitch in his hand that brought back all those years at Jensen and Sons. Being slapped, hit, kicked, beaten behind the trailers. My body tensed, knowing the situation well and readying itself for the coming blow.

But, they never came. I opened my eyes, watching the doctor through squinted slits, still not convinced he wouldn't change his mind and let his clenched fist fly.

"You think I'd hit my own patients?" he asked, the words broken up between his arrogant laughter. Shoulders shaking with mirth, he backed away from me, striding toward his ornate desk. A relieved breath escaped my lips as my personal space regained its freedom from the doctor's overbearing presence.

I watched him, never letting my eyes wander from his form, as I wiped my palms against my skirt to get rid of the sweat. I needed to escape this volatile situation. Every instinct in my body screamed it at me and my legs itched to run as far away as possible.

"I'm not an ill-bred man, Ms. Thornton. I don't stoop to barroom brawls to get my point across. I like to think of myself as a man much more sophisticated than that," he said, his unsettling smile setting me on edge as he pulled open one of his desk drawers. He stared down into it, stroking whatever sat in it with an almost loving expression on his face.

If the terrified lump in my throat grew any larger, it would have ripped my esophagus in two, I was sure.

With tender movements, he grasped whatever laid in his desk drawer and pulled it into my view, revealing the rough brown texture that haunted my dreams. The one thing sure to make Power break her end of the bargain and surface.

And surface, she did. As soon as her eyes laid on the burlap sack, she surged forward with such force that my hands flew to the sides of my head, fists curling into my hair as I doubled over in agony and slammed my burning eyes shut.

She screamed inside my head, fighting and clawing at the stone wall, her raging words indecipherable through the intense power of her angry screeches.

"No!" I cried out, my kneecaps taking the hard impact of my fall to the ground. Deafeningly loud ringing blasted my ears as I fought her off, feeling each scratch and punch she threw at my defenses, wincing in the excruciating mental pain.

"Look at it, Ms. Thornton!" Shilling demanded, curling his fist into the hair on the back of my head and yanking me, hard, to my feet. My teeth gritted against the sting and Power grew wilder at the attack, throwing her body against the wall. A long, solid crack erupted from the center, where her shoulder hit, lengthening and weakening my only defense with each smash of her berserker onslaught.

Hold the wall together, I chanted, doing my best to focus solely on that all important task rather than the doctor's rage. I was no fool. While Shilling took place as the primary threat to my body, Power was much more than that. She would destroy much more, including the doctor. Her attack was the more dangerous one, and she alone held the power to completely destroy me, from inside out. Something the good doctor, no matter how badly he broke my body, could ever accomplish.

"Open your eyes, you filthy criminal!" he roared, shaking me by the roots of my hair. The pain from the strands ripping from my scalp stung my eyes. My heart racing, pounding itself against my chest so hard I was certain it left a dark and ugly bruise, I squeezed my eyes closed even harder. Hot, salty tears beaded at the corners of my eyes and trailed down the sides of my face, while Power strengthened her attack to be freed.

My undoing came as Dr. Shilling shoved the burlap sack over my head, squeezing his ivory hands around my neck.

Loud, shrill giggles burst from my mouth, making a wide, painful grin spread across my covered face. My back arched as my muscles tensed, sending me into an upside down U shape, still laughing that maddening sound. The wall, my precious wall, crumbled down as my resolve disappeared into thin air. I curled my body further until my head and hands sat between my feet. Through the tiny holes in the sack, I saw Shilling's polished shoes retreat two precise, measured steps.

Power shoved me back behind the destroyed wall, her eyes spitting fire at me, furious that I'd fought her for this moment. My body continued to giggle and contort as I reached out for Power, begging her to stop before she did something irreversibly devastating, but she met my pleads with a glare that would have split me in two had it been a knife.

She had nearly made it to the surface, breaking the invisible barrier to take control over my seizing body, when everything in the room froze.

The knock on the door repeated, more persistent this time than at first.

"Dr. Shilling," a muffled voice called, alarm clear and present in his voice. In a slow haze, I drifted back to the forefront, past the startled Power, who shoved at my shoulder in an aggressive show as I passed her. The string that seemed to keep her tethered behind the wall pulled her back behind it, reconstructing the stones until the wall stood tall and firm again. I broke through the barrier, taking a huge, shuddering breath and yanking the burlap sack off my head in the same motion.

Shilling fumed as he watched me stand straight and hurl the offending sack as far away from me as I could with two fingers, too afraid to feel the fabric in my hands. I stood before him, trembling as my adrenaline rush diminished, leaving me an emotional, terrified mess.

"Dr. Shilling, I know you have an appointment, but I really need to speak with you!"

As he moved toward the door his eyes never left mine, their coldness jolting me into an uncomfortable tenseness that took over my entire body. But, I realized, with a sense of astonishment, that I recognized the voice on the other side, and for the first time, that voice sounded panicked instead of jittery or content.

Ed's hulking body filled the door frame and then some when Shilling pulled open the door, letting it swing with more force than necessary. Ed's wall of a chest rose up and down at an alarming pace, his large lime green eyes wide and trained on me the instant Shilling let him in. His gaze flicked from my face, down my body, then back to my eyes, boring into them as if asking me something.

'Are you alright?' they seemed to ask.

As Shilling glared at my gargantuan savior, I gave a quick, sharp nod to answer him, while doing everything I could to send my eternal gratitude through my expression at the same time.

"What is the problem, Mr. Warton? Ms. Thornton and I were in the middle of an important session," the doctor snapped, shoving his hand through his mussed hair, pressing the strands that had fallen from their gelled positions back into perfect place.

Ed frowned, rubbing the back of his neck and averting his eye to look at anything but the two of us.

“I-uh… I’m ready to talk about it. My crimes. I want to get better. So I want to talk. Now. Before I change my mind and chicken out,” he blurted, eyebrows raised as if he were just as surprised by the words stumbling from his mouth as Shilling appeared to be.

The doctor threw his shoulders back, a genuine pleased smile gracing his lips as he stood straighter, as if he’d singlehandedly “fixed” Ed already. He looked at Ed, then back at me, pondering which of us held more precedence.

With a quiet scoff, he swiveled on his heel to look at me. “You are dismissed, Ms. Thornton. I’ll see you Tuesday.”

Chapter 15

I sprinted all the way from Shilling's office to the cafeteria, only slowing once the double door to the food hall clicked shut behind me. My chest heaved in rapid succession as I scanned the back of the room for the table my ward usually claimed. John, Esther, Lottie and George sat in their normal spots at the round lunch table, chatting between bites of their sandwiches. Except, of course, for Lottie, who played with hers in her hands, making slight indentions with her fingers to make it look smaller, as if she'd eaten some of it when we all knew she hadn't.

I took a moment to gather my nerves into a somewhat composed state before walking to them and sliding into my seat beside John. He jumped, startled by my sudden appearance, and looked at me with wide eyes for a moment. Did he know Shilling had called me to him? Did he even know we'd been caught? His face scrunched up in confusion at my frazzled state, answering both questions before I could ask.

I smiled and swallowed the nervous lump blocking my airway. A change of subject to his own unasked questions was needed before I had to answer him and alarm everyone else.

"Where's Marcie?" I asked, feeling guilty for being thankful for her absence, giving me a quick excuse to move his attention elsewhere.

"She's having an episode. She flipped her switch from happy to sad yesterday and won't come out of her room," Esther replied, sympathy thick in her words. "What about Ed? I know he's come back from wherever he goes already. I saw him in the hallway. He never misses a meal..."

I couldn't be sure if any of the others saw the way my eyes averted the instant she mentioned my Goliath sized rescuer, but the way John's shoulders tensed told me he noticed. Guilt rose up in my throat and I caught his gaze, nodding toward the hallway so we could speak in private. Surprise filtered through me when he denied my request, nodding instead toward the entire table.

He wanted me to say it in front of everyone.

Why?

I bit my lip, as the shaking in my limbs started up again. His stance softened as he took my trembling hand under the table, squeezing it for support. I gazed at him, begging him silently to let me tell him privately, but he shook his head again, then inclined it toward Esther, Lottie, and George. The three ward mates watched us, confusion written clear as day all over their faces, with a dose of suspicion dotting the edges of George's expression.

The deep breath I took burned all the way through my lungs as I prepared myself to be blamed and hated by the people I trusted and had come to care for over the past six months.

"Ed's in Shilling's office. Shilling called me in this morning and attacked me. Ed interrupted and bought my way out by telling him he'd talk about his crimes."

John and George stiffened as Lottie and Esther adopted expressions filled with fear for their ward mate.

"Attacked you, how?" John asked, scanning my body up and down much the same way Ed had when he'd entered Shilling's office.

Every breath from my lips shook as fear overrode my senses. "He tried to trigger an episode. Or, rather, he tried to force one. If Ed hadn't come in when he did..."

George cursed, earning a sharp look from Lottie, but he didn't seem to care. Tension filled the air everyone took in what I revealed.

"He's targeted you," Esther mumbled, shaking her beautifully coiffed curls sadly. "He has you in his sights and he's going to stop at nothing, now, Kate. Shilling wants you on the thirteenth floor."

The hairs all over my body rose on end, alarm racing through me at warp speed. Robbie's description of his cousin filled my mind, replacing me with the shell of a man with missing digits and tiny scars, making me panic all the more.

"Stay here," George instructed to the three of us women as he and John stood, pushing their chairs back from the table and abandoning their lunches.

"You did well, Katie," John whispered just before he and George disappeared from the table, his lips brushing my ears with his reassurance. "You can trust them."

My fists clenched in my lap. He hadn't exactly given me a choice in the matter, and the times where I relied on him to take complete care of me were coming to a close. Maybe I'd made a mistake in clinging to him so quickly so soon and for so long. But what else was I supposed to do, being sent to an insane asylum and him being the first friendly, helpful face? Wouldn't anyone have clung to him like I did? Even Marcie had.

Marcie...

Had everyone really left her alone in her state? Didn't she need someone, too? To care about her, and show her that? Why had she been abandoned to suffer alone in her depression? Anger rose up, consuming the fear I'd bathed in all day since being summoned to Shilling.

Esther and Lottie jumped, startled, and only then I realized that I'd slammed my fist on the table. My tongue darted out to moisten my dry, chapped lips. Marcie had been kind to me. She'd been kind to all of us. Why wasn't she entitled to that same care and affection?

Much like John and George had, I shoved myself up from the table and stalked out of the cafeteria. Esther and Lottie called out behind me, reminding me that we'd been ordered to stay put, but I ignored them with more ease than I would have thought.

"Someone could hurt you!" Esther cried, sounding much less confident and composed than normal.

Really, I couldn't help but laugh. Her cool, put together demeanor seemed to have wafted through the air into me as I scoffed, rolling my eyes at the ridiculousness of her statement.

"I'm a mass murderer, Esther. I slit the throats of almost two dozen people in one night. Who, exactly, do you think can hurt me?"

The color drained from both womens faces, and I took that cue to turn and leave.

"Marce?" I called, knocking quietly on the cheap, hollow door. Two orderlies strode by, and I wondered if the disgusted grimaces they seemed to give me were all in my head- a figment of my imagination left over from the attack from Shilling earlier that day.

No answer came from the room, and I waited only a few more seconds before cracking open the door and sliding inside, making sure no more of Rosenton's increasingly suspicious staff were around to see me.

At first, with a quick glance around the room, my first impression was that she wasn't in her room. But, just as I turned to leave again in search of her, a single tuft of shimmering, golden blond hair poking out from the wadded up blankets on the bed closest to the window caught my attention. I slid the door closed all the way, only satisfied when the soft click of the lock anchoring in place resounded.

"Marcie, it's Kate," I whispered, walking to her bed and sitting beside her curled up body. Still, she remained quiet. I glanced over to her face, my heart dropping at the pitiful sight.

John's description of her being two people rang true as I studied her muted, pale and lifeless features. With no makeup, nor her usual bright, sunny smile, Marcie Greene looked like she could have been a corpse. Her large doe eyes fell unfocused to the window in front of her, barely blinking every few seconds, and her lustrous hair seemed dead and dull, tangled and greasy from not bathing. Even her beautiful skin looked grey, like the dead.

It was hard to believe the bright and bubbly woman could have been thrust into her current state in just two days, especially when I'd yet to have seen it in the six months I'd been at Rosenton. Two weeks, everyone had give her, before the switch in her brain flipped and she became catatonic. Yet those two weeks had passed and kept going, until we'd forgotten her condition altogether, it seemed, taking advantage of the happiness she brimmed with at all times.

The woman I studied now made me wonder if all that happiness she exuded had been real. Surely no one could truly be that lovely and vivacious with the sadness she now portrayed living inside her.

I laid my hand on her head and began combing through her hair with my fingers, taking note from all the times Esther had done the same for me, and the comfort it had gifted.

"I guess you don't fell very well. It's alright if you don't want to talk. I'll just talk to you and you can listen. Or you can ignore me, if you want. The only thing I won't let you do is be alone. You don't deserve to be alone."

I waited a few moments for any reaction, even the tiniest one, but received none. Only the faint rise and fall of the bedding on top of her proved she still breathed.

My fingers continued their path through her limp hair, catching on ratted tangles that I tried to smooth out as my hands came in contact with them. "Lottie told me your mother is coming to see you this week. I wonder if she has another trip to town planned for you. You seem to rather enjoy them, not that I can blame you. I wish, just once, Martha would approve me to leave this place for the day with everyone else. I've never been in trouble here, before today, anyway. Am I truly that terrible a person, I wonder?" I kept my voice light and curious, rather than pensive as I spoke about my own insecurities. No need in adding any more of a somber mood to the air in the room.

"In any case, I'm sure you'll have more delicious gossip about your hometown for me. Was it Sandra you said got pregnant recently? Or was that Samantha? I get the two mixed up. I probably wouldn't if I actually knew them. Funny how people you've never met can know intimate details about you through word of mouth, isn't it?"

This time, a single tear careened down her paled cheek and onto her mattress, though she made no motion to swipe it away. But, progress was progress, so I took the little bit of hope it offered.

A frustrated sigh flew from my lips, blowing my hair from my face. I grimaced. "This is stupid," I decided. "We both know I don't make small talk like this. I feel as though I'm insulting you by treating you like a fragile little girl, trying to indulge and entice you into coming out of this horrible place. But, you know what, Marce? I think it's alright to be sad sometimes. You're entitled to it occasionally."

Her unmoving eyes squinted so very slightly that I nearly missed it. The tiniest shred of relief flitted down my body.

"I don't know why you're sad, and it's not my business unless you choose otherwise. But, I'm not going to leave you to wallow alone, either way. You're probably my closest friend here." I paused, shaking my head with a smirk. "Who am I kidding? You're the closest friend I've ever had."

At that, she rolled her eyes and scoffed, pulling the blanket over her head. I stared at her hidden form in shock.

"What on earth was that for?" I asked, yanking the blanket back to reveal her face once more. Her tear streaked face turned, allowing her to glare at me full on.

"You're lying!" she accused, her voice cracking with the shrill volume.

My mouth fell open as I processed those two words. "I am not! What do you think I'm lying about?! That I won't leave you here alone?"

She sat up, nearly jarring me off the bed with the quick movement. Her dainty ivory finger pointed at me, stabbing my chest as she spoke. "How can you call me your closest friend? How dare you dangle that thread of hope in front of me! All I've wanted since you came here was to be close to you! You were so skittish! So alone! You looked how I felt! I've never had a sister or a best friend or even a true friend, period! But, I thought you could be different from all those evil, backstabbing hens back home. I was always second hand trash to them, and they loved just tossing me away for bigger and better things the moment they could! I thought you would understand me and I would understand you! But you're just like them! No matter how hard I tried, you always went running to John! John, John, John, John, John! You spend all your free time with him or Esther! You never look for me! I always have to come to you for us to act like friends! You're just as mean as all those tittering broads back home! You're mean, Kate! And I don't want to be your friend anymore! Leave me alone!"

I stared at the furious girl in front of me, my jaw hanging open stupidly as she fumed, gesturing for me to leave with her hand extended toward the door.

"A-are you kidding me, Marcie?! For the longest time I was sure you hated me! I was scared to get too close to you! It was so obvious you were in love with John, and I could see how upset you got every time he even looked my way-"

She cut me off with a burst of shrill, mocking laughter. "In love?! With John?! That's ridiculous! He's my friend! In what world would

I, coming from the top tier of social hierarchy, be a match for a man who's too kind and naive from a simple farmland upbringing to understand a drop of the universe I live in? Are you out of your mind?!"

I threw my hands into the air as a lead weight splashed at the bottom of my stomach. All this time I spent thinking she was jealous of John's affections toward me. All this time I spent walking on eggshells around the girl, thinking she'd turn on me and stab me in the back at some point for her jealousy! No! The silly woman was jealous of John, not his affections to me!

"Maybe because you turned into a green monster and threw yourself at the nearest man every time you saw John and I together! I thought you hated me!" I repeated, this time stabbing my finger at the center of her chest.

Marcie shoved her hands into her lifeless, stringy hair, letting out an animalistic shriek of pure frustration. "You're so stupid! Why would I try so hard to be your friend if I wanted your man?! I just wanted you to be my friend!"

The two of us stood, though I couldn't remember either of us moving from the bed, in the center of the room. The only sound permeating the air came from both of our heaving chests, hers due to rage, mine due to stupefaction.

Minutes passed as we glared, the room filling with such angry tension I could barely stand it. How could we have misunderstood each other so tragically? I'd spent six months seeing a situation that did not exist, and completely missing the one that did.

No wonder we were in an insane asylum. No real world drama could have unfolded so exuberantly as this.

I closed my eyes, forcing my breaths to steady themselves before I opened them again, calmed, to look back at Marcie.

"I didn't know you wanted to be my friend earnestly, Marce. I misunderstood your intentions, like you misunderstood mine," I told her, taking care to choose words that wouldn't offend or rile her. "But now that I know, I really do want to be as close a friend to you as I consider you to me. Do you think we could do that?"

Her glazed eyes bore into me, flicking all over my face for signs of something I could never know. Even her eyebrows furrowed in incredulity, making her suspicions write themselves clearly across her beautiful, but haggard, face.

"You really want to be my friend, then?" she asked, narrowing her gaze at me and crossing her arms over her ample chest. The girl still wore her nightgown, and the deep set wrinkles and creases told me she'd been wearing it since she fell into her depression. No more than six inches at a time laid smooth over her body, from the scooped neckline to the ruffled hem at her toes.

I nodded and moved to sit on her bed, my energy waning. Even through the confrontation, Power had kept her promise to leave me be, and it felt strange, not having her running commentary spilling into my own thoughts. On some deep seeded level, I'd subconsciously welcomed her intrusions and my head felt oddly empty and wanting without her presence.

A soft rustling noise made by her nightgown accompanied Marcie as she lowered herself onto the bed beside me. She clicked her tongue, rolling the cottony fabric of the bedsheets between her fingers.

"I'm sorry," she whispered, swallowing. "For calling you mean and telling you I didn't want to be your friend. I just thought..."

"I know. And I'm sorry I didn't trust you enough to be a friend back to you. It's hard, you know? Being the newcomer in an insane asylum. I had to guard myself, and I didn't know what you were capable of, since I thought you wanted John."

A gentle chuckled filled the air while Marcie tilted her head up to look at the ceiling. Watery tears distorted and exaggerated the shape of her innocent eyes. "I don't know what I was thinking when I tried to kill him and me. My whole world just flipped on its head and everything crushed down on me. It was the only way I could see out."

It took me more than a few seconds before I realized she was talking about her ex-husband, but when I did, I took her hand in mine and squeezed for comfort. Tears overflowed and dripped from her jaw when she looked back at me.

"I would have gotten a divorce, but my parents wouldn't allow it. Too scandalous. Too much shame on the family name. But, all I could think about was how much better he deserved than me. I mean, look at me, Kate!" she cried, hiccuping through the words. "I'm not normal! Who does this?! Who goes from insanely happy to suicidal within seconds, for weeks at a time? He deserved better..."

My own eyes began to sting with unshed tears for the woman, and I pulled her into a tight hug, rubbing her back in large circles. "There's nothing wrong with you. You just need a little bit of help, is all. All of us here do. You are normal," I pressed, wishing she'd see that, but knowing by instinct she wouldn't believe me.

Not long after Marcie stopped crying, Lottie entered the room. Her footsteps fell light and tentative as she approached, glancing at me, as if to ask if her presence was safe. I nodded at her in confirmation and she let out a noticeable breath of relief, although

I still felt a little frustrated with her and the others for not coming to Marcie themselves. What happened to family? Weren't we supposed to take care of one another? Or was that just until things got too difficult or uncomfortable?

Marcie clammed up, becoming a corpse like being again when she saw Lottie enter the room. The three of us sat, speaking softly about trivial things for a few hours, though it was mostly Lottie and I talking. Marcie only spoke if it was necessary, and even then she only spoke in nearly indistinguishable whispers.

As the sun began to cast brilliant pinks, purples, and blues across the sky outside their small window, I took my cue and left, hugging the two girls before heading back for my own room.

CHAPTER 16

It took making a deal with the devil, but after promising her the reigns over my body for one hour in exchange for Power's charismatic gift of persuasion, I managed to convince all of Ward F to meet in Marcie's room at seven in the morning. She surprised me, doing exactly what she said she would without trying to attack my friends or having a psychotic meltdown. Did that mean we were easing into one another? Meshing and compromising until we both lived together in harmony?I scoffed. Not bloody likely.

While I'd gladly admit to having been painfully naive my entire life, experience had taught me over and over that Power did nothing that wouldn't benefit her first and foremost.Esther, Lottie, and I met in her room before the men arrived, waking Marcie up with gleeful cries of happiness. The poor girl nearly hit the ceiling, shucking her blanket off and sitting up in bed, her eyes huge with shock an fear as she stared, dumbfounded, at our smiling faces."What on God's green earth-!""Get up!" Esther cut her off, grasping Marcie's hands and hauling her to her feet. "Get dressed in something beautiful! Ward F is having our own little psychotic party, and you're the guest of honor. Up and at 'em, Atom Ant!"Marcie's jaw hung open as she struggled to find words. I grinned at her, pulling her into a hug before shoving her down into the little plastic chair in front of their desk. Like in our room, Marcie and Lottie had propped a large square mirror up on the desk, transforming it into a makeshift vanity.

Marcie glanced up at me, bewilderment written across her face so brightly I was surprised I couldn't see each letter etched into her perfect skin."Have you all gone mad?" she whispered, her eyes flicking to and from each of us.Collectively, we chose to ignore that comment, though with wry smiles plastered on our faces at the irony.Esther pointed a long, tanned finger with fire engine red polish on the nail at me. "Find her something to wear." I nodded and headed to the far corner of the room, where the girls' armoire, a carbon copy of ours, stood. I flung the doors open and gaped at all the magnificently luxurious clothing nearly bursting from the wardrobe, as Esther instructed Lottie to begin painting Marcie's nails while she did the shaking girl's makeup.My smile grew wider as the fact that we were actually helping someone in this awful place sank in. Maybe we didn't have medical degrees or syringes filled with drugs strong enough to sedate a fleet of elephants. But we had something better than that. We cared about each other. The cheesiness of the thought formed a slight grimace on my face, but I couldn't call it a lie.

The doctors here simply could not manage what we could, and I wasn't sure if I was more comforted or terrified by that.We had barely finished primping and prodding Marcie into a perfect little porcelain doll in scarlet lipstick and an ivory silk dress when the men entered the room, without so much as a knock. John walked straight to me, a smile full with warmth and pleasure poised on his lips, while Esther gave them an earful for intruding without announcing themselves first. Ed seemed to be the only one who looked the part of the thoroughly scolded schoolboy, which I found hilarious considering he stood a full two feet taller and a breadth wider than the rest of us."It wasn't you who asked us here, was it?" John asked, the corner of his mouth twitching upward in amusement. Heat filled my cheeks."You could tell?" I replied, chewing my lip sheepishly.He took my hands in his, chuckling as his eyes reached up at the ceiling."Somehow, I just couldn't picture you telling me to, 'get my perfect little rear end to Marcie's room at seven-thirty in the morning, and get ready to party like a drunk clown on fire'."I groaned as the blood in my veins transformed into lava, and dropped my head into my hands. "She's impossible!"A gentle kiss to my knuckles brought my head back up.

"But effective. I'm here, aren't I? Just please tell me she didn't make the same remarks about Ed's and George's posteriors as she did mine. That could make things awkward."I laughed, my chest aching with the force of it. John's eyes lit up and his grin grew. "I closed myself off from her while she did it, so I have no idea. But, rest assured, she'll be reprimanded if she did."At the word 'reprimand' his light countenance faded. His eyes turned serious as he bore their intensity right through me. "Actually, I do need to talk to you about something. Why did you run off yesterday? George told you to stay there, together. If one of the orderlies or nurses had been told to intercept you by Shilling, it would have ended badly for you, Kate."I frowned, my eyebrows furrowed at his authoritative tone. As far as I knew, my participation in the "John knows what's best" club had been optional, not mandatory."I can take care of myself, you know. I have for almost a quarter of a century now," I told him, forcing myself not to speak snappily. More flies with honey than vinegar, I told myself. Something inside me, connected to Power but not directly from her, swelled with pride at my attempt to stand up for myself. Power arched an eyebrow at my words, clearly impressed, and something about knowing she was proud of me for something pleased me."He nearly had you in a psychotic episode in his office.

What would you have done if Ed hadn't interfered?"Killed him, Power supplied, her tone simple and curt in my head. The implication echoed off the walls of my skull, making me swallow the nervous ball of emotion in my throat.I decided on a much more watered down version of her blunt truth, choosing to repeat what I'd told Esther the day before. "John, I'm a mass murderer. My body does things no other can. He couldn't have hurt me before I hurt him."His shoulders flinched as I spoke the harsh words and his hands tightened around mine. "Kate, I-""Everything's fine, alright? I appreciate your concern. It's more than anyone else has ever given my way. But, I'm not helpless or weak." The words were whispered from my lips,and for the first time, I was the one placing a comforting kiss to his cheek. Red splotches worked their way up his neck, but he schooled his features to remain hard."You're changing, Kate," he replied lowly, so only I could hear. "I don't know what's happening, but you're becoming more like her. More confident, less scared. I just hope it's a good thing."***"How did you manage this?" Marcie asked in a breathy voice.

The whites of her eyes became visible all the way around her irises as she took in the modest cake Esther had sneaked into the ward lounge. It was nothing large or elaborately decorated, but the box cake she and Lottie had crept into the asylum kitchen to bake the night before was far better quality than the usual gruel we were given on a daily basis. And because none of us had tasted the sweetness of sugar on our tongues aside from the chocolates Marcie brought home with her from her trips with her mother, the spongy cake tasted like all the pleasure of the world combined.Esther scoffed, tossing her curled hair over her shoulder, as if the idea that she'd have difficulty doing anything whatsoever was preposterous. "I'm Esther Martinez," she replied, raising one perfect, sculpted eyebrow as a self-satisfied smirk made itself known on her ruby lips.Lottie burst into giggles, burying her face into the smiling George's cotton shirt. He wrapped his arm around her twitching shoulder, her giddiness rubbing off on him. He shot me an arrogant but pleased look, and once again, a confusing, backward sense of pride that someone was pleased with me bubbled up in my stomach.Marcie turned her face up to all of us spread in a semi circle around her to block her from the sight of any wandering staff.

I was already on Shilling's bad side. A nosy nurse reporting a mysteriously appearing cake from my ward would only serve to draw more unpleasant attention my way.Tears gathered over her eyes, spilling onto her cheeks to drip off her jawline and splash on the cold tiles at her feet."Why?" she croaked, turning to look at each of us, as if we'd laugh and tell her it was all a joke and she had to return the cake to go mope in her bed once more.I tried to take an inconspicuous step back to keep an eye on the door, but two gargantuan hands on my shoulders pressed me forward. I stumbled, glancing back to see an apologetic expression on Ed's face. Was it truly a surprise that he didn't know his own strength?"It was Kate's idea," he mumbled, hiding behind his thick mop of inky black hair. "She said you needed us."Expectations of her running from the room sobbing, thinking they only cared because I asked them to, filled my mind and I braced myself to go after her. Instead, my body jolted ramrod stiff in surprise when she shoved the cake into John's hands and tackled me to the floor in the tightest hug I'd ever experienced."Thank you!" she cried, her tears staining the expensive dress she had bought me so many months before. My hands gripped at the hem, struggling to keep myself covered and decent from my sprawled out position on the floor."You don't have to thank me.

We want you to know we care for you," I wheezed, clawing at her shockingly strong grip around my neck. Power crouched behind the stone wall, doubled over from the intensity of the hysterical cackles wracking her body. Whether it was due to my embarrassing position in a dress on the floor in front of everyone, or my flustered emotions that kept me perpetually unsure of how to deal with situations where someone thanked me, I didn't know. Whatever the case, she spared none of my pride as she rolled around on the dusty ground, holding her stomach as tears of mirth ran in a constant stream down her cheeks.Thankfully, John saw my stressed condition and hauled Marcie's body from mine, chuckling as he placed the cake back in her hands. "Give her some room to breathe, Marce," he teased, tweaking her nose before extending his hand to me. I placed my fingers through his and let him pull me to my feet again, tugging at the hem of my dress and patting around my legs to make sure everything was modestly covered.Oh, please. You wore skin tight leotards that left no room for mystery whatsoever in front of thousands of people over the years.

And not even two days ago you wore one in front of John. Stop acting like it would even matter, you prude.My cheeks flushed with liquid fire at Power's snippy chastisement, but I held firm. Performances felt worlds away from the pathetic little social gathering I found myself in. How could she possibly compare the two? In the three rings, I was no longer Katherine Thornton. I transformed into Kate the Great, filled with confidence and stage presence that could charm an entire fleet of Russian soldiers if I so chose. No one dared look at me in an inappropriate fashion, despite the second skin quality of the spandex leotards. You don't look at birds in flight and wonder what they look like plucked.

You simply admire the way their wings flap to help them defy gravity, letting them do what you only wish your body would allow."You alright?" John asked, snapping me out of my rather poetic inner speech.I offered him a smile, weaving my fingers through his and resting my head on his shoulder as we moved to sit on the scratchy, dilapidated couch. "I'm great. Just glad we pulled this off. Hopefully none of the staff feel the need to seek any of us out and catch us," I murmured so only he would hear. We hadn't gone through all the trouble of organizing this mini party for Marcie just to have it ruined by a wayward nurse or orderly on a mission from Shilling.He squeezed my hand, reassuring me best he could. "Don't worry about it. I'm sure everything will be fine. Relax and enjoy yourself. George, Ed, and I will keep watch."And relax, I did. For the next several hours, miracle of miracles, not a single nurse, orderly, or doctor walked through Ward F's lounge. Even when all of us missed breakfast, feasting on the contraband cake in place of the flavorless, soggy oatmeal, they left us to ourselves. I would have found it suspicious and been nervous had I not been having so much fun. Ed's deck of cards gained their own popularity, being used to play Old Maid, Speed, and even Texas Hold'em.

Through the poker games, we came to discover George possessed a phenomenal blank face, and Marcie couldn't school her expressions to save her life. George won all but two hands, and because we only had our last pieces of cake to bet with, he ended up with a small mountain of the crudely cut slices.Marcie hopped up from her chair after losing the white chocolate truffle she'd laid down for bets when she lost her last piece of cake to the master of the poker face. "You have to have cards hidden up your sleeve, you cheat! But, I'll let you have it because I'm an exceptionally kind woman!"The room roared with laughter at her outburst, and soon after she fell into her own fit of giggles as George smirked at her, amusement gleaming in his eyes and arms crossed over his chest. The scene was perfect, really. For a while, I forgot about the fact that we were all in an asylum, fighting to stay under the radar so we don't get sent to the looming thirteenth floor. I forgot about halfwit escape plans to appease Robbie.

I even forgot about the extra attention Shilling bestowed on me the day before. For those few hours, the seven of us were simply a group of good friends, getting together to laugh, listen to the radio, and play cards.I stood, arching my back as I stretched my pent up muscles. My shoulder popped loudly, earning me a wince from Lottie."I'll be back," I told the room at large when everyone gave me strange looks for disturbing the happy ambiance with my sudden movements."You're not leaving, are you?" Lottie whined, shooting big, puppy dog eyes at me alongside a pouted lip. The poor girl seemed even thinner than normal lately, and while I hadn't told any of my ward mates, I'd heard the nurses talking about her fainting more often than usual. If only she would just eat..."Of course not," I assured her, ruffling her short hair as I walked by. "Just the ladies' room."My hand rested on the handle of the thick wooden door when I heard a cacophony of different feminine voice shouting different versions of, "I'm coming too! Wait up!"I turned, completely bewildered. "All of you have to go to the ladies room as well?"The three women, who I was beginning to fear their scary ability to seem so in sync with one another, all shot me varying expressions that all but shouted, "don't be stupid".

Except, I had to be stupid, because I couldn't think of a hidden reason for all of them to accompany me to the bathroom, of all places. Was this some ritual I'd never been introduced to?"Oh, Kate," Esther sighed, rolling her eyes in exaggerated exasperation. "You have so much to learn."My brow furrowed in pure confusion, but I let the trio drag me down the hallways into the womens restroom, regardless. Behind the wall, Power let out a single haughty laugh at my apparent naivety, crossing her arms and looking up to the ceiling. How did I get stuck with someone so clueless and useless?Had I not seen her point, I would have argued. But, seeing how I had no idea what had just happened or why I was being looked at like I had three heads, I pressed my tongue to the roof of my mouth and let the insult slide.Lottie closed the door with a gentle hand as soon as the four of us were safely inside and standing in front of the mirrors.

I turned, leaning back against the porcelain sink and looked each of them in the eye. "What am I missing? Why did I need a posse to go to the bathroom?" I demanded, figuring the blunt question would yield a higher chance of being answered.I didn't miss the way Lottie placed her skeletal hand over her mouth to stifle a giggle. My gaze narrowed on her, causing Power to laugh again, inside my head."You never had any girlfriends in the circus, did you?" Marcie asked, her smile soft, but still twitching at the corners with amusement at my expense."I never had friends, period."That seemed to turn the trio's sloppy grins into guilty grimaces. Marcie looked at the ground to her left, fidgeting with the hem of her skirt. "Sorry," she muttered.I waved her apology away. As long as they weren't laughing at me I didn't care how much they patronized me.

Mocking laughter, though, brought out the still unearthed memories of being beaten at Jensen and Sons, and those were memories I had no intentions of freeing from their confines at the back of my mind, where not even Power would venture."What's going on?" I prodded, patience wearing thin.The fluorescent light above us flickered, flashing back to life with a disconcerting buzzing noise. Esther turned her face toward the mercurial light, frownin g."It's like a thing, you know? Girls just go places together," Lottie answered me, finally. Her floral print a-line dress twirled around her legs like a trumpet as she swished her knees back and forth, giggling like a child at the pretty movement of the fabric.My mouth turned down in disgust and I looked to Esther and Marcie for confirmation."Even to the bathroom? Isn't that... I don't know. Isn't that just gross?"Esther swiveled her gaze back at me, her frown transforming into yet another amused smirk. Marcie hopped up on the edge of the sink, swinging her legs beneath her as she held back the mirth in her expression."You're silly, Kate. We don't really go to the bathroom.

We just come to the bathroom together to talk away from the boys," she explained, chuckles making her voice shake."But, to the bathroom?""Yes, child! Women have been doing this for ages!" Esther cried, smacking the back of my head with her palm. I winced, shooting her a dirty look as I rubbed the spot she hit."It's gross," I insisted, hoping the three women would get the hint and leave me alone. Either it flew over their heads or they saw it and chose to ignore it.Marcie twisted around to examine her makeup in the mirror, pulling and prodding at her eyebrows and cheekbones. "So, I heard you got in trouble with Shilling."The groan that I let out was impossible to hold back."I had a meeting with him the other day. When you and John left. Shilling called me into his office to discuss something with me," she continued, watching Esther, Lottie, and I through the mirror. Her lip quivered and she sniffed, focusing on freshening her makeup again. "He said I was doing so well lately, and it was time I knew the truth."Esther tensed up beside me, her hands curling into tight fists at her side.

Something told me she knew what Marcie was going to say already, and it wasn't good.Marcie produced a golden tube of lipstick from her dress pocket. She snapped off the cap and twisted the bottom until the pale pink wax emerged from the top. It slid gracefully on her lips, painting the chapped surface a moist, salmon color before she replaced the cap and slid the tube back in her pocket. Her lips puckered in the mirror and she used her index finger to swipe at a few smudges of pink on the outside of her lips, removing the excess."He told me about Bobby. He's not dead, like everyone else told me. I didn't really kill him. But, he left me, and ran off to a whole other state to get hitched to some frilly little twit. They're expecting their second... offspring," she rambled, struggling at the mention of the couple's child bearing status.I sucked the air in through my teeth, glancing at Esther for some sort of guidance. The older woman's face was a blank slate, though, and I could plainly see that she intended to tread carefully with this new revelation. Lottie shuffled her feet beside her, looking all over the small restroom except at Marcie."I just don't get it. We took vows. Why wouldn't he try to help me instead of running off with some other girl?" she whispered, flicking the tears from her eyes before they could run and leave thick black streaks of mascara down her cheeks.I doubt their wedding vows included him experiencing a near death experience by his humble, submissive wife either.

She can't be serious, Power scoffed, rolling her eyes. She laid, draped over a plush velvet chair, twisting her hands and fingers into intricate shapes, creating crude animal pictures against the lit up stone wall. Could she have made her disinterest in the wellbeing of my friend any more apparent?"It doesn't matter now," Esther told the crying woman, her eyes hard and authoritative. "You've lived for years in this place thinking him dead. You will continue to do so, because there is no changing what's been done. All you can do is get over it."The light above us flickered again, coming back on with one less bulb lit.

My mouth parted in shock at Esther's hard words, but there could have been no other response the older woman could give. She wasn't one for useless coddling or sugar coating. Marcie had enough pity for herself, and Esther, I knew, would add no more."T here's more..." Marcie warned, drawing shapes on the mirror with her fingertip. Her eyes flicked to us, then back to her musings again. "Shilling said I'm much better now. He said I can go home soon." The air in my lungs whooshed out, leaving a burning sensation in my chest. Home? Home? Marcie could get out! She had a chance, unlike the rest of us! I grabbed onto the sink for support as the full weight of her revelation hit me.Unbridled, raging jealousy rose up in my chest, making my limbs ache with envy at how easily she could be free of this place. She could be normal again. She could live.She won't, Power muttered, exhaling hard. She's too ingrained here. She doesn't want to leave. Can't you see that?No.Mark my words, Sane. She won't leave unless it's kicking and screaming.

A blood curdling scream jolted me from sleep late that night. Esther flew from her bed, tossing her blankets to the floor and rushing for the door to the hallway. The scream went on and on, piercing my ears with its shrill, agony-filled shrieks. I jumped up and followed after Esther, snatching my silk dressing robe from the hook and wrapping it around my body as I ran to catch up with her. Images flashed through my head like the flashbulb of a camera. The man from Ward J arched and pulling against the nurses and orderlies as he screamed, just like the woman screaming now.

The sobbing nurse holding what was left of her cheek, trying to staunch the blood bath pouring from her face. The resident's glazed eyes as they made contact with mine, just before he lost consciousness. The chunks of bloody flesh falling from his lips, landing on the pristinely waxed floor with a sick, wet thlump.Y ou won't like this, sweet Sane, Power literally sang in my head, laughing as she mocked me. I ignored her and struggled to catch up with my roommate. The screams came louder and shriller the farther we ran down the hall. Lottie met us halfway down the womens dorm section and kept up with us without a word. As the gut wrenching howls grew in volume and intensity at the ward lounge door, John, Ed, and George came barreling from their hallway, all three men wearing masks of confusion and alarm.

"Where's Marcie?" George snapped, his eyes flicking methodically over each of us. I realized, with surprise, that he'd done a head count and immediately assessed the safety of our own. He was the first to notice the beautiful woman's absence.

All eyes went to Lottie, who began sobbing, shaking her head and admitting she had no clue. Her roommate wasn't there when she was woken by the cries coming from the lounge. George grabbed her by her thin arm and pulled her to him, shielding and comforting her with a detached coolness that she basked in and took too eagerly. I swiveled my head to look at the heavy wooden door separating the lounge from the hallway where we stood. The screams grew in intensity, piercing my heart and making nervous beads of sweat form at my temples. I knew who the screams belonged to. Two hands grabbed me by my upper arms, pulling me backwards and making me realize I'd gone for the door without realizing it. "Let Ed and I go in first," John murmured in my ear. Frustration bubbled up in my stomach, but I swallowed it down.

Come off it, Sane. You're angry that he underestimates you. You're mad that he treats you like you can't handle yourself. Stop acting like it's no big deal and get mad! You're the biggest pushover! Useless!But, John didn't treat me like I couldn't handle myself, did he? Being the protective alpha male seemed to be in his nature, and I couldn't bring myself to believe he actively thought of me as incapable. Does he act this way toward Esther or Lottie or Marcie? He doesn't, Sane. Just you. He thinks you're weak.John and Ed pushed open the double doors, exchanging anxious glances as the anguished wails tripled in volume with the barrier gone before ceasing altogether. There she hung, suspended by her porcelain, delicate neck from a rope tied to the support beams in the ceiling, one of the ugly, scratchy orange armchairs tipped backward beneath her feet. Her shadow on the back wall cast an obsidian halo around her limp and now quiet body as it swayed in the air.

Two nurses held onto her legs, the one to the left gripping an empty syringe between her yellow and grey teeth.I stepped into the room, past John and Ed who reached out to keep me from walking any further. Sidestepping them proved easy with their own shocked and appalled states. None of my other ward mates moved, and not a drop of color could be found in any of their paled faces. "I've got her! Go get Ernie!" the younger of the two nurses barked at the other, the one with the needle in her mouth. The elder nurse dropped her arms from Marcie's thighs and sprinted past me and the others, screaming Ernie's name down the hallway. A thin stream of blood dripped from Marcie's thigh, where I assumed the older nurse had injected the syringe she'd held between her teeth. The ruby droplets collided with the white tiles below her, staining its pure surface. My feet worked of their own accord, taking me to my friend and righting the overturned chair. I stood on it then, and reached up to the noose around her neck. Every muscle in me quivered, and red hot tears pressed the back of my eyes, but I gritted my teeth and forged past it all.

My hand stilled halfway to the yellow rope.The noose wasn't tightened. I felt my eyebrows furrow as I studied the old fraying rope, caressing the worn fibers in my fingers. Trembling, the pads of my fingers found the vein in the side of her unbruised throat. Her pulse pumped through her neck, strong and unhindered. The syringe must have held a sedative, meaning she hadn't been thrown unconscious from trying to hang herself. She didn't try to kill herself, you twit. Take a closer look at that noose. You, of all people, should be able to see the obvious flaws in the knots. She never intended to die, stupid.My eyes followed the twists and knots in the rope, confirming the weak attempt at making a noose. Even Marcie would have known better than to use a rope that someone had sawed half the fibers through, if she truly wanted to kill herself. But why? Why the show? Why want anyone to think she wanted to commit suicide? Because she's insane.I blinked. Ernie burst through the already opened doors as John strode toward me, holding out his hand to help me down from the chair. His eyes flicked from me to the furious orderly, sensing the danger he posed.

A wave of relief washed over me that he noticed the strange, unsettling way Ernie paid a bit too much attention to me, but disappeared just as quickly when confirmation of his own reservations about Ernie's behavior proved the threat was real, and not just in my head. "Go call Shilling. He'll want her on the thirteenth floor for this," Ernie snapped at the older nurse, who seemed more and more like a gopher than a medical service provider with every order handed her way. John's grip tightened painfully around my finger, the bones grinding against each other, making me wince and try to yank my hand away. "You and Esther take Lottie to your room for the night. Do it now. Ernie and the nurses will get Marcie down, but you can't be here when he does. So go," he instructed in my ear, low enough for only me to hear. Without waiting for a response, he let go of my hand and bounded from the room, his body disappearing down the long hallway as he ran at full speed, like a man desperate to fulfill some role the rest of us knew nothing about. And this time, despite Power's constant mockery inside my head, I had no issues following his command.

Chapter 17

I spent all of the next morning waiting for something, anything, to happen. But, had it not been for Lottie waking up in my bed, the one sign that what had happened the night before wasn't some terrible nightmare, I would have never guessed it had been anything other than a normal night. No mention of Marcie was made. Not from Lottie, not from Esther, and not from George or Paul in Group Therapy. I was just beginning to wonder if I had imagined the entire thing, despite the proof in Lottie staying the night in our room, when it all came rushing back in the form of a rare and serious altercation in the ward lounge. George, Lottie, and I walked back from Group Therapy, George with a protective and commanding hand on each of our shoulders, when the sound of furious shouting reached my ears. A glance up at George made my fears solid. The slight tic in his jaw, as if he knew exactly what was happening behind the door, gave it away.

Lottie faltered a few steps until her body became shielded by his. The movement looked practiced and certain, like she saw him as her own plastic bubble to keep harm away from her. "What were you thinking?!" John yelled from the lounge. I flinched, then straightened up and let my jaw hang slack. John never raised his voice. He never talked to any of us like that. "I'm sorry!" Marcie's distinct, lilting voice cried out between sobs. "I just couldn't leave! I had to make sure they didn't discharge me!"Pushing past George proved uncharacteristically easy. Pressing my ear to the door while he watched on would have made me uncomfortable any other time, but after pulling my friend's body from a noose the night before, the only thing running through my mind was the desire to find out why I'd been put in that position.

She didn't want to kill herself, I was sure. The nicks in the rope, the loose noose, the lack of bruising around her neck... It all pointed to the fact that she'd done it for.... What? Attention? "Did you know that they were taking you to the thirteenth floor?! Do you realize by how little you escaped that fate, Marcie?! What you did was stupid! Stupid and reckless and it would have killed everyone in this ward to see you get taken up there!" John roared. My tongue left the security of my dry mouth to lick my lips as a tremor of unease and fear dripped down my spine. I'd never heard him so infuriated before, and, quite frankly, it scared me. I'd only just pressed my ear closer to the cool wood when a hand on my upper arm pried me away. George's intense glare focused in on me, commanding me to step back without a single word.

How was it that this sixteen year old boy thought to protect a full grown woman? A woman and a frail teenager, at that? He dismissed my calculating frown and twisted the doorknob, watching it swing open and land against the wall with a soft thud. Three sets of eyes swiveled our way. Marcie stood, dainty hands clenched together at her chest as tears streamed from the corners of her doe eyes. John towered over her, his face scarlet with rage and his knuckles white. Fire loomed in his gaze, daring on of us to say something to set him off. Esther, bless her soul, stood between the two friends, a hand to each of their sternums, pushing them away from each other with her face twisted in anxiety. I knew John would never lay his hands on Marcie, and Esther knew that as well, but it didn't mean he wasn't livid with the young woman. The tension in the room suffocated my thoughts, and judging by the looks on everyone else's faces, it suffocated theirs also. John's shoulders heaved as he struggled to calm down. I took a tentative step toward him, questioning him. My heart dropped when he looked away from me, clenching his fists tighter. But, I couldn't let him shut me out.

Not out of this. If he could look at a situation concerning me and make a judgment call on my behalf, he owed me that same courtesy, and I planned on cashing it in. Squaring my shoulders, and giving Power, who was watching then entire scenario fold out with morbid interest, the slightest amount of freedom so I could siphon off her courage and boldness, I glided over to him and took his fist in my hand. He turned, glaring at me through narrowed slits. "Come with me," I whispered, focusing all my energy on sounding calm and collected. Was this what he did when he took over a situation for me? Did he feel the panic and swallow it down like I found myself doing that very moment? If so, he deserved a lot more credit than I gave him.He stood firm, refusing my gentle pull, for a solid ten seconds. Ten tense, terrifying seconds, where he bore his eyes into Marcie's. His anger rolled through the air toward her in tidal waves, so thick we might have tangibly touched it if any of us had dared move. But then, as if the gates opened and his resolve to verbally berate Marcie fled, he flicked his earthy eyes back at me.

With a neanderthal-like grunt and a stiff nod, he motioned for me to lead the way. I wasted no time. After a cursory glance at Esther to make sure she'd comfort Marcie, I squeezed his fist in my hand and tugged him out of the lounge with me. The lounge doors slammed shut behind us and I walked the two of us further down the hall, until satisfied we wouldn't be interrupted and he had adequate space to cool down. I leaned against the wall, sliding down to sit on the frigid tiles that felt like ice against my thighs. "What's going on, John?" He glared daggers at me, but I knew enough to know I wasn't the cause of them. He shoved an irritated hand through his blond hair. I noticed for the first time how much longer it had grown since I'd arrived at Rosenton. It had barely touched the top of his ears then, and now it grazed his chin, though he normally shoved it back away from his face. Doubled with the stubble he tended to let grow recently, I was astounded at just how much older he looked. You look different, too. You look better than you ever did before. You look more like me and less like a hobo you'd find on an empty train, Power quipped, unable to resist commenting on anything that made her out to be better, stronger, or lovelier.

Though I was loathe to admit it, she was right. Every day, with every round of primping and prodding Esther did to me before bed, I seemed to glow a bit more. Some mornings the image in the mirror shocked me when I couldn't tell if I was staring into my own reflection or one of Power's parlor tricks. Yet, it always showed me, without any glamor infused by my counterpart. I wondered, if the two of us stood side by side, could anyone tell us apart?

John's gruff tone snapped me back to reality, a faint pinkness in my cheeks that I'd dazed off so easily. "She was reckless and stupid. She knew what happens to people who try to kill themselves the way she did. She knew what the consequences would be, and she pulled that stunt last night anyway! If she knew what I had to do... If she knew how close she was to being taken..." he ranted, barely acknowledging my presence. He paced the hallway, yanking his hands through his hair and raving so quickly I barely caught a few words at a time. I watched him stalk back and forth like an enraged, caged panther. When he paused in front of me, I half expected him to bare fangs like a furious jungle cat. "What do you mean? What you had to do?" I asked, tilting my head up to meet his eyes. He stood there, fuming, looking like he hadn't heard me speak at all before something clicked and he blinked. "Huh?" he replied, as if he'd been in a trance the entire time. My teeth sank into my bottom lip for a moment. "You said you had to do something to keep Marcie from being taken.

What do you mean?" All the pent up aggression in his body released, leaving him a slumped mess as he sank to the floor beside me, leaning his head back on the hard white wall. He stared up at the ceiling, eyes unfocused. "I had to bargain with Shilling. Again." If his words had been any quieter, I wouldn't have heard them at all. Something foreboding and sinister rolled in my stomach as I took them in. "Bargain?" I whispered, covering his hand with mine. The chill in the unforgiving floor seeped through his hand and into the tips of my fingers. "I had to give him some details I didn't want to give, Kate. He's been working on me for years, and I've never told him a thing about Normandy. Never told anyone. Never wanted to and never will want to. But, it was the only thing I had to bargain with anymore. I've already used up everything else I have to haggle with."Every functioning cell in my body stopped. "You... He makes you tell him things to keep from hurting us? Why?" I blabbed, nothing in my head forming into coherent sentences. Without moving his head, he looked sideways at me. "He doesn't make me tell him anything. He just knows that I'll do it if there's a threat to any of you. But, now... Now there's nothing left to give him. And, the only reason he hasn't sent me to the thirteenth floor is because he doesn't know that. He's sick, and wants every ounce he can squeeze out of me before he decides he's the top dog in here. If anything else happens, Kate, I'm done. He'll send me to the thirteenth floor, knowing he's taken everything he can."

"Then leave! You told me you can go at any time! Get out before that happens!" I cried, twisting my body to face him. I grabbed his face in my hands and forced him to look me in the eye. His stubble itched at my palms, and I took a split second to savor that before putting myself back to business. "It's only a matter of time before one of us screws up enough to get sent there. You have to get out!" Power grasped at the strings to my sanity, nudging me to let her take control. My breath quickened and I nearly choked. I wasn't being threatened, and there was no burlap to be seen to trigger her desires. There was no reason for her attack, albeit a gentle attack. More of a strong suggestion than a demand. Unless..John stared at me, studying my the emotions I knew were flashing across my face. Let me out, Sane. I can convince him to go. I can make him leave so he doesn't get hurt, Power purred in my ear.

She wanted to protect him. When had she become anything but self serving? What benefit could she possibly gain from his safekeeping? Don't be so dramatic. You know I like him as much as you do. "I would never leave any of you here without my help. You know that," he replied finally. The despair and hopelessness swimming in his eyes told me his self-implied duty wasn't so much out of care and honor as it was obligation and responsibility. We relied on him. We looked to him to guide and protect us. John was our leader, and by seeing him as such, we'd all inadvertently chained him here. He may have had the means to leave whenever he wanted, but his code of ethics, his moral guide, prevented him from leaving and casting us off to the wolves. And then, it hit me. Like a train crash exploding in my head, it hit me. The realization left me breathless. John planned on dying in this place. People like us, we didn't get better. We didn't get reintroduced into the real world. Esther and I were lifers, and as long as he held onto this moral obligation to see us protected and safe, he knew he'd never get out of Rosenton Home for the Criminally Insane alive. "Oh, my gosh." The words breathed from my lips as the impact sank into me, wrenching my heart into painful, impossible knots. "I won't leave any of you here. That's why I've been talking to Robbie. If I can get all of you out of here, we might all have a chance to live," he murmured in my ear as I crashed into his chest, letting the sudden burst of tears soak through his cotton shirt.

His arms wrapped around me, pulling me tighter to him. "John, what are they doing on the thirteenth floor? I know you know! Please! Just tell me!" I sobbed, the thought of losing him to an unknown menacing force too much for me to handle. I had to know what we were up against. I had to know what I was fighting. But, just like every other time I asked about it, his body and voice became like stone. Cold, calculating, and hard. He wrapped his hands around my upper arms and pushed me to sit on my own. A flicker of emotion ran across his face when he took in the tear stains on my cheeks, but it was gone just as fast. He looked me dead in the eyes, piercing me so hard I was sure I'd be nailed to the wall when I tried to stand. I begged him with my eyes to open up to me, tell me what he knew, but I got nothing else from him. "It. Doesn't. Exist."

I twisted and twirled my plastic spoon between my fingers, a nervous habit I'd picked up with Jensen and Sons, except the flags and batons I used to play with were much larger than the utensil in my hand. I imagined an extra foot on either end just to sate my nerves. No one at the cafeteria table spoke to one another. Even George and Lottie remained silent, him eating what I assumed was supposed to be mashed potatoes and her pushing the food around on her plate, only bringing the spoon to her lips when the tiniest bit of potato remained on it. Ed seemed oblivious to the thick tension, but he rarely spoke anyway, so maybe he didn't notice. Esther watched each of us, her ample chest rising and falling in short bursts, showing just how anxious she felt. Marcie was back to being catatonic, her platinum hair damp and stringy, and her eyes watery as she gazed at the far wall with unfocused, enlarged pupils. For once, she had eaten even less than Lottie. John seemed to be the most normal of us all, clearing his plate and leaning back in his chair.

He studied Marcie, biting the inside of his cheek. So quick I nearly missed it, he glanced at me, asking for reassurance for what he was about to do. I nodded, offering him a small ghost of a smile for encouragement. "Marce," he spoke. Every set of eyes at our table turned to him in shock. Except for Marcie, who didn't even hear him for all her reaction. He reached over and placed his hand over hers on the table to get her attention. In an agonizingly slow motion that had my insides twisting at the unnatural feeling it gave, she turned her head to look at him, cocking it to the side the tiniest bit as a replacement for having to use her vocal chords to ask, "what?" They stared at each other for a moment as the rest of us took in the scene. As long as I'd been at Rosenton, there had never been an altercation between any of us, and the rift in our dynamic left us all on edge and jumpy. Except for Ed, of course, who simply looked around at all of us as if he had no idea what was going on. "Marce, I'm sorry. I'm sorry for upsetting you. You scared me, is all," John expanded, giving her dainty hand a little squeeze. She didn't respond at first, but as we all grew more and more uncomfortable, shifting in our seats and trying to decide when the best time to bolt would be, she gave a slight nod alongside an even smaller smile. She accepted his apology.

Chapter 18

Tuesday and Wednesday rolled through without anything out of the norm. No special calls from Shilling, no extra attention from Paul, and Ernie had called in sick Wednesday, so we were relieved of Physical Activity. After John's apology to Marcie, the dynamic between us all shifted back to normalcy, and by the time Thursday rolled around everyone had gotten over the little spat. Marcie was still in her stupor, but little things changed over time, signaling her gradual return to her normal, cheery self. Group Therapy consisted of a new addition that week. Instead of the chairs being arranged in a circle with nothing in the middle, Paul had brought in a large card table. George eyed the new piece with a strange, curious suspicion, but stood at one of the chairs and pulled out both on either side for me and Lottie. He'd just pushed Lottie's chair closer to the table with her in it when the door opened. "Katherine Thornton?" the receptionist, who I'd grown to like for her constant sunny disposition, beamed.

George pulled my chair away, allowing me to stand. I thanked him and walked over to the bubbly woman. "Visitor!" she chirped, grinning as though nothing could possibly ever be wrong in the world. I looked back at my ward mates to make sure they heard where I'd be going. Lottie nodded, but George stared blankly at the receptionist. The more I studied him, however, the more I realized his expression wasn't actually blank, but observant. He seemed to be taking her in, as if she were a rare species of bird and he was a top notch ornithologist. But that description didn't seem to quite fit either. It was more like... like he was a method actor, studying for a role. His eyes caught her every expression, every movement, every word to be stored for later. But, for what? My musings shut down when he finally looked at me. Like Lottie, he nodded and turned back to the odd table as Paul began handing out construction paper and crayons. As if we were all in elementary school.

The insult rang loud and clear, though only those of us from Ward F looked lucid enough to catch it. George's nose wrinkled in disgust and even the childlike Lottie seemed put off from the implication that we were so unintelligent we had to share our feelings via crude crayon drawing. I took my opportunity to skip that particular catastrophe and followed Miss Receptionist down to the first floor, where an orderly did his usual routine of leading me into the visitation room and cuffing me to the table. A few more residents were sprinkled throughout the room this time, all from different wards and all looking terrifying to varying degrees. I wondered what they'd done, and if all of them were fully evil. I couldn't imagine there being so many people who were solid evil that they would fill an entire institute. Even in our ward, the one Shilling had called the worst of the worst, I saw far more good than bad in my ward mates. If that was the case for us, how much more unfair and traumatizing was it for the residents in the other wards? Robbie walked in while I observed those around me with a studious eye, reminding myself of George a little bit. Except something in the way he had watched the receptionist had set me on edge.

Something strange and unnatural.I smiled at Robbie when he sat down in front of me, across the table. "I'd give you a hug, but the whole handcuffs thing makes it awkward, and that orderly is looking at me like I might spring you from the place with a secret key or something," he blurted, turning to give a rebellious thumbs up and cheeky grin to said orderly. I laughed as the orderly crossed his tree trunk arms across his chest while shooting my ring master a dirty look. "Anyone ever told you that you have a problem with authority?"He scoffed, rolling his eyes. "I'm a Jensen. Of course I do. That's why I'm always the boss, Kate. Where have you been for the past decade?" God, the banter felt so melodically normal, and I basked in it, absorbing the familiarity. I'd missed it. Eating dinner in his cabin while we laughed over stupid things. Making quips at each other during practice. Why had I never seen that sibling bond he'd tried so hard to foster before? Had I been so blind? You were too busy having the snot beat out of you by his employees. Power spoke as if she hadn't been the one to insist on slicing Robbie's throat also. As if I hadn't begged and pleaded for her to not include him in the massacre.

My hatred for her fueled by her arrogance, I caged her in behind the wall, binding her so tightly I hoped it hurt her. I hoped the wires sliced her perfect pink flesh like she had sliced my brother's. I felt her fury, and made a point to ignore it, dubbing it part of her punishment. "Hey, you okay?" I snapped back to the real world, jumping when his voice startled me. "Yeah, sorry. So, what's up?" I asked, plastering on the most sincere grin I could muster. A heavy sigh blew from his lips so hard it moved pieces of hair from my face. He leaned back, propping his legs up on the table and weaving his fingers behind his head. "Trying to get you out of here. The more I find about this place, the less I like it. And that's saying a lot, because I hated it from the get-go. Even if I can't get you out, you need to find your own way. You can't stay here, Kate."

"Feet on the floor!" the orderly at the door barked, making me flinch. Robbie rolled his eyes and dropped his legs back down, then turned to face the brute with a mocking salute. I stifled a giggle at the raging look in the man's eyes. Over the past six months, between visiting weekly for both John and I, Robbie had become almost overly comfortable with his visits, often poking and prodding the staff, just to get a rise out of them. Of course, that only resulted in subtle retaliations directed at me, but I never let Robbie know about that. Just seeing him so alive and boisterous was worth more than any amount of bruised wrists from purposefully-too-tight handcuffs. And I hadn't missed the sly flirtations between him and Miss Receptionist either. I knew he often stayed for a few minutes after I'd left, hanging out at the front desk and charming the glowing woman until her cheeks burned red. I tried to imagine having her as a sister-in-law, and the idea appealed to me. Robbie wasn't a playboy by any means, but when he did want something or someone, he got them, one way or another. And, in the deepest crevice of my heart, I hoped he did snag her for himself. Maybe he'd even reinstate his circus and she'd travel with him. With us, if life turned out the way he wanted.

Assuming he had changed his mind and would reinstate it. "You know I can't leave without my ward mates," I said, bringing his attention back toward me, expecting him to give me an exasperated look or say something along the lines of, that's impossible. Instead, he pleasantly surprised me by nodding in agreement. "I know. I'm working on it, day and night. As many law books and public records as I've looked up, I should have a degree by now." My face screwed up in disgust. "You? A degree? That thought is revolting. You're a performer. Putting you in a grey suit in a courtroom would be like caging a peacock so his feathers couldn't show." That earned me a loud burst of laughter. People all over the room jumped at the sound, shooting wary eyes at our table. Most likely questioning which one of us actually belonged here with the way he was acting. Robbie reveled in the attention, like a true master of performance shows. He beamed at everyone, his presence seeming much larger and overbearing than it actually was. But, that was his gift. His charm. I'd never met someone more charismatic and suited for the title of ring master than him. He could fill a whole town and then some with his presence when he wanted to. "So," I began with caution, "have you thought about it?"His eyebrows drew together in confusion.

"About what?""Performing. Rebuilding Jensen and Sons." His enigmatic air wilted and he slumped over the table, not meeting my eyes. "I can't, Kate. I wish I could. I wish I could think myself worthy to bring it back, but I just can't. I failed once, and it hurt my sister more than anyone else. If I fail again, who knows who'll get hurt? Innocent people this time? I just don't feel responsible or worthy enough." I actively chose not to point out that I was far from the person hurt the most from my attack, and that innocent people were slaughtered the first time. We'd had that very argument too many times to count, and he had it in his head that I was the victim, nothing more. It felt like he thought some third party person committed the heinous murders and not me. Though, how close to the truth that was, I couldn't be sure. It sure didn't feel like Power was some part of me, aside from sharing my head. I couldn't read her thoughts like she could mine. I couldn't predict what she'd do or say.

I couldn't control her. She had her own agenda and plans that I didn't know about. Yet my hands held the knife that slit over twenty throats. My body crawled across ceilings and through windows, moving like a snake to her intended targets. How could I ever begin to understand that? "How will I make a living if you don't? You're far more than capable, and you know it. What happened was my fault, not yours. If you-""Kate! I don't want to say it again! It was not your fault! It was theirs! Stop taking the blame for their injustices!" he snapped, anger written across his features as he banged his palms on the table for emphasis. Again, all eyes drew our way, but neither of us paid them any heed. I glared at him, frustrated with his blindness and insistence that I was some kind of avenging angel and not a murdering psychopath. "They hit me! How does that begin to compare with me killing them? I'm still here. They aren't. You can't say what I did wasn't far worse than-""Who wouldn't have snapped?! I can't think of a single person who wouldn't have retaliated somehow.

God, Kate, it was self defense as far as I'm concerned!" My heart raced in my chest, my head spinning as I began to feel faint. I closed my eyes and counted, trying to calm down before I got too riled up and Power took over. In a voice so low I hardly heard it myself, I replied. "What about you? What reason did I have to take a butcher knife and slice your throat open like a pig at the slaughter, Robbie? What reason did I have to watch your blood spill from your gaping neck? I all but made a Pez dispenser out of you. For what reason? What did I have to retaliate against you for? You never hit me, kicked me, or beat me. So, why?" I whispered, glowering at him as the world around us faded to black, leaving just the two of us alone at the small table. He had to see that I wasn't innocent. He couldn't keep placing me on a pedestal. At the end of the day, no matter how much I resembled that little mouse my co-performers had so cruelly dubbed me, I was dangerous. I was a murderer, and nothing could change what I'd done in cold blood. For the first time, the confidence in his demeanor faltered, leaving him confused and unsure. A grim sense of satisfaction that I finally got through to him settled in my stomach, but I couldn't be happy about it. Why couldn't I have just kept letting him believe the best of me? Why did I need him to think the worst? That I was a monster with no conscience? With no heart? A coolness overtook him as he leaned forward on his elbows, putting his face just inches from mine.

I waited, curious about his sudden change. "I didn't protect you. I didn't protect my sister. That's why." All the air evacuated my lungs in one fell swoop. "I slit your throat! I tried to kill you! Why are you taking the blame for my actions?! I don't understand!" I cried, wishing I could lift my hands from the table and shove them through my hair like John had earlier that week. Hot tears pressed the backs of my eyes and I didn't bother trying to hold them back. They fell, without restraint, in a constant stream down my face as I struggled to keep from screaming in frustration. He grabbed my chin, forcing me to look him in the eye, where fire snapped and crackled just beneath the surface. "I know I haven't shown you much of what a family means, Kate, but when you fail someone you care about, there is nothing that can take the guilt away. I failed you, not just as your boss, but as your brother. If you... If you knew half the things I know, you'd understand.

But, because of my own faults, you don't. So you're just going to have to listen and accept it. There is nothing you could say or do to make me hate you or be disgusted with you, when my own guilt feels like it will swallow me whole. So stop trying to paint yourself as a monster to me. I've grown up with you. I've trained you and spent more of your life with you than anyone else. I know you, and I know you're not this evil demon you're trying to portray yourself as. So shut your mouth and stop arguing with me and trying to scare me into hating you. It's not going to work, you stupid, stubborn girl."Of course he was right. I didn't understand the dynamics or emotions of a family. I couldn't begin to understand his reasons for forgiving me and burdening himself with any amount of blame that he should have been casting at me. But, I couldn't excuse myself either. Not just because he wanted me to, and nothing could change my own guilt. He pierced me with his steel colored eyes for what seemed like forever, both of us in a stubborn stalemate. It was me who faltered, giving in first. I swallowed the emotional lump in my throat and looked away. His breath of relief knocked into my face and he leaned back in his chair, crossing his arms over his chest. "Can I ask you something?" I began, knowing the time for a change in subject was far overdue. "Anything." I stared at the cuffs keeping me attached to the table.

Asking him felt like a betrayal to John and Esther, who had spent every opportunity trying to convince me not to acknowledge the existence of the thirteenth floor, but I had to know. The need to be prepared overwhelmed me. All I could think about to justify my question was that it was better the devil I knew than the one I didn't. So, I shoved my reservations aside and met his gaze. "Do you know anything about the thirteenth floor here?"Robbie frowned, squinting as he searched his memories for information. "I can't think of anything I've heard. Why?"I mulled around the possibility of telling him my suspicions and everything that had been happening so far, but one look into his concerned expression made my decision for me. I couldn't put any more on his shoulders. He was already working himself to the bone, and the added pressure of the thirteenth floor would exhaust him. And he looked far too energetic and happy again for me to justify that. I couldn't add more to his already loaded plate. "No reason. I just saw that it wasn't listed on the sign out front," I lied, shrugging in what I hoped was a nonchalant manner. Power snickered at my lame attempt at lying. He nodded, smirking from one side of his mouth. "A lot of buildings are like that.

It's bad luck or something to have a thirteenth floor, so most big buildings like this skip it. Kinda weird, having a superstitious mental asylum." The smile I offered felt weak and hollow, but he didn't seem to notice. In fact, his face lit up and he leaned forward, excitement suddenly flooding off him toward me. It'd been a while since I'd seen him so animated and the sight transformed my grin into something genuine and warm."I almost forgot!" he started, whispering as if we were conspiring. "I've been visiting John Kingwood a lot lately. What do you think about him?""He's a good guy. I like him a lot. Why do you ask?" I replied, twisting my fingers together as he ate up my response. My teeth pressed into my lower lip as curiosity over his odd behavior overtook me. Even Power perked up, cocking her head to the side like an interested puppy at his giddiness. A smug expression took over him and he pushed himself even closer to my face, nearly climbing on top of the table in the process. The orderly standing guard watched the interaction with suspicious eyes, his lip curled in disgust at Robbie's almost comical animation. "How much do you like him? Enough to be with him?" My eyes widened as liquid lava glowed beneath the skin on my face and ears.

"What?!" Robbie laughed, sitting back down in his seat with a loud clank when all four feet on his chair met the ground again. "He's asked my permission to court you when you all get out of here. He's smitten, Kate! I needed to make sure you liked him back and he wasn't some crazy stalking nutter before I gave him an answer, though. So, can I give him my blessing?" Everything in the room halted as my pulse skipped over itself. Then, as if in fast forward, the walls spun around me. My mouth fell open as Robbie chuckled at my response. "What? Why-why would he ask you? You're sure he asked you that, and not something less... committed?" I blabbered, shock setting in as the weight of what that meant settled in the bottom of my stomach. Courting? As in, the step before marriage? I knew we had something, but I hadn't dared hope for anything more than that. Did he truly feel that much for me? Was I in the realm of possibility for something so permanent to him?Robbie slapped a hand to his chest, feigning hurt. "I'm your patriarch, Kate. Dad's long dead, and there's no one else. Of course he asked me! And, do you think I'd mistake the verbatim phrase,

'Robbie, I'd like to court Kate, with your permission'?" Bewildered, I stared at him in open speechlessness.

He rolled his eyes and smirked at me yet again. "Don't look so surprised. The guy created a whole circus for you in an underground cave, and even orchestrated the plan to get you out to it. I have no doubts he'll take care of you. I just want to make sure you'll be happy with it." Stupid, caveman-like sounds spurted from my lips as I blinked and tried to come up with some intelligent reply. "Nod for 'yes', shake for 'no'," he prompted, laughter dancing in his eyes as he made fun of my stupor. For six long months, we'd made it clear we cared about each other, but I'd never looked any further into it. I didn't have the luxury, and hoping he felt something more for me had seemed ludicrous. How could someone as good as him want someone as flawed and cracked as me? The fact that he did want more... John wanted me. Unable to form the syllables required for words, I nodded.

Chapter 19

"Kate." I lifted my head from my paperback and scanned the room. Not that I'd actually been reading it. All that seemed to reside in my head anymore was the knowledge that John had asked to court me, if we ever got out of here. I hadn't said anything to him about it, getting the distinct impression from Robbie that I wasn't supposed to know, but I also didn't want to change things between us yet. There was a certain quality that altered in relationships when things became official, and I couldn't afford that as long as every bad thing at Rosenton loomed over my head. George stood in the lounge doorway, eyebrows drawn in anger and mouth pursed in displeasure. Everyone else had already left for the monthly trip to town- the trip I'd never been approved to go on."Yeah?" I asked, already knowing he needed to me to stay with Lottie, maybe not knowing she'd already left. He only showed his emotions so easily when his parents visited, and I couldn't say I blamed him. Too many times, I'd been visiting Robbie at the same time George's mother and father came for him, and the horrible things his father snapped and yelled at his only son would have made me less than eager to meet with them, too. How George managed to sit there, across from that monster, every visit with a cool, mocking smile on his face, I'd never know. But, there were a lot of things I couldn't understand about the hardened teen.

At that point, I just counted myself lucky he was on my side, it seemed. "Lottie's in her room. It'll be a while," he replied, voice cold and commanding. "She didn't go with the others?" I asked, surprised. Of all of us, she and Marcie tended to get the most excited to go shopping and eat at the diner they'd described to me a million times. Envy didn't begin to describe the feelings swirling in my gut for the juicy hamburgers and root beer floats they gushed on and on about when they came back each time."She wasn't approved this week. Go to her. Now," he snapped, his impatience with my questioning ringing loud and clear, though I suspected it was more a result of having to go greet his beast of a father than anything to do with me. Sliding the small scrap of fabric I'd been using as a bookmark between the pages, I closed my book and left it on the coffee table, following George out into the hallway. We split ways when the hallway divided into two directions, him taking the way that led to the stairs and me turning down the corridor to the womens dorms. He never so much as looked back at me, knowing our routine well enough to trust I'd obey and go straight to his little shadow, keeping her company until he returned. Why do you let him walk all over you? You're weak and stupid.

Do you really think letting him order you about is any different than when Charlotte and Gregory did it? I rolled my eyes at her attempt to manipulate me into turning against George. Power had been extra cranky and snippy all day, and I couldn't help but wonder if she was jealous that John wanted Sane Kate, and not her. It had to be a blast to her enormous ego. Funny, I thought, directing the notion to her loud and clear. Wasn't she the one who cowered like a scared puppy when George had threatened her so long ago? The strong and unbreakable Power, put in her place by a young teen who couldn't even grow facial hair yet. Power, a vision in a sparkling white leotard with red trim and an elaborate feathered headdress, stepped from the dorm room just in front of me. Her eyes held a fire I hadn't seen in a long time as she strolled toward me, hands on her hips as her scarlet heels clicked against the cold floor. Her mouth moved as if she were speaking aloud, but her voice only reverberated inside my head, making me shiver at the odd discombobulated combination.You'll die one day, Sane. And you'll be dead and gone and you'll still be the scared little mouse you've always been.

You'll never stand up for yourself, and you'll never live a normal, disgustingly happy life, she sneered, halting only when her body was mere inches from mine. So close I could feel her body heat radiating on my prickled skin. I hated when she showed herself like this. Why couldn't she stay in my head, locked away like the animal she was? But, you know what will happen to me? She continued on without waiting for my answer, which I expected. I'll find someone else's head to live in. I'll look just like a better version of them. I'll have the better version of their voice, their eyes, their skin... And I'll live on while you rot. I closed my eyes, forcing myself to take deep, calming breaths as she circled me. A predator inspecting its prey, pinpointing and exploiting its weakness. But, I would give her none. No fear, no trembles, no tears. What about Marcie? Could you imagine her living with me in her head? She's beautiful. Much prettier than you, she said, disgust poisoning her tone. Or little Lottie. She's young. Malleable. I could do wonders with her. Such fresh fruit, ripe for the picking.She stopped in front of me again, and I opened my eyes to meet her furious glare head on. With a coldness so scathing I could have only learned it from Power, herself, I peered at her through narrowed eyes and stepped around her, continuing on to my destination without giving her the satisfaction of a reaction.

Her chilling laughter followed me as I strode down the hall, making all my senses run on high alert, aware that I'd made the choice to turn my back toward her. Hallucination or not, there was no doubt she'd be able to harm me if she was presented with the opportunity. Walking away from her, my back to her, shed a blinding spotlight on that chance, and I became aware of that a fraction of a second too late. Two hands rammed into my shoulder blades, shoving me forward to crash into the wall. One of the metal doorknobs caught the underside of my ribcage, and bright, unbridled pain blossomed up from the impact point, making tears spring to my eyes as I tried to catch my breath. Both my hands flew to my side, cradling the agonizing injury. Ignore me again, Power dared from inside my head, all mocking and warmth gone. Taking a long, cleansing breath, I straightened up and locked my eyes on Lottie's door, meeting her dare head on by dismissing Power with the cold assurance that I was no longer scared of her.

"Why is George here?" I asked Lottie, spinning in circles on the desk chair one of the older nurses had left in their room by mistake. It had wheels and a lever to adjust the height, and the novelty still hadn't worn off on me as I savored the feeling of spinning so fast that everything went out of control. Lottie looked up at me from her perch on her bed, her previous smile faltering. An assortment of dolls and stuffed animals hogged the bed space at her cheap headboard, but she didn't seem to care. The young woman scratched at a loose thread on her blanket, twisting her mouth in a grimace. "He's here because he has a problem with bullies." "I wonder if there's more than that? It's so strange..."Lottie's fingers twitched uncomfortably, her face paling under my inquiry. I hadn't meant to interrogate her, but aside from Ed, George was the only one in our ward that neither Power nor I could quite figure out. And he knew about my crimes and diagnosis. Why shouldn't I know his? John had made it a point to show that I could trust in our little family. Didn't that courtesy run both ways? "I think it's time for lunch. We should go," the girl muttered, glancing every which way but toward me. She knows. She just doesn't trust you.Oh, to be able to block Power out completely...My feet skidded to a stop below me and I waited for my brain to catch up with the rest of me that was no longer spinning. With a few hard blinks, my sight and perception went back to normal and I stood, smiling at Lottie.

"Alright. Let's go." Lottie hopped up and nearly sprinted from her room and all the way to the cafeteria. Guilt rose up in my chest for my questions making her so uncomfortable, but I was too busy trying to keep up with her to dwell on that. Her skeletal frame burst through the cafeteria doors, and as what I could only guess was a gesture of good will, she glanced back at me over her shoulder and smiled as she got in line for her lunch. Ham sandwiches today, with a tiny bowl of grayish macaroni and cheese as a side. Utterly unappetizing, but it got the job done as far as nourishment went. We had only been at our table for ten minutes, grinning and chatting about silly things as if our earlier conversation about her strange protector hadn't happened, when the doors opened and our other ward mates, sans George, poured in. Smiles decorated their faces, as they always did after the monthly trip to town. Even John seemed rejuvenated and airy as they skipped the line for food-darn it, they ate at that diner!-and headed straight for us. Marcie bent at her waist to wrap her arms around my neck in a short hug, startling me into looking to Esther for guidance. The Latino beauty shrugged and turned her attention back to Ed, who smelled of smoke again. Black smudges decorated his fingers, the very tips of them a bright scarlet color. Like burns, I realized, eyes wide as the metaphorical light bulb clicked on with a blinding light in my head.

But, from what? Lunch carried on, as it always did, with just a little more enthusiasm and life infused into the conversation as a result of the trip to town. I focused my attention on Lottie as a way to not think about John's request to be with me if we ever got out of Rosenton. Every time our eyes met, heat flooded my cheeks and embarrassed me, so I opted to pretend he wasn't there to save myself from the humiliation of answering why I kept blushing when I looked at him. Lottie and I had just calmed down from a fit of giggles over the burly man-woman nurse in the corner jolting herself awake after falling asleep at her station behind the cafeteria food line. The man-woman had nearly fallen from her tiny stool, throwing her hands out to the front just to have her chin collide with the edge of the counter, and Lottie and I were the only two to witness the scene. Then it happened. I didn't even realize it at first. But when the rest of the table went quiet in stunned positions, mouths hanging open, it hit me. Lottie took a bite of her macaroni.

"Then Esther told him we were from Rosenton, and he about fell out, trying to get as far away from us as possible!" Marcie snickered, holding her hand over her chest as she held back the unforgiving laughter. Lottie and I giggled at her story. It felt good to see Marcie smiling and chattering again. Her dive into depression had been short lived, and for that we were all thankful. She skipped ahead, twirling her platinum strands around her manicured fingers. Every bounce to her step radiated life and childish happiness, something I found contagious as I followed after her with Lottie at my heels. Marcie tilted her head back, basking in the moonlight as she grabbed the hem of her lace skirt and twirled in a circle. Her a-line dress billowed out in graceful waves around her as she spun, embodying the very picture of sweet madness and beauty. A nymph, trapped in a lantern to never shine her light for the wood fairies ever again. It seemed too much of a shame that her spark wouldn't leave the asylum, where it could never be appreciated as it should be. "It's turning autumn," she breathed, dropping her skirt to raise her hands above her head, like a novice ballerina. "Can't you smell it in the air? It's my favorite time of year. I'd always sneak out to go to the marshes for the bonfires back home. It's too bad we can't have one here. They'd probably never let a bunch of lunatics play with flame on the asylum grounds, huh?" Lottie laughed, shaking her head.

"No, probably not, Marce. There are arsonists here. It'd set them off, I guess. But, I still think we should sneak out! Just us girls, one night. We could get into some fun mischief, I think. Especially if Esther comes!" Marcie rolled her eyes, sticking her tongue out as she ruffled Lottie's cropped hair. "Where exactly would we sneak? There's not a foot of space on the property that isn't watched by the hounds. It'd never work." Without meaning to, my eyes swung over toward the vegetable garden before sliding to the left, to the overgrown bush hiding the tiny hole in the chain link fence. Escape would be so easy, so simple. If we wanted, we could all gather together and make a run for it that very night. But, where would the seven of us go? I knew of no way to contact Robbie, and I really didn't even know what state we were in. Some of our families might take us in, but the chance of being double crossed by well meaning relatives who wouldn't believe our stories of the sinister staff and the thirteenth floor, which was just speculation more than anything, was too great.

I couldn't be sure Lottie especially would be able to take the consequences of that. "Let's just enjoy the roses for a while," I suggested, far too tempted to let my friends know about how easily we could escape. Marcie was too volatile and unpredictable to burden her shoulders with such hope. The two girls walked by my side as we strolled down the floral pathway. The rose garden glowed with an otherworldly aura after the sun set, casting everything in melancholy shades of navy and black instead of the lively pinks, reds, and whites of the daylight hours. I felt like Alice, tumbling down the rabbit hole into a land of unholy, twisted sights and smells. Yet, it was still beautiful, and I found myself thinking how much I preferred the nighttime scene as opposed to the daytime one. Aw, how sweet. You're attracted to the darkness. How utterly cliche for such a woman as yourself."George's parents came to visit him today," Lottie spoke up suddenly, sounding unsure of her decision to divulge that information. I raised an eyebrow at her, curious. "Isn't his father just awful?" Marcie blurted, cringing at the mention of him. Lottie nodded. I stayed quiet, too cautious of spooking her loose lips into hiding by asking any more questions. "He's not the reason George is here, but he sure didn't help matter any."

"Do you think he made him the way he is? The way he's so... odd?"Lottie bristled at Marcie's words, placing her hands on her protruding hipbones. "He's not odd! He's the best friend I've ever had! And, like you have any room to talk about being odd!" Marcie threw her hands up in surrender, eyes wide. "I didn't mean it like that! I just meant he doesn't act human. I'd probably be the same way with a dad like his, though. He doesn't scare you at all?"Lottie's brown hair flew through the air as she shook her head, glaring at the older girl. "No. I'd never be scared of George. Why would I be? So what if he's not like the rest of us? We're in a mental asylum, Marcie! I'd say his differences are a good thing!" I caught Marcie's eye with a discreet hand gesture and pulled my thumb and pointer finger across my lips in a clear gesture for her to zip it before Lottie lost her temper. We had enough to worry about as a ward. Inner turmoil would only hurt us and make us all weaker as a unit. With a sigh, Marcie's shoulders drooped and she sent a gentle smile at the young woman fuming in front of her. "You're right. I'm sorry. I didn't mean anything by it." The three of us sat in a stalemate, watching each other for signs of aggression, before Lottie's stance deflated and she dropped onto the stone bench behind her. "He's not a bad person. He just has prob-"Her words halted in midair and she froze, staring at something behind Marcie and I.

Gooseflesh rose on the back of my neck and my hair stood on end as a feeling of 'not right' washed over me. Sucking in a deep breath, I turned my head over my shoulder."Hello, ladies. Isn't it getting close to light's out?" Ernie asked, addressing all of us but keeping his rat-like, beady eyes focused on me. My body stiffened under his scrutiny and I grabbed Marcie's hand, taking two steps backward with her in tow. She stumbled over her feet, clinging to my arm. I felt Lottie's long, thin fingers wrap around my upper arm from behind me. The two women were looking toward me for protection. Somehow, in some way, through my attempts to help them, they saw me as their shield, and terror raced through my veins, because I had no idea how to protect them. What could I do against Ernie? What was it you told John and Esther in a fit of false bravado, Sane? Something like, 'I'm a mass murderer. Who can hurt me?' Where's your courage and arrogance now?Power... I could let Power out. But could I deal with her aftermath? I turned my head toward Lottie, keeping my eyes firmly on the corrupted orderly as he stood over me, daring me to run or fight. "Go back inside. Get John or George or Ed.

Whichever of them you find first. Run," I commanded, hoping my attempt to sound in charge and in control like Robbie worked. Her fingers slid from my arm and she took off, making Ernie sneer at me in a way that brought me back to days under Jensen and Sons. The same sneer I'd get from Gregory before he attacked. I knew the look all too well and my body tensed for it, ready to lunge back. "Kate, what are you doing?" Marcie whispered, horror ringing in her voice. I flinched at the sudden sound I hadn't been expecting."Go with Lottie," I snapped, angry with myself for forgetting her presence. I couldn't let her witness this. Over six months had passed without anyone else learning of what I'd done, what a monster I could be. Now that we were friends, I couldn't let her see that. She shook her head, hands tightening around my wrist. "No! I won't leave you here." "How sweet," Ernie guffawed, his grin too large for his thin face. "You think she'd need you for help? Do you even know who she is?" "Shut up!" I cried in a panic as the thought of my secrets being laid out so openly sured through me like a tidal wave. I threw my arms out to shove Ernie away from me, the force knocking him back a few steps.

Fury snapped a raging fire in his face and he came back for me, knocking me to the ground and driving his fists into my face and torso. That almost forgotten, but still so familiar pain erupted beneath my skin as I tried to block the heavy blows. He let loose his rage on me, blow after blow raining down on my much smaller frame, each punch harder and more painful than the last. I'd been a fool to compare him with Gregory and the others. Their attacks were cold, calculated, and mocking. They wanted me to know they controlled me. This was in a different world from that. Ernie's attack was wild and untamed, like a berserker with no thought or rationality to his actions. Somehow, I'd found something even more terrifying than the years of abuse I'd been dealt in the circus, and it sent my mind reeling in pure alarm. Without hesitation, I crumbled the wall in my head that held Power captive, begging her to help me. My mental cries echoed against the walls of my skull, receiving no reply. The realization hit me like a bucket of ice cold water and I felt the color leave my face as my stomach rolled. She'd left me! She had left me alone to deal with this! Why?! Hysteria, pure and primitive, overrode every shred of sense in my body and I began to fight back, like a wild caged animal.

My fingernails met the rough, pocked flesh of his face, dragging down and pulling skin with it. My knees crashed against his spine as I bucked my hips, doing everything I could to save myself. Loud, shrill screams for help filled the air, resulting in a backhand to my face and his calloused hand covering my nose in mouth, blocking my airway. Above him, Marcie shoved her weak attempts at punches into his ribs. When that failed to so much as phase him, she wrapped her arms around his neck, pulling back with all her might, trying to tug him from me. She yelled for help, her voice cracking and shaking, before he shoved her off him, sending her crashing to the ground and tumbling several feet away. Her footsteps then fell loudly against the concrete path, growing softer as she ran away, screaming and crying out for anyone to come save me. Black spots danced in my vision as I struggled to breath. The pressure in my eyeballs felt as though they'd explode any minute, but I kept fighting, begging Power to come back to me. I fought him back until the black edges around my vision closed in toward the center, threatening to take me from consciousness. I couldn't welcome death peacefully like I'd always thought I would, but the weaker my limbs got, feeling like lead flowed through my veins instead of blood, the more I realized how real the possibility was. Everything could stop there. No more plans of escape.

No more days with John. No more friendly chats with Marcie, Lottie, and Esther. I'd be gone, leaving nothing behind but a trail of grisly bodies, nearly decapitated, but not quite. I had long since quit calling for Power, recognizing her abandonment. She must not have needed me as much as I thought, and that sent the strangest sense of sadness and guilt traveling at breakneck speed down my spine. Acceptance took over what little was left of my mental capacity, washing me over with a peaceful sense of finality, when the air around me poured, unrestricted, into my lungs again. My eyes shot open while my lungs overcompensated for the minutes they'd been denied their nourishment. I coughed, gagging as my body's reflexes freaked out, trying to right itself. A loud, familiar sound pounded into my ears from my left, and I looked up through watering eyes to see what was happening. My breath caught in my throat. Bright, crimson blood flew through the air in sprays, splattering over my bruised and bleeding face as George's fists pummeled into Ernie's unmoving head. George's blows rained down on the unconscious man, tainting the air with sickening wet crunches and snaps.

He hunched over him, back turned to me as he continued on with cold precision and merciless efficiency. How long had it taken him to put Ernie in such a state? Had I been struggling for my wits to return for so long that this had happened? Or had George taken the orderly out in one fell swoop before continuing the job without pause, effectively "double-tapping" and making sure he wouldn't be getting back up? A particularly thick spray of blood splattered across my face, making me snap out of it and wipe furiously at my cheeks to get rid of the offending liquid, still warm from the veins it had coursed through only minutes before. George's fists kept up with their assault, and by the sheer volume of blood pooling like a black shadow around Ernie's unmoving body, I gathered he was long dead. Dead... Clutching at the dirt and grass beneath my hands, I scrambled to my feet and ran to George, trying my hardest to not look at the spot his blows were marking. After the events of the past hour, my stomach would turn even quicker than normal, and the thought of shaming myself by vomiting in front of my rescuer was in no way appealing. I raced around the carnage to face the man still pummeling my dead attacker, wet, shining blood coating his hand and arms all the way up to his elbows as he landed blow after bone crushing blow. I'd only just faced him, reaching out a hand to grasp his attention when I heard it.

Excited, joyous laughter slipped from between his wide smile. His eyes sparked with the untamed and overly eager enthusiasm of a man savoring every moment of his actions. Shock held me in place as one thought ran through my head, over and over. Had Power jumped to him? Had she done what I thought impossible and infiltrated someone else's mind? Dread coursed up from my toes to my throat, making me light headed. You'd prefer that, wouldn't you? If I left you alone and bothered someone else? Sorry to disappoint, but he's just a run of the mill psychopath, no extra baggage necessary, Power spat, finally speaking up from the shadowed corner she'd hidden in for the entirety of the attack. Sweet, satiated relief. I'd never felt so thankful for her presence in my head before and a wave of comfort and wholeness surged through my panting chest. Thank God. But why hadn't she helped me? Answered my frantic calls? To prove a point, idiot. You're nothing without me. I am everything powerful in you, and without me you're just a sniveling child who can't take care of herself. You need me, and there's nothing you can do to change that. George's white teeth shined from beneath his widely stretched lips, speckled with the scarlet blood of his victim. They glowed almost as bright as the excitement in his eyes. It was the first time I'd ever seen any emotion in those hazel orbs.

Chapter 20

"George!" I cried, my heart pounding against the walls of my chest. He shook me off, glaring at me with ice in his veins for interrupting the only thing I'd seen give him real, tangible joy since knowing him.

And that thing was murder. Murder with his bare hands, pounding his fists into what was left of Ernie's now unidentifiable face.

"Please! George, stop! He's-he's dead! Please, stop!"

He shot up to his feet, a feral grin adorning his young face as he tilted his head back to bask in the moonlight. He ran his bloodied hands through his dark hair, slicking it back with Ernie's useless liquid life and leaving scarlet hand prints on his smooth cheeks and forehead. His chest heaved, grinning mouth hissing in pleasure as he sucked in deep, satiating breaths.

I stumbled to my feet, feeling my bones crack against each other as I trembled with adrenaline.

"What? No 'thank you, George, for saving my life'?" he asked, looking down to meet my shaken gaze. I took the sight in, memorizing every sick and twisted detail of the scene without wanting to.

"Y-you killed him. I... I..."

Tears didn't spring to my eyes, even though I begged them to for the loss of life. It didn't matter that Ernie was a bad man. He was someone's son, maybe a husband or father. Someone had to love him, and someone would now have to mourn him. No, I couldn't be sad that Ernie was dead. In fact, I felt more relieved than anything. It was those who knew and cared for him I wanted to break down and plead for forgiveness from.

George stared at me, an amused smirk playing at his lips. "Are you really so shocked, Kate? It's not like you haven't killed before. Would you rather I had let him turn you into pulp?"

"No... I..." My voice cracked with the hard lump of emotion in my throat, threatening to rip through my esophagus.

He tossed his head back and laughed, gripping the ruby stained strands of hair in his fingers, as if he'd just won the lottery and couldn't believe it. Bile swirled in the pit of my stomach, threatening to make its way up my throat. He'd enjoyed the thrill of the kill.

"You're no virgin to this, you know! You've slaughtered more people than any of us! You can't tell me you didn't feel the adrenaline! The rush! God, it's exhilarating, isn't it?"

Tiny, pathetic whimpers squeezed their way past my quivering lips as I sought for some kind of rationality in what I was seeing right in front of my face. "I... I..."

He swooped down to stand right in front of me then, taking in my white face with sparkling eyes filled with pure bliss. His wet, sticky hands gripped both sides of my jaw, stroking my cheeks with his thumbs and no doubt leaving blood smears all over my skin. "Red is such a striking color on you, Kate. You should wear it more often," he whispered, his excited eyes flicking between mine, searching for my compliance.

It's such a lovely color. It looks spectacular with your skin tone. I would know, remember? Power said, nodding her agreement with George and his implications. Her delicate, yet deadly, hands caressed the stone wall like a lover, stroking every dip and cranny made by the rough exterior.

"Kate! What happened? Are you alright?!"

George snapped his hands away from my face, still glowing with the life he had taken just minutes before. He took a step back just in time for John to round the corner, face paled and eyes searching frantically for what I could only assume was me. When his eyes landed on their target, he barreled over, crushing me to his chest so hard I thought my ribs would crack under the pressure.

"You're okay! You're okay. Marcie and Lottie said... Good God, are you okay?" He thrusted me back, holding me by the shoulders while his panicked eyes scanned over my body, cataloging every bruise and scrape.

My trembling lips parted to speak, but only strained whimpers and squeaks poured out. My eyes darted from his face to George's, dozens of conflicting emotions and thoughts racing through my head at light speed. His warm thumb stroked my bottom lip, encouraging me to say something intelligible and satisfy his need to know I wasn't harmed.

Except I had been harmed.

Gnarled, hideous purple and black bruising bloomed like beautiful, yet deadly, tropical flowers on my porcelain skin. Every touch, every movement, felt more painful than the last as my adrenaline rush began to slow and shock set in.

And, ironically enough, the only reason I knew shock had taken over was the fact that my first thought upon seeing the black welts and contusions decorating my arms was, 'Esther is going to kill me for making her have to cover these monstrosities up with more makeup until they go away.'

"She's fine," George said from behind him, his voice as cool and calculated as normal, but his eyes sparkling and his teeth glowing in a cheshire cat smile that made me shiver. "We need to take care of the body, though. Send her upstairs to stay with Marcie and Lottie. She's too weak to handle this."

Weak. Weak. An insult to my mental capabilities thinly veiled as a concerned statement for my physically battered state.

Can you blame him? Look at you! You can't even speak! You should just run along upstairs and leave the heavy work to the people who can handle a few minor annoyances, unlike yourself.

Unwillingly, my eyes drifted down to the mangled remains of Ernie's corpse. The bitter odor of copper and death swirled in the air around us, trespassing on my disgusted olfactory glands. Minor annoyance, indeed.

"No," I spat, wrinkling my nose as the smell assaulted my nose. "I'll stay. I'll help."

I didn't miss the way John's eyebrows scrunched up in concern, nor the way he studied me as if I were a creature he'd never seen before.

"Are you sure? George and I can handle this."

Matted strands of limp hanging hair stuck to the blood drying on my face as I shook my head at him. "I'm going to help."

His fingers squeezed my shoulders before lifting from them to let him inspect the dead body on the ground between us and George. A string of highly uncharacteristic curse words flew from his mouth as he took it in, walking a tight circle around the corpse.

"This is bad," he muttered. He wiped down his face with his hand, pausing on his mouth and rocking back on his heels. "This is really bad. We have to find a way to hide him before the girls get here. They shouldn't have to see this. Then, we need to send them to bed and get rid of him." John spun around, glaring at George, who looked far too pleased with himself as he eyed his handiwork like a prize trophy. "How did this happen?"

Almost humorously, George stepped back and extended his arms toward me, much like Robbie used to do when he announced me under the big top. He tried to hide how wide his excited grin spread, but failed miserably. "Why don't you ask the object of Ernie's affection? She seemed to be a great catalyst in bringing his crazy to the forefront."

My jaw dropped and I stared at him in shock. Was he making a joke? At a time like this? After taking another person's life with his bare hands? I'd never so much as seen him crack a smile other than a mocking smirk, and now he acted as though he'd just hit the game winning home run. Not only that, but he seemed proud of me for being the one to provoke Ernie's attack, and then stayed after to help clean up.

"Kate?" John asked, his tone growing weary and maybe even fearful of my answer.

I pleaded him with my eyes to understand and not think I'd wanted what had happened for a moment before I spoke. "The girls and I... We were walking in the garden and he just... popped up out of nowhere... I... I didn't know what to do, so I sent the girls back inside before they got hurt. He got too close, so I shoved him back and he jumped me, I swear! I didn't meant to provoke him. I just wanted to get away... Then, he started hitting me and strangling me, and I was almost gone when George showed up and... and did... that," I stammered, like an illiterate fool with no grasp of the English language. I motioned with flailing, helpless hands to Ernie's body, my throat constricting as tears threatened to well.

"So you didn't... You didn't kill him?"

"No!"

Behind him, George scoffed, possibly disgusted with the fact that I looked horrified at the thought of taking credit for such a heinous crime. Suddenly, the young man I'd come to sort of brush off as slightly harmless and innocuous stepped out onto the stage in a whole new terrifying light. He wasn't harmless. I should have never underestimated him. He was a man who only gained joy by having control over lives other than his own, and craved for me to be the same way. He was his own version of Power, and that made me want to run. Run as far away as fast as I could. I wanted to bolt past them and crawl through that hole in the fence and never look back.

John's shoulders slumped in relief before tensing up again when the sounds of Marcie calling out to us met all our ears at the same time.

"Help me get him behind the bushes. We'll get rid of him when the women leave," he instructed in a quiet tone, flicking eye contact between the two of us. George stepped forward, into action. Without so much as a grimace, he linked his arms under Ernie's shoulders and waited for John to pick up the legs. Disgusting, clotting goo from what was left of Ernie's head slopped onto George's shirt, but he didn't look like he minded at all. If anything, he seemed pleased with it, making my stomach turn dangerously.

I darted in the direction they were moving and held back the branches of the large rose bush standing there so they could deposit Ernie on the ground behind it, out of view of anyone else who showed up. Ernie landed with a hard thump and the two men walked back out within seconds. John looked past me as he walked by, focusing on the bench across from him, his fists clenched and his gait tight. He didn't like this any more than I did.

I glanced over at George, my heart fluttering in a frenzy of panicked emotions against my ribcage. He met my stare with his own intense, overwhelming one. My body flinched back as his entire presence spoke out to me, commanding me to let go and revel in what he'd done. He didn't just expect it. He needed it. He needed someone to share his glory with.

"George!" Lottie cried out, shooting into view as she raced from around the corner to the three of us. She collided into George's bloodied chest, throwing her arms around him and squeezing so hard I was sure her brittle bones would break. He hugged her back, but only barely. His eyes didn't leave mine, even as she fussed and sobbed over him.

Marcie and Esther followed in quick succession behind her, both wide eyed and pale, while Ed brought up the rear with a solemn expression that told me he knew how dangerous and tricky the situation was about to get. He offered me a weak, closed lip smile, but I couldn't gather the appropriate effort to return it. Me, a seasoned performer. As many years as I spent grinning through the most painful attacks and abuse, I couldn't even find the strength I needed to pull the corners of my mouth upward.

"What's going on?" Esther asked, eyeing the blood on my cheeks and all over George. "Marcie and Lottie said George attacked you."

I nodded, biting my bottom lip. "He did. George... took care of it."

Her eyebrows rose nearly into her hairline and she spun on her heel to study him. "You took care of it? By that, you mean... you took care of it?"

George held his arms out in a show of openness. "Would you ever expect me to take care of it in any other way? You know what I do."

My stomach rolled, threatening to evacuate its contents at any moment. Tiny beads of sickness vibrated in my chest, making me dizzy and nauseas.

A loud sigh cut through the air, snapping everyone's attention to its owner. John stood from the bench, unfolding his body to stand tall and determined, a cold glint in his eye and his mouth set with purpose. No one spoke, waiting for our unofficial leader to tell us what to do.

"Take Lottie and Marcie back upstairs. Keep the orderlies from asking questions about our whereabouts. We're going to get rid of him," he instructed Esther, who nodded and led both girls by the shoulders back toward the asylum without so much as an eyebrow raised in question. The impact her absolute trust in him made was staggering, and I found myself wondering how many messes John had to clean up over the years.

He can't take another one, you know. He's out of bargaining chips, remember?

My stomach stopped rolling and simply sank at Power's reminder. If anyone found out about this, he was as good as done for.

And, it would be my fault. Just like with Robbie, I would be the reason behind the ruin of his life.

No.

I wouldn't let it happen.

"Can you find a shovel and ax?" John asked Ed. The large man nodded and lumbered away without question, further proving just how much we'd all come to depend on him and look to him for guidance. Were we really such sheep?

"Wait!" John cried, snapping his fingers as if he'd just remembered something important. Ed looked back over his shoulder, paused mid-step. "Matches! Do you have matches?"

A smile that sent chills straight down into the very core of my bones spread across Ed's face, and he nodded once before walking again toward the garden shed near the fence.

"Are you sure you want to stay?" John asked, turning toward me. I saw no warmth or comfort in his face. Instead, cold logic and duty replaced those features, proving just how seriously he was taking the situation. He wanted me to leave, I could tell. But one reminder of how easily everyone else had obeyed him without delay made that impossible. I needed to know what kind of man he was when things weren't going well, and if I should reconsider his request to court me. I couldn't bind myself to someone who would use force or manipulation to bend me to his will, and as inappropriate and horribly timed as my little test was, it was the strongest opportunity I had to see the man behind the shell of all things good.

"I'm staying. I need to help," I answered, lifting my chin in a dare to try to convince me otherwise. Out of the corner of my eye I noticed George's smirk broaden as he crossed his arms across his chest in a show of pleasure mixed with amusement.

John let out another defeated sigh and nodded in recognition. "Alright. I don't like it, though."

I tried, I really tried, to dampen the elation at his reaction from soaring through my veins like burning alcohol, but I failed miserably. It must have shown on my face because he stared at me, confusion written across his expression, for a minute before shaking his head like a dazed dog and turning his attention to Ed, who was in view and carrying a shovel and ax. The equipment looked like child sized toys in comparison to his gargantuan size, somehow making the scene a little less intimidating.

John thanked him as he took the ax from his hands and held it out for George to take. George must have known exactly what to do without any further instruction because he walked back through the rose bushes, and the bile inducing, sickeningly wet snaps and crunches of the sharp blade meeting every joint and bone in Ernie's lifeless body echoed all around us.

Without another word, John gave Ed a look, communicating something I couldn't decipher, then took the shovel and my hand and led me out of the garden and to a spot between the garden shed and fence. Barely three feet laid between the two, and because the shed had been placed crooked, the space only narrowed the further up it went. Weeds took over the entire space, telling me no one paid much attention to it.

"Keep watch?" he asked, refusing to meet my eyes. He stood in an uncomfortable, almost insecure stance, staring at the space beside my left ear. I took in the way his body seemed to shrug down, the limpness testifying to his mental exhaustion and stress over the entire ordeal. It made me wonder how I looked, blood smeared over my face, beaten to a pulp, and still trembling like a leaf.

I turned around, scanning the darkened area as his shovel met the earth, cutting through the weeds and breaking up the soil in the tiny space. We didn't speak as we worked, and I could just barely make out the sounds of the ax in George's hands meeting flesh over and over again being carried through the wind. When it stopped close to an hour later, my trembling had calmed down somewhat and I'd been making a point not to think about the evening's events so I wouldn't lose what little sanity I had left.

A warm weight fell on my shoulder and I looked over, meeting John's dirt smudged face. Worry etched itself into every crevice and the fresh, earthy scent of new and broken soil clung to him like it belonged there all along. He wore it like a professional. Like a farmer.

"We're going to burn him. You don't have to stay," he whispered, squeezing my tensed shoulder in support. "You don't have anything to prove. If you don't want to see it, it's alright." Behind him, a small but deep hole marred the earth, and the realization that Ernie's rather large body was to fit in such a small place made my heart work overtime against my chest like a hammer beating a nail.

With a woeful smile, I shook my head at him. "Thank you. But, I need to stay. If I leave, it won't sit right with me for the rest of my life. I swear I'm alright."

His fleeting glance over all the purple and black contusions decorating my body told me very clearly that he thought otherwise, but to my satisfaction, he left any arguments or protests behind his tongue.

He gripped my hand in his as we made our way back to the other two men. Ed poked his head around the rose bush when our footsteps shuffled close enough for him to hear. Within moments both men were standing in front of us, Ed scanning my features doubtfully and George appearing far too chipper for the task at hand. The four of us stood in silence for a little while, the moonlight casting an eerie light over us, turning the ruby blood splattered everywhere black. The macabre sight sent waves of unease coursing through me, but I stood firm under the scrutiny of the night air.

You're in over your weak little head. You know this type of thing is my territory. Do you really think you can live up to it? Can you look at burning flesh without breaking down into a sobbing child? Power mocked, sneering in a way that made her anger and jealousy of my control evident.

I waited for someone else to speak, not wanting to be the one who broke the disturbing ominous silence we seemed to be trapped under. Maybe it was sinking in with the other three. Maybe they were using the time to come to terms with what had to be done. I doubted it was the case for George, and I didn't know enough about Ed to say for sure, but John's pensive and unfocused stare made it easy to believe that at least he was doing those things.

The air felt weighted, pressing down on my lungs and making my chest feel unbearably tight with each inhalation. The stars glittered above us, twinkling in the cloudless night sky to cast a decent amount of muted light down on us.

“Are we just going to stand here all night?” George asked, crossing his arms over his soaked chest. Blood dripped from every plane of his body while tiny specks of splattered blood clung to his cheeks and forehead. He inspected the back of his hand with a raised brow, the corner of his lip twitching upward as he took in the grisly sight.

“There should be a canvas bag or some kind of tarp in the shed. Ed and I can get started on the body,” John replied, not sounding pleased in the slightest.

With a bright grin, George turned and headed toward the shed, whistling and swinging his arms happily as he moved.

I started to follow John and Ed behind the bushes to help, but John paused in front of me, stopping me in my tracks. He swiveled around on his heel, looking flustered and upset. His eyes strayed from mine as he rubbed the back of his neck and inhaled a sharp breath.

“I know I shouldn’t tell you what to do,” he started, clearing his throat uncomfortably. My heart sank as I waited for the inevitable ‘but’. Power lifted her chin in arrogance, as if she knew he was too good to be true. “And I don’t want to be the kind of man who orders women around. My ma would skin my hide if she ever heard me disrespecting a woman.”

Power snickered. I’m sure his ma would be so very proud of the way he’s about to set fire to and bury a dismembered body, too. You’ve caught yourself a winner, Saney Sane.

“But, I’m not going to lie to you, Kate. Something in my gut is telling me that it would be horrifically wrong for you to see this. It’s twisting my stomach just thinking about you carrying the images around for the rest of your life. Please, please make my conscience happy and stay out here? Keep watch or something. Please," he begged, grasping my upper arms and pulling me to his chest. My entire torso and face sprang to life in agony, the bruises and cuts still fresh and untreated as I collided with him. His chin rested on top of my head as I squirmed to find a less painful position.

He released me and took a shaking step back, his head bowed low so that I couldn't see the torment in his eyes at the situation. Something told me John Kingwood was not a man accustomed to begging for anything, and that fact alone made me set aside my pride and think about what he was asking of me.

Did I really want to see this? Was I so desperate to assert my independence that I'd watch a corpse be set on fire and burned? See the flesh melt and the bones turn black under the white hot flames?

Weak, Power hissed in my head, flitting around and bouncing off the walls of my skull as she repeated the word over and over.

Her taunt nearly made my mind up for me, and I squared my shoulders, ready to tell him I insisted on being there. But, then, as I looked at his state- the trembling fists, the lowered head, and the hunched, insecure stance of his shoulders- my will softened. John didn't want to control me. At least not on this. Scraps of what he'd trusted me with about his time in Normandy strung together in my mind, making my guilt fester into an overbearing wad of clenched teeth and aching hearts. If I participated in this, it would probably kill him. I couldn't put him through that. Not when he'd been so kind and so caring toward me all this time.

No.

I'd rather be forever scarred with the label 'weak' than 'selfish'.

We walked back into our prison covered in dirt, dried blood, and ashes. It had taken hours and the moon had hoisted itself high into the sky by the time Ernie's remains were buried in the small hole hidden by the garden shed. None of us spoke, though George whistled incessantly, as if he'd experienced the best day of his life. John and I, though, were too enveloped and suffocated by the events of the evening to even think straight. We walked like the living dead, feet shuffling sloppily against the cobblestones and concrete, both our minds in similar states, I assumed.

Ed brought up the rear, his breathing heavy and labored. I hadn't missed the way his eyes had lit up, filling with sparks and excitement when he'd struck the first match. His gaze had lingered on the flame, watching it as if it were the most beautiful woman on earth. He'd ran his fingers through the flame over and over as he'd waited for John and I outside the rose bush. John had failed to notice him, but because I'd been facing him while we talked, the orange light flickering through the branches and leaves had caught my attention, leading my eye up to the pure lust and admiration Ed's entire body had encompassed as it had danced in his hand and reflected in his entranced and excited eyes.

Robbie's pretty receptionist jumped, startled, when the four of us appeared in the lobby so that we could get to the staircase and return to our ward. I spun my head around to look at John, silently asking him what to do. She'd seen us, and if anyone ever found the corpse pieces, she'd have all the evidence needed to make our sentences even worse than they already were. She was a witness now.

John, with a slump of his shoulders and an exhausted sigh, motioned George over to him with two fingers. Still whistling,

George made his way over and smiled, apparently already knowing what John wanted.

"Just... talk to her. Don't hurt her. Don't even touch her. Just convince her she didn't see us, and that you're not covered in blood," he instructed the teen, scrubbing his cheeks with his blistered hands. It had been a while since he'd worked manual labor, he'd said, and there were no gloves in the shed for him to use with the shovel.

"You're just no fun tonight, are you? Fine. I'll just talk to her," George replied, waving his hand in the air, dismissing us. John shot him a warning look, not at all amused with his flippancy, before shaking his head like a Golden Retriever with water in its ears and leading the way to the stairs with me and Ed in tow.

Marcie, Lottie, and Esther were waiting in my room for us to return, the younger two wide eyed and quivering with each other and the older watching me with such a profound sadness in her eyes that I nearly burst into tears on the spot.

"I'm going to shower," I croaked, biting back tears. My movements fell jerky and unsteady as I gathered my shower supplies and clean pajamas from around the room before exiting.

I showered hastily to curb my exhaustion. Every muscles ached, expanding and twitching under the hot waterfall in my shower cubicle. My bruises and cuts cried out in agony at every droplet, but I couldn't find it in myself to care. My body had undergone much worse. At least nothing felt broken. The memory of how being beaten felt had nearly escaped me in the past six months, and the familiarity frightened me. Surely it couldn't be normal to know such pain so intimately.

After scrubbing the filth from my skin, I toweled off and slipped into the pink silk pajamas Marcie's mother had sent to me two weeks before. The smooth material caressed my marbled skin with material that kept cool and soft, feeling heavenly against my injured body.

When I returned to my room, everyone except Esther had gone on their way, leaving the two of us alone in our room. I collapsed onto my bed, not bothering with the blanket or sheet. My eyelids felt like they were made of lead, and I laid there with feelings of hopelessness and guilt soaring through my veins at breakneck speeds.

Esther moved to my side, humming a soft Mexican lullaby as she pulled my bedding up around my shoulders. I barely groaned out a hoarse grunt of thanks.Her delicate hands began sliding through my hair, gently separating the knotted clumps of hair as her song continued on.

Something hot and wet landed on my cheek just before exhaustion finally claimed my consciousness.

Chapter 21

"Now, tie the ends together in a knot. Does anyone need help with that?" The same man who had been teaching the class the entire time I'd been at Rosenton stood at the front of the room, a goofy, hopeful smile glued on his face.

A man up front who hadn't stopped rocking back and forth since walking into the craft class rose his twitching hand and another woman who didn't seem to be able to manipulate her fingers lifted her arm up, muttering angry gibberish under her breath.

I glared down at the beaded necklace in my hands. The crafts seemed to become more and more juvenile every week. The white yarn and macaroni and plastic beaded creation screamed at how little the staff thought us capable of. I couldn't help but be jealous of John, who never even showed up this morning. I hadn't seen him since the night before, right before I'd gone to shower. I'd asked Esther at the beginning of class if he was alright, but had received a biting response that led me to believe he was fighting his own demons. The ones that got him in Rosenton to begin with.

"This is stupid," Esther muttered, jerking the two end of the knot tighter, breaking the yarn and sending uncooked pasta and little plastic beads flying in every direction. An older man with white hair and a protruding pot belly sitting diagonal from us cried out, then spun around and started cursing at Esther, his face cherry red and eyes bulging in unwarranted fury.

"Shut your hole, Pat! Turn around and make your little trinket before I take it from you and shove it up your-"

"Hey!" an orderly snapped, stalking toward us with a cautionary needle filled with sedatives glistening in his palm. "Cut it out! Pat, go back to work! Esther, shut up and get back to your necklace! Leave each other alone!" He yelled as if he were breaking up two growling dogs instead of people. I sank down in my chair and focused on turning invisible.

None of us had been ourselves all day. Marcie had begun to sink back down into her depressive state. Lottie had clung even tighter and closer to George, who had never looked more satiated and pleased in all the time I'd spent at Rosenton. Esther had been extra snappy and wary of everything, and John was nowhere to be seen. The only person who vaguely resembled himself was Ed, and that was more because he always seemed so mysterious and brooding anyway.

And the previous night's effects didn't skip over me. The tightness in my chest had only crushed my insides further and further, as the stress began taking its toll by making every dark corner lunge out at me and trick me into thinking we'd been caught already. My brain flipped and tumbled, tripping over itself as the pressure and impact of what we'd all done pounded into it.

“I need to go to the bathroom,” I said, glancing up in time to see Esther nod in acknowledgment. I stood and speed walked out the door and into the stark, sterile hallway. The walls breathed around me, constricting and closing in on me with every breath.

You’re losing it, Power sang, laughing as she walked around the corner and stood in front of my sweating, clammy body. Black edged around the corners of my vision, threatening to overtake me and leave me at the mercy of whichever staff member came across me first.

Power tweaked my nose, then went to inspecting her nails with an amused grin on her painted lips. She wore performance makeup, the heavy kohl and mascara making her eyes look larger and foreign. Despite the heavy makeup reserved for the spotlight, she wore a simple practice leotard that highlighted her smooth curves, the simplicity making her appear even more attractive than normal.

“You look like a tart,” I blurted, reaching out to lean against the inhaling wall beside me. Sweat dripped from my temples, trailing down my jaw and making my skin feel tight and grimy.

And you look like you can’t handle a little stress. It’s been a day, Sane. You’re just chomping at the bits to be caught. All of you are. You don’t think Shilling doesn’t notice how all of you are acting like your dog died? You need to stop being so weak and stupid. Get over it and move on. If I end up on the thirteenth floor because of you, I swear I’ll rip out your tongue and mop the entire ward with it.

I glared at her from beneath the arms propping my forehead against the wall. Her presence made everything around me press closer and closer to me, taking up all the air and leaving my breaths quick and my my fingers and lips tingling. I was fairly certain I was hyperventilating, but the only thought racing through my head was, GET OUT GET OUT GET OUT.

Power disintegrated into millions of tiny particles as I bolted for the staircase, straight through her. Had she been a real, tangible person, I would have barreled them over with the force of motion my legs used to propel me toward freedom. Everything around me was too close, too tight, and too suffocating. My inner walls of sanity cracked and shifted, threatening to crumble to the ground and let loose all my demons while destroying me in the process.

By the time I made it outside, my body was working solely on some base instinct that knew more than I did, because while it headed in a straight direction like it knew where it was going, I had no idea where my legs were carrying the rest of me. I flew through the rose garden, past the vegetable garden and to the overgrown bush I'd come to dream obsessively about. I dove behind it and crawled, smearing soil and wet sludge down the front of my clothes, under the hidden hole in the fence.

The moment the fences of Rosenton Home for the Criminally Insane no longer trapped me within its morbid walls, fresh air filtered into my lungs and I knelt in the grass there, soaking in every drop of clean, untainted air. Nothing bad happened outside the walls of Rosenton. No murders, no horrible doctors, no nurses with scary medications, no orderlies with needles in their pockets. Out here, the weight lifted from my chest and I sobbed with overwhelming relief.

I could run.

I could leave and never look back.

I could be free.

So, do it.

I frowned at her intruding voice. It was too much for me to hope to be completely free. She would always be there, causing more trouble and stress than I could handle properly. Though, I wasn't sure anyone knew the proper way to handle having a second person in your head. A murderer at that.

A deep sigh traveled past my lips. I couldn't leave my ward mates. Not after all they'd done for me. Not after all John had done for me.

I uncurled, standing barefoot in the cool grass, the emerald blades greeting my clenched toes. With my shoulders back and determination flowing through my limbs, I walked into the forest.

Chapter 22

The sharp edges of the broken chain links left bloody trails of superficial scratched down my bare arms, catching on my blouse and ripping holes in the expensive lace. Not that the top was in pristine condition anyway, with the abundance of mud, leaves, and cave water staining the material. Impulse and strong emotion had led me to make unsavory and unwise decisions before in my life, but never ones with such consequences as the ones I knew Shilling would reign down on me once I re-entered the building. The leaves of the overgrown bush rustled and grabbed at my clothes as I shuffled by it, in some way warning or begging me not to go back.

Admittedly, my night of freedom from Rosenton tempted me beyond what should have ever been possible. Spending my second night away from the imposing building and terrifying staff left me wanting more, despite the fact that I'd slept on a hard, unforgiving cave ground all night. My body may have been stiff and sore, but my mind felt refreshed and capable again. The only problem being what Shilling would do to me once he found me back in my ward.

Of course, Ernie's death replayed in my head, over and over again all night long. Like some sick picture show, where I was the only one in the audience. The blood, the scent of charred human flesh, the sight of his severed limbs being tossed in a canvas bag and thrown unceremoniously into a shallow, hidden grave. We'd given him no funeral or even so much as a peaceful moment of silence. No prayers to admit his spirit into heaven. If he hadn't taken care of his spirit in life, I couldn't see what good the prayers of his murderers would do for him, anyway.

Stop being so cynical. You didn't even do anything. George killed him. Ed burned him. George dismembered him. John buried him. What did you do? Sit at the sidelines and watch for the guard who never showed up? You think you're so bad, Sane, and that's hilarious. You didn't even want to me kill those evil piles of garbage that abused you for fun at Jensen and Sons. You're no murderer. You're just an emotional little girl who feels bad for things she didn't even have the guts to do.

I thought back to the electricity in George's eyes that night. How he'd been excited and more than elated to have done what he did. He'd been proud of his work, and had gained real, pure joy from taking another man's life. Then, he'd expected me to feel the same thing, when all I could truly feel was shock and horror. Ernie had attacked me, but I hadn't wanted the man to die.

It would have happened again and again until one of you died anyway. You should be thanking George for cutting your suffering short and making you come out the winner so soon.

I scoffed as I limped down the garden path, staying in the shadows and scanning the area for orderlies to avoid.

You know it's true. George is strong. Much stronger than you could ever hope to be without me. Come on, Sane. Why don't we strike up a deal, hm? Something to benefit us both?

No way under the sun. I'd been down that path one time too many. Power had lost her mind if she thought I'd even entertain the thought of striking a deal with her.

She pouted. Don't be like that, Saney. We've had good times together. You're just too uptight to properly enjoy it. Will you just listen to my idea?

No.

Well, it's a good thing you're forced to listen to my voice inside your head anyway, isn't it? Look. You give me complete control when things get out of hand again, because you and I both know that will happen in this hellhole, and I'll stop insulting you.

Oh, please, I thought, picking up my pace to make it to the back door to the building. I'd been insulted my entire life. Her petty words had never affected me the way she wanted them to.

I heard her huff in exasperation before getting the distinct impression of her arms being crossed at her chest while she rolled her eyes. If I didn't know she was a manipulative psychopath, I would have thought her childish pose funny.

Alright. Then, if you give me control when things get out of hand, I'll stop fighting you for it the rest of the time.

Fat chance of that happening.

A guttural noise of frustration sounded low in her throat and she stamped her foot, sending dust fly around her. She eyed the particles with disgust.

I'll stop showing up.

A slow grin spread across my face. It scared me, how I'd manipulated her for once, herding her in the direction I wanted. But, after all the times I'd spent seeing her in the shadows, hanging from the ceiling, and laughing at me in the mirror, the need to feel safe and stable mentally overtook every ounce of guilt about it. I'd have done almost anything to keep her from randomly popping up in my vision again.

With a curt nod, I accepted her terms and entered the building.

Being pulled into the same closet John had pulled me into months ago sent a massive wave of deja vu over me, before I realized that I was being borderline kidnapped because I had no clue who had grabbed me or what they planned to do with me once that closet door shut. I jerked away from the stiff grip, resulting in having my body yanked even harder into the closet. The momentum caused me to crash forward into another body. A body that was decidedly smaller than John's, but still male.

The door clicked shut behind me, making a sense of pure alarm race through my head.

"Where were you?" George demanded, shoving me against the door and pinning me there with one hand on my shoulder. His voice registered in my head and I relaxed for a moment before my hackles rose again at his tone. Power smirked behind the wall, watching in apt interest.

In an attempt to stand my ground and not give in to his rudeness, I placed my hands on his chest and tried to shove him away, but the boy didn't move an inch. So, in true feminine fashion, I settled for giving him my best angry glare in hopes he would cower back.

Of course, I'd never been lucky. In fact, my actions only produced his own frustrated glower that held ten times the fury mine had ever held in their life.

"I'll ask again. Where. Were. You."

A can of paint wobbled on the shelf beside his head, still reeling from the vibrations the slam of my body hitting the door had set off. It balanced, precariously, on one side, leaning further and further toward his head. Using reflexes I hadn't had the opportunity to exercise in a long time, I shoved George back, hard, just in time for the paint can to fall from the ledge and land with an ear-splitting clang on the tile ground, right past where his head had been. Blue paint exploded everywhere, which I found irritating since I'd yet to see any color aside from the patented mental asylum white anywhere in the entire institute.

George glanced down at the can, taking in the powder blue mess all around us and all over the two of us as well.

"Marcie is going to kill me," I groaned, snatching a box of unopened paper towels from another shelf and dabbing at the paint drenching my skirt and blouse in a futile attempt to rescue the ruined garments.

"She won't get the opportunity if you don't answer my question within five seconds," he growled hoarsely in response, then coughed as the chemical fumes from the spilled paint began to fill the room.

My head shot up in surprise. It seemed so unreal, so silly, for someone as powerful and strong as George to do something as mundane as cough. It was enough to remind me that he wasn't some almighty being, but a human being just as susceptible to human conditions as the rest of us.

Don't get too comfortable, Power teased, rolling her eyes. Not even thirty minutes ago you were lamenting and just twisting your guts silly over the fact that he killed Ernie with his bare hands, and liked it.

My eyes began to water as the overpowering chemicals made their way to my lungs and nose, burning a path throughout. I reached down for the doorknob in hopes of opening it to ventilate the tiny room, but George's hand snaked around my wrist and held me still.

"Let's say the door will open when you tell me where you were last night, hm? Until then, we'll just keep all this paint company," he wheezed, somehow managing to sound domineering and in control through the obvious physical pain he was in. My lungs ached as the fumes became thicker, making breathing near impossible. The scene around me faltered back and forth as my head swam in clumsy circles.

"I'm going to pass out," I begged, leaning for the door, while coughing against the sharp odor infiltrating my nose.

"Then answer the question, Kate!" His grip tightened and he shoved me against the door again, stepping over the busted paint can to pin me in the exact same position as before.

"I had to go clear my head! I snuck out!"

Nothing in the massive amount of appalling things at Rosenton had ever rendered George speechless that I had seen. And yet, my quick, wheezing confession that had nothing to do with the atrocities of the staff and the elusive thirteenth floor had his jaw loosen in surprise. Beside when he had killed Ernie, it was the only flicker of human emotion I'd seen of him that seemed genuine in all my time at the asylum, and I found myself with the upper hand for once. I had information he wanted.

"Let me out and I'll tell you more. Please, George. I feel faint in here with the paint fumes," I groveled, while Power shifted in her chair, leaning in close with one fist under her chin to watch how it all played out. She smiled at my weakness act, then shook her head. That won't work on him. He doesn't feel empathy. Flatter him.

"I wanted to ask your opinion on it anyway. No one else would think it through as well," I continued, finding the manipulation easier than I felt entirely comfortable with. But what other weapon against him did I have? I wasn't even certain Power could take him.

You're right. I wouldn't be able to take him physically. But, we're one and the same. I understand him. He's a kindred spirit to me, and I'm finding myself enamored. I could at least get us to a stalemate.

George's hand left my wrist and he twisted the doorknob before pushing it open with more force than necessary. I tumbled from the closet, gasping in the fresh, untainted air. I reached out for the opposite wall, leaning against it as I tried to steady my spinning head.

He stepped out of the closet, stalking toward me with a thoughtful look on his face. "We'll talk more about this tonight after lights out. Be in the rose garden. I don't need to tell you what will happen to you or Lottie if you don't show up."

I gaped at him. Threats to me, I'd expected. But to Lottie also? The girl he protected like he actually cared about her?

"She trusts you," I whispered, my hands gripping at my now blue shirt.

He chuckled, a sound so chilling I flinched back even further against the wall. "I'd hope so. I haven't kept her under my wing for nothing."

I jumped up, every protective, mothering instinct I possessed rising up like cavalry against his coldness. "You can't do that! What are you planning to do with her?!"

His shoulders lifted and dropped, a nonchalant show of carelessness. He leaned against the wall beside me, inspecting the paint on his trousers with an amused glint shining in his cool hazel eyes. "I can do whatever I want, Kate. I'm not shackled down by emotions and useless sympathies like you are. She's safe in my hands as long as I get what I want from you and everyone else here."

Every red blood cell in my body ran cold at his words, said so casually, as if Lottie truly didn't matter at all to him. "She's just your pawn," I mumbled, horror blazing a trail down my spine, leaving goosebumps in their wake.

"Don't look so stricken. Does she have it so bad? All she's ever wanted is protection, and I give it to her. Nothing anyone could say to her would change her deluded little white knight fantasy of me. She's getting what she wants, and I'm getting what I want." He explained it like a game. A terrible, horrible game.

"But, it's wrong!" I cried, backing away from him, all my rejuvenation from my night in the cave thoroughly banished in the face of his indifference to Lottie's place in his elaborate ruse.

"Wrong..." George flipped the word around on his tongue, trying it out like an exotic delicacy. "Who says it's wrong? People? I'm a person. Don't I have stake in what that definition should be? Men set all these rules in place, but who's really enforcing them? Who's the top of the pyramid? We're all on level ground, aren't we? Equal?

Why is their definition of wrong better than mine? It isn't. Everyone is getting what they want here, Kate. Your silly notions of right and wrong are skewed and close minded Open your eyes."

The white walls of the hallway spun around me, threatening to close in and collapse in on me any second. Tingling sensations filled my lips and the tips of my fingers and toes as I backed away from him, desperate to run. Power had been right when she'd labeled me as the 'flight' side of survival, because it was all I seemed to do in the face of danger. Enough time barely passed for me to wonder what her reaction might be to the situation before I gave in and ran from George. He smiled, watching my paled face take in his ridiculous justification and excuses for the wrongdoing he felt no remorse for doing.

With his admission of his heartless nature, the threats he made against me so long ago flitted into my head in a brand new, even more sickening light. I no longer thought of his words about ripping Power's throat out as an exaggerated wordplay to catch my attention. He'd meant it, and he would do it the moment I messed up any aspect of whatever game he had going.

I turned tail and ran for the showers, the need to escape bearing down on me in an attempt to suffocate the life directly from my lungs.

All eyes turned to me when I took my seat at the end of the couch in the lounge, after coming back from a long and exhausting shower. George's words played on over and over again in my head, the haunting syllables like a sick subliminal monologue as the scenes I'd unwillingly memorized of him killing and desecrating Ernie's corpse rolled behind my closed eyelids. I'd turned the hot water up as high as it would go, not even touching the cold, and let it burn my skin. The scalding water left me raw and steaming, but it felt like the only thing I could do to rinse myself of the overload of despicable atrocities I'd witnessed in the past week alone. Shilling's first attack after we'd returned from the cave, Marcie's depression, Shilling's second and more brutal attack on my psyche, Ernie's attack and subsequent appalling death, Marcie's fake suicide attempt, John's revelations about his own fate and last chance, and now George's display of his true colors.

I would have given my left foot for a break.

I settled into my seat, closing my eyes and ignoring the curious eyes pointed toward me. Six months of peace and ease left me softened and unsuspecting. I should have been on guard for everything. I should have never let myself relax or think that things could be simple.

A warm weight intertwined between my fingers and tugged, asking me to stand rather than demanding it. The urge to stamp my foot and whine out a petulant, "no!" against it overwhelmed me, but I swallowed it down.

A break? In this place? You had six months worth of a break.

I know! I snapped at Power, my irritation rising as she reprimanded me. The conniving murderer reprimanded me. The irony fell on my thoughts with the force of a speeding bullet, but I actively chose to ignore that.

So, with an insurmountable amount of grudging reluctance, I peeled myself from the couch and hauled myself to my feet. John tugged me behind him, leading me from the room with a gentleness that soothed my frustration away, smoothing over the sharp ridges of irritability and snappishness. Behind me, a lighter set of footsteps followed us, but no one spoke.

John led me into the hall and around the corner, near the mens' dorms. When he turned to face me, instant guilt washed over me. Dark, purple circles colored in the spaces beneath his bloodshot eyes, and his tanned skin lacked the healthy glow I'd never seen him without. His shoulder slumped forward, as if he was a rag doll being held up by a string in his neck. Concern etched itself into his paled face as he scanned my form for clues to wherever I'd been. His focus zeroed in on the long scratches from the clipped fence edges.

"Where have you been? We were worried sick," he asked. The words were the same as George's but with far more weariness and desperation replacing the anger. Esther stepped from behind me to join him, standing by his side. She hadn't bothered with makeup, revealing just how much older than us she was for the first time. For her to neglect her strict beauty regimen meant my departure had affected them far more than I'd thought it would.

I had the good graces to look down by way of shame for putting them through such stress.

"I had to go clear my head. Everything just overwhelmed me, and I had to go before I lost control," I whispered, pressing my lips in a thin line afterward.

A thick breath of relief blew from John's tensed lips and he leaned back against the wall, running his large hands through his hair, slicking it back over and over again. "So, Shilling didn't get to you, then?"

Esther's hand flew to her chest and her eyes squeezed shut. She murmured something sounding like a quick prayer before opening her eyes again and sliding against the wall, to the floor. As if the knowledge that the doctor hadn't gotten his hands on me had pulled all the bones from her body, leaving her a melted, formless heap on the tiles below.

"No. I didn't want to give him the chance to take advantage of my stress. So I did what I needed to do."

"Where did you go, mija?" Esther asked, staring up at me through bare lashes. Wrinkles carved their way across her colorless face, deep and long, accentuating the leathery texture of her skin that she normally covered with a flawless application of makeup.

My eyes darted to John as I pulled the hem of my skirt between my fingers, twisting the fabric nervously. My body wilted in relief when he nodded in understanding. Esther studied the exchange, but inclined her own head in acceptance that she wouldn't be let in on the secret. No one but Robbie, John, and I knew about the cave, and it would stay that way. My private circus was too special, too intimate, to let the others know about it. I wanted it close to my heart, guarded as an ultimate secret for only the three of us to treasure.

"I'm sorry I worried you," I offered in a small voice. "Did Shilling find out?"

Esther shook her head, wisps of black hair falling from her severe bun. "No. I bundled sheets and pillows under your blanket last night when they came for lights out. You should be safe."

Gratitude welled up in my stomach at her kindness. Who was I to deserve such a wonderful mother figure? I knelt in front of her and pulled her to me in a tight embrace, fighting the emotions swirling around my head. "Thank you, Esther. I'm so sorry I worried you."

She returned the hug, though her arms felt limp and weak around my shoulders. Pinpricks of remorse over my selfishness prickled over my skin, making me feel like the world's worst friend. She didn't deserve to be worried or abandoned.

"Que esta bien, mija. I'm just glad you're alright."

My vision traveled up from the socked feet that stepped in front of me and to John's face. The tension had left his frame and he stooped down, helping both of us to our feet by our hands.

His fingers began to release mine, but I held them firm. He hadn't deserved to worry so much over me either, and with a mountain of resolve to show him how sorry I was and how much he meant to me, I leaned up on my tip-toes and planted a small peck on his cheek.

"I am sorry," I whispered close to his ear, then settled back on my heels to look up at him, searching his face. Like before when I'd initiated the small, intimate contact, a red flush worked its way up his neck - the only sign that he felt flustered by my actions. Despite that, his lips curled up into a heartwarming smile that had me mirroring my own version back at him.

"We should get back to the others," he murmured, clearing his throat. Esther grinned slyly, amusement sparkling in her dark eyes and highlighting the deep crow's feet bordering them.

"Your children will be beautiful," she declared, then straightened her shoulders and sauntered back to the lounge without another second to spare, leaving John and I to stare after her in embarrassed shock.

This time, the red flush took over John's entire face, neck to hairline.

The coolness of the stone path seeped through my thin socks that night as I made my way into the rose garden. My heart hammered out a steady, pounding rhythm as the wind picked up and lifted my tangled hair off my shoulders. I hadn't exactly made it to the garden at the time George had specified, since neither John nor Esther had let me leave their sights all evening. I'd waited until Esther's breaths had come slow and deep from beneath her blanket, signaling her slumber, before crawling from the room with a silk robe around my nightgown, and sprinting down the stairs to the garden. Hopefully George had waited. I knew without a doubt that I would die of guilt if something happened to Lottie because of me.

I scanned the area for him as I jogged through, smelling the heavy scent of rain hovering over top of me. Thunder growled in the sky to the east, close enough to warn of its presence, but far enough away to tell me we'd have some time before the storm arrived.

"Come on, George. Please have waited. You knew John wouldn't have let me out of his sight," I mumbled to myself, peeking around corners and behind alcoves. Lightning cracked across the sky, a thin, hair-thin bolt crawling across the sky far enough away to make me a little less nervous.

"I'm feeling generous, so consider yourself fortunate."

I spun around, hair flying in every direction, to face him, letting out a sigh of immense relief. "Oh, thank God."

A sly smile worked its way onto his lips. "Let's walk and talk about this little nugget of golden information you've been stowing away." I nodded and fell in line beside him, wrapping my arms around myself to keep from shivering. Autumn was on its way, bringing the cooler weather with it. I wondered if the roses would hold up through the fall and winter months. Did roses wilt and die in cooler weather? I knew next to nothing about them. I'd never been in one place long enough to watch flowers grow.

"I admit I underestimated you," he began, strolling with a confidence I found unsettling. "I wouldn't have pegged you as the type to let us all stay trapped here while you knew of an escape all along. Maybe you are as evil as the news reports said. I didn't know you had it in you."

My teeth clenched while Power laughed inside my head. If only he were a decade or so older! I'd leave John to you and take this one for myself. He's a master at his craft!

"That's not what I was doing," I protested, shivering against another breeze.

He chuckled, kicking a pebble from the pathway. "Is that so? Then you just found it yesterday? When Marcie was having her episode and Shilling wanted her on the thirteenth floor, you didn't know we could have sneaked out to safety?"

I said nothing, knowing, somewhere in my reeling head, that he was pressing my buttons on purpose to manipulate everything he could get from me.

"I've known about it."

"So you are just an evil little psycho, wanting us all to rot here while you keep an escape secret from us?"

"No!" I snapped, turning to face him. He paused, watching me with a raised eyebrow in expectation. "I was... waiting. Where would we go? Do any of us even know what town we're in? What state? Shilling would send people to find us, and there are too many do-gooders out there with no clue how awful this place is, who would turn us in the moment they saw us! How would we eat? Where would we sleep? It would be evil to let us traipse out there without a plan!"

"And what kind of plan do you have in mind, oh wise one?" he mocked.

I sucked in a deep breath, feeling the oxygen infiltrate my lungs alongside the humid heaviness of the air. "That's what I've been working on. Robbie has been helping. We've been trying to find a way to get all of us out."

George squinted, thinking back. "Robbie. The man who visits you? Your brother, right?"

I nodded, too frustrated with him to speak.

"Yes, the two of you have the same eyes."

My mouth opened to reply, but the oddness of his seemingly random observation held me stock still as I tried to decipher it. "No, we're not blood related. He's my adoptive brother," I explained, but he waved off my clarification and continued walking, motioning for me to hurry up and follow when I didn't move. My feet slapped the stone walkway as I rushed to catch up with him.

"Show me where you escape from," George commanded when I fell beside him again.

And I did. I took him to the overgrown bush hiding the damaged portion of the fence, pressing my hands against the chain link to demonstrate how it gave way. He bent down, studying the fence and prodding it with his hands for several minutes while I stood watch.

"What's out there?"

"Hm?" I asked, shaking myself from the sarcastic diatribe with Power in my head.

"Out there," he repeated, rolling his eyes as he gestured to the tree line on the other side of the fence. "What have you found? A town? A road? Anything?"

My shoulders lifted and drooped. The day I told him about the cave was the day I ate my pinky finger for the fun of it. "Just woods. Trees. A few footpaths, but nothing substantial."

"How far out have you gone?"

I pointed straight past the damaged portion of the links. "Straight in that direction a few hours. Which direction is the town they always take you guys to?"

"The opposite directions. Out the front gate. It's called Gaineston. But they won't let us know what state we're in. If we're even in the United States anymore."

"We'd have to be. We're all American citizens, and our families visit often enough that it can't be more than a day or two's drive for any of them," I muttered, chewing on my thumb nail as I mulled the possibilities over in my head.

"Your brother hasn't mentioned it?"

"What?"

"What state we're in, Kate. Pay attention."

Power snickered, but I ignored her and shook my head. "I've never thought to ask. He probably doesn't know we don't know. Do you think they tell our families not to let us know?"

"Of course they do. They don't want us to have the confidence of familiarity if we try to leave," he scoffed. I glared at him as a metaphorical light bulb lit up over my head.

"You already know all the answers to all these questions you're asking me."

He grinned at my accusation. "Most of them, yes."

My lips curled in disgust. "You belong here, George."

That earned me a hearty laugh as he stood and brushed the dirt off his trousers. "You act as though I don't know that."

Chapter 23

"I know! Peter and Harold stopped by his house to check on him and he wasn't there either. It's like he just disappeared into thin air."

"Well, I can't say I'm surprised. Ernie was a strange man. Something was always off kilter about him. He probably packed a bag and took off just because."

"But, who leaves ground beef out to thaw if they're leaving for so long? He didn't plan on going anywhere. I still say something happened to him. He's probably in a ditch, dead, somewhere."

I stood, ramrod straight against the wall of the adjoining hallway as the nurses' voices drifted into my ears from where they stood, gossiping at their station about Ernie. His disappearance had finally been noticed, and that did not bode well for us. Fear ran a marathon through my limbs and I began to shake, the adrenaline commanding I flee the scene.

Run, run, run, Sane. It's what you're good at.

I wasn't sure why that particular comment hurt when I'd heard her say variations of it so many times before, but for whatever reason, a bolt of pain shot through my chest and I winced, biting my lip against it. Power caught onto it and held fast, taking the opportunity to add more jabs in hopes of tearing me even further down. Why she wanted to protect me, but destroy me at the same time, I didn't know. But I wouldn't satisfy her by taking the time to dwell on it, so I swallowed down the lump in my throat and blocked her out the best I could.

With a renewed vigor due to my desperation to run, I peeled myself off the wall and hurried down the corridor. I needed to talk to someone, anyone, from my ward. We had to be prepared for the coming storm.

As if on some cosmic, ironic cue, the downpour that had descended and stayed on top of us since the early morning hours released a deafening clap of thunder. The lights flickered, emitting a faint buzzing sound before winning the fight against the storm and brightening back up.

I quickened my pace, nearly running on the freshly waxed floor, sliding on my socks as my body rounded corners too rapidly. The absolute last thing I wanted was to be caught in Rosenton, alone, in a pitch black hallway. Finding even one of my ward mates to cling with until the threat of losing electricity passed would boost my confidence and kill off the fear.

My luck paid out as I passed by the stairwell. The door opened, revealing Ed, most likely coming back from his daily outing. Without a second thought, my legs pumped harder to carry me closer to him, needing the security of another trustworthy friend. He saw me coming and his eyes widened when I tried to come to a stop two feet away from him. Unfortunately, between the momentum I'd built up running down the corridors and the new wax on the floor, I failed and careened into his chest, unknowingly inhaling the aroma of thick, burning smoke off his clothes.

He steadied me by my shoulders and set me back on my feet while I hacked and coughed at the way the smoke choked my lungs.

"You okay?" he asked, scratching the back of his head and flicking his eyes all around. I would have laughed at how much like an awkward, teenage boy he seemed had I not been trying to expel the offending odor from my body through my burning airway.

"Yeah," I wheezed, flicking the tear that had gathered at the outer corner of my eye away. "I had... I was near the nurses' station...Th-they figured out... They know Ernie's missing." The words tumbled out haphazardly between bouts of coughing.

Ed frowned, his massive hands clenching into fists the size of sledge hammers. The wave of unease rolling off him felt tangible as the implications of my discovery sank in.

He looked down at me, his jaw clenched. "We need to get to the lounge so we can let them know."

I nodded, my throat finally clearing of the sharp smoke, and followed him to the lounge. I couldn't bring myself to let more than a foot or two come between us, just in case the electricity went out and I needed to reach out to find him. The ability to just keep that contact, that touch, if we were cast into complete darkness, would keep me on the safe side of panic.

Ed pushed open one of the double doors, the action so soft I wondered if he loathed being the one to break the news. The man made it habit to stay in the background, unnoticed and overlooked. Being the one to bear bad news like this put him at the center of attention, and I doubted he enjoyed that.

Another stroke of pure luck had all the rest of our ward mates already relaxing in the lounge, hypnotized by the rain pelting the window. A sense of deja vu overcame me and I smiled before remembering what I had to reveal to them. Dread formed a concrete block in my stomach.

"We need to talk," Ed spoke up, letting the door fall shut to grab everyone's attention. Looks of surprise decorated each of the faces staring in our direction.

John caught my gaze, scrunching his eyebrows in a tight chevron in question. I bit the inside of my cheek and tried not to cry.

"About what?" Marcie asked, pulling her hand away from the window where she'd been drawing simple pictures with her finger in the condensation. A childish stick figure family and stick house with little flowers popping out of the stick grass filled the bottom of the pane.

"They've discovered Ernie's missing," I said before Ed would feel pressured to take the lead. After saving me from Shilling, it was the bare minimum I could do to try to repay him.

The temperature of the room, already at a nice chill, seemed to drop another ten degrees as everyone froze.

"So soon?" George asked, standing from his chair with a little stretch and a sly lift of the corners of his lips. Lottie remained perched on the arm of said chair, her wide eyes following his movements. A sick, twisty feeling swam through my gut as I remembered his callousness toward her affection and admiration. Did she know he held her life in his hands? That he could be her ultimate protection or ultimate demise, depending on something as trivial as his mood?

Esther shot him a look that screamed, "can it."

"I heard two nurses talking about it. Someone went to his house and found food thawing, so they know he's missing," I added, clenching and unclenching my fists to keep myself from crying.

Esther cursed and began running her hands up and down her arms, like she was trying to banish a sudden chill brought on by our certain demise.

George smiled. His teeth gleamed under the harsh florescent lights, an evil, vile sight that told the world just how comfortable he was with murder.

"So what?" he asked, shrugging his shoulders. This time, John shot him a warning look since Esther's jaw had fallen open at his blatant nonchalance.

"This isn't a game," John snapped, his knuckles white as they gripped the arms of his chair.

"I know that. They know he's missing, but why would they suspect any of us? For all they know he's just a victim of a random criminal out there, in the real world. They have no reason to think we had anything to do with it unless we lead them to believe it," he countered, his arrogance shining through like the sun in the summertime.

He's right. You just have to stop panicking like an idiot and pretend you don't know a thing.

I hated how right she and George were. I hated that she acted as an anchor to my hysteria. I hated that she liked George so much and wanted to find a kindred soul in him.

But I couldn't bring myself to hate her, or George for that matter. She was part of me, and he was a friend. Neither very good at their roles, but they held those positions just the same. And try as

I might, I just couldn't harbor hatred alongside the care I felt for them both.

You're such a sucker. But, I appreciate the kind thoughts. Her words were laced with sarcasm, but I thought I may have detected the slightest hint of sincerity somewhere in the jungle of cynicism she thrived in.

"So," George continued, stretching his arms over his head to further prove how little he was concerned about the situation, "We just go on with life like nothing happened and pretend we don't know a thing. Easy. Getting worked up over it is a red flag, so everyone just shut up and forget about him."

As if it were so easy. So simple. To forget the sight of blood, the sound of bones crunching, the scent of a burning body.

Simple. No problem.

But, looking around the room, I seemed to be the only one thinking along those lines. Even John nodded his head, agreeing with George's calloused idea. I turned to view the entire room, seeing each face beam with agreement that his plan was best. The first word to slam into my head was "cowards", but I shook it away. Ernie was dead. Nothing would bring him back or take back what had been done. My ward mates weren't cowards. They were just trying to survive.

With all my internal moral compasses spinning out of control, still not sure which way to turn, I met George's cold eyes and nodded.

Group therapy felt like a punishment for my submission to George's plan. Paul had come after me before, pressuring me to share and open up to the group, but I'd become somewhat of a prodigy of George's in manipulating the conversation to reveal nothing about myself. He had even trusted me enough to keep watch over Lottie while he took care of other business during our sessions at times. I never knew what that business was for sure, but I always suspected it had something to do with the frequent visits his mother and father made to the asylum because of the way he nearly always came back agitated and amped up, like he wanted to fight something.

Or kill something, Power piped up, all too pleased with her addition to my inner monologue. I grimaced. While her promise to remain unseen still went unbroken, she was making a habit of interjecting disturbing little quips to shake me up. The worst part of it being that she knew it worked.

Paul swung his head to look at me, as if he'd felt my inner struggle with the demon in my head. My insides churned and I looked away, hoping, like a child who didn't know the answer to the teacher's question, that not making eye contact would make me invisible.

"What do you find difficult to deal with?" he asked, swaying the conversation to inflict everyone's attention on me. "What frustrates you, Miss Thornton?"

"I don't get frustrated," I replied, squirming in my seat. I technically hadn't lied. Power got mad, and acted on it. Sane just cowered in a corner until the offending situation went away.

"Everyone gets angry sometimes," he insisted. "What are your pet peeves?"

"Nothing. I'm a calm person."

George snorted beside me in amusement, low enough that Paul didn't hear it. Lottie shoved an elbow in his rib and shot him a stern glare. A small wave of pride for her little reprimand coursed through me and I smiled at her, hoping it would encourage her to do it more often.

"That's not entirely true, is it, Kate? Dr. Shilling and I often share notes, you know. Why don't you open up and release the burden you're carrying?"

The thought of losing my burden, Power, felt far too panicky on my mind than I was comfortable with. I wanted to want to jump at the chance to rid myself of her, but just the notion made me feel guarded and protective, almost hysterical. I needed her like I needed a drug, and that sent in overwhelming amounts of self-loathing to my very core.

"I'm alright. Really. I just don't get mad anymore," I tried to assure him anyway, uneasy with the determined glint in his eye and the way his pink lip curled down at the edges in a mocking snarl. His pen tapped at a rapid speed against his clipboard, telling me exactly how invested he was in getting me to talk. He wouldn't be giving up easily today.

"Come on, now. Let's be serious. We both know why you're here. Do your ward mates know?" he pressed. My foot began vibrating against the tiled floor, giving away the fact that he'd struck a nerve. My jaw clenched as the rest of my body began shaking, readying itself to bolt. Power rumbled beneath the surface of my psyche, readying herself to take over as well.

"I get angry when I think about my cousin," Lottie blurted, making me freeze. George frowned beside me, his shoulders tensing as he turned a stormy warning look at her. "I get mad when I remember the things he used to do to me, and why I'm here. I get angry that I let what he did affect me so much that I ended up here."

I tried to catch her eye, hoping a subtle shake of my head would make her stop giving Paul ammunition against her, but she refused to look at me or George at all. Instead, she focused on the far wall, where a large yellow poster depicting "5 Steps to Calm Down". As if there were a steadfast recipe for that. Cartoon boys and girls acted out each step, looking awkward with disproportionate limbs and black dots for eyes.

"I get angry that I let him affect me so much that I tried to hurt my sister," she continued while Paul scribbled down notes at lightning speed, scrawling across the paper so fast the pen knocked hard against the wood, producing loud clicking sounds each time he started a new word.

"I get mad that my sister hates me because of the way I let him affect me," she kept on, yanking her arm away from George after he pinched her, trying to get her to stop talking.

"I'm angry that my parents refused to believe me."

Anger, bright and unbridled, rolled off George as she disobeyed him and continued spilling her soul, putting herself in danger. He snatched her hand back, crushing her fingers between his, making her wince and whimper before turning her pleading eyes to him.

Anyone else would have thought he cared for her with the way he loosened his grip and softened his gaze to reassure her. Any normal person would have assumed he didn't want her putting herself in danger with Paul because he might have even loved her. But, I knew the truth even if Lottie didn't. Even if the rest of the world didn't. George didn't really care about Lottie. He only cared about what having her under his wing would benefit himself. Without her, none of his ward mates would tiptoe around him. As long as he held her reins in his grip, he knew the rest of us would have done anything to make sure she stayed stable and happy.

By one sly maneuver into the youngest member's heart, he'd effectively caught the rest of us in his manipulative trap.

George Baker, actor extraordinaire, knew exactly what to do to get exactly what he wanted. And somehow, though all of us except Lottie knew that, we were all still twisted and sick enough to care about him. Maybe because of the hypocrisy we would have been guilty of if we judged him based on his diagnosis and crimes. He'd even said it himself. I'd killed more people than any of them combined, except maybe John if his time in the Army counted for anything. Esther had murdered the man she loved the most, and Marcie had attempted the same. None of us were blameless, except perhaps Lottie, if her vague confessions were anything to go by.

"I'm mad that I can't make myself eat, because I don't want to grow up," the young girl added, her lip curling in disgust as her fingers gripped the edge of her chair. She looked ready to bolt, and all I could do was sit and wonder why on earth she'd do this to herself.

"I'm so mad that sometimes I can't even put order to my thoughts or the reasons why I do the things I do. And I hate that I'm so freaking hungry, but this dictator inside my head just won't let me eat anything."

Paul grinned, the expression chilling me to the bone. The heel of his foot bounced against the floor, like he was genuinely excited that she'd spilled so many of her secrets. George glared at the therapist, daring him to speak. I shuddered at the thought that the sixteen year old held control over a grown man. The testament to his manipulation and control sent a panicky feeling up my spine.

"And what is it your cousin did that affected you so?" he asked, tapping his pen against the clipboard again.

Lottie never got the chance to answer. Her mouth opened, but before any sound came out, a deafening crash jolted everyone's attention to the ruckus. Across the room, a metal chair lodged itself in the sole window in the room, glass shattered and scattered all around it. Beside me, George stood, fists clenched and mouth set in a menacing snarl.

It's strange that the cool and composed little psycho just had an emotional outburst, don't you think?

I agreed with Power mentally, but resisted the urge to write it off as just that. Esther's words from months before haunted me. He doesn't do anything without purpose, she'd said. What purpose did throwing a chair through a window have? Nothing about it seemed characteristic of the detached teen, but one look at his face and tense body told me that even if it was an act, some portion of genuine anger shined through.

Had killing Ernie set him as much on edge as it had the rest of us?

No. He wouldn't even give that a second thought. He's angry that the power dynamic changed over. He doesn't like not being in control.

The glass still holding the chair in place in the window cracked out even further, forming a delicate spiderweb of broken glass all around it, crackling and shining with each minuscule movement.

George took a threatening step toward Paul, who smirked in response, furthering his aggressor's fury. My knuckles tightened on the edge of my seat as the scene played out. Anything George did could be turned against him, but he had to have known that already. The boy wasn't unintelligent. Then again, if his need to be the puppeteer, in control of the rest of us, was what made him snap, maybe he'd lost his wits altogether in favor of regaining the upper hand.

Take control, Power whispered in my ear, like a sinister devil on my shoulder. Her voice curled around my psyche, slithering and hissing with liquid temptation.

I took the bait, jumping from my chair to grab George's arm and pull him back before he could incur Paul's wrath. A simple, commanding look that I'd learned from the master manipulator himself aimed at Lottie had her hopping up to follow us out the door of the group therapy room.

I took one last look back at the demented therapist as I dragged my two ward mates from the room. His face lit up, excitement glowing from his posture that he'd managed to possibly break one of us. George seethed in my grip, then shrugged me off before stalking from the room with the grace of a panther.

I turned away from Paul and hurried after George and Lottie, letting the door slam behind me.

Chapter 24

George threw his fist into the mirror above the sink, sending a hailstorm of shattered glass crumbling around his arm, projecting reflections of the bathroom in a thousand different directions as each shard caught an image as it fell. The pieces made sharp tinkling sounds as they crashed to the dingy floor until they settled still, the sudden silence ringing in my ears even louder than the obscenely loud collision of his knuckles meeting the smooth surface.

Lottie hovered by the door, her hands brushing her throat as she fretted over whether to approach him or not. I didn't give her the chance to be his scapegoat. Where I wasn't sure she could handle him, I knew Power was at least an even match.

I took a hesitant step toward the fuming boy, shooting a stern glance at Lottie, telling her to stay put. He gripped the edge of the sink, hunched over the faucet as his shoulders heaved in his struggle to keep control. Every breath he took shot from his nostrils with force, drawing my attention to the way his jaw clenched so hard I was sure his teeth would shatter.

"George," I stated, fighting to stay calm. My hand, with reluctance, settled on his tensed shoulder. "Get it together. You're in control here, not your emotions."

A dark, sinister sounding chuckle erupted from his mouth as he moved to glare at me. "Emotions," he spat, curling his lips back in disgust. "Useless. They're a sign of weakness, and I am not weak."

"Of course not-"

He spun around, shoving me backward until my back hit the hard wall of the small bathroom. "Don't you dare try to patronize me!" he yelled, storming toward me with something closely related to what I had seen in his eyes the night he killed Ernie swirling around his hazel depths. From the doorway, Lottie gasped, her eyes welling up with unshed tears.

"George, please!" she cried, reaching out to touch him.

He turned on her, allowing me a brief second to catch the breath that had been knocked from my lungs.

"Sit down!" he snapped at her, shocking me cold. I'd never heard him use such a harsh tone on her, and judging from her own wide eyes and limp limbs, she'd never heard it either. Within a half a moment, she'd obeyed and slid to the floor, staring up at him with such fear that it gutted my heart from the inside out.

"You're scaring her," I said, evoking all the serenity and calmness I could into my voice, though my knees knocked together as they shook. I swallowed, eyeing the broken shards of the mirror closest to me in case I needed a weapon.

It didn't go unnoticed, of course. His gaze followed mine to the glittering glass pieces and he grinned as if he'd read my thoughts completely. "Not just her, it seems. What are you planning to do, Kate? Slit my throat, too?"

A violent wave of shivers caressed my spine at his tone. I bit my lip, pushing my fear of his unstable state back down. "If it protected Lottie and me, then yes," I told him, choosing to answer honestly because he clearly was not a fan of the careful handling I'd already tried.

His face twisted. "Lottie? You think I'd hurt her? After all I've put into protecting her?" After I've worked so hard to use her as my shield and manipulation tool? The words went unsaid, but I heard them all the same.

"You're not exactly predictable right now," I answered, not bothering to hide the fact that my fingers wrapped around of particularly large shard of glass. The jagged edges sliced into my own hand, producing fresh wells of scarlet blood to appear and drip onto the white floor. How much blood had the floors of Rosenton seen over the years? How many times had the pristine white tile been stained crimson?

George scoffed. "I would sooner cut off my own foot than harm her." Because she's what's keeping everyone else under my thumb. Again, more unsaid but clearly heard statements filled the air between us, and he knew it.

"He won't hurt me," Lottie whispered from her spot on the floor. I looked at the willowy girl, feeling the twisting of my heart tighten. The look of young love in her face, complete with adoration and idolization for good measure made me want to cry. He would never return the feelings. I didn't think he even could if he wanted to. But, the fierce protectiveness over her and his constant care blinded her to the obvious, and in that moment all I could feel for Lottie was overwhelming pity and sadness.

George grinned, pleased with her input. Lottie smiled back like a little girl basking in his approval.

"I know," I whispered, unable to look at her anymore. I could do nothing to help her. She would have to learn her lesson the hard way, and in that moment I knew the only thing I could do to help her was to be there when that lesson was learned. Before that, nothing and no one would be able to convince her of George's real motives.

"He protects the underdogs, Kate. Don't you see it yet? It's been so long since you got here. Surely you can see it? It's what he does. It's why he's here," she continued on, preaching at me with all the conviction of a fire and brimstone reverend. She walked over to me, one twiggish leg stumbling in front of the other. With gentle hands, as if I were the unstable one, she pried my fist open and plucked the shard of mirror from my grasp, dropping it to the floor. My eyes wouldn't move from the young girl, locked on her with such horror and fascination that there was no chance I'd be able to ignore anything she said.

"Why are you here?" I asked, directing the question to George, but never looking away from Lottie, who smiled up at me like a little girl trying to coax a stray dog to be petted. "You've killed, haven't you?"

"Of course I have. I'm too good at everything else to get caught. Of course, I could have killed more discreetly and no one would have ever been the wiser, but it was a calculated move. I needed to leave," he replied, as if 'needing to leave' justified murder perfectly well.

My gaze finally swung over to him, and my nose wrinkled at his disregard for human life. "What did you do?"

And just like that, at the snap of a finger, he was back to arrogant, gloating George. The George in control. The George that scared the daylights out of me every time he opened his mouth. The furious fire behind his eyes faded, replaced by an excited spark, and the tension in my body fled to make way for a giddy disposition that disturbed me on one too many levels.

He rocked back on his heels, crossing his arms over his chest and grinning like a Cheshire cat.

"I disposed of the threats to my..." He glanced at Lottie, sending the message loud and clear. "Friends. A bunch of kids at school liked to take advantage of the weaker specimens, so I eliminated the problem. With my father's .38 revolver."

My blood ran cold. "You shot up a school?" I stammered, the tingling in my fingers and toes warning me of the coming panic attack.

Kids. He'd killed other kids. For what? Bullying? What did he care? Did he have more like Lottie back home? More... friends? No, more like assets. Tools. Someone threatened his possessions, so he killed them?

There was no way to stop the vomit rising up my throat. I flung myself at the toilet at the far wall and heaved into it until all traces of my lunch left my stomach. Tears streamed down my face, a result of the vomiting mixed with the intense sorrow choking me alive.

A small, bony hand rubbed light circles on my back, while a quiet feminine voice shushed me, like a mother to a sick child. How did she find what he'd done okay? How did any of my ward mates find it okay? How did they converse with him every day, knowing what he'd done?

Shilling's words came racing back to me. 'Ward F is quite the ward. We put the most dangerous of our residents in your ward. Do you know why they're so dangerous? Because you are all perfectly aware of your capabilities. Your minds work on a level that is conscious and present. And yet, you've still done despicable things. You are very fortunate to not be in prison instead of here.'

I'd brushed it off at the time, thinking he couldn't possibly be telling the truth. My ward mates were good, inherently. I'd been so convinced. But this... What George had done... There was no good in it, no silver lining. Just a child himself, still, he'd killed other kids. Kids with moms and dads and futures. Kids who could have turned from their bullying, given the opportunity to mature and learn from it. Kids who might have apologized, had they the chance. Kids. He'd killed kids, and he held no remorse whatsoever for it. He all but bragged about it, like a trophy in his psyche, on a shelf.

And yet, here he stood, doing the even worse to not only Lottie, but the rest of the ward. He used an innocent girl as a shield and loaded gun at the same time.

"You're just a bully, too," I whispered, the revelation sending hot, steaming jolts of fury through me. "You're a bully, just like the kids you killed."

He laughed from behind me, as if I'd told a hilarious joke that only he got the punchline to. "How do you figure?" he asked, purely for amusement's sake.

The silver handle of the toilet lever gleamed at me, reflecting George's figure in a grotesque, distorted vision. I stared at it instead of turning to face him head on.

"You're no different. You pick on the weak. You even blackmailed me!" I snapped, glaring at his reflection still.

More laughter, even harder that time. He doubled over at the waist, clutching his stomach as he fought for air between loud, undignified guffaws. "You think I blackmailed you because you're weak? That little psycho in your head really has done a number on you, hasn't she? Weak! Weak! The very idea is ridiculous!"

"Blackmail?" Lottie asked, startling me. I'd forgotten her presence entirely.

"Then, why? Why use me? Why target me, if not because I'm weaker than you?!"

"Are you kidding?" he cried, thrusting his arms out wide, eyes bulging as his grin stretched to impossible lengths. "I picked you because you're not weaker than me! I picked you because you're probably the strongest person in this asylum, Kate! And if I have you, I have dominion over everything!"

The air, still heavy and wet with the remains of the storm, felt clogged in my lungs as I walked with the rest of my ward mates past the rose garden and toward the vegetable garden. Inside my head, Power fussed with her ponytail, griping about the humidity making her hair frizz.

"Do we have to?" Lottie whined, dragging her feet along the stone pathway like petulant child. Her bottom lip stuck out in a pout, reminding me of a toddler who wasn't getting her way.

"It's either work the garden or spend yet another day cooped up in that lounge," Esther replied, shooting a reprimanding look at the young girl. "John went through a lot of trouble to get it approved, and we'll have fresh food afterward, so stop complaining."

I hung back, grabbing Lottie's hand and offering her a small smile. All day I'd tried to purge our earlier fiasco in the bathroom from my mind, if only for my overstressed brain's sake. The weight of the world already crushed me beneath the burdens of everything pressing on my mind, fighting for resolve. George's revelations would have to take a back seat until I was sure I wouldn't have a mental breakdown when I thought about it.

"It'll be fun. And just think, Lottie. Fresh tomatoes. Fried, garden fresh squash. Cooked carrots. We'll eat like kings when we're finished. And it's good to be in the sunshine anyway."

She scoffed, making me realize the absurdity of my statement, trying to convince a girl who didn't eat to work by using food as encouragement. Maybe I was finally losing what was left of my mind.

Marcie bounced up to fall in step with us, intertwining her fingers with Lottie's free hand and shooting her a megawatt smile.

Look who's back to being happy. Thank goodness. Pitiful, sad, pathetic Marcie isn't nearly as entertaining.

"Come on, Lottie! We'll work together, yeah? We'll make a game of it or something. Anything is better than spending another day up there," she told her, hitching her thumb over her head to gesture at the skyscraper behind us.

With a frustrated growl in the back of her throat, Lottie nodded with reluctance and cracked a small half-smile at Marcie. The two girl began chatting, waving their free hands around and laughing. I took that as my cue to leave them to their own company, and I hung back even further, falling in step with John.

"Hard to imagine Marcie digging in a garden, but she seems eager," I quipped, eliciting a good natured smirk from him.

"She acts like she wouldn't be caught dead in anything less than a thousand bucks worth of jewelry and that a speck of dirt will give her cancer. But she loves it. I think it's relaxing for her, but we both know she'll never admit it."

I muffled a burst of laughter, giggling beneath my hand. His smirk transformed into a full grown grin, and he looked proud of himself for making me laugh.

He wants to impress you because he likes you, stupid.

"You'll have to show me how to tell which ones are ripe. I've never worked a garden before," I admitted, tucking my hair behind my ear. Dozens of unsolicited insecurities raced through my head, heating my cheeks. Things like, will a farm boy like him even want a woman who doesn't know how to work a garden? And, what good will I be to him as a wife if my only skills involve circus performances? Why would he want to be with a woman who doesn't know how to cook? Will he second guess his request to court me once he sees how clueless about normal life I am?

"I'll teach you. You'll pick it up in no time," John assured, casting a furtive glance around for orderlies or other staff who might witness the act of affection before taking my hand into the warmth of his and squeezing it in comfort. His entire form glowed with contentment and strength, lighting up the grin he sent my way.

You're flirting now? How do you even know how to do that? Power asked, tinkling laughter ringing in my ears. It's like you're a teenager!

Her blatant call out created a flood of heat that took up residence in my cheeks and the tips of my ears, but knowing John couldn't hear her words made me feel less self conscious about it. He still didn't know that Robbie had told me about his request, and every time I thought about it, huge, overjoyed butterflies took off in overzealous arches and figure 8s all over my stomach.

He wants me. He wants me. He wants me. The phrase repeated itself in my head over and over, as if hearing it enough times would make be believe it. The idea was just too good to be true, especially for a murderer like me. In a way, it terrified me because knowing how good it was cemented the fear that giving me that hope only to have me fall victim to Rosenton's demented games seemed like an appropriate cosmic consequence for my crimes.

You're such a drama queen. The adolescent angst is killing me, and you're twenty-four!

John's fingers tightened around mine, as if he knew Power was ridiculing me and wanted to comfort me. Impossible, of course. But I let myself pretend for just that moment that someone else could see her and tell me I was okay. That I had support, and someone to lean on when she pressured me too much.

The day grew older as the seven of us worked in the garden, pulling vegetables from the still moist soil. John's hand only released mine when he had to pull a particularly stubborn root, or when I needed both hands to pull something from its vine. True to his word, he not only told me, but showed me, how to tell which ones were ready to be picked and the best way to eat them. Patience and a lovely sense of gentleness that I'd forgotten him capable of emanated from his body as he instructed me on every detail, giving me handy tidbits of information about gardening and the harvest season that I stored in my brain, hoping I'd be able to use them in the years to come.

I had to wonder if John's intention to court me had anything to do with Robbie's decision not to reopen the circus, as well as his confidence that I'd be fine living a life as a non-performer, a normie. He'd told me several times that he'd teach me anything I needed to know, but the excuse had seemed so flimsy and breakable. Had he had some inkling all along that John would take care of me? Teach me how to survive off the land and walk around as if I'd never experienced the high of death defying acts and exaggeratedly beautiful performances? Was I even capable of that life? Could I be fulfilled, never showing off for an audience again?

I glanced up at John as he dropped a sunshine yellow squash into the canvas bag he'd brought with us, shuffling various vegetables inside it around to keep the crushable tomatoes at the top. Maybe my passion hadn't been destroyed so much as it had been transferred. I certainly felt the same warmth and overabundance of humbled ecstasy with John as I had with the circus. The same sense of peace and comfortableness cocooned me when I was with him, when before, the only thing to make me so content and happy had been soaring through the air, getting high off adrenaline and risk.

"It'll be dark soon. We should probably head on in," he commented, standing straight with a hand to his back to ease the aching, bunched up muscles there. Beads of sweat huddled around his hairline, gifting me with a glimpse of what he'd looked like on his farm in Texas, working all day in the sweltering heat. For a moment, I pretended that was the case. Rosenton didn't exist. We'd met in his hometown, gotten married, and worked his farm to make a living. In my alternate universe, I already knew everything he knew about gardening, alongside some delicious recipes I'd use to cook him supper with. We'd go back into the paint-chipped, white, wooden farmhouse, listening to the creaks and settling of the planks on the front porch as we made our way inside. He'd run himself a bath while I got to work in the kitchen, and, like a true gentleman, he'd wait for me to finish my own bath and join him before digging into the elaborate meal. We'd clean the dishes and go to bed together, exhausted and satisfied from another long day's work, content with the simple and fulfilling life.

"Finally!" Lottie exclaimed, throwing her too-thin arms in the air and breaking me away from my imagination.

How can such a drama queen be so incredibly boring? I nearly fell asleep there in the midst of your 'simple farm life'. Will you honestly give up the thrill of the performance for that malarkey?

The sight of John grinning at Lottie and ruffling her short hair like an older brother was all I needed for my short answer.

In a heartbeat.

Chapter 25

"Welcome back, Kate. Have a seat."

I lowered myself into the new leather chaise lounger Shilling had replaced the nice, normal chair with. The man had probably known that replacing a basic, comfortable chair with this confusing piece would set us on edge. Finding an acceptable position to sit in on the chaise felt impossible. I would have put my left arm through a meat grinder before dropping my guard and stretching my feet along the elongated cushion, but sitting sidesaddle only left me with the interesting and uncomfortable feeling of spending an hour without a backrest, with the arm of the stupid thing digging into the side of my thigh.

"We've had some interesting developments this week. Have you heard anything about it?" he asked, entirely too relaxed for me to believe that he was actually so apathetic about it. Of course, I knew what he was talking about. Nurses and orderlies hadn't been able to keep their gossip from leaking into every crevice of Rosenton's halls. News of Ernie's mysterious disappearance spread through the staff and residents alike like wildfire, though it seemed to be more entertaining than worrying to most. Apparently, Ernie's creepy advances and too-friendly touches spread over many different women, all brunettes and all petite. But, as relieved as I felt over that revelation, the fact that no stories of any of his other targets ever feeling anything more than mildly annoyed with his antics rather than scared settled uneasily in my stomach. He'd found something different about me that took his interactions with me to a higher, more disturbing level.

So, with the full knowledge that Shilling knew for a fact that I'd heard, I shook my head 'no' and stared at him with what I hoped was a blank expression. Power stirred beneath the surface of my mind, not liking the way he led the conversation. We both knew, from experience, that he often used that tactic to launch an attack of some sort, usually resulting in me fighting Power back down. Which, in turn, caused Power and I to be at odds for hours afterward, both angry with each other. Her, for my refusal to let her have control, and me, for her tendency to want to shoot first and ask questions later.

The doctor smirked and shifted in his leather desk chair, leaning back with his spidery fingers spread across his thin and fragile looking torso. He watched me, studying me with a gleam in his eye that told me to stay on guard, even more so than usual.

"It seems one of my employees has gone missing, and all evidence points to foul play. Would you know anything about that?" he prompted, raising one thick eyebrow over the golden rim of his oval glasses.

"I don't see how I would. I barely know most of your employees' names, much less their personal lives or schedules." Aloof confidence seeped into my tone, all impressively faked considering how shallow my breathing was becoming.

He hummed, tapping his pen against the ever present clipboard. Memories of my first ever session drifted to the forefront of my mind, reminding me of how much the incessant tapping had made me feel even angrier and crazier. Compared to then, I felt more sane than ever. Maybe all the events from the past few weeks had grounded me. Maybe the seriousness of every insane thing that had happened had snapped me out of my crazy for my own good.

Maybe it's been almost a year since it happened and you're coping. You over analyze everything.

I blushed at her simple, logical explanation. Why couldn't I have been the more logical one? Why was I, Sane, the one who always tried to look too deeply into things that were clearly cut and dry? I wanted, so badly, to believe her to be completely evil and useless. Admitting someone who murdered without a conscience possessed good qualities felt like a betrayal to the human race in general. But, I couldn't deny it. As much as I hated her, I cared about her and I needed her.

The similarities between the way I felt about her and George were astounding.

"That's interesting. Because we've come across some evidence that point in your direction, Miss Thornton."

My stomach flipped over and took a nose dive for my toes, before shooting back up to lodge itself in my throat. My head filled with static and heat rushed to the tips of my ears, while my lungs forgot how to do their job at all. I stared at Shilling, wide eyes and slack jawed.

Let me out! Power screeched in my ear, reminding me over and over of my promise to let her have control when situations like this happened. But, it wasn't out of control just yet. I needed to hear what he had to say. Maybe he was bluffing. Maybe he just wanted to rile me up for a reaction. A reason to send me to the thirteenth floor.

The thought of that possibility sobered me up and air rushed back into my chest, banishing the black and white static in my brain.

"That's preposterous. How could I have had anything to do with anything like that?" I asked, my voice light and breathy. Trying to regain some semblance of confidence, I cleared my throat and sat a little straighter, looking him in the eye.

"I'm sure we'll figure it out. His journals made your relationship with him very clear. I never thought you were the type to string along two men at once, but maybe I held too many expectations for a mass murderer. It must have slipped my mind." He said it with such flippancy, as if we were having a perfectly normal conversation.

He talks like that to make you feel uneasy. And it's working. Get it together and act innocent, stupid.

"Journals?"

"Yes. You didn't know? He kept them meticulously, apparently. A whole bookshelf full of them from this year alone. He had quite the obsession with you. I have to tell you, Katherine... The things we found out about the two of you would have made me fire him immediately. He knew intimate relationship with residents was strictly forbidden. I can't punish you, no matter how much I wish

I could. After all, you're not capable of making wise decisions. It's part of your diagnosis."

I gaped. "I never had a relationship with him! Ernie harassed me, but I never would have done anything to him!"

Chilling me to the bone and sending a thick sense of unease up my ramrod straight spine, Shilling burst into a wide grin, showing more teeth than I'd ever seen him show before. His lips disappeared into his mouth as his eyes lit up and his posture straightened with excitement. My body immediately recoiled and I prepared to leave my fate in Power's hands.

"So you have heard, then! I never mentioned his name on purpose, you know. How easily you tripped. Katherine!"

My blood ran cold, and without another moment's hesitation, I pulled the pin from the stone wall, watching it tumble down around Power. She surged forward, shoving me back as she fit herself in my body, cracking her neck side to side and wringing her limbs, as if settling into my skin for a good fit. I sank back, landing with so much force I rolled, on the dusty ground of my subconscious.

"Nice trick, doctor," she hissed, moving with the grace and fluidity of a snake preparing to strike. She stood and made her way toward him, trailing her fingers along the table and desk as she glided closer to him.

Think about the consequences before you do anything, Power, I reminded her, knowing if I didn't at least try to hold her back a little, she'd end up doing unspeakable things that landed us in even more trouble than we already were in.

Hips swaying in smooth circles and walking on the tips of her toes, just like the night she slunk through the circus campground to slit dozens of throats, she stopped in front of him and perched herself on his desk, knocking a few knickknacks to the floor with a quick flick of her wrist. With half hooded eyes, she pulled her fingers closer to her face and examined her fingernails, smirking at his discomfort. Shilling knew, judging from the guarded expression decorating his wary face, the stable Kate was no longer in the driver's seat and that he was dealing with the highly volatile Power. Though he couldn't have possibly known the details of the transformation. The fact that Power hadn't attacked him outright, as he'd expected, left him with tense shoulders and an unwavering gaze on her face, looking for any sign of the aggression he could use to send us to the thirteenth floor.

I felt her pleasure in his discomfort rumble beneath my feet as she reveled in the control she held over him.

"Now, what, exactly, are you hoping to accomplish by this little session?" she asked, flicking his nose with her thumb. My thumb. I shuddered at the thought of my skin touching his. "You want me to get violent? Lose my temper? Attack?" Her voice slid from between puckered, moist lips like silk ribbons, her tongue tying the pretty bows packaging each word.

"I'm a doctor, Kate. My aim is to make you better," he replied, suddenly very serious.

Power scoffed. "Oh, please, Shilling. We both know you want me," she paused for dramatic effect, raising her eyes to look at the roof as one slender finger pointed at the ceiling. "up there."

His arms crossed across his chest in a show of false arrogance. His bravado fell short of its desired effect, though, since the fear rolling off him saturated the air between Power and him. Even recessed into my own mind, I could taste the bitter emotion on my tongue, and Power grinned at the fact that she caused it.

"I'm sure I don't know what you mean, Miss Thornton. Are you have delusions of grandeur now? Thinking yourself more important than you are? Or maybe you're growing paranoid."

Her tongue clicked as she shook her head, smiling with a knowing gleam in her eye. "Defensive, I see. Trying to pin it back on me, because you know it's true." She looked back up into his wrinkled eyes, tilting her chin up and speaking into his ear with a lover's whisper. "You think that just because this body looks like something you could crush with your bare hands that I don't see the game you play with us? The fact is, doctor, one day I'll take everything from you. I'll take this building, your employees, your madness, and your life. I'll have it all in my pretty little palm, and you'll beg me for mercy. You'll cry and sob like a child, and it won't do you any good. You'll be terrified, and you'll crawl away on your hands and knees to escape. But... You won't be able to. You might not believe it yet, doctor, but you belong to me. You, and this entire establishment, and all the people and things in it. So, keep up your delusion of control over the situation. It won't last much longer."

I watched a bead of sweat form at his temple before racing down as he swallowed. His adam's apple bobbed, encased in the skin of his throat. Power caught sight of it as well, and leaned forward to pluck the fancy, gold plated pen from his shirt pocket.

"You're quite high on yourself, and you've hidden that exceptionally well behind this facade of insecurity, Katherine," he commented, his attempt to recover his cool obvious. His voice shook at the beginning, only smoothing out once Power leaned away from him, removing the cap from his pen with her nimble fingers. She studied the elegant personalization scrawl on the side of it, then flicked her eyes back up to catch his gaze on her.

"You're so frail. About forty, maybe fifty since I doubt you've ever worked outside a day in your life. And you had it all, didn't you? A prominent asylum with all the funding the government could ship, no government check-ins, because who cares about a bunch of criminals, right? They're just happy to not have us running amok with the rest of society. You have your secret thirteenth floor, where you do God knows what. You had it all, Shilling... You had it all. You lost it the day you accepted my admittance to your lovely home for the criminally insane."

He sat, frozen, when she leaned in, flipping the pen between her knuckles with ease. So quickly that he barely registered what was happening in order to react, she thrusted her hand out toward his neck, slashing a neat, thick, black line across his throat with the ink of his own pen. His hands flew to the mark, eyes bulging out of his head as he realized she could have killed him.

However, as soon as the shock melted away, a raging wildfire of fury swept in. He slammed one fist on the table while yanking open his desk drawer with the other. A cold, malicious glint filtered through his eyes and he drew up to make himself appear taller, stronger. A trick Power used often.

"Isn't it funny how one piece of material can make the most terrifying of demons buckle at the knees and lose that control they so cling to?" he asked, one corner of his lips lifting in premature triumph.

Power raised her hand with the pen in it, ready to stab him. I slammed my eyes shut so I wouldn't see her killing him, only to hear a knock at the door, freezing both Power and Shilling in their tracks.

"Your ward mates often make nuisances of themselves by coming to your rescue at oddly appropriate times," Shilling sneered, his chest rising and falling so quickly I wondered how he hadn't hyperventilated yet.

Power tossed her head back and let out a truly menacing ring of laughter. "Rescue me? Oh, sweetie! They just rescued you! I would have had your pretty little pen halfway buried in your throat by the time you could have even grabbed anything from that flimsy drawer."

"Enough!" he snapped, his face transforming into a rather horrifying shade of red. "I will not-"

Another knock at the door interrupted him, and he jumped, startled.

"Go ahead, doc. Answer the door," Power teased, tapping her fingers on the underside of his clenched jaw before sliding out of his path with a mockingly calm smile. He shot one last glare at her, then huffed an angry puff of air and stomped over to the door, flinging it open.

"Open them in your room," Robbie told me, sliding a box of drugstore chocolates across the visitation table toward me. I raised a puzzled eyebrow, but took the box, already opened and closed again judging by the lack of shrink wrap, between my fingers to fiddle with while we spoke.

"Um, thanks?" I replied, tilting my head in question.

He seemed off kilter. Below the table, his feet tapped and vibrated ceaselessly, and he drummed his fingers over the tabletop in the same fashion. But his facial expression gave no clues as to whether his actions were due to excitement or nervousness.

His eyes flicked to my face for the first time since I'd sat down, and all the itchy energy in his body came to a screeching halt. The color fled from his entire face and his jaw hung slack.

"Kate! What happened to you?!"

I looked away, trying to make myself seem smaller by shrinking into myself under his scrutiny. I'd been a fool to hope he wouldn't notice the bruises and injuries Esther's magic makeup still couldn't hide completely. She had layered the makeup so thick before that my skin had broken out in hives beneath the caked on oils and pastes. For the sake of my own already questionable sanity, she'd refused to put anything else on my face for the next week or so, putting the bright, blooming bruises on clear display for everyone to see.

Shilling said nothing about them. Asked no questions. Made no offhand comments. What does that tell you, Sane?

That, somehow, he knew more than he let on. Maybe Ernie had written even more, less vulgar, fantasies in his journals. Violent scenes in his head that Shilling and his staff assumed to be true events, explaining the injuries nicely. The thought that maybe I'd killed Ernie in a fit of rage and my wounds were a result of his defense might have crossed his mind also.

Though that still didn't explain why he hadn't dangled that in front of me.

"It's been taken care of, Robbie," I muttered, rubbing one of the nastier, darker blotches with the back of my hand and wincing.

"That wasn't what I asked," he snapped in return, leaning across the table to get a closer look. Concern settled into his visage, creating a deep frown in his brow.

A heavy sigh escaped my lungs. "An orderly. But, a friend took care of it."

Vulgar words that were new to even my ears flew from between his lips, and he rested his elbows on the table, shoving his hands through his long hair. "Eat all of those chocolates, okay? Make sure you eat them all, especially the ones at the bottom, do you understand?"

My mouth twisted into a still perplexed grimace, but I nodded anyway. "I will. Are they drugged or something?"

The smile he gave didn't reach his tired, hollowed eyes. "No, they're not drugged. Just make sure you eat them all. Preferably tonight."

"That's going to be one heck of a stomach ache tonight."

"Then share the top layer. But you eat the bottom layer, okay? I mean it. I... I picked them especially for you. To, ah... show how much I do care and to assure you of how hard I've been working."

Hearing Robbie stumble over his words sent up immediate red flags in my head, and my eyes widened in alarm. He was trying to say something, without saying it. Which only meant whatever he was trying to tell me could have no chance of being overheard. Loud, almost painful thumps of my heart beat into my chest.

"So what happened to the guy who did that to you? Did he get fired?" he asked, switching topics. The heel of his foot resumed its quick tapping against the tile floor, and he leaned over to inspect the injuries. I winced when his finger brushed one of the nastier bruises and he muttered a quick, quiet apology before leaning back in his seat.

I pushed my hair behind my ears, looking down at the speckled table and the shackles around my wrists. They were too tight again, but that hardly seemed like something to complain about considering everything else going on.

"Something like that," I muttered. "He won't be a problem anymore."

It had been a long time since the air between Robbie and I had been tense or heavy hearted, but as he studied my face, and most likely the way I refused to look at him, period, the atmosphere felt so thick that I could barely breathe it.

"By, 'a friend' who took care of it, you do mean a real friend, right? Not... Not the part of you that..."

"No!" I said, shaking my head back and forth in horror. "No, nothing like that has happened since... that night. It really was a friend who took care of the situation."

Though, what type of friend George was, and how much I actually trusted him as a friend, was still a puzzle to me.

Relief released the tension in Robbie's face and his eyes fluttered closed, as if he were saying a silent prayer of immense gratitude. "Good. Good. Okay. Alright. Good... Look, I... There's something that- I mean..."

I felt sick. Robbie didn't do this. He didn't lose his cool. He didn't stutter. An overwhelming sense of nausea swept around my insides as beads of cold sweat materialized on the planes of my forehead and cheekbones.

Drawing his hands through his hair, the motion making me see how oily and disheveled the strands seemed, he shook his head, as if clearing all the stumbling away. Taking in a deep breath, he leaned close to me, his mouth close to my ear. His hot, hurried breaths blasted the skin there before he spoke in a low whisper.

"You need to get out of here. You should have never been sent here. My cousin- I mean, our cousin freaked out when I asked him about the thirteenth floor. He screamed and fought and had to be sedated for the first time in years. He said the doctor cuts people open, while they're awake, up there. He experiments on them, from what I could gather out of the hysterical thrashing. Kate, you and your friends need to get out, now."

Chapter 26

White hot tears sprang to the backs of my eyes as the blood in my body all rushed around, panicked, before settling at the tips of my ears and limbs. I couldn't breathe. Oh, God, I couldn't breathe!

A string of the vilest, most vulgar curse words I'd ever heard in my life filled my head as Power's rage bubbled up and boiled over into my own psyche. She paced behind the wall, fingers dug into the roots of her shiny hair, gripping and yanking the silky strands as her chest heaved up and down.

Out! We need out! Not tomorrow! Not next week! Now! We need out! She shrieked as her long legs made jarring, shaky strides back and forth. Her hysteria added fuel mine and before I knew it, black spots were dancing in my vision and my tongue felt made of cotton. The cuffs around my wrists clanged and jiggled together against the table as what felt like ice water filled my body, producing such violent shaking and trembling that Robbie grabbed my shoulders and held me still.

"Kate! Kate, come on! Don't do this! Calm down, breathe. Breathe, dang it," Robbie said, his fingers digging into my shoulders. The pressure and pain of that simple motion grounded me, somewhat. Enough for the world to stop spinning out of control around me. I looked up at him, feeling like the blood vessels in my eyes would burst at any moment as tears trailed down my cheeks and jaw, leaving dark, wet spots on the table separating us.

"Hey! What's going on over there?" the burly orderly in the corner snapped, making his way toward us with an awkward, lumbering gait.

A fierce emotion I hadn't seen in Robbie's eyes before flickered up like a flame and he glared at the balding man. Just like his ability to attract and entrance thousands within a five mile radius, he seemed able to put off a threatening vibe that made him seem like a terrible nightmare for anyone who crossed him. The orderly's eyes widened, and he took a hesitant step back, crossing his arms defensively, as if he expected Robbie to attack him.

"Nothing of your concern, dip stick. Go sit in your corner and leave my sister alone," he answered, standing and squaring his shoulders as he stared down the chrome dome three times his size.

"Robbie, no!" I cried, trying to stand. My hands, still locked to the cuffs on the table, jerked me back down and I fell back onto my seat. "He probably just wanted to make sure you weren't hurting me!"

Fat chance of that.

I didn't even try to hurl an insult back at Power for stating the obvious. I just needed to reason with Robbie enough to not get him arrested or kicked out. I still needed him. Especially after what he'd just told me. I had to have more information, and I had to have his help in finding a way out of here.

"That true?" Robbie asked the nervous orderly, who shifted from one foot to the other, breaking eye contact.

"Yeah," he replied. "She just seemed upset. I'll leave you to your visit."

He didn't even verify Robbie wasn't hurting you, Power noted, rolling her eyes as she sank to her knees in the dust, calming down from her hysteria.

Within seconds, the orderly had returned to his post in the corner of the room, and Robbie sat back down in front of me, his face lacking any of his mischievous mirth from our previous meetings. He shook his head, then ran his hand through his hair again and left it there, resting his elbow on the table.

"Your cousin survived, right?" I whispered, twisting my fingers inside my hands.

"Yeah. Our cousin survived, but only because his mom felt guilty about leaving him here. She got a lawyer and brought him back home, under the stipulation that he not leave the property, ever again. I... I've already tried finding a lawyer who will do the same for you, but none will come within a ten mile radius of your case." He looked down as he said the last part, fists clenched under the table.

"They think I'm a monster. Of course they won't take it on. Would you, if you didn't know me?" I asked, holding no grudges against men who thought they'd be pure evil by aiding in my release. "Plus, I think Shilling would fight it tooth and nail. Esther said he's targeted me."

"Targeted you, how?"

I took a deep breath, inhaling the scent of bleach and old medicine. "He keeps trying to trigger an episode where I lose my mind again. Like he wants me to attack him. I think it's so he can send me to the thirteenth floor."

Every ounce of color in his face drained, leaving a ghostly white, horrified shell of my ringmaster.

"We've gotta get you out. You and your ward mates," he said, absolute fear swirling in his grey eyes. "I'll work on everything day and night. You just get back to your room and eat those chocolates. Every last one, do you hear?"

This time it was my eyes that widened as he stared into them, commanding me, not as my brother anymore, but as my boss. "Yes, Robbie," I replied, old habits rising up to meet the somewhat familiar situation.

We sat in silence for several seconds while he stared at me, searching my face with desperate eyes for something I couldn't possibly decipher on my own. Finally, he spoke again, taking my hands in his and squeezing.

"I have to go," he said, making my heart drop into a pit in my stomach. "But, I'm coming back in three days. I need you to work on finding a way out, just in case my plans fall through. You have to be your own backup plan, got it?"

My chest tightened as more tears surfaced as a result of the resounding fear echoing all around me. I squeezed his hands and my eyes slammed shut against the terror taking over my body.

"Please don't leave. Please. Don't leave me here, Robbie. I'm scared," I whimpered, trembling as my voice cracked against the emotion building in my throat. I laid my forehead down against our clasped hands, unable to control the quiet sobs making their way through my chest. His hands tightened around my fingers, and I felt him lay his head on top of mine, shaking and quivering just as much as me.

"I'm so sorry," he breathed, over and over again repeating those three words. His deep, always confident voice cracked and I knew he was either crying or on the verge also. "I'll be back, I swear. I won't leave you here. I'll get you and your friends out, somehow. Please, just eat those chocolates. I left something special for you at the bottom, Kate. I'm not abandoning you here. You won't die here. I swear."

It was a miracle of itself that my legs carried me all the way back to Ward F's floor. They shook like a newborn foal's new legs the entire way, and the jarring hiccups that made my weak body even more unsteady only made the trip more difficult. My chest spasmed and jerked with each sobbing breath, and by the time I made it through the door to my floor, I knew I wouldn't be able to hide my blotchy, hysterical state from any of my ward mates.

Just go to the shower room, Power mumbled, her head aching and her body drained from the emotional whirlwind. Clean yourself up and pull yourself together. We have work to do.

I obeyed her without a moment's hesitation, almost as if I was on autopilot. My legs moved on their own, without instruction from my brain, toward the women's showers, the white tiles even colder than normal through my thin socks. Or maybe shock was settling in and my body wasn't registering everything properly.

As had become habit, I let the shower water pelt me, the temperature up as far as I could get it without leaving blisters on my black and blue skin. Everything ached, and my muscles screamed in protest, begging to rest. I soothed their wails, promising only a few more minutes of standing before I'd shuffle along to my room and pass out on my little bed.

Are you stupid? Power asked, sounding genuinely curious more so than insulting. You can rest all the time in the world after we escape! Did you not hear what he said? Medical experiments, Sane! Look, I know you're technically crazy and all, and so am I, but this is a whole new level. He's sick and demented, and he has you in his sights as the next target for those experiments! We need to get out!

Her words terrified me, rattling my very bones down to the core, but years training while exhausted left me with some perspective on fatigue and the failures brought thereof. Creating an escape plan on such short notice while my brain wanted to shut down from all the pressure overwhelming me would only lead to absolute catastrophe. Much less actually carrying out that plan. To do so would mean doom from the start. I had to give myself and my friends a chance.

Power took in my thought process, mulling it over with a scared, critical eye. I don't like it. I think you should go get everyone right now and make a break for that hole in the fence within the hour. But, I gather you're not going to do that. You're going to regret that, Sane... Her voice sounded so melancholy, so prematurely remorseful, that I had to clench my jaw against more tears.

She had the right to disagree with my choice, but at the end of the day, it was my choice to make.

And I needed to wait long enough to prepare a solid, steadfast plan.

I finished the rest of my shower with graduated slowness and stiffness. The bruises hurt, my face felt tight and swollen from the constant tears, my legs trembled with the effort to stay upright, and my brain pleaded with me to just let it shut down for a little while to recoup.

Sliding my clothes back on, I scooped up the box of chocolates Robbie had given me and popped one in my mouth. I'd share them with everyone else. It was the only way I could see them being eaten as quickly as he wanted. Had I been in my right state of mind, I would have been curious about his intentions behind the strange gift, but as it was, all I wanted to do was stop thinking and using my imagination. Too many horrifying images filled my mind each time I opened the possibility.

Moving slowly, I exited the shower room and walked, with a stiffness that belied my desire to just drop to the floor in a useless heap, toward my room. My eyes wandered up the sides of the pearly walls until they landed on one of the many utilitarian clocks gracing the many hallways. Just after noon. Everyone else would be at lunch, but the thought of food made me want to burst into tears all over again.

I leaned against the wall, pressing my forehead against the frigid surface as I tried to regain some semblance of strength. Footsteps approached from the adjoining hall, coupled with another set of heeled ones. Staff, not patients, judging by the fact that they wore shoes at all. A loud internal groan of frustration made its way up my gut. They'd make me go to the cafeteria if they saw me.

Forcing my body to exert just a little more effort for my own sake, I stumbled into one of the supply closets and closed the door. My back slid down against the door until I sat in a crumpled heap on the tiles below. The scent of bleach and mop water filled my head, sending my perception into a frenzy of dizziness. If I never smelled bleach again after escaping this prison, it'd be only too soon.

The footsteps drew closer, near enough for the voices accompanying them to come into range also. A man and woman, I gathered, while waiting for them to get even closer so I could make out their words. I pressed my ear to the cool wood of the door, straining to listen in.

"I know it was on purpose." My heart began to race. I couldn't have mistaken Paul's silky, snake like voice in a million years. "The remains were burned and buried, for goodness sake! Anyone with half a functioning brain could tell you that it was murder. And if those remains don't belong to Ernie, I'll eat my own socks!"

"I'm not saying it's not. I'm just saying the girl you're trying to pin it on makes no sense." The woman's voice fell familiar on my ears, but I couldn't place it. I turned to face the door, pressing myself even harder against it in an attempt to recognize the firm, authoritative tone.

"Then who? She's been seen flirting with him, trying to get his attention. She's the only suspect, Martha."

Martha?

Slowly, for which I'd blame on sheer exhaustion, an old rusty light bulb seemed to click on over my head. Martha! Martha West, the woman in charge of the nurses and orderlies. The one who approved our trips to town and supervised over our floor. The one Marcie had pleaded with to let me go on a shopping trip with her and her mother.

"You saw Ernie's journals. He was obsessing over the other girl. What if he made a move on her? She's clearly the most unstable person in this entire establishment. You need to look into the possibility that she did it. She's capable, and it's probable."

"I don't need to do anything. Are you forgetting who the employer is, Mrs. West? I tell you what to do, not the other way around."

"Yes, and your employer is Dr. Shilling, Paul. If you don't look into the matter the way you should, I'll go straight to him and make sure it gets done anyway. I don't want to see an innocent girl get taken away because you don't want to listen to a woman. Your pride is going to get an innocent girl killed."

He laughed then, making me shudder against the door. "Innocent? This is a home for the criminally insane! No one here is innocent, and they're all capable of doing what was done to that body downstairs. You need to get your head out of the clouds. This has nothing to do with you being a woman, and everything to do with your obvious favoritism toward your niece. The evidence-"

"Then why put me on her floor, Paul? You know I care about her, and I promised her mother I'd look after her! And evidence? What evidence? A bunch of circumstantial crap that wouldn't hold up in court? You'd be laughed out by the judge."

"So you admit to blatant favoritism?"

The silence rang around me. Their footsteps paused, leaving an empty void of nothingness while I waited, sweat dripping from my neck, for them to continue.

"That's not what-"

"You're fired, Martha, for impeding a federal murder investigation with favoritism. We can't have uncooperative staff here at Rosenton, as you well know."

"You can't do that! You haven't even called the police yet! If you do at all!"

"I just fired you, Mrs. West. Now, I suggest you pack your things and leave before I have to have an orderly who used to work for you escort you from the premises."

The heeled shoes scuffled around before taking off in a furious hurry. They paused one last time before disappearing completely.

"I'll see to it that you hear from my lawyer, Paul. Be expecting a phone call by the end of the week."

"Looking forward to it, Martha. Now run along. Wouldn't want to get you in a tizzy."

Martha said something back, but my eyelids felt far too weighted down to comprehend it. Finally, the fatigue took over and I nodded off against the supply closet door, drifting away into a swaying, ocean-like slumber.

Chapter 27

I woke some time later. An irritating, thin layer of film sealed my eyelids together, having been produced from the sharp chemical fumes of the various cleaning agents surrounding me. My legs stretched out as I pushed myself up to sit upright, and I palmed at my aching eyes and temples.

Too much had happened too quickly. It seemed that one horrible thing barely passed by before another took its place, and the ache in my teeth from the constant grinding they'd been doing in my sleep attested to my never waning panic and stress. I closed my eyes and sighed, leaning my head back against the door with a dull thud.

Martha had been Marcie's aunt. That explained why the young woman had been so comfortable with her and had expected her to roll over and let me go to town with her so long ago. She must have been the only other thing keeping Marcie from going to the thirteenth floor after her episode. Aside from John's great sacrifice, anyway. No wonder the girl had flitted around without a care in the world. She had someone who could do something on her side the entire time.

I wondered if any of our other ward members knew about it. Surely I'd have heard something in passing conversation by now if they did. But, why would she keep it secret?

Stop playing psychiatrist. Just go ask her, stupid.

Another weighted breath inflated my chest and I let it fly from my lips in a disgusted raspberry sound. Did it even matter if anyone else knew? Did it matter at all? What difference did it make? Marcie didn't want to leave anyway, so Martha was most likely only there to make sure she stayed on the safe side of the asylum. And, that was a good thing.

Right?

Either way, I needed to get off the dingy supply closet floor and go find her. I hadn't checked on her in days, and there was no telling where she was on the limited, yet volatile, spectrum of emotions she possessed. I could only hope for the happy side, because it seemed no one except me wanted anything to do with her during the other phase.

With every muscle crying out in protest, I stumbled to my feet and left the closet. The bright florescent lights in the hallways felt like scalding water on my eyes, and I groaned as they tried to adjust past the pain.

Your body is shutting down, because of the stress. You can't handle it, Sane. We need to escape before you're even more useless than you already are.

I ignored her and gritted past the aches and pains in my stiff body, walking in a jagged line toward the lounge. I passed by Marcie and Lottie's room on the way and poked my head in the door, hoping she'd be in there so I wouldn't have to walk any further. Lottie shook her head with a small smile when I asked if she was in there with her.

"I haven't seen her all day," she added. Then, "Are you alright? You look... tired."

In other words, I looked like death warmed over, chewed up and spit out. It didn't surprise me because that's how I felt, too.

"I'm fine," I replied, waving my unruly hair from my face. "Just need a few more hours of sleep at night, is all."

"Well, you do that. You look like you need it."

And you look like you need a sandwich, anorexic brat.

I mentally scolded Power for her insensitivity, then left the room in search of the blond beauty.

The lounge doors squeaked horribly when I opened them, causing everyone's heads to turn to me. I smiled a tired, apologetic smile and scanned their faces for Marcie, only to come up empty.

"Has anyone seen Marce?" I asked, flicking my gaze from John, to Esther, to Ed. George and Marcie were nowhere to be seen.

"Not since earlier today. She's not in her room?" Esther asked, raising a sharply penciled in eyebrow. Her makeup seemed slightly off. Her usually elegant eyelashes were clumpy and thick. Her eyebrows had been penciled in with a heavy hand. Her red lip stain feathered out around the minuscule wrinkles surrounding her lips. All things she had drilled into my head as felony grade beauty faux pas.

The stress is eating her, too. I'm telling you, Sane. We need to get out now, and make a plan once we're all out. This won't end well, the way you're wanting to do it. Everyone is breaking down.

"No. Lottie said she hasn't seen her either."

Ed stood from his seat, where his knees had nearly reached his ears in the chair that seemed three sizes too small for him. He unfolded himself until he stood straight, his shoulders brushing the top of the tall window frame beside him. "I'll go ask an orderly if they've seen her," he said, then left the room without waiting for a reply.

The three of us remaining stared at each other in silent tension, feeling the dangerous shift in the air. The timing of her aunt's pink slip and Marcie's disappearance was too obvious to be a coincidence, but I shoved the thoughts aside to keep myself from panicking. But did Esther and John know about it?

"She may be in the shower room," Esther offered, scrunching up her nose at how weak the excuse sounded, even to her own ears.

John said nothing then entire time, his tanned face pale and cloaked in a thin layer of nervous sweat. Dark grey circles framed his eyes, giving him a skeletal appearance that pulled at my heartstrings. Had he been having nightmares like I had? Did he see Ernie's scarlet blood dripping behind his eyelids when he closed his eyes, like I did? Did the guilt of taking yet another human life eat at him until he felt like nothing but bare bones, like my guilt did?

"Did you guys know the head nurse was her aunt?" I blurted, desperate to get my thoughts away from the dark and twisted imagery Ernie's death brought. Their wide eyes and stunned faces gave me the answer better than any words ever could have.

"What?" John asked, cocking his head at an angle.

"The head nurse? You mean Martha?" Esther said at the same time.

I nodded, biting the inside of my cheek and hoping Marcie wouldn't be too angry with me. "Yeah. I heard Paul talking to her, and he fired her. He said since she was her niece, she was showing favoritism and hindering an investigation. He fired her on the spot."

The two ward mates turned to look at each other, an impossible to decipher silent conversation flicking between their eyes. So they hadn't known. What did that mean? Why had Marcie hidden it?

"No wonder she never got taken to the thirteenth floor. Martha was her buffer. No one can be taken without the head nurse's consent." Esther began to pace as she spoke, hands perched on the curve of her hips.

John shook his head slightly at me when I opened my mouth to protest that he'd been at least half of the reason Marcie hadn't been taken. My mouth snapped shut and I shuffled on my feet, biting my lip.

"Paul was blaming Marcie for Ernie's disappearance... And..." Tears pricked at my eyes as the impact of what I'd heard finally came crashing down. "And, they found Ernie. They were arguing about who'd done it. Paul is sure it was Marcie, and Martha was trying to tell him it was me. I don't know what to do or say or..." I trailed off, swiping the back of my hand across my wet cheeks as my vision blurred with more tears.

A loud thump had me looking back up to see John slumped over in one of the scratchy orange chairs. He held his face in his hands, the rest of him limp as a rag doll, as if he were defeated beyond the brink of hope. My lip trembled as I took in the broken form of the man who'd been the source of strength for all of us for so long. He'd given us too much. Too much, and now he didn't have anything left for himself. I felt horribly, criminally selfish for taking and taking and taking from him. No one could shoulder it all alone. Not even the golden boy, John Kingwood.

I made my decision then. I couldn't add more to his plate anymore. I had to take on the ward's problem, myself. I'd make our escape plan, myself, and allow him the right to follow instead of lead for once. He, of all people, deserved that reprieve, especially after all he'd already done for us and how much of himself he'd given for our wellbeing.

Drying my tears, I sniffled away my emotion and channeled Power and her ability to be in control of every situation. She would know what to do. Her ability to remain calm and flippant would anchor my worries and inner hysteria. I couldn't afford to be the sniveling, scared little girl anymore. I had to be strong. I had to be a woman instead of a child relying on everyone else to take care of me. It was my turn to take care of them.

"I'm going to find Lottie," I announced, clearing my throat of the emotion clogging my voice. "She might have seen which direction Marcie went when she last saw her."

Neither Esther nor John so much as looked at me, both too drained to acknowledge anything but their own concerns. They seemed broken. Like a pair of boots that'd been worn too many times over rough ground.

Not waiting any longer, I turned and fled the room, heading straight for Lottie once more. Even if she could just point me in the direction Marcie had left in, it would be better than the nothing we had to go on currently.

"Lottie!" I said, barreling into her room and closing the door behind me. She jumped, startled, and looked up at me with wide eyes. “Which way did Marcie go when you last saw her? Do you remember her telling you anything at all?” The words flew from my lips in a breathless heap, small wheezing sounds punctuating the end of each syllable.

“What’s going on?”

This time it was me who jumped, pressing my hands to my chest to try and slow down my thrashing heart. George stood behind me, somehow having sneaked into the room after I’d closed the door.

So, in a bout of near hyperventilation, I recounted the information I’d given Esther and John. George took the news in a much calmer way than they had, but it was to be expected. Nothing shook George Baker. Nothing upset him. Nothing made him lose his cool.

“Well, aren’t the secrets just flying from the woodworks now,” he muttered, rubbing his smooth jaw with the palm of his hand. His eyes narrowed as he stared at the far side of the room’s ceiling. “And no one has seen her all day, yes?”

My head bobbed up and down affirmatively.

“The last time I saw her, she was heading for breakfast. I assumed she’d be in the lounge or that maybe she got a visitor,” Lottie’s timid voice peeped. The skin of her throat clenched as she swallowed nervously. “Do you think something’s happened to her?”

Yes! Something horrible! Something that we can’t even imagine!

“I don’t know. But nothing good happens here once the staff gets involved. We should find her,” I said instead. She nodded, and for the first time in a while, I paused to take the time to really look at the fourteen year old girl. Her dress hung from her skeletal frame like a depressed, hopeless tent. Her body held no womanly curve, like it should have been beginning to hint toward at her age. There seemed to be no muscle between her skin and her bones, with the way every joint protruded, jutting out so far that I wondered how she didn't have bedsores sleeping in a body so uncushioned. The veins in her hands looked like mountain ridges on a map, and her pale skin looked weak and translucent. But, it was her eyes that haunted me. Surrounded by a deep circle of mottled red and black, with chapped lips set beneath a red nose, her eyes looked nearly hollowed out in their sockets.

What had brought someone so young and seemingly innocent to a place as tainted and blackened as Rosenton?

And maybe the more important question... What had brought her to the decision to live her life, wasting away into nothing? What had happened in her childhood to make her decide that denying herself the very thing responsible for keeping human beings alive was her enemy? Where had such a mindset come from, and how did she justify it?

"I know what you're thinking," she whispered, looking back and forth between George and I. Like she wanted to tell me a great secret, but needed his permission first.

"What am I thinking, Lottie?" I asked, my voice just as soft as hers. My heart ached for her and whatever mental torment she lived in.

"That it's not so hard to just pick up the fork and eat something. But, you're wrong. It's near impossible, not that someone perfect like you would understand."

I scoffed. "I'm not perfect. Not by a long shot. If you knew-"

Go ahead. Tell her why you're here. Tell her about me. It's high time the rest of the ward know the completed Katherine Thornton.

"Please. You're as close to normal as it gets. You shouldn't even be here and everyone knows it," she said, her bony fists clenching and unclenching as tears pooled in her eyes.

"You're so wrong, it's not even funny. But, I don't think it's easy for you to eat. It's easy to everyone else, but not you. And I know you have a reason for that. I won't judge you for that. We just want you to be healthy, is all."

George remained silent behind me, where Lottie could see him but I couldn't. Whatever signals, if any, he gave to her went unnoticed by my eyes as I waited for her reply. Lottie fidgeted with the material of her dress as she looked out the window, refusing to meet my gaze.

"It was my cousin," she finally spoke in a deceptively calm tone. "My aunt and uncle died in a car crash, so my parents took him in. In the beginning, everything was fine. He mostly just stayed in his room. My parents said he was grieving. But, eventually, I guess he got over it because he started sneaking into my room at night, doing horrible things to me. He was fifteen and I was only nine. It was awful. So, when his nightly visits lessened, I thought it was over. But, I caught him looking in my little sister's room one night, his hand on the doorknob like he was about to go in there."

Her jaw tightened as her teeth gnashed together in her mouth, producing loud clicking sounds that made me wince. "So, I stopped him and told him to leave her alone. I'd take whatever he wanted to dish out to her, and I wouldn't tell anyone. He agreed, and it all started again. But, eventually, I wasn't enough, I guess. And I was so broken and scared all the time. He did awful, twisted things to my mind, making me believe all sorts of things about myself that I know aren't true. George has shown me that," she added, looking at the teen behind me with such utter adoration that I nearly wept.

"Go on, Lots," he urged, his tone gentle and encouraging. Somewhere in the back of my mind, I knew better. I knew he was acting.

Like a danged professional, he was acting. But, she idolized him and worshipped him with so much sheer love that I couldn't bring myself to shatter her by letting her think the truth, even for a moment.

"Then, he started going to my sister's room at night. I'd stay up til dawn, knowing I had to stop him and catch him each night before he got to her. I never slept, and everything just started feeling not so right in my head. Things didn't add up. Normal, everyday things. I couldn't remember how to use a fork. I would forget to bathe for days. But, it was all in the back of my mind. Protecting my sister was all I thought of. I obsessed over it. So, when her birthday came around, and I caught him with her in his bedroom, it all came crashing down. What little bit of myself I'd kept was gone. It was her birthday, for crying out loud. I wanted to kill him! I wanted to hurt him so badly he'd never recover. But he was much stronger than me, and I'd never be able to pull it off. So, I told my parents what he'd been doing..."

I knew what was coming next, and I hated myself for listening to it. For letting her speak something so hurtful and sickening that it made me want to vomit.

"They didn't believe me. Told me I was a liar and to apologize to him. Then, they sat me down and told me how serious the accusation I made was, and how things like that ruin peoples lives when they aren't true. But it was true! I kept trying to tell them, but they wouldn't have it. And the only thing that made sense at the time was to take what he wanted from him, while saving my sister from him at the same time. I put arsenic- a lot of arsenic- in her cake. I didn't want her dead. I just didn't want him to hurt her. I wanted her to stay pure and innocent and small. Small enough that he wasn't interested in her. I wanted her to stay as small as I wished I was." She sucked in a deep, trembling breath, as if she wanted to say more but stopped herself.

"So, that's why you don't want to eat? You want to stay little? You don't want to become a woman?" I asked, tucking some of her short hair behind her ear. She shed no tears as she told her story, and she didn't break down and cry afterward either. Maybe she'd cried too much over it already. It'd been five years ago, and already she showed signs of mental defense mechanisms to rival adults with life spans filled with trauma. Had George taught her that? Like a machine that was broken, had he "fixed" her to get her up and running again so he could use her for his own personal gain?

Lottie nodded in answer to my question and looked over to George again. His shoes scuffed the tiles behind me as he walked leisurely over to her, pressing his hand onto her shoulder. She smiled up at him, seeing the gesture as kind and comforting, while I bit my lip and saw it as controlling and a way for him to steer her where he wanted her.

"We should go to the lounge and see if they've found Marcie," I mumbled, unable to look at his trickery anymore. She'd left her life with one evil mentor just to be thrust into life with another, and I wasn't sure which of the two were more dangerous.

Without waiting for them to follow, I turned and left the room to go meet back with John and Esther in the lounge. Every problem we faced raced around in my head, bouncing off the walls of my skull and begging for resolution. The problem lied in my lack of possible answers. Power screamed at me to just gather up my ward mates and escape through the hole in the fence that very moment, but with no provisions, shelter, or outside support, I wasn't sure we'd make it alright.

I shoved my hands into my skirt pocket in frustration. The smooth edges of the box of chocolates Robbie had given me reminded me of its presence, making me pause.

"Is there a problem?" George asked from far too close behind me. A sharp, startled intake of air from a little further to the left signaled Lottie's presence as well.

I shook my head, the ends of my long hair whipping to and fro with the exaggerated force of it. "No. I'm just trying to come up with a plan," I said, yanking my hand from my pocket as I continued my journey to the lounge room in a dead sprint. George and Lottie ran to keep up with me, somehow knowing the severity of the situation without asking a single question about my sudden burst of panic.

I flung the doors open and pulled the small box from my pocket, prying the tin lid off and flinging it to land on the coffee table in the center of the room.

"Here! Eat!" I snapped, shoving a chocolate truffle at each person.

"What the heck?" John asked, grasping my shoulders to try to calm my frantic movements. I shrugged him away and handed piece after piece of chocolate to him, George, Esther, and Lottie until the box was empty. I stared at the bottom of the empty box, eyebrows drawn together in a deep chevron of confusion.

There was nothing there.

Nothing but the blank bottom of the box. No hidden message. No magical master key to help us escape. No phone number to reach Robbie at. Nothing.

My heart deflated in my chest and I sank to one of the scratchy armchairs in defeat, still clutching the empty box in my hands. "I don't understand," I whispered to no one as a wave of hopelessness cocooned me in its weight. "He said to get to the bottom of the box..."

Warm, heavy hands took the box from me and laid it on the coffee table with a slight clink as the tin box met the wooden surface. The hands returned to me, wiping my tangled hair from my face and holding my cheeks between them. Hands so warm they could have only belonged to John.

"What's going on?" he asked, in a tone one would use on a hysterical child. "What was supposed to be in the box?"

"I don't know," was my weak, whimpering reply. I met his earthy eyes with my own, pleading with him to believe me and not think I had finally lost my mind completely.

A film of something resembling sadness, or maybe pity, covered his gaze at my words. He did think I'd begun to lose it. I groaned and pulled his hands from my face to hold them in my own. My fingers squeezed around his as I implored him to believe me silently.

Before he had a chance to answer, the door swung open yet again, making all our faces jerk to see who'd entered.

Ed stood in the doorway, sweat pouring from his ghostly pale brow. His eyes were wild and panicked as they flicked between each of us, his huge body trembling so much that his hand jiggled the doorknob he still held onto, as if it could support him.

"They've got her," he stammered, looking weaker by the minute.

That's what raw fear looks like, Sane. No filters, or attempts at bravado. Just pure, uncut fear.

"What do you mean? Who?" Esther asked, though we all knew the answer.

"The staff. They've taken Marcie to the thirteenth floor."

Chapter 28

The doors to the gymnasium opened with a loud creak. I kept my eyes on the floor, still seething about my ward mates' decision to do absolutely nothing for Marcie. They'd left her to her fate, saying there was nothing we could possibly do. But, there had to be something, and I intended on finding out what.

John had tried to hold my hand, like normal, on the walk from breakfast to Physical Activity, but the anger at him and the others had me yanking my hand back while shooting a nasty glare at him. The guilt and sadness written all over his face would have softened me toward him on any other day, but all I could see when I looked at him was his silence when George took over as unofficial leader of our little group and proclaimed it too dangerous to try to get her back. Like mindless drones, they'd all nodded. Except for John, who'd sat slumped in his chair, looking like a corpse as he acted as if his input couldn't change the outcome. He hadn't nodded, but he hadn't opposed it either, and for that I lost a large amount of respect for him.

His hand slipped over mine again, and again, I jerked back. But, this time, he only squeezed harder and pulled me to a stop. Opening my mouth to dish out a scathing reprimand, I spun to face him. The colorless shade of his face and fearful, panicked eyes made me stop.

"Kate," he whispered, sounding very much like a scared little boy. It was strange seeing the man I'd come to see as an alpha male reduced to something so broken and tired. "Don't turn around. Get out of here."

My eyebrows crinkled up in confusion. "What?"

"Just go. I'll tell them you're sick," he demanded, his shoulder squaring as some of the old John seeped into him.

"Why?"

His lips parted as he prepared to speak, but another hand on my shoulder shifted my attention from him and to the person touching me. John's eyes blanked over before he squeezed them shut, as if he'd lost or regretted something important. The hand on my shoulder turned me to face the owner of it. Paul stood in front of me, a deceptively warm smile fixed on his face.

"Hello, Kate. Ready for some sack races?" he asked, a kind expression frozen on his face. Like he'd practiced that one expression, but none of the natural movements associated with it. Chills ran down my back, making me shiver and take a pronounced step back away from him and into John.

"Uh, sure," I stammered, not missing the satisfied glint in his eye as he nodded and walked back toward the center of the room. Before I could examine the contents of the gymnasium, John had spun me around again to face the doors.

"Just leave, Katie. Please," he begged. His chest heaved with his building panic.

"What's going on? Why?" I repeated, fear crawling around like tiny insects in my belly.

"They're trying to trigger you. They're acting on the target they've painted on your back. Please. Don't look. Just go."

"Kate! John! We're about to begin!" Paul called. A rustling sound floated into my ears from the center of the gym, causing Power to perk up and me to turn, seemingly in slow motion, to see what the fuss was about.

At the sight of dozens of large, industrial sized burlap sacks lying on the polished wooden floor, every muscle in my body locked in place. Before I could think a single, comprehensive thought, I felt myself being yanked from my neck below the surface of my mind. Power shoved me down, landing her sparkling red heels in my torso and using the momentum to kick off me and surge up to take control.

My body seized up, head lolling backward as my legs and arms shot ramrod stiff at my sides. I felt my fingers and toes curling with the strain my muscles were exerting. Loud, cracking sounds popped from the joints in my spine as my back began to curve backward, leading my body into a back bend without the support of my arms to steady my balance.

I watched from inside my head as John rushed to me, gathering my mangled form into his arms as he tried to bring me back. He couldn't have known how useless his attempts were. None of my ward mates had ever seen Power's reaction to burlap, and how it brought such a strong nostalgic reminiscence of her night of glory that I was powerless to deny her. John only knew to warn me because I'd told him of it.

How stupid I'd been to not listen to him when he'd told me to run and not look back. Like Lot's wife in the Bible, I'd looked back when I should have been fleeing, discarding his frantic warnings, and paid dearly for it.

Fire burned up and down my throat, ripping my esophagus as my muscles struggled to contort and writhe against John's frantic, but soothing, touch. Dozens of footsteps scrambled toward me as Power slid into my skin, forcing it to relax and allow her to guide it. It must have sensed the danger in bowing to her wishes, because, like a wounded dog to a stranger, it shied away and rippled in distaste from her touch.

Eventually, though, it couldn't overcome her strength and sheer willpower. Power broke the surface with the force of a speeding locomotive and lifted herself into my body. Exhausted, all the muscles gave up their fight and flopped down, going limp and pulling John down with the sudden dead weight. He landed on top of me with a surprised sound of pain when his face hit the wooden floor beside my neck.

Tinkling, feminine laughter rose from Power's throat, jolting her chest in bouncing, jarring spasms. She reached down and stroked John's hair as he struggled to stand, clutching his bleeding nose. She wiped the blood from his upper lip and grinned at him.

"Well, hello again," she teased, fingers running through his long hair. Bubbling green jealousy rippled through me, hating her for touching him so intimately when I hadn't dared yet.

"Power," he whispered, untamed horror written across his paled features. He stumbled to his feet and backed away from her, turning his eyes to take in every single detail of the gymnasium surrounding them. I screamed at Power, pounding my fists against the un-giving stone wall. She couldn't do this! She couldn't take over! She'd have us both sent to the thirteenth floor!

Her excitement vibrated the ground beneath my feet. A new, thrilled light lit up her eyes and her smile widened as she propped herself up on her elbows. My elbows. "You remember my name this time! Oh, I knew you cared!" she cried.

John was much less enamored by her. His lips curled back in disgust and he swiped the the rest of the blood under his nose. Around her, standing in a large circle, stood all of my ward mates, looking on in pure astonishment. She beamed a blinding, megawatt smile at all of them, particularly George. He smirked at her extra attention, clearly enjoying her presence and what it meant for him.

"Is there a problem here?" Paul pushed himself between Esther and Ed, stopping short when he found my body propped up on the ground. One look at the cocky stance Power held, even on the ground, and he knew that Sane was gone and Power was in control, even if he didn't know the logistics. He chuckled deep in his throat and pushed his glasses up the ridge of his nose with his middle finger.

"Not a single thing in the world is wrong today, Mr. Therapist," she cooed, lips curled in a saccharine smile that made me want to vomit.

"I'm glad to hear that, Ms. Thornton. I assume you're up for some sack races, then? And, you, Mr. Kingwood, should get to the nurses' station to have that bloody nose looked at," he replied, his stern voice letting him know he would tolerate no arguments.

John clenched his jaw, working his tight fists at his sides. "It's just a busted blood vessel. It's not even bleeding anymore. I'm fine."

"I'm in charge here, John. Now, I told you to go do something and I expect it to be done. I can't have you bleeding all over the polished floor. So, go," Paul snapped, again phrasing his authority in a way that made me realize just how much he thrived on that power over us and the staff under him. He didn't like to be second guessed, and he didn't want anyone challenging his role as head honcho.

Chocolatey eyes turned to me, hesitation and wariness etched into their depths like engravings on a tomb. He didn't want to leave. Not while Power had control and there were a couple dozen giant burlap sacks in the corner. I wanted to reassure him and beg him not to leave me trapped in my own mind at the same time. Power wouldn't let anything happen to my body, but I couldn't say the same for the bodies around me. And who knew what antics she'd stir up, and what trouble those antics would brew?

With great reluctance, he turned to Ed, giving him a look that the giant man seemed to understand immediately. "Watch out for her and keep an eye on her. She's not stable," I heard him murmur to him as he passed him by, walking so slow that it looked like every motion that took him farther away from me pained him. Ed nodded, flicking his lime eyes over to Power like beaming spotlights. She smirked and tapped her fingers against the cool wooden floor.

The door closed with a quiet clasp as John disappeared behind them and Power stood from her seat on the ground. She stretched her arms out, grimacing with the motion as if my body had been cooped up for a long time. "Oh, how I love a good healthy competition between friends," she said, grinning at my ward mates like a cat in a room full of canaries. Injured, scared canaries.

While the rest looked on with varying versions of shocked and horrified expressions, George stood apart, seemingly unperturbed by Power. A lazy smile curled up the corners of his lips from where he stood, leaning against one of the support beams in the large, sparse room. His arms crossed his chest, fingers flexing back and forth.

"Then let's begin," Paul replied, striding to stand beside me with an air of arrogance I wished he would choke on. "Why don't you pick your sack first, Kate? Since you're so eager."

She reached up and ruffled his slicked back hair, earning a break in the cocky demeanor so that one of annoyance could take its place. "You're too kind," she cooed, and spun to face the pile of sacks. Tingles fluttered beneath the skin of her fingers, translating to my own, even in my head. A strange sense of giddiness bubbled up under my feet, and she traipsed over to them, fingers itching to feel the rough texture.

It's going to overwhelm you. It'll take over, I tried to warn, but she scoffed as if the idea were insulting and kept going. The closer she got to the sacks, the stronger the desire to lose herself came. I felt it in the air around me, infiltrating my head and thickening until dizziness took over me. I stumbled back, landing on my butt, to watch her move.

Laughter exploded from her mouth the moment her fingers made contact with the burlap material. Something feral grew at an alarming speed inside her, pounding at the floor beneath me, and screaming to be let out. Wild, untamed recklessness took off like silver bullets through her veins, begging her to lose all sense of control or sanity. Take what you want. Do what you want. Unleash, it whispered in her ear, swirling around her thoughts and emotions with the grace of a snake. Power kept laughing, doubled over and nearly in pain, as the slithery temptations kept her hypnotized.

The jarring of the snap in her control reverberated all around me, making the stone wall shudder and creak under the pressure. Before I could fully process what that meant or how to react, Power was shooting off to the far wall of the gym, clutching the coarse material of the burlap sack between her trembling fingers. Her laughter rang out in a constant, unrelenting stream, echoing off every surface and bouncing back into my ears over and over. I jumped to my feet, desperate for a way to rein her in again. Power was bad enough without the added catalyst of the burlap sack. No one and nothing could predict anything she would do anymore. Everyone was in danger, friend or foe.

She gripped the sack between her teeth, leaping for one of the metal support beams lining the gymnasium wall. Her fingers and bare toes latched onto it, several feet in the air. Shouts of surprise and sharp, demanding commands floated all around from where the others stood as they all ran for her.

Power ran her tongue along the course fibers of the bag held in her teeth, muffled cries of laughter huffing into and around her mouth as tears of hilarity gathered in the corners of her eyes.

Control yourself! I snapped, fury rising in the pit of my stomach at her weak attempts to hold the raging insanity back. You belittle me for being weak, but you can't even keep yourself together for three seconds once a stitch of burlap enters your sight. Get it together, Power! I hoped with everything in me she couldn't feel the fear and nervousness sharing space with the indignation in my tone. The idea that she could hurt any of my ward mates made hard balls of bile to form like lead in my stomach.

Using muscles and grips my body hadn't had to use in a while, Power shimmied all fifteen feet up the steel beam. Her head grazed the ceiling, shifting the hair on top and making my scalp itch.

"Kate!" Esther cried, pure panic clothing her voice as she dug her hands into her mussed hair, sending midnight colored strands flying all over her head like a demonic halo. "Oh, my gosh. Oh, my gosh, Kate, what are you doing?!"

Power didn't grace her with an answer, still laughing maniacally. I watched, through her eyes, as she arched her back to take in the rest of the adjoining ceiling. Her arms strained against the effort, pulled straight while her legs crouched down, vertically, against the beam. I held no reservations that my body could hold the position and keep itself up on the beam for a long time. Robbie had trained me well, after all. Hours upon hours of strict, near impossible practice that could have left me broken and unable to function, had he not been a professional who knew my limits and cared about my wellbeing.

No, it wasn't falling from the ceiling I was worried about.

It was the excitement humming beneath my feet. Her breaths came quicker and more hysterical. She zoned in on Paul and the orderly dressed in the normal crisp white uniform, her wide smile letting the burlap sack fall from her mouth and flutter to the ground.

"Oh, what fun we're going to have," she whispered between giggles. Without warning, she hunched down before using the force behind her legs to launch herself into the air. For a split moment, I was brought back to the big top at Jensen and Sons, soaring the air, arms outstretched to reach for Gregory's hands on the opposite trapeze. Adrenaline raced through my muscles and veins, sweat beading along my forehead and collarbone with a heady mixture of excitement and anticipation.

Power's fingers wrapped around the thick cord holding the hanging light, momentum yanking the rest of her body forward, then sharply back again as her grip anchored her to the wildly swinging light. Shadows and white beams of light whirled around the gymnasium, casting distorted images of every object in the room all over the place, like a tornado of nightmares and demons. She giggled again, flipping herself upside down before the swinging even slowed down, and wrapped the semi flexible cord around her ankle and foot, allowing her hand to release the cord to hang from her tangled foot. Her hands splayed across the large plexiglass half globe shade on the top side of the bulb, stabilizing her movement.

"Go get the tranquilizers!" Paul yelled at the stunned orderly, who watched her movements with a dropped jaw and eyebrows raised clear into his receding hairline.

"What is she?!" the orderly asked. "She's not human! No human can do that!"

I found myself rolling my eyes at his dramatics while Power laughed on and on, letting the wind rush through her hair as she pushed more momentum into the swinging light, making it her own demented little trapeze act.

"She's human, you stupid moron! Go get the tranquilizers before I have your job!" Paul screeched, sounding very much like a spoiled child not getting his way.

"Calm down, Pauly!" Power taunted from the forward swing, extending her arm in a graceful, show stopping flourish. "You're sounding a bit flustered! Where's your control, love?"

"Kate, stop! What are you doing?!" Esther cried out again, while Lottie and her stepped forward, almost directing underneath Power. Maybe they underestimated us and thought we'd fall. They couldn't have known otherwise, as I'd never revealed myself to them, but it still burned down my chest as a sort of insult.

Paul pointed a furious, shaking finger at Power, other hand clenched in a white knuckled fist. His jaw clicked and teeth grinded in his anger. "You will come down from there this instant, Ms. Thornton!"

Power tossed her head back and laughed, swinging wildly from her upside down perch. "Or what, sweetheart? You gonna climb your stiff, awkward little body up here and get me, yourself? Make me!"

The orderly took that moment to spin around and run for the door, most likely to the nurses' station for a sedative. Though how they expected to get it into Power from fifteen feet below her, I didn't know.

George's eyes never left her contorting body, taking in every movement, even as he pulled Ed toward him by the sleeve. "Go stand under her. You're the tallest and can catch her when the tranq hits her," he instructed in a low voice. But, not low enough that Power's ears didn't pick it up.

"Look at you, Georgie!" she cried, clasping her hands below her chin. Shorter strands of her hair caressed her cheeks as she continued to sway back and forth, the waves cascading down toward the floor, away from her face. "Aren't you just the little leader! You always get what you want, don't you? Hmm... I wonder what I'd see if I looked inside your cold, calculating little brain? A lot of self, but no personality, I bet."

He flicked his eyes to meet hers, raising one eyebrow with a wide grin splayed across his lips, revealing his shining teeth. "At least you'll only find one of me in there, sweetheart."

A delighted squeal erupted from Power's throat. "Oh, you're a catch, aren't you?! Too bad you're so young, dear. We could set this whole place on fire! Of course, Ed could definitely help with that, couldn't you, honey?"

Ed's face paled, but he stayed stayed quiet where he stood beneath her, ready to catch her.

"Let's not bring innocent bystanders into this. You called me out, Psycho. Don't be a weakling by bringing the weaker ones into your fight."

"So chivalrous!" she gasped, placing her hand on her heart in mock shock. "And yet, so hypocritical! Should you really talk about using weaker specimens for your own selfish desires?"

"That's not fair! He's not using me!" Lottie broke in, thin, fragile hands perched on her hips. Her usual dull, subdued green eyes looked like they'd like to spit fire at Power for daring to insinuate anything negative about her white knight. "Why do you keep saying things like that?! You don't know anything about our relationship!"

A dark chuckle rumbled in Power's chest. Don't say anything, I snapped at her. She's just as much an anchor to his sanity as he is to hers. If she gets cut loose from him, there's nothing holding him back from turning on us. For now, let him use her.

She twirled a little more from the cord, spinning until her foot and calf were unraveled from it, leaving her only holding onto the swaying light by her hands. I sighed, unabashedly enjoying the movements and contortions and acrobatics despite the precarious situation. Maybe I was finally losing what was left of my sanity. For all the chaotic, awful things happening, my mind felt as though it was in a pleasant, numbed and calm daze. The strained panic and fear etched into my ward mates faces called out to my sense of sympathy, but it never responded. And Paul's rage and promise of ill omen didn't go unnoticed, but I found I couldn't care less. Power was in control, and for once, I could sit back and not worry. Not make the decisions. Not be in constant control. The illusion that she would take care of our shared body masked over every single reservation and fear I had of her control.

"I suppose I don't, Lottie, dear. I apologize," Power conceded, with a wicked smirk cast George's way. "He's your savior. Your hope, I suppose. I shouldn't have poked fun." Every letter she spoke was filled with false, mocking repentance. Her eyes batted for a moment at Lottie, turning into large, innocent doe eyes, before she situated herself upright, legs straddling the cord as she sat, legs dangling, on top of the light shade.

Lottie bit her lip, suddenly looking unsure of herself. Her moment of bravado vanished, she stepped back into the hollow shell of insecurity, crossing her arms over her chest and averting her eyes. "S'alright," she muttered, voice shaking.

"Come down, please!" Esther begged, pacing back and forth behind Ed. Tears streaked down her face, leaving trails of thick, black mascara in their wake. Power cocked her head sideways, studying her frantic movements.

"Esther, love, whatever is the matter? You don't think I'm going to fall, do you? I'm Kate the Danged Great! I don't fall," she sneered, like the word "fall" was a curse, nasty and bitter on her tongue. She opened her mouth to add more to her mocking degradation, but a sharp sting in her thigh, accompanied by a whooshing sound, stopped her. Instead, a startled gasp flew from her lips and she looked down at the fleshy part of her leg. A brightly feathered dart penetrated the meat there, stuck in her skin to the hilt of the needle.

As everything around her began to spin and the corners of her vision went black, I screwed my eyes shut, dread filling a pit in my stomach. Her fists loosened from the thick black cord of wires and her eyes rolled in the back of her head just before she went limp in my body, shoving me back to the surface before we fell, hurtling through the air, toward the polished wooden floor.

Chapter 29

I woke to the intense pounding of a thousand hammers in my skull, accompanied by rolling, swirling balls of bile playing bumper cars in my stomach. A loud groan escaped my lips while I tried to remember where I was and why I felt like I'd been hit with ten flus, all rolled into one. Even my muscles, usually limber and languid, felt stiff and achy.

"Don't move too much. The sedatives have... lingering after effects. Wouldn't want you to lose your lunch all over the new rug."

The voice from my right added another hundred or so hammers to the group in my head, eliciting a pained whimper from my own voice. What had they tranqued me with? Elephant doses? My eyes, sealed together with a thick film, tried to open, but the tiniest amount of light sent lightning bolts of pain shooting straight to my temples. I squeezed them shut again and focused on trying to remember where I'd been before.

Marcie's on the thirteenth floor... Robbie's box of chocolates was a dead end... The gym... Power... The burlap sacks!

It all came crashing back down to me in one huge, weighty heap, yanking my breath from me and crushing my chest like an anvil being dropped from ten stories up. I'd fallen! Fallen from fifteen, maybe twenty feet in the air! I, Kate the Great, fell for the first time in over seven years.

There you go again, being dramatic. In case you don't remember, you were drugged. Of course you fell.

Except it wasn't me that fell. It was Power. Not that she'd call attention to that.

"We're going to have a little chat, Ms. Thornton," that darned voice spoke again. A thick shuffle of footsteps traveled across the room, followed by a quiet metal-on-metal click.

He's locked the door.

The rolling in my stomach intensified. Nothing good could come of that. Bad things happened behind locked doors in this place. Fear made a trail up my spine, leaving a cold sweat in its wake.

"What's going on?" I managed to ask with a hoarse, croaking voice. My throat stung and ached as I tried to find some kind of moisture in my mouth.

"I'm sure by now you've noticed the absence of your fellow ward mate. Marcie Greene, yes?"

Shilling, Power realized about a half a second before I did. You're locked in a room with Shilling, and he knows you're vulnerable.

"She's been transferred to a floor better equipped to handle her and her... situation."

"The thirteenth floor," I murmured, more to myself than to him. But he heard anyways, smirking in demented satisfaction that I'd heard of the mysterious, menacing, and non-existent floor of the huge building. My eyes finally cranked themselves open against the agonizing light. Better to be in pain but watching the doctor than the opposite.

"Clever girl," he mocked, walking in long, confident strides across his office. I looked around the room with wary eyes. Every time I found myself in it, there seemed to be more elegance worked into it. Cheap, basic furniture seemed to be magically replaced with expensive, opulent pieces little by little. Where was his money coming from? More residents?

"She didn't do anything to get sent up there. Bring her back," I demanded. Still, my voice crackled and broke over the syllables, as if I hadn't used it in years.

Shilling stopped, turning on his heel to look back at me, an evil glint swirling in his expression that I didn't like one bit. "On the contrary. Ms. Greene is under suspicion of murder, again. We've already established that you've heard of our dear Ernie's departing? It seems his remains have been dug up behind the garden shed, and the evidence we have points directly to her."

I froze in place. No. No, no, no, no, no!

"But... But, she didn't-"

"Didn't what? Kill him? What pieces of him we could still recognize had bits of her hair and fingernail scratches in them. My best guess as to what happened is that she made yet another advance on him, which he rejected, like the good employee he was. She became enraged and attacked him, most likely with the shovel she buried him with. It seems she then dismembered him and burned the pieces. That pesky torso, though... It just didn't burn all the way through. She should have been more patient and waited for it to burn through instead of rushing the process and burying him.

Otherwise we'd never have the evidence we do in order to send her where she belongs."

"She couldn't have! She didn't do it! You have to bring her back! It wasn't her!" I stammered, struggling to sit up on the stupid chaise lounger. How the heck was I supposed to sit on this blasted thing?!

He quirked an eyebrow and moved to take a seat on top of his desk, crossing one leg over the other. "You seem to know an awful lot about something you previously claimed to know nothing of. Do you have something to tell me, Ms. Thornton? Were you involved in the murder?"

"Of course not!" I snapped, too quickly. "I would never..."

The awkward silence filled with tension around us as he looked on at me, expectantly.

I would never... I would never... Except that I already had. I'd killed over two dozen people in a single night. "I would never" translated to "I certainly would".

"It wasn't her. I know it wasn't," I insisted instead, hanging my head in shame of the reminder of my crimes. Power sighed, rubbing her manicured hands over her face.

"And, how, exactly, do you know this?" Shilling asked after a beat, straightening his posture to seem taller, more intimidating. It didn't work, but it was in my best interest to pretend it did.

My teeth sunk into my lower lip for a moment. "I was with her every night for a week. She couldn't have done it." The lie slid easily from my tongue, but the frown on his face told me he'd caught it anyway.

"Unless you can give me the name and details of who murdered my employee, and how it was done, Ms. Greene will remain on the thirteenth floor as the prime suspect. The only suspect. If you can provide me with other information, I will trade her presence for the guilty party you name," he said in slow, deliberate syllables. I recognized the way he was leading me. Like Esther said, he'd targeted me from the beginning, it seemed. The entire thing played out into an elaborate ruse to get me where he wanted me. He knew that, and at this point, I was sure he knew I knew that as well.

The pendulum of the ornate, expensive looking grandfather clock ticked a steady rhythm on the far wall, like a timer counting down to my demise. A weight poured itself into my lungs in liquid form as I faced the inevitable. No one would go down if I could help it, but it was still better that I be sentenced to death than any of my ward mates. The constant swing of the pendulum seemed to slow down with time, marking my gradual acceptance of my fate.

"I killed him. He hit me, so I knocked him unconscious with a shovel, beat him even more, tore him limbs apart with an ax, set the pieces on fire, and buried him in a canvas sack behind the garden shed," I told him. My voice, as a testament to my non-wavering loyalty to my friends, never shook as I spoke the words that would seal my fate and give the disgusting doctor exactly what he wanted.

"And Ms. Greene's hair that we found with the body?" he led, unable to take my confession without dogging at every single bone he had.

"I was with her all day. Some of her hair must have been on my clothes. She wasn't there. It was only me."

He said nothing in return for a while, letting the quiet grow louder and louder. The strange limbo where my expectations for my false admission met the reality of it fell in a dull, anticlimactic release. No earth shattering moment where Shilling hauled me up by my arm and shoved me to an orderly to be take upstairs. No giant needle of fear injecting shivers over my body. No "aha!" reaction from the doctor, even. Just the quiet, almost lazy silence, interrupted intermittently by the thunking tick of the grandfather clock.

It stretched on and on, until my tensed body could stress itself no more, and finally relaxed just enough to keep me from panicking over the unknown as of yet.

Finally, he sighed and slid off the top of his desk. He strolled to the other side while I sat up straight, ready to bolt if the need arose.

"I didn't expect it to be this easy, I'm afraid. I knew you cared for your ward mates, but maybe something should have happened sooner. Before you could form attachments that keep you grounded enough to not do as I'd planned. It was a sin of sloth, on my part. I've just been so... busy, that I haven't properly invested the time I should have into poking the bear, so to speak," he began, looking down at his desk with such sorrow in his eyes that I almost pitied him.

"I guess I'll have to take the easy way out, since you won't rise to the occasion without provocation," he added, a wistful lilt to his voice that had my fingernails digging into the leather chaise. I watched with an eagle's eyes as his hand slid down the desk, sliding open the top drawer while he shook his head in disappointment.

"What are you doing? I gave you what you want. I confessed. Just take me and bring her back down." I stood, inching toward the door I already knew was locked. There would be no ward mate to save me by knocking on the wooden door this time. I swallowed the nervous lump in my throat as my hands began to tremble.

"See, that's the thing, Katherine. Your confession? It's just... not... good enough for what I want. You're too level headed. Too... calm. I need more to justify sending you to my private floor. And, since you won't give it willingly, I'll just have to make it happen the other way." His vein-riddled hands delved into the drawer and pulled back, bringing the burlap sack with it.

I didn't try to fight it. In fact, I called her out before she even had the chance to register what had happened. The last little slip of the course fabric rose from the drawer just as Power swam past me in the little purgatory between the surface of my mind and her prison behind the wall. As what I could only imagine to be a gesture of good will, or maybe comfort, her hand reached toward mine, grasping it solid for a single second as she floated up and I sank down. Her fingers caressed my palm, like she was telling me everything would be okay. Then, I was back behind the wall, a quaking mess, and she was breaking the surface, molding herself into my skin for the second time in one day.

Before Shilling could make a move, Power had bounded onto his desk, shoving knick-knacks and papers in all directions. She crouched there, swiping her hand out to snatch the sack from his hands. The material itched at her fingers, sending jolt after jolt of electric currents up and down her fingertips. Excitement hummed beneath my feet, vibrating the floor until I began bouncing with the force of it.

"A present?" she purred, rubbing the material against her cheek, soaking in the memories it brought back to her. "For me? You shouldn't have. You know I get emotional when you give me gifts, doc."

"How do you do this, Katherine? I'm quite enamored. The change you exhibit is breathtakingly quick, and so markedly different. I'd love to see what's in that lovely little head of yours," he replied, his wide eyes flicking over her form.

"I didn't take you for a cradle robber, doc. A psycho in disguise, yeah. We all know you're worse than any of us. But, really, you're what? Forty? Fifty? Don't get your hopes up, Pops," she teased, slipping her hands into the sack, savoring the sensation of the jagged fibers scratching against her softened skin.

Something strange flashed across Shilling's face. The softness in his gaze morphed into cold steel. His slightly feminine jaw set, teeth clicking as he clenched them together. Even his posture went rigid, like a stone statue in his leather desk chair.

"I assure you, Ms. Thornton, it was never you I wanted in that sense. I can see her in you, though. It's fascinating how similar you look. The difference, however, is in the eyes," he said. His fingers wrapped around her calf, squeezing until she shot him a warning look for the bruises she'd be sure to have once he released them. He rose from his seat, towering over her as waves of sudden hostility rolled off him, filling the room until it felt suffocating. "Those stupid grey eyes. Hers were hazel. A beautiful starburst of green, blue, and brown. You. You have his eyes. The little halfwit who took her from me. I worked hard to make sure you were sent here, Ms. Thornton. It will be my greatest honor to finally see your brain and heart throbbing in my hands."

A flock of shivers rolled down my entire body, head to toes, and I curled into myself, leaning against the stone wall for stability and protection. Power, however, uncurled herself from her crouching position upon his desk. This time, she loomed over him. It was a dominance game, I realized. Like animals, the person on the highest ground would be the winner in it. And, unless he planned on sitting on top of his bookshelf, she'd won.

"Shilling, baby, are you finally losing your mind in public now? Is that what all this is about? I look like your long, lost, love interest? How humiliating for a man of your stature. You sound pathetic. No wonder she left you for someone else."

For a man in his middle aged years, Shilling struck hard, and he struck fast. Within the short time it took Power to flick her eyes to her nails, then back up at him, his pretty, polished pen knife was poised at her right eye, millimeters away from her surprised grey irises.

"I think those hideous grey abominations will be the first thing I remove from your skull," he whispered. His hot, damp breath collided with the skin of her flushed cheeks, even from the foot or so below her at his stance on the floor. My heart raced in my chest, the beating feeling like hundreds of wild horses stampeding from inside my ribcage.

Thankfully, Power proved herself a much braver, confident woman than me. Though obviously taken by surprise, she wasted no time in clamping her hand around his wrist and twisting it until his face scrunched up in pain and he dropped the small knife. It clattered to the floor, clinking back and forth for a moment before rolling underneath the desk.

"Don't be a tease, sweetheart," she spat, shoving him backward. He landed back in his desk chair, while Power took her time stepping down from the desk itself. She moved like a panther, full of grace and purpose. Like a predator who knew her prey was caught. His glare burned into her face, uncensored hatred coloring in every wrinkled crevice of his face.

"Now," she started, running her hand over his hair, like a petulant pet, "You're going to-"

The sensation of being punched in the jaw felt so achingly familiar, bringing a strange and disturbing sense of nostalgia that did the trick in sending Power over the edge, yet again. Nights at Jensen and Sons, being hit, kicked, and abused filled my vision, while scenes of slit throats and gallons of ruby red blood filled hers. Ear blasting, shrieking laughter filled the office as her head snapped back to look at the doctor full on. She had pounced on him, fingers clenched around the delicate skin of his throat, in a nanosecond, squeezing so hard his eyes bulged from their sockets.

"I've never killed a man by strangulation before, doctor. Do you feel honored, being the first?" she whispered, her grin so wide the muscles in her face began to ache and cramp. The loss of her control sent black tendrils through the floor, grasping at my feet, as if it wanted to pull me into it also. Shilling, gripping her wrists with one panicked hand, raised his other hand and sent his palm rocketing into the side of her face, making contact with the spot just above her temple. Whether it was bad aim, or he meant to miss her temple by so little I didn't know, but it succeeded in knocking her body away from him.

"Guard!" he yelled, voice strained and breaking as he struggled to bring his windpipe back to full working order. "Guard!" he tried again, louder. He jumped from the chair, white coat trailing behind him, and leapt straight for the lock on the door, flicking it unlocked just as Power regained her senses and stumbled back to her feet.

"Bit off more than you could chew, daddy-o?" she groaned, palming her eyes in an attempt to see straight again.

He turned, taking her by surprise again. "Not me, Katherine. No, I bit off just enough. It's you who took a bigger serving than you could handle." My breathing picked up pace even more at the wild, feral way his shoulder hunched in, an animalistic match for the crazed expression on his face.

He planned this! I shouted at Power, though she most likely had that figured out from the beginning. My suspicions confirmed by the quick shake off she gave me, not even acknowledging that I'd done more than watch in rapt horror at the entire scenario.

A guard in a dark blue jumpsuit jogged into the room, scanning the scene with hard, wary eyes.

"Cuff her and have an orderly bring her to the thirteenth floor. She's confessed to the murder of Ernie Keller. There is no help for some unfortunate souls in this world," Shilling ordered, false pity written across his face, concealing the unadulterated pleasure hiding just beneath it. My heart slammed against the inside of my chest in a frantic fit of frenzy.

No! Don't let him do this, Power! Yet, even as I screamed at her to not do it, I knew it was our only hope of freeing Marcie. She proved her loyalty to our ward mates by ignoring my cowardly pleads for self preservation.

The guard, an older man with greying hair, moved toward her with cautious steps, like one would do to a wild animal in their front yard. He held one hand on the silver revolver holstered at his hip and the other outstretched toward her.

"Ma'am, I'm going to need you to cooperate so I don't have to harm you," he said, moving forward in tiny increments that told unspeakable truths about the fear making his voice tremble.

"You know who I am, then?" Power mused, cocking her head to the side like an inquisitive puppy. "I'm Kate the Great. I bathed in the blood of twenty some-odd people in one night, you know. Are you really so sure you can handle this job, sir?"

He gulped, beads of sweat forming at his temples while his footing stumbled and his hand twitched on his gun. She sighed, gifting him an uncharacteristic genuine smile. "Don't you worry, Mr. Guard. It's not your throat I plan on having in my hands today." With that, she thrusted her wrists out to him, offering herself to his handcuffs without hesitation. He snapped them around the porcelain skin lightning quick, still very clearly afraid she would attack him.

He began leading her from the room, but at the doorway she dug her heels in and spun to face the seething Shilling again. A smile more suited to her sinister nature grew across her face, and her eyes widened to the point that the white around her irises became fully visible. "Aren't my eyes pretty, Doctor? Remember what I said before. You belong to me," she told him, laughter bubbling up to boil over the threshold of her grinning lips.

The guard, undoubtedly terrified and possibly clutching at a hidden rosary in his pocket somewhere, nudged her forward to keep walking, a slight tremor to each of his steps. Power bounced along beside him, then opened her mouth to speak again, an old nursery rhyme floating in the air back to Shilling.

"Mary, Mary, quite contrary. How does your graveyard grow? With silver bells, and cockleshells. And pretty maids... All in a... row," she taunted, tossing one last triumphant look back at the doctor before allowing herself to sink back behind the wall, thrusting me back to the forefront of my mind and body. She relinquished control with eyes sparkling with utter delight, almost like a 'thank you' of sorts.

Before the door to Shilling's office closed, I heard the unmistakable sound of that cursed burlap sack sliding back into his desk drawer, which he closed with a resounding click.

Chapter 30

The scared guard couldn't have shown how much more grateful he was to hand me off to the burly, bald orderly if he'd dropped to his knees and pledged his life in allegiance. It might have had something to do with my drastic change in demeanor after Power gave control back to me. From what he'd seen, I'd gone from psychotic, evil demon spawn to tearful submissive kitty cat in less than a heartbeat. No doubt, the poor man would go home to rethink his career choice. I know I would have, in his position.

What I hadn't expected, though, was to meet warm, chocolate eyes the moment I stepped away from the office. John walked, just a few steps behind the guard, following us until the guard made the hand off to the orderly. A dark bruise spread across the top of his nose where he'd fallen on the gym floor earlier, and his eyes were filled with panic, though he said nothing until the orderly secured me by my cuffed wrists and began walking me toward the staircase.

"You can't do this," he told the orderly. The bald man shrugged, not even gracing him with a verbal answer. "She didn't kill Ernie.

What do you want? I have money. I'll give you whatever you want if you just let her go," he added, nearly tripping over his socked feet as he jogged to walk backwards in front of him, facing us.

"I'm employed by Dr. Shilling to follow orders, boy," the orderly barked, his voice gravelly and deep. He shoved John away, but John was back in front of him in the blink of an eye, stopping in his tracks and forcing the orderly to stop also.

"She lied. She didn't kill Ernie. I know because it was me. I killed him," he tried, fisting the orderly's collar in his hands, stepping forward, into his face. I saw the challenge in his bowed up posture, even as desperation laced his false confession. The way his eyes flicked nervously, and the lump in his throat that he swallowed with great difficulty gave him away.

"John, don't," I started, but he shot a silencing glare at me that had my mouth slamming shut as the tears in my eyes began to spill over.

"You did not kill Ernie. I won't let you go down for it. I won't let them take you," he replied. His posture straightened even further, and his eyes regained the hard determination and confidence that had been lost from his defeated form for a while now. Slumped, drained, tired John was gone, replaced with the alpha male avenging angel who had everything under control I'd come to know him as before the recent events at Rosenton had stolen it from him.

"Go tell Shilling he's wrong. She lied when she confessed," he ordered, the words booming loudly around us, bouncing off the white walls of the stark dormitory hallway. An air of absolute authority radiated from him, and he seemed to grow taller and more intimidating. A spark of hope swelled in my chest. Maybe he could save me from my fate. Maybe all his and Robbie's efforts wouldn't be in vain.

The hope died out, slumping into crushed pieces, when the orderly, with barely a twitch of his lumberjack muscles, shrugged John off and kept walking, frog marching me closer and closer to the staircase. The commotion of my sudden attempts at release coupled with my own desperate begging must have alerted the other residents to the scene, because the sound of the heavy wooden doors to the lounge slammed open and several sets of footsteps raced toward us.

"John? What's going on?" a voice asked from behind me. I recognized the Mexican lilt immediately. Esther. Who else had been in the lounge?

"They're taking her to the thirteenth floor. She lied and confessed to killing Ernie," he answered, his gaze not moving from the orderly's face for a moment.

"They can't do that. She didn't do it!" Lottie cried out. In a moment of uncharacteristic bravery, she leaped into my peripheral vision, wrapping her stick thin arms around the orderly's tree trunk bicep, and began trying to pull him back. "She's innocent! You can't let them take her, John!"

"She lied! She confessed!"

Tears poured down my cheeks in miniature rivers, dripping from my jaw to land with even smaller splashes on the tile floor. My mouth opened to speak, but the ball of emotion in my esophagus prevented any sound from making its way out. I stood there, my mouth opening and closing like a stunned goldfish as the orderly tried to walk the thin balance between pushing me forward and keeping my ward mates from creating a disaster of the situation.

He spun me around, trying to swat Lottie's hands from his arm and yelling at the rest of my ward mates to stop trying to interfere unless they wanted to be sedated and punished. My eyes flicked up toward the connecting hallway that led to Shilling's office just in time to see George disappear down it. He hadn't uttered a word the entire time, but the determination in his movements as well as Lottie's presence told me he had been there also. Even Ed stood in the hallway, hanging back with his jaw hanging open and a colorless pallor to his face.

The cacophony of all their shouts and protests fell harsh on my ears, making me wince against the noise. John gripped my arm, trying to pull me from the orderly and to him, but the orderly yanked me back, making me stumble, with a simple grunt of effort. He shot a nasty warning look at John before snapping orders at the rest of my friends.

I had to wonder why none of them had felt so passionately about Marcie's abduction. Compared to their reaction to mine, they couldn't have cared less that she'd been taken, and that possibility made me feel ill. She was innocent. Far more innocent than I'd ever be. So why did I deserve their fight for my life, and not her? The young beauty queen deserved to be wanted and fought for far more than me. At least she'd brought joy and laughter to our ward. It seemed all I brought along with me in my nonexistent suitcase of emotional baggage was an ever looming sense of dread and cautiousness.

"What is the meaning of this?!"

Every pair of eyeballs in the hallway snapped to attention as Shilling stomped toward us from the connecting corridor. George slunk behind him, steering clear of any area where he'd be easily spotted.

"What is going on, here?! I send one little harlot to the thirteenth floor, and a group of well behaved lunatics suddenly lose their minds?! Mr. Baker even came into my private office, unannounced, trying to tell me he'd been the one to kill my employee!"

"No!" Lottie shrieked, the animalistic, pain filled cry strangled with emotion at the thought of her savior, her white knight, being taken from her.

"Hold you tongue, Ms. Holbrook!" Shilling snapped, jabbing an angry finger in her direction in warning. "I will not have my asylum turned into a madhouse by you lot!" Even I struggled to contain my snicker at the failed logic behind his furious rant. "Each and every one of you will return to your rooms, immediately! Is that clear?! I'll hear of no more outbursts from any of you, or you'll all be joining her, understood?!"

Where the corridor had been a chaotic mass of cries and physical altercation a moment before, it sat now in complete silence and stillness. Like a photograph, frozen in time. None of them would have dared risk being sent to the thirteenth floor. Maybe they hadn't realized that their attempts to have the blame put on themselves would have landed them there anyway. Either way, the terror encompassing each of my friends froze every muscle in their bodies.

Shilling took a moment to glare into the eyes of each of them before making a clenched fist with his pointer finger extended toward the dorm rooms. "Go!" he snapped, pieces of his greying hair falling from its perfectly gelled coif into his eyes.

As if time had regained its senses, the hallways erupted into action again. My ward mates fled for their rooms, excluding John, who stayed clutched at my side, staring down his nose at the doctor in a dare for him to object to his presence. Shilling glared at John, sizing him up, before scoffing with a shake of his head and stalking back to his office.

The orderly's meaty fingers squeezed tight around my cuffed wrists, and with John following and holding onto my upper arm, he began to lead me toward the staircase again. My lungs expanded too far as real, raw fear crept up into my very soul. I should have gotten us all out when Power wanted it. I shouldn't have waited. I should have had all of us out of Rosenton already. Sharp pain etched its way up, in a scorching straight line, from my abdomen to the base of my neck. The tears kept flowing, without restraint or pause.

"I'm scared," I whispered to myself as the realization of what was about to happen to me settled down into my psyche. "I'm absolutely terrified."

John's thumb rubbed what was supposed to be a comforting circle on my arm. He offered me a watery smile that he didn't believe in any more than I did. But, he couldn't tell me everything would be alright, because nothing would be alright.

More likely than not, I would see my own death as a result of my escape delay. Power had been right, like she always seemed to be about such things.

The orderly paused at the staircase, casting a wary look at John. I noted the way my hands and knees shook in fear, the cuffs jingling together to make rapid clinking sounds over and over. How could

I climb several flights of stairs when it felt like a miracle that my legs were holding me up just standing still?

The two men holding onto me exchanged meaningful looks for a fraction of a second. The orderly gave him a curt nod, alongside a murmured, "Two minutes. If you do anything other than talk, I'll have to tell Shilling about Holbrook's regression." My brow furrowed into a deep, confused chevron, but John simply returned the nod, as if the two men already had an arrangement. The orderly passed my cuffed hands from his grip into John's, and he opened the door to the staircase, propping it open and standing just inside the doorway, his back to us.

John turned to me then, his hot chocolate boring into mine with an intensity that twisted my gut into a thousand and one knots. "I'll get you out. I'll do something. I'll find some way," he whispered, pulling me to his chest in an embrace that supported my trembling legs. "I swear I won't let you die there."

My voice choked on a shuddering sob. I reached out for Power, begging her to let me siphon some of her strength, but she hid from me. Whether she was as terrified as I was, or she was angry with me for letting the situation come to pass at all, I didn't know. I just hoped and prayed fervently that I'd live long enough to find out.

My tears eased a moment later, enough for me to speak. Two minutes gave me almost no time to possibly say my last words to someone so important to me.

"I'll look for Marcie," I choked out. Spasming hiccups jolted my voice and chest, making his warm body tighten around mine, as if he could protect my vulnerability from the inevitable. "Robbie's coming back tomorrow for a visit with me. Go to him. Please.

Maybe… maybe between the two of you… Maybe you can get Marcie and I out alive," I added. A fresh wave of hopeless tears dripped from my chin and onto his flannel shirt, leaving dark spots all over.

"I will. We'll get you out, Kate. I swear, you'll be alright," he whispered, nearly crushing me with both the physical and emotional weight of his embrace. He held me as if he didn't believe the words he spoke. As if he didn't think he'd ever really see me – alive – again. I couldn't help but wonder if that would be the case.

"Time's up," the orderly snapped, turning back around and eyeing us with a cautionary look that set my blood boiling.

"That was nowhere near two minutes," John snapped, but I heard the desperation in his tone all the same. How could I not recognize his when it sounded exactly like my own?

"You're lucky you got anything at all, Kingwood. Now, get on out of here. There's nothing else you can do." With that, the burly man pulled me from John. The coldness that settled over me at the lack of his touch chilled me to the bone, and my shuddering fear gave way to a growing sense of hysteria that showed itself in the wideness of the eyes I had locked on John. I used up everything I had in pleading silently for him to not let the orderly take me.

For a split moment, as he grabbed onto my hand and yanked me back to him, I thought he'd answered my silent request. Air sucked up between my teeth in a sharp, but quiet, gasp just before his hands traveled from my wrists to my cheeks. Holding either side of my face in a gentle, yet firm, grip, he set his lips on mine.

The kiss was quick. I felt no fireworks or sparks of electricity like the heroines in Charlotte's racy novels. What I did feel, though, was much better. If I thought the comforting warmth he gave off with his touch was a good thing, the purity and, dare I say, love transferring from his lips to mine was remarkable. His fingers stroked the tear stained spots under my eyes, and I only just relaxed into his hold when two gruff hands yanked me back again.

The orderly yelled something at John, but I didn't hear it, and I don't think he did either. His gaze held mine captive, telling me a thousand words I'd never be able to translate. But, that was okay, because I was quite sure the kiss we'd shared had been worth more than entire novel's worth of words. And, still, behind that warmed emotion, a layer of almost tangible fear laid like a dark netting over the top of it.

The orderly barked one last reprimand that fell on unhearing ears at him, then began shoving me, none to gently, toward the propped open door to the stairwell. To my death. To my fate. To wherever Marcie was.

'Be strong,' John mouthed just before my own stumbling forced me to spin around and be manhandled into the doorway. He might have said it aloud, though, because the sensation of my first kiss still had my ears ringing and my senses dulled.

I licked my quivering lips and nodded to him as he stood there, looking hopeless and frustrated. Every step back I took seemed to exaggerate the cacophony of emotions swirling in his body, seeping out through his every pore. His posture, his eyes, his scowl, his clenched fists, even the tiny hairs standing on end along the back o his neck.

He remained there, still as a statue, with the most pained face I'd ever seen on another human being, as I crossed the threshold onto the stairwell, letting the door slam shut behind me.

CHAPTER 31

Gut wrenching screams and agonized wails permeated the thick steel door before the orderly even opened it. My knees trembled, knocking together, as my heart banged against my chest. Every instinct in my body shouted at me to run, but the thick hands leading me by the handcuffs around my wrists prevented it. I had no idea how I'd made it up so many flights of stairs in my terrified condition.

"Please," I begged, unashamed at my lack of dignity. "Please, don't make me go in there. Please."

Pity, loud and clear, swam in the orderly's eyes as he walked around me to unlock the reinforced steel door. "Doctor's orders," he mumbled, by way of apology.

A pained whimper squeezed between my pressed lips as I fought everything in my head screaming at me to flee, like I did during any altercation or complication I'd faced in my life. The screeching sound of rusted metal grinding against more rusted metal tainted the sound barrier between us and whatever stood on the other side of the door. The orderly shoved his keys back in his pocket and pushed me in front of him. His palm pressed against my trembling shoulder blades as he reached around me to pull open the door. One solid shove sent me sprawling across the threshold, whereupon I slammed my eyes shut in a last ditch effort to pretend it was all a demented, horrible nightmare.

"Wake up, wake up, wake up," I whispered to myself, begging everything in the universe for it to not be real. The cuffs dropped from my wrists, and less than a second later the steel door slammed shut behind me.

I stood in the doorway, my eyelids squeezed together and my fists clenched, pleading with the fates of the world to show me that I'd somehow been drugged into a hallucination or something similar. Each breath I took wheezed in and out in short, shallow bursts as my lips mumbled plead after plead. More agonized screams erupted from further away, causing my muscles to tense and twitch. I shoved the palms of my fists against my eyes, desperate prayers dancing off my tongue in a constant stream.

You're out in the open, Sane. Find a hiding place, Power instructed. Her voice sounded far away, as if she were muffled with a sea of cotton balls separating us.

The joints in my fingers cracked and popped as I forced the fists they created to relax. Of course, she was right. Cowering in the open left me a target. A vulnerable, defenseless target with a bright crimson bullseye washed right over me.

But, a target for what? Shilling? Paul? The other residents here? You've really done it this time, you bumbling imbecile. I'm done letting you have your way all the time. The deal is off! Get ready to be stuck behind this stupid wall forever, because as soon as I've gotten my strength back, you'll never be in control again! Now move!

Yet another pathetic whimper leaked between my quivering lips. Wonderful. Not only was I in danger of only who knew what on this blasted floor, but the psycho in my head had become yet another threat. A thick mixture of frustration and hopelessness bogged down my mind, mingling with the fear and anxiety already present. My body shook and tensed even further, not sure how to react or what to do with all the emotions flying around my head.

Power's fury snapped like a surge of fire through me. Get it together, dimwit! I won't die because of you!

Whether from force of habit from taking orders from her for so long or shock, I didn't know, but my back straightened, pulling my posture up properly and my hands fell to my sides. Through wide, humbly chastised eyes, I took in the sight in front of me for the first time, sucking in a deep lungful of air through my teeth as I did.

The first thing my brain registered was the pale green tint cast over the entire area. Green, the universal color of illness. Sickly, nauseating, heavy green. The walls of the long, dim hallway were halved by two colors, unlike all the other levels of Rosenton. The top half might have once been a nice eggshell color, but was now the color of day old snow sludge, while the bottom half was a dull, dirty green that I suspected was the culprit for the colored cast over the room. As far down as I could see, filth and dust blanketed over every surface while chipped paint speckled the walls, revealing the white base underneath.

Of course he'd only bother to paint his private play floor. But, you'd think a man with so much money and power would hire a maid to clean it, too.

The hallway stretched on until darkness shrouded it, lending no clues to how much or little further was left. Like Ward F's floor, a nurses' station jutted out at one point and a dozen feet from that, an orderlies' station did the same. Doorways to other rooms – what I assumed were the equivalent to our dorm rooms downstairs – stood like unmoving soldiers down either side.

But, there were no actual doors.

I couldn't place my finger on why that simple fact sent shivers racing down my spine and a soft gasp of air hissing through my teeth, but the sense of foreboding it brought fell heavy on my chest. I swallowed nervously, flicking my eyes from doorway to doorway in search of a door to any room whatsoever, only to come up with nothing.

My head tilted up, taking note of the ceiling. Unlike the other floors, the thirteenth floor housed no florescent lights. What little visibility granted looked to be the result of the waning sun shining in the rusty barred windows flanking the opposite walls of each of the door-less rooms.

That realization gave way to another startling mental notation.

Shadows, though light, shuffled and danced against the hallway walls. Which meant there were... things... or people... inside those rooms, and they were mobile.

Calm down, Power snapped, though her own panic was nearly tangible in her voice. You're Kate the Great. Slinking around and finding hiding places is what you do best. Now, start scoping out safe places.

Loud, painful groans wafted from a room four or five doors down. Almost in reply, it seemed, whimpers and other moans of discontent sounded from the surrounding rooms, floating into the air and haunting the dim, dirty air around them. My back met the solid metal door behind me, and only then did I realize my feet had stepped back of their own accord, anxious to get away from whatever or whoever inhabited this dilapidated, imagined floor.

Hide. I needed to find a place to hide. Fighting the ingrained habitual gut reaction to flee, I forced my socked foot to take one tentative step forward. My toes barely touched the grimy floor before motion in my peripheral vision had my head jerking up to look in the direction it came from.

A scream so primal it felt as though it was ripping the inside of my throat raw, tore from behind my teeth and out into the tainted and sickly green corridor.

Knees drawn tight to my chest, and arms wrapped around them, I pressed my forehead down against my kneecaps and struggled to stop my hysterical rocking. Visions of what I'd seen only moments before flashed behind my eyelids, sending my heart to race as the full horror of what it meant sank in.

No eyelids. Just abnormal, too large, bloodshot eyeballs staring directly at me. No eyelashes. No blinking. Just the startling, eerie sensation of being watched by a silent monster.

Every breath shot in and out through my lips in rapid succession as the fresh memory assaulted me.

Scars and boils covering every inch of visible skin. Rotten, stinking pus oozing from infected wounds. And, no hands. In horror filled shock, my gaze had drifted down from the unsettling lack of eyelids, down his bulging, tumorous neck, following the line of his bloody arms to end at… nothing. Jagged, bloodied scars sealed the ends of what should have been his wrists, leaving only two useless stumps that hung at the tortured man's sides with no life or use.

Leaving behind only the remaining charged atmosphere my horrified scream had filled, I'd bolted from the spot and ran. Slow, barely coherent heads attached to more tortured and mangled bodies had turned to see my own body flee past the rooms they filled. Footsteps had congregated behind me, heavy and shuffling, as the residents of the thirteenth floor had all lumbered toward their doorways to watch me try to find some safe place. None had come after me, but I placed no stock on that fact, because I had no idea if it would remain that way. They all seemed too far gone, too dazed and half dead, to care too much for chasing me. But, I couldn't rely on that. Shilling had created monsters by taking his victims and making them as inhuman as he possibly could. My only wise choice would be to expect the unexpected.

I shoved my hands through my tangled hair, gripping at the roots and tugging hard. The slight pain pulled me back from the ledge of panic, grounding me just enough to slow my speeding breaths and calm my hysterics. With time, my body began to still, until I became a limp, tired, useless heap of crumpled limbs and salty tear tracks on the floor.

Check your surroundings, Power snapped. You're in enemy territory and you need to know what you're working with.

I nodded, submitting to her amazingly level headed instruction. With a timid lift of my aching head, I rose to sit on my knees and began to absorb as much of the empty room I had chosen as possible.

It harbored no structural differences to mine and Esther's dorm room in Ward F. The same size, with the same barred window in the same spot. The similarities came to an abrupt halt there. Chips in the awful greenish-teal paint littered the walls, while trash and soggy debris sat in hunched piles all over the room. Where the strong odor of bleach had burned my nostrils in the lower floors, the sharp, musty tang of the unbathed stench of dozens of bloody bodies reigned in this place. The smell of sweat, mixed with coppery blood, alongside the stink of human waste drifted from every crevice, though I saw none of the substances responsible anywhere.

Perhaps the most disturbing of all, though, was the absence of any kind of door to the room.

You have no shield. No barrier between you and whatever else is out there, Power offered, always the wiser to the inner workings of my twisted mind.

Cold dread worked its way up my throat. The most basic element of protection was missing. Again, like a snake ready to strike, the world 'vulnerable' slithered up the walls of my mind, haunting me with its implications. Safety was a far off illusion, cast by the misguided encouragement and sugar coating of my ward mates for the lethality of Rosenton. Esther and John knew about this place. Their refusal to speak of it told me as much. Maybe even George knew, though expecting anything except the unexpected out of him was a foolish endeavor.

The desperate need to find a safe hiding place reared its head again, demanding I uncurl myself from the floor and take preemptive action. No longer could I play the defense card. In this place, on this floor, I had to be two steps ahead, on the offense and ready to take action at all times.

With the chill of the damp floor stinging my bare feet, I stood, joints popping and clicking, to prepare myself to explore and scout the area.

That's my girl, Power encouraged. Steadily, I noticed her voice gaining strength and volume, as if the distance between us was shortening. Pretty soon she would be able to fight me for control again, and my overworked, emotional brain wasn't so convinced that was a bad idea anymore.

The hallway loomed outward on either side of the doorway to my room. I braced myself on the useless door frame and leaned out just far enough to study what lied in either direction. To my right, where I had run from and where the door to the stairway sat, no fewer than a dozen mangled and deformed residents shambled around, eyes dead and unfocused. One man bumped into a smaller woman with a large dent in one side of her shaved head. She stumbled back, hitting the wall and sliding to the floor while never moving her eyes from straight ahead. The man, with one eye socket empty and both ears gone, shuffled his feet forward, seemingly unaware of the woman he'd knocked down.

I studied the oblivious and trance-like state of them all, taking as many mental notes as I could before dashing down the other empty side of the hallway in search of a safe place to hide. None of them seemed to make any motion that they knew where they were, or what had happened to them. A small, startled gasp flew from my lips as one middle aged man pulled himself, barely conscious, by them arms along the filthy floor. It was only as he turned to enter one of the rooms that I saw why. He had no legs, and barely a waist.

Close to death, and covered in his own dried blood, he dragged himself across the threshold, like a dog fleeing to the solitude of the underside of a porch to die in peace, painting a thick, dark red trail of his own blood with him. I didn't understand how he could possibly be alive, being cut in half the way he was. No man could survive that.

You know he won't survive it, Sane. He's been sewn up, but he won't last. It must have happened recently.

I swallowed thickly. A pained groan emanated from one of the patients further down the hall, snapping my attention from the half-man, and back to my target objective. Safety. Even if flimsy, some sort of safety had to be found.

Falling back into the feline grace I'd been gifted with under Robbie's strict training was far easier than I'd expected. It'd been so long since I'd had reason to use it, aside from the two nights I'd spent in my cave at my dark circus, that I half expected to trip and fall at some point. Thankfully, though, my years of ruthless training stuck, and combined with my inherent ability to stick to the shadows and go unnoticed, I made quick, quiet, and easy work of sneaking down the left side of the hallway.

I swept over each room I passed with a rapid, but critical, eye as I moved by them. Each one dashed my hopes of finding security a little more than the last, especially when I caught sight of a catatonic, experimented on resident or two in several of the rooms. And just like each room discouraged me a bit more with each failure, the tortures and inhumane treatment I saw of each of the anguished residents screwed the nails into my heart deeper every time I saw one of them. Never did the next one seem better than the one before it, but if I compared the unique torture and deformation of the last to the first, I'd still be unable to decide which nefarious fate was worse. How could a person compare the terror of having their eyelids cut away to the horror of having holes drilled in their teeth so that wire could be laced through them to sew the teeth shut? I saw no mercies given, in any form.

By the time my feet, numb and turning purple, slunk over to the abandoned, dilapidated nurses station, the bile swirling and tossing around in my stomach demanded to be released. A small, forgotten plastic trashcan layered in dust and mold met an unfortunate fate as everything I'd eaten recently made a reappearance into its depths. I tried to keep quiet as I retched, but there was really no need. Not only did none of the zombie-like residents pay any sound any mind, but their own screams and wails of agony made sure to drown out the sounds of my sickness.

I fell, limbs limp and weak, onto my bottom when I was finished, leaning back against the inner cupboards inside the nurses' station. My fingers curled around the small metal handle of the cabinet nearest me, and I pulled, trying my best to be silent. To my relief, the opening click was minimal in volume, and I pulled the door open the rest of the way. Soggy, molding cardboard boxes filled with equally destroyed messes of goopy remains of old patient records sat inside. I grinned, glad for the little beacon of hope, when I saw that the shelf splitting the cabinet space in half was removable.

Goosebumps erupted from my palms and knees as I shuffled backward and opened other cabinets around me until I found one with enough extra space for me to move the boxes and shelf to it. I shoved them against the various items already housed in the new cabinet, then waited for another scream to sound from down the hallway before putting all my weight into slamming it closed again.

With a firm resolve and solid focus on completing my job, I managed to keep from panicking or giving into the mounting fear. I grasped the bottom hem of my cotton dress and ripped a long, narrow piece from it, tying on end to the handle of the empty cabinet. The space was a tiny fit and filled with more mold and rat droppings, but I squeezed myself into it anyway, tugging the free end of the tied fabric to pull the cabinet door fully closed.

Perfect.

I found myself preening under the uncharacteristic praise from Power's glossed lips. She no longer felt very far away, but she wasn't strong enough to fight me for control yet, either.

I let a deep breath release and sighed. The hiding spot would be adequate enough, I hoped, but I needed to figure more out about this place if I wanted to be ahead of the possible, and probable, danger. Becoming one of the creatures shuffling through the hallways without cognitive thought or focus... I wouldn't allow that to be an option.

My palms hit the damp, frigid floor first as I tumbled out from the cabinet. I stumbled to my feet and glanced around the hallway again, swallowing back the fear once again. I no longer had the luxury of paralyzing emotion. The sensation of taking control felt foreign to my body, since Power wasn't the one exerting it, but I chose not to linger on it.

I winced every time my feet made any sound as I tiptoed further toward the end of the corridor that had been shrouded in darkness. The actual desire to investigate the area resided nowhere in my being, but my will to survive, as well as Power, demanded it. My teeth ground together the closer I got, but I refused to pause for even a moment, because it would give me the opportunity to talk myself out of acting on my own initiative. No one here would stand up for me or rescue me. For the first time in my life, I had to save myself.

Before I knew it, due to my internal pep talk, I had crossed into the unknown, standing in the dark area as I waited for my eyes to adjust. When everything around me finally came into focus and a somewhat acceptable sense of clarity, I found myself staring at a thick steel door, much like the door to the stairwell. Unlike the door I'd been shoved through onto this floor, though, the door before me was stamped with heavy metal bolts around all four sides, and a small rectangular window at eye level.

Licking my dry lips, I took the two tentative steps forward, until the little window stood less than six inches from my red, numb nose. The air around me seemed to freeze over even further, to the point that my eyes automatically grazed over the corners of the grimy glass window, looking for signs of actual frost. An ominous heaviness spread from the door toward me, washing over the area like a plague of hopelessness and rage. It settled over my lungs like hundred pound weights, crushing me into oblivion, spreading its malevolence until it infiltrated every crevice of my soul.

Look in, Power whispered, nudging me forward even as the door itself loomed overhead, projecting itself as the nefarious guardian of whatever evil laid inside.

Rising up on my tiptoes, pressing the pads of my toes even further against the icy tiles of the damp floor, I leaned up, gripping the one inch wide ledge of the peephole and peered inside. At first, I could make nothing out of the inky blackness inside the room. But, then, shapes began to form to my widened eyes. Within seconds, the form of what looked like some kind of gurney or operating table took shape, surrounded by rolling carts piled high with tools of every kind. I squinted, making out several scalpels darkened with blood that whoever had used them hadn't bothered to clean off. More recognizable doctors' instruments laid all over several of the carts, but as my gaze slid from one to the next, tools not so common to the operating table began to appear. Rusted pliers, circular saws, piles of archaic looking power drills splattered with dried blood and what my queasy stomach assumed to be tiny white bone fragments. My mind conjured up the image of the man I'd seen with holes drilled into his teeth, followed by a demented scene where he laid, awake, on the operating table while Shilling stood over him with the drill whirring, just so he could capture the man's terror in his own memory to savor.

I shook the images away, thoroughly repulsed and horrified, to continue my examination of the surgical room. More objects, morphed by the darkness in the room, appeared and I took note of each one. Mostly items clearly used in Shilling's torture of the residents, reinforcing the unease slithering around in my gut.

Before the scene could disturb me any further, I pushed away from the intimidatingly large door and sighed, taking a step back.

However, a rather solid, fleshy mass connected with my back, freezing me in my tracks. Shilling, my mind whispered, while another scream built up in the back of my throat. I spun around, throwing my arms up as shields as I backed straight into the steel door to the torture chamber.

"No!" I cried, though the reason behind the denial remained unclear. No, don't hurt me? No, don't be Shilling? No, stay away?

No, all of the above? My heart slammed against my chest with the force of a hammer swinging in such rapid succession that I feared myself about to be victim to a heart attack. I'd known fear before, but the sensation coursing through my veins put the rest to shame.

The person I'd stumbled into breathed in deeply, the effort producing a scratchy, rasping noise that was decidedly not Shilling. That knowledge was enough for my eyes to pry themselves open and my arms to lower slightly, though still guarded. I looked up, shrinking back against the door still, despite the small relief. When I got a good look at the mangled creature in front of me, though, all the air left my lungs in a forceful, jarring heap.

Three orderlies and two nurses stood in the area, restraining a single man in a hospital robe. The man's eyes were wild, overflowing with fear and anger as he fought against them, thrashing and biting everything he could. Blood dribbled down his chin as he roared like an enraged beast. An orderly snatched the syringe from the new nurse and jammed it into the man's kicking leg.

Across from them, huddled against the wall, another nurse stood, doubled over and sobbing as she held her hands against her face. More blood poured like a waterfall between her violently shaking fingers. Her sobs got louder and louder as she began to scream, crashing to her knees against the shining linoleum.

My eyes shot back to the man as he let out one last, terrifying roar before he, too, fell to the floor in a lifeless heap. He looked up at me as his limbs gave out, making eye contract and keeping it even as his body collapsed onto itself. I watched as his eyes rolled into the back of his head, leaving nothing but the whites of his eyes to stare back at me. The man's mouth fell open and huge fleshy chunks of blood and tissue flopped down with a sickening fwop from his mouth and onto the floor in front of him. The crimson liquid spread around his head, staining the pristine linoleum. Horror overtook me as I realized what had just happened, and what those fleshy chunks were and where they came from.

"You!" I gasped, fingers shaking as they reached out to him before thinking better of it. Just because I felt pity for him didn't mean he wasn't a threat. My own condolences and care for what he'd been through meant nothing about any kindness he may or may not have reciprocated. Who knew what Shilling had done to his mind up here? Six, seven months was a long time to be trapped here. Any number of horrible things could have done... any number of horrible things to his mind.

The man stared at me, though the emptiness in his eyes unsettled my very bones. Red, jagged scars covered his arms, and I suspected the rest of him that was covered by his tattered shirt and trousers also. His dark head had been shaved, making the scars crossing all over the patchy stubble stand out even more. Fingers were missing from his hands, a pattern I'd noticed among many of the residents so far. My own fingers curled into my palm, as if that would protect them from the same fate.

Other than that, he didn't seem as deformed and maimed as the rest of the people I'd seen so far. Was that by Shilling's wishes, or had he managed to avoid much of their fates somehow?

The man's face remained empty of any emotion or recognition, not even showing if he was studying me the way I was him.

Is this what George would look like if he didn't play act at emoting? Power wondered aloud, as if she'd forgotten the dire situation we'd found ourselves in.

I shrugged her away and focused on slipping away. I couldn't be sure of his intentions, if he had any at all. With a single backwards glance, just to be sure I'd really seen him and not imagined him, I took back off down the hallway, into the lighter but still dim part, and reentered the room I'd claimed for myself earlier, huddling in a ball of nervous energy in the only corner not visible from the doorway.

Chapter 32

"Do it again, Kate. You've gotta get it perfect."

A frustrated rumble sounded off in my throat, and I stood, ready to try Robbie's newest act again. The fire lighting in his eyes, coupled with the big, cheesy grin highlighting the lower half of his own sweating face, eased some of my aggravation away. Thick, wet clumps of his black hair stuck to his forehead, escaped from the ponytail he'd tied away from his face with a small strip of leather. I'd told him countless times that a regular elastic ponytail would hold much better, especially with the rigorous training, but he held to the notion that that stupid leather strip felt "authentic", whatever that was supposed to mean, or why it was even important.

"You can do this. I know you can," he urged, grinning and nodding his head at me, excitement bubbling beneath the surface of his words.

My eyes closed, and a hot, thick breath of air filled my aching lungs. Without a word, I nodded and took my position again.

"You've got this," he encouraged, stepping forward to lift me up to the horizontal metal bar. "It's hard, but you can do it."

I practiced for another two hours, until the quivering in my strained muscles made any more attempts a danger to myself. Without Robbie's constant encouragement, I would have given up hours ago. But he had a way of shining his enthusiastic light so brightly that it was impossible to tell him, "no".

My body slumped to the floor, a sweating, shaking mess. "You're trying to kill me," I accused, too exhausted to grin through my lame joke.

"Am not," he scoffed, dropping down beside me with a canteen of iced water. He shoved it to my mouth and I drank greedily, savoring the crisp sting as it rushed down my parched throat. "You're just capable of so much, Kate. You may not have it down yet, but you will. And, by this time next year, you'll have it as second nature and we'll be working on something even more advanced."

I groaned, slamming my forehead into his shoulder. "That's not helping! I don't even want to consider anything more difficult than this right now!"

The chuckle in his chest vibrated his shoulders, bouncing my head a little. This time, I found just enough strength to smile along with him. He stood, offering me a hand up. I took it, with reluctance, and wobbled to my feet. The lengths of my legs trembled beneath me, but I made it back outside the practice tent without incident. After a quick signal to Charlotte, letting her know Robbie was ready for her to practice her routine with him, I hung my head and made my way to the lions' cages.

"Kate!"

I turned, the ball of my foot grinding into the crunching dead grass beneath it. Robbie stood at the entrance of the small white practice tent, waiting for me to answer him.

"Yeah?" I asked, praying he didn't want me to "help" Charlotte with her routine, like last time. That had ended with an infuriated attack later that night, where the beating had been more personal, and therefore more painful. But more painful than the physical blows, had been the words that haunted me most nights recently.

"You're nothing!"

"Who are you to be his teacher's pet?!"

"You don't deserve to breathe the same air as me, much less act like you're better than me!"

"What worth do you have?! None! You're worthless!"

"You're weak and pathetic! If you died, it'd takes months for anyone to even notice!"

"Go to my trailer and pull the set list for me, please. I can't remember if I put Charlotte in the trapeze act this week or Ellie," he said, instead. My chest released a relieved breath, and I tossed him a quick affirmative smile before turning back around and changing course for his trailer.

Once I got there, I ducked under the awning and stepped inside the crowded space.

"Set list, set list, set list," I mumbled to myself, sifting through the ominous stacks of paper threatening to collapse all over his desk. He didn't allow any of the other performers to come into his private quarters, so I made it a point to never let my special exception be found out.

My eyes narrowed as I stood, unable to find that one sheet of paper among the sea of chaos, and studied the rest of the room for other possible resting places. They zeroed in on the rickety wooden shelf standing beside his unmade bed. A single mint green sheet of paper hung halfway from the edge of it, held in place by what looked like a small, singular jewelry box. I reached out for it, scouting around various objects lying around his unkempt floor. My fingers brushed the thick paper, just as my foot slipped into his velvet top hat, lying haphazardly on the ground. The brim extending from the bottom of the hat rolled to the side, catching my ankle with it and sending me flying to the messy floor. I gripped the corner of the paper on the shelf just as I fell, bringing it and the jewelry box down with me.

The small, dark wood box clattered to the ground, bursting it's rugged, well worn lid open. The wristwatch I recognized as the one Robbie's father had given him before he passed away tumbled from the black velvet pillow inside, landing in an undignified heap on the floor beside my head. Forgetting the set list, I grasped for the precious watch, knowing it to be of much greater importance to Robbie than the little piece of paper that changed each week.

The gold felt smooth and cool against my fingers, the black leather strap a stark contrast to the yellow metal of the faceplate. My other hand found the little pillow it had rested on, and I scrambled forward to pull the box to me so I could place it all back inside, and safely back on its perch on the rustic, old shelf.

I slid the box toward me, pulling myself up on my knees, then picked it up with the other two items poised to be placed inside. And, I would have placed them there immediately, without hesitation or suspicion, if I hadn't seen my full name scrawled across an old, yellowed envelope at the bottom. A thin slice of wood, identical to the other wood of the box, laid a few feet away, just the right size to fit in the bottom of the jewelry box.

A false bottom.

The envelope crinkled dangerously under my touch, threatening to fall apart in its old age. The handwriting spelled my name out in full swirls and fanciful swoops, the letters exaggeratedly beautiful and luxurious. I flicked the flap on the other side open, turning the fragile parcel over in my hands. Inside, a single page was nestled, folded in perfect, almost uncreased thirds. But, the envelope felt too heavy in my hands for a single piece of paper. The weight was far too unbalanced, with the majority of it hanging onto the bottom corner. Only a slight bulge reaffirmed my suspicions.

The letters slid out with ease, almost as if it'd been waiting for me, and was excited to finally be read by the recipient. I held my breath as I unfolded the paper, flattening it against my lap gently, so as not to harm the aged material.

Katie, it started, and I squeezed my eyes shut for a moment. No one called me Katie, though the thought of being called by that particular nickname sent warmth to my belly, like a comforting cup of hot cocoa on a winter day.

I am under no illusions that I'll ever get to see you after you're born. I've been locked away for so long that even if they did let me out, I'd have no idea how to live back in the real world again. And, maybe because of the bluntness I've endured over the past six months, this letter will be short, to the point, and just as blunt as I'm accustomed to nowadays.

I love you, first of all. Let no one ever tell you I did not. You aren't even born yet, but I know that the love I shared with your father could have only created you as something magnificent and wonderful. You have a brother, only a couple years older than you, who is already showing promising signs of being the same kind of strong, kind man your father is. I can only hope that you are able to meet him and bond, knowing that you will always have each other. Your father is the best kind of man. A little reluctant to love, at first, because he's lost someone dear to him already, but the moments where you question his love for you will be worth it when he finally does open up to you like he has to your brother. I can only hope that what I've told you about him remains the truth after I'm gone. Death does strange things to strong men, and he will have had a double dose of heartbreak by the time you go to him. Just give him time and patience, and love him even when you fear he might not love you. Cling to your brother for comfort when you need to, because I know that little boy, and I know he'll always take care of you.

There are things I imagine you'd like to know about yourself and me. I'll give you as much as I can on this single page, because I'm sure to not be given any more than this. They don't even know I have this. Your father snuck it in to me, with no idea that I'll truly never be able to leave here and be with him again.

I have a feeling you'll have your father's eyes. If they're a stormy, steel grey, then I'm right. If not, I suppose they'll be my color. A muddy, nearly brown, hazel.

I also already know you're a girl. I've known from the beginning. My family always gives birth to girls first. Though, if you do turn out to be a boy, my heirloom gift I'm enclosing will look a little silly on your wrist.

Speaking of, the bracelet was my grandmother's. Keep it, and treasure it. It's likely the only thing you'll have of mine, besides my blood.

The writing began to shrink as the woman who claimed to be my mother neared the last few lines of the page. I held the paper closer to my face, trying to make out the thick, murky ink.

Some will tell you I'm not well. I suppose they're right, in a sense. I'm not always myself. Sometimes, I'm Chaos. My grandmother – your great grandmother – had one called Mayhem. It seems to be a family curse, and I do hope you aren't burdened with it.

Lastly, a word of wisdom. No matter what you have or don't have, be content, but never complacent. With that mindset, even if you fall from a great height, you will live to be happy and unbroken. Never let the temptation of power overtake your good will toward others.

I love you, I love you, I love you.

Your mother,

Evelyn

I stared at the confusing letter, reading over parts I didn't understand over and over. The fact that she said her family – our family– had girls first, and yet I had an older brother. I couldn't even begin to decipher the bit about a supposed family curse. Were Chaos and Mayhem my ancestors' versions of my own Power? But, how could Power be a curse? She protected me. She fed me strength when I had none of my own. It didn't make sense to call her a curse.

Then, of course, was the bit about her being locked up. Was she a felon? A criminal? Incarcerated? Why would she think she wouldn't survive to see me? So many more questions rose from the ashes of my ignored, yet unknown, past, and I wasn't sure I wanted that.

Wouldn't I rather be content to simply live, even without all this information that only raised more questions? That had been her last bit of advice, after all. Though, how to be content without being complacent eluded me, completely.

The sound of the door to the trailer slamming startled me from my thoughts. I shoved the letter and envelope, tearing them in the process, back to the false bottom of the jewelry box, sliding the sliver of wood that disguised itself as the bottom of the box over the top.

"So, this is Robbie's private area, huh?" Gregory mused, glancing around the chaos around him. My heart sank into the depths of my stomach, and I pushed the wooden box under his bed, behind me. He reached back, flicking the lock on the trailer door, then turned back to me with that familiar, sinister grin stretched wide, showing off all his white teeth.

"Not here," I begged, unashamed. I'd follow him to be beaten willingly anywhere but Robbie's trailer, my only untainted, safe haven.

"I'll try to make sure you don't remember it, Little Mouse. But, even if you do, you will tell him you fell and hit your head. Got it?"

I think it was the fact that my heart was ready to explode out of my chest in fear that woke me from the dream of my memory. I sat up, hands squeezed to my chest as I struggled to bring my breathing back to normal. Power smirked, beneath the surface, and I instantly knew she'd known about the letter I'd found so many years ago. How many other occurrences had I forgotten through all the head injuries and mental torture I'd been the victim of over the years?

Then, more questions were taking up every spare inch of space in my mind, like floodgates had opened. Many of them were the same as I remembered having immediately after reading the letter. Why was my mother imprisoned? How could... whatever condition is what that led me to have two people in my head be genetic? How had she coped? Was her version of Power, Chaos, to blame for her imprisonment? And, how did I have a brother if she claimed her family always had girls first? Who was she? And, maybe more importantly, who was my father?

Or... was she just insane? Did none of her information make sense because she'd lost her mind? Was it all just mindless ramblings of a lunatic? Was that another curse to be handed down to me?

A shuffling sound from across the room jerked my attention away from the internal, and back to the real world. My eyes shot over toward the source of the noise, and I froze, remembering exactly where I was. The thirteenth floor. No safety. No protection. No barriers. No doors. I'd chosen to hide out in one of the rooms the other deformed creatures seemed to pass by more often than the others, but my luck had run out, apparently.

A dark shadow filled the doorway. At first, I saw no distinguishing anomalies that pointed toward torture or experimentation. No missing limbs or strange placement of other body parts. And the figure only stood at a few inches taller than myself. Long hair would have normally told me it was a woman, but in this place, where no hygiene care was offered, much less hair maintenance, it didn't quite work the same way.

We stewed in tense silence for several minutes, neither of us moving or taking our eyes from each other. Or, so I assumed, anyway. The lighting from the room behind her cast her whole body in obsidian shadows, leaving her as a dark blob of lifeless depression in the center of the entrance to the room I'd chosen. Cold chills enveloped me in an uncomfortable cocoon as I took in every detail I could.

The figure shuffled on her feet, taking one hesitant step forward. My body repelled itself, pressing itself into the wall behind me.

"Kate?" The voice coming from the formless shadow left her lips as barely a whisper, but I'd have known that voice anywhere. A deep, sinking sense of dread settled at the base of my stomach.

"Marce?"

The slumped figure took another step toward me, the light from the barred window in my own room casting her face in its grimy light. This time, my body moved forward instead of back. I stumbled to my feet, anxious to get to my friend. The filth and damp trash beneath my bare feet squished between my toes, filling me with disgust, but I paid no mind to it, only focused on getting to her.

"Why are you still here?" I borderline whined, disbelief and defeat lacing my voice. "They were supposed to take you back down to our ward if I..." I paused a foot away from her, taking in her harrowed appearance with appropriate horror. Mildew from the window, with the sunlight cast behind it, reflected dirty greenish brown spots on her sallowed and bruised skin. Thick, jagged stitches kept her left eyelid sewn shut, while an unhealed, but clean cut, from what I could only speculate as coming from a scalpel, ran the length from the height of her beautifully feminine cheekbone down to the corner of her lip. Blood dripped from the gash, trailing down her cheek and staining her tattered silk dress.

"What have they done to you?" I whispered, reaching for the disfigured portion of her face. She shied back, hiding her left side from me. Her only functioning eye refused to meet mine.

"You came for me?" she asked, instead, glancing all around her with twitchy, uncoordinated movements.

"Of course I did. You're my friend. They told me... they told me they'd send you back down to our ward if I confessed to Ernie's murder. They thought you did it."

Stupid. You've been had. I told you, and you didn't listen.

A humorless laugh forced its way from between her chapped lips. "You know they don't let anyone leave here. You're so dumb, Kate," she sobbed, throwing her arms around me in a sudden show of affection. I tripped backwards with her weight, struggling to return her embrace while keeping us both upright.

"What has Shilling done to you?" I asked, running my fingers through her dull and greasy hair, hoping to instill some sort of comfort to her battered form.

She snorted, though it sounded forced and pitiful. "Compared to the others here? Nothing worth mentioning. I can still speak, and I haven't been sawed in half and left to die. Just a few broken fingers, a missing eye, and a cut on my face. I'm lucky, really," she choked, tears building in her eyes. A clear, salty drop fell from her right eye as a bead of water and blood pooled in the corner of her damaged one. It dripped down, disappearing into the deep bloodied gash in her cheek.

My eyes scanned the rest of her thin body. Sure enough, her left hand hung in a mangled heap of twisted, swollen fingers below her hip. An unstoppable wince twitched my features as the thought of how how much pain she must have been in hung around my mind.

"Kate, they do awful things here," she whispered, her trembling breath burying into the side of my neck as I continued to hold up her body weight. She hung limply against me, as if it had taken all her strength just to get to me in the first place.

"I know. I saw the others."

"We're not going to make it out of here alive."

My teeth sank into my bottom lip, nearly drawing blood. The lingering feeling that her words rang absolutely, irrevocably true wrapped itself around my mind in a hopeless cloud. Despite that, I lied to her anyway, because what else could I do? To agree with her felt far too much like the final nail in the coffin. Like giving up. So, I gathered every ounce of bravado still hiding in the dark corners of my body and shook my head.

"No," I told her. "We're going to be fine. I'm getting us out of here. We won't become like the others here."

Marcie swallowed, her eyes flicking back and forth between mine as she leaned back to try to see me. "You swear it?" she asked, making me wince. I nodded, anyway. Maybe some hope, even if it was vastly misplaced, would be the deciding factor between life or death in this place.

Marcie slid to the ground then, holding her palms over her watery eyes. Her broken fingers on her left hand stuck out in odd, painful looking places. It had only been a few days since she'd been brought here, and already half her body was an unfixable mess, disfigured by Shilling to a horrible degree.

"Can we sleep?" the girl asked, looking up at me like a scared child, asking if she'd be okay in her dreams when the real world held too many atrocities. And again, as if my word could banish evil dragons bent on hurting innocent girls, I nodded and sank down beside her, where we used each other's laps as pillows to guide us both into that blissful dreamworld.

The foggy haze of sleep still hovered over my thoughts and body while my eyelids creaked open, like old, unused doors in need of oil. The room around me spun, sending my head into a dizzy mess, before settling down so I could raise myself from Marcie's lap and sit up properly. I palmed my eyes, grimacing at the disgusting way the grime sticking to my hands rubbed against my face.

Marce groaned, shifting in her sleep. Even unaware, she seemed to know to keep her left side from putting too much pressure against anything. Streaks of blood from her face wound puddled down the lap of my dress, where she lay. I closed my eyes and looked away, the guilt swimming in my stomach for her condition too much for me to bear.

It was the moment my sight moved from her mangled face to the area in front of me, that I froze. Cold, humid air sucked in through my teeth in a sharp, but quiet gasp, and my chest tightened as waves of fear mingled with anxiety crashed down on me.

They were all there.

Most stood, but some, with damaged legs or other atrocities that kept them from standing, knelt or sat in front of me. They stared, collectively, as if all of them were one solid being, split into separate bodies. Cold, dead, hopeless eyes, filled with pain and suffering, aimed at me with such decisiveness that I couldn't have looked away if I'd tried.

Power pushed the soft limits of the limbo separating us from each other. Even without speaking, I knew she saw the very real threat in front of us. These people, as much as what had happened to them wasn't their fault, were unstable and unpredictable.

Shilling could have done anything to them. He could have even brainwashed them or taken their will to make their own decisions. It wasn't unheard of, especially in some of the concentration camps used during the war. Horror stories, alarmingly similar to what stood before me in person, had come back with many of the soldiers, shedding light on the awful nature of some corrupted human beings.

Had John seen things like that, I wondered, before scolding myself for losing focus and setting my attention back to the matter at hand. The dozens of thirteenth floor victims surrounding Marcie and I, staring at me without any cause that I could decipher.

With exaggerated caution in keeping my eyes trained on the walking dead surrounding me, I slid out from under Marcie's limp form and rose to my feet. Not a soul so much as moved, though their own empty sights kept attached to my every motion.

We stood like that, in a stalemate of uncertainty and fear, for what felt like ten thousand years, to me. Each disfigured person held in their own place of the semicircle crowd of other victims, and as I looked from face to face, I realized that not a single one of them blinked. Their enlarged pupils hinted at the possibility that they'd been drugged or medicated, perhaps with the same "medicine" I'd been given months ago. But, it wasn't just their black pupils that seemed too large. Each of the disfigured stared at me with unchanging, enlarged irises as well. Far too little white surrounded their disturbingly disproportionate irises, only adding to the blank, empty appearance in their faces.

Movement to my right startled me, causing me feet to take an involuntary jump backward. I swiveled around to watch, my heart pounding against my chest like a wrecking ball against my sternum.

A single male limped forward. Those surrounding him shifted out of his way, never breaking their eyes' contact with my form. Clouds passed by the window, casting the room in an even dimmer light. But, I could still make out the man's face. Air struggled to fight past my own hyperventilation to fill my spasming lungs.

He continued forward, stopping only a couple feet away from me. His gaze never wavered, just like the ones surrounding us. My throat constricted, while Power began tugging at the threads of control I held onto, nudging me to give them to her.

The man who'd torn the young nurse's face off studied me, his eyes narrowing toward me, eliminating all the white space around his eyes. His dilated pupils sharpened the tiniest bit, as some recognition or intelligence seeped through to his barely conscious brain. The calm, lazy breathing of dozens of thirteenth floor victims coupled with my own hectic, terrified breaths filled the room with its eerie sounds.

His arm raised, then, straight from where it hung at his side. His tattered and filthy sleeve shifted against his thin, papery white arm, showing the angry red scars decorating his body like a road map. Despite the missing fingers and scars, he seemed in much better condition than the others, still.

His hand reached for me, arm extended fully from his body. Only three fingers remained on the hand he held out, but compared to the torture of those around him, I hardly expected him to complain. Or talk, at all, really. So far, no one had spoken a word. Not even a moan of pain or terror stricken scream.

He stared at me, waiting, with that lacerated arm outstretched. Power yanked at my subconscious, threatening me against doing anything stupid. I shoved her back down, resolute to give her control if things got hairy.

With trembling muscles, I mirrored his actions, bringing my own hand up until only a few inches separated our hands from touching.

What are you thinking?! Don't touch him! Power raged, kicking at the stone wall holding her back.

His stare bored into me, telling me I knew what he wanted me to do, and he expected me to do it. And so, against Power's frantic demands, I took the smallest step I could manage forward. Our palms met, cold grime against cold grime, three fingers against five. The man took a step forward, until our elbows bent to allow him to stand directly in front of me, so close I could smell the bleach and old medicine on his skin.

His mouth opened, dry lips splitting and blood beading along the splits. My own lips rolled into my mouth, pressed together so tight my teeth hurt. How long had it been since he spoke? His teeth weren't missing, nor were they experimented on. The pink flesh of his tongue still hid in his mouth, too.

Three fingers curled over the tops of my more petite ones, and I pulled away from him, ready to bolt. However, his hands wrapped around mine, and he used that leverage to pull himself even closer. And, barely inches away from me, he bent his head to meet my eyes with his. Something, however brief, sparked for a moment. Intelligence, again, or maybe something even more complex than that.

His oversized eyes flicked over mine for half a second more, before his lips parted again and he spoke, sending a violent wave of horrified, confused goosebumps down, then back up, the entire surface area of my body.

His voice barely a crackling whisper, he said, "Kill them all."

Chapter 33

The world stopped spinning as I stared, horrified beyond my wildest nightmares, into the enlarged eyes of the man in front of me. The spark of clarity that had flashed in them before he'd told me to "kill them all" had vanished, replaced with the same cold, dead, empty look all the other tortured souls around him wore.

"Kate?" Marcie's quiet voice drifted from behind me, trepidation coating the single syllable.

Waving my hand in a jerking fashion, I shushed her. The thirteenth floor victims didn't seem to act aggressive toward me, but nothing could be certain toward Marcie.

She's one of them, you know, Power reminded me. Her usual scathing tone was replaced with an uncharacteristic gentle one. For all her callous actions and quips, my evil twin did care for my ward mates - Marcie in particular.

With extreme caution, I took a hesitant step forward, knees shaking as I tested out the reactions of the other inmates. In silence, one by one, they each took shuffling steps backward as I neared them. I motioned for Marcie to follow, keeping my hand held out for her to grasp. Her broken fingers slid against mine, jutting out at odd angles that made my stomach roll. Would her fingers ever be the same again? How would she survive, mangled as she was, once we got out?

If we get out.

As I did any time Power shoved the truth in my face so bluntly, I ignored her. Marcie's socked feet padded along behind mine, her shallow, scared breaths hitting the back of my shoulder in warm, jarring puffs. The residents continued to part, leaving a thin but open path for the two of us to pass through. Tiny, nervous spasms fluttered in my chest, keeping the air trapped in my lungs. My breath held there while we took tiny steps past them, waiting for the unstable, unpredictable inmates to attack suddenly.

However, they never did, and when Marcie and I reached the doorway, I turned back around to take in the puzzling, disturbing scene again. Aside from the narrow path we had passed through, none of them had moved, and they all still faced the opposite wall, where they'd found us sleeping. I swallowed the fearful lump in my throat, wincing past the pain of it sliding back down to the base of my stomach.

I glanced over at Marcie. Her body trembled and a thin layer of tears glassed over her one uninjured eye. The thick black cords holding her left eye sewn shut looked wrong, so wrong, in her once perfect face. Not only that, but the deep cut on her face had begun to show signs of infection. Though only a small amount, the yellow pus in the meat of the gash could only mean bad news. Obviously she needed medical attention - real medical attention - but the knowledge of how quickly an infection could take her from somewhat okay to... to dead... It hit home with me, finally, how dire our situation was. The redness and slight swelling surrounding the gash only intensified my concerns.

"What?" Marcie asked, eyebrows drawn.

My eyes squeezed shut as I looked away from her and into the empty, dim hallway. "Nothing," I whispered, and tugged her with me as I entered the corridor. "We need to find an escape. Or at least a place to hide, or a weapon. We just have to do something."

She said nothing, but nodded meekly and allowed me to lead her down the hallway. We made our way to the only exit, the reinforced steel door. I don't know what I hoped to find. There was no chance of us escaping the foolproof blockade. Shilling would have made absolute sure of that. He was not a stupid or naive man. But, I couldn't think of any other option. Waiting around for something to happen was what had gotten us into this mess in the first place. Power had warned me to take preemptive action, and I'd denied her. No more. I wouldn't allow her control, but I also wouldn't cast her wise judgment aside again.

I'm not sure there's anything I can help you with anymore, but the sentiment is nice, she snapped, clearly angry with my too-little-too-late change of heart.

If I could have apologized to Power without making Marcie wary of my already questionably sanity, I would have. As it was, I could only send her my most contrite emotions in waves to her, hoping it was good enough.

I jerked to a halt. There she stood, upside down yet again, her red stiletto heels pressed against the top of the door frame of one of the rooms closest to the door to the stairwell. Her hair had grown longer, reflecting the lengthened state of my own limp and dirty locks. The tips caressed the floor as she leaned against one side of the entryway, arms crossed as her head swiveled to follow my movements. As always, she looked beautiful, times a thousand. Her hair curled, makeup immaculate, and positively glowing in one of my favorite old red and gold performance costumes.

However, her mouth marred the beauty of the rest of her. Literally stretching from one ear to the other, it brought me back to the vision I'd had of her months before, where she'd thrown herself against the window of my underwater circus cabin. Power grinned at me, reading my thoughts. The smile showcased every tooth in her head, and then the gums and the insides of her cheeks encasing them. Disgust for the unnatural scene rolled up and back down my body, producing a humored scoff from her.

In some perverse moment of curiosity, I glanced at Marcie, wondering if she could see Power hanging just a few feet away from her.

"You keep acting strange," she blurted when she caught my stare. "What's wrong?"

I sucked in a sharp breath. "Can-can you see it?" I asked, nodding toward Power. Whether I wanted her to be able to see my alter ego, I couldn't say, but I had to know.

I'm an 'it' now?

Marcie stepped closer, stopping in the doorway. Power glared at her closeness, but refused to move from her perch. My question was answered when Marcie stared directly through Power, though, and the nervous breath I held onto released.

So, she really was all in my head.

Marcie spun on her heel, shooting daggers at me with her one eye. "That's a horrible thing to do, Kate. You think I don't know what could happen? I didn't need to see that or have it pointed out to me," she snapped, storming past me to get to the stairwell exit. Confusion marred my features as I watched her leave, my eyebrows drawn in a deep V. Next to me, Power giggled, covering her massive mouth uselessly with her dainty hand.

That was perfect. You're a piece of work, always screwing up without even knowing it.

"What?" I asked, not sure what had just happened.

Look in the room, stupid.

My body sidled past hers, making the extra effort to make sure no part of my made contact with her. Her grin never faltered as I stepped inside, waiting for me to discover whatever had set Marcie off.

Oh.

Thick, congealed black blood puddled around the man who'd been sawed in half, framing his dead, graying remains. His glazed eyes stared to the side, directed at Power, more or less. It didn't seem to bother her, her stance nonchalant, but shivers overtook my spine at the thought of his lifeless eyes being attached to a version of me. It disturbed me on a deeper level. Something about the fact that someone living couldn't look at Power and know she was there, but this disfigured, dead thing with no life left to brighten his eyes seemed to stare straight at her, unflinching. It felt too much like symbolism I didn't want to consider.

"You did that on purpose," I accused, quiet enough that Marcie wouldn't be able to hear. Power shook her head, her silky corkscrew curls dancing in waves with the movement.

I wish I could take credit for that disaster you just created. No, that was all your doing, Sane.

Twisting my fingers in the filthy fabric of my skirt, I turned from her smirking face and followed after my offended friend, feeling like an absolute heel. My fingers gripped onto her shoulder as I caught up to her, pulling her back to face me again. We paused in front of the steel door, setting aside our mission of finding some kind of weakness within it for escape to fix the kink in our friendship.

"I didn't mean that. I didn't even see the man there. I saw something else, Marce, I swear. I just wanted to know if it was all in my head or not. I'm so sorry," I blabbered, desperate to mend the broken trust I'd caused.

She lifted her chin, looking down at me past her nose from her one good eye. Somehow, she still seemed to put off an air of regality and poshness through the injuries to her face. Inside, I smiled at that fact. Unlike the rest of the thirteenth floor residents, she hadn't been broken yet.

"Just what did you see that could have possible overshadowed the sight of a man sawed in half on the floor?" she seethed, anger dancing in what little light was left to shine in her face.

Unable to break the bad habit, I bit my bottom lip again and looked away, unable to meet her firm gaze. "I'm in here for a reason, you know," I started. "Not everything I see is real, and I just... didn't know. I'm sorry."

The haughtiness blanketed over her softened into understanding, laced with some measure of pity. "Oh," she said, then lapsed into a silence uncomfortable to both of us. I wondered, vaguely, if it would be a good time to explain who I actually was to her. My time in the circus. Power. The massacre.

I scoffed. No. Of any time in the world, now was the most inappropriate time to divulge my identity. None of us needed the extra stress at the moment.

The rusty clanking sound shaking the door to our right shook us from our inner battles. The skin surrounding my eyes tightened as they grew wider in panic.

Someone was coming in.

"Run!" I whisper-shouted to Marcie. She wasted no time. In seconds she was fleeing back down the empty corridor, skidding to a sliding stop at the old nurses' station. "Get into the cupboard underneath!" I called, at least a dozen feet still behind her. Her head swiveled to look back at me, surprised at my distance.

The door creaked, metal grinding on metal in an agonizing cacophony of sharp scrapes as it was pushed open from the other side. Without waiting any longer, Marcie dropped to the floor, out of sight, and, judging from the soft click that somehow made it to me through the rush of blood pounding in my ears, was able to make it safely into the hiding spot I'd cleared the day before.

The screeching, awful noise assaulted my ears as it grew in volume, signaling the further opening of the impossibly thick door. My legs pumped against the damp floor, feet slapping against the chilled tiles. A resounding boom echoed down the hallway, the sound of the door hitting the wall beside it. I chanced a glance back, sliding and slipping until my body careened into the crumbling counter. The edge of the laminate surface caught just under my ribs, shooting flares of pain into my core. I grimaced under the lingering ache, but refused to close my eyes as they searched out the person who'd just entered the thirteenth floor.

Paul watched me run, then crash into the station, a sickening grin of satisfaction gleaming on his face. Sheer delight fluttered in his eyes as he took my form in, as if he were a starving man and I was the first steak he'd seen in years. It didn't take a genius to know that was nothing but bad news for me. Would he torture me, like he and Shilling had done to the others? They'd certainly taken no time in doing so to Marcie, who'd only been there a few days.

We won't let them, without a fight, Power said, walking from the shadows of the stairwell to stand behind him. Her mouth, again, stretched from one ear to the other, but she no longer smiled at me. Instead, her glare focused on the back of the oblivious Paul's head. He walked toward me, his gait excited and nearly bouncing. She matched him, step for step, only inches from his back.

"Katherine Thornton! How lovely to finally see your mousy little face on this fine floor!" he cried, his exuberant voice bouncing off the walls closing in around us. I backed up against the cold counter, the gritty dirt and greasy grime digging into the pads of my fingers. My eyes darted all over, searching for another escape. Too bad he'd closed and locked the door behind him, though I hadn't expected an escape to come that easily anyway.

"Your little boyfriend is making quite the ruckus downstairs, demanding you be set free," Paul began, closing in on me. Power seethed from behind him, her manicured hands clenched into white knuckled fists. "He's actually in the visitor's room now, with your brother and that tramp, Martha. I imagine they're working on equipping the best lawyer money can buy, hoping that they'll rescue you from your pitiful fate. In fact, Kate, I hope that is what they're doing. Collaborating, gathering hope that they'll win. That way, when this all goes to court, I can stand witness to how utterly unmanageable and violent you've become. Then, Shilling can crush every shred of hope they built up in their little pea brains, and I get to watch it all play out across their pathetic faces when they realize they've lost."

Lawyers.

Despite his morale crushing speech, a spark of hope flared up in my chest. Robbie and I were past the point of equipping the help of lawyers, and had been for some time. That meant... That meant Paul and Shilling knew much less than I'd feared. They didn't know of our escape plans, not that we had constructed a solid one yet. But, that still meant we had the element of surprise on our hands, and that lifted the dark cloud from my shoulders, just the tiniest bit.

Paul continued on toward me, until we stood nearly toe to toe, his shining brown leather dress shoes nudging the tattered remains of my thin socks. Power bristled, not pleased with his proximity to the body she so badly wanted control over. Her jaw clenched, and her hands rose to wrap around his head, not quite touching him yet. He stood, still oblivious, with that menacing grin stretched across his bright face, as her scarlet nails dug into the flesh of his cheeks and dragged back toward his temples, ripping the flesh until only bloody chunks remained.

Horrified, my jaw fell slack, while Paul's grin morphed into a satisfied smirk. Power leaned forward, her talons still sunk into the bloody bits hanging from his face. Her chin rested on his shoulder, and she smiled, revealing the rows of needle sharp, crimson stained teeth inside her far too wide mouth.

We haven't lost, Sane.

"By the way, how is Martha's niece faring? Ms. Greene, I believe? I helped Shilling with her surgery, you know. Isn't she much lovelier now?" Paul taunted, still not seeing or feeling the terror he should have, considering Power's closeness and clearly violent intent.

Words refused to leave my opened mouth. My tongue flapped uselessly as I tried, but nothing came of my efforts. Blood ran in tiny rivers down his face, staining the clean shaven skin there. The color drained completely from my cheeks as Power rose to her tiptoes and flicked her tongue across one of the rivulets, catching drops of the ruby liquid on her tongue.

He's ours. Shilling is ours. This whole place belongs to us. We'll show them that, soon, she whispered into his ear, though her firm gaze remained locked on me. Paul made no move to show he'd heard her, or that he felt the gashes mirroring each other on either side of his face. Was it real? Or was I stuck in another demented vision, brought on by Power?

"Surely you've seen her already? There's no use lying, but I'll let you gather yourself. You've always been a tiny little nothing, haven't you? I don't know why Shilling wants to destroy you so badly, but I can't say I'm not eager to see the results. Or to help him achieve those results. I'll be seeing you again soon, little mouse. Take care," he continued, finishing his monologue with a dramatic flourish of his sweeping hand.

Power stepped away from him then, pulling her nails from his flesh and licking the blood from them with long, feline flicks of her tongue. I shook my head, pressing my palms to my eyes in an effort to bring my sanity levels back down to normal. Another tentative opening of my eyes revealed that it'd worked. Power had disappeared, and I caught sight of Paul's unmarked, smooth, clean skin on his cheek just as he turned to leave again.

The door slammed behind him, but I found I still couldn't force myself to move. Power had regained her strength, as well as her confidence. Not a shred of the uncertainty she'd shown earlier remained, and the arrogant, overwhelming presence I'd come to know so well was back in full swing. The only question was, would her evil powers be used for good this time?

Movement all around me snapped me from my thoughts. Trembling, moaning thirteenth floor victims revealed themselves from their hiding places all over the area. For the first time, real, coherent emotion resided in their oversized eyes.

Fear.

Then I realized. I'd been the only one not to hide and cower when Paul had arrived. For once in my life, I'd been the brave one.

I was no longer just the little mouse.

Chapter 34

Hunger pangs drove me from sleep early the next morning. Gray light, a sign of dawn's approach, filtered through the mold and filthy film layering over the single window. My stomach rumbled, demanding the daily gruel it'd become accustomed to. But, did the residents ever receive food? They had to. The man who'd bitten the face of the nurse had been locked away up here for months. The only other possibility my fuzzy mind could conjure was far too horrifying, even for what I'd already seen. Sure, I'd heard of the Donner Party – almost everyone had. But the idea of experiencing cannibalism firsthand fell to my shoulders with much more weight than hearing about it.

Even Power shuddered at the unwelcome image of residents eating other residents, so I shook my head and opened my eyes in an attempt to banish the unpleasant, early morning thoughts.

Dozens of mutated torture victims stood in my room again, but this time, they all stood facing away from me. A sea of pale, zombified people in dirty, threadbare clothes spread themselves out across the area, all facing the eerie doorway on the other side.

I squinted at the mass, confused by the situation. The day before, Marcie and I had already come to the wary conclusion that the residents meant us no harm, but I was far from anywhere close to trusting them.

Pushing myself up on my elbows, I began to sit up, only to stop at the distinct sound of shoe-clad footsteps approaching from down the hallway. Adrenaline picked up speed, humming in my veins and waking my groggy brain as I froze, on alert for an escape route if need be. I moved to kneel, hunkered down behind the bodies of my fellow inmates. The steady tapping of walking shoes got closer, revealing a second set of quieter, but still shoe clad feet. None of my new ward mates moved a muscle, except to sway back and forth ever so slightly at random intervals. Was that due to hunger? Or perhaps whatever medicines they'd been pumped with to keep them sedate and under control?

The two people coming down the corridor stopped in the doorway to the room we were all in. I held my breath, the temporary silence making the hair on the back of my neck stand at attention. With movements so tiny I almost didn't notice them, the residents closest to me closed in together, forming a solid wall separating me from the people on the other side. Whoever it was couldn't see me, but I couldn't see them, either.

"I know she's here, my pets. Step aside and I won't take one of you to my playroom today," Shilling's cold voice rang out across the room, loud and domineering.

None of the residents moved, keeping me sheltered from his sight.

He huffed, shoes squeaking against the moisture gathered on the cold floor. The same cold floor that was slowly making my kneeling knees numb.

"Fine," he quipped after a moment of unwavering silence from his steadfast victims."Paul, choose a resident to take with us today."

My heart thudded angrily against my chest. Yet another innocent person, taken and hurt, because of their loyalty to me. Why? I was nothing special. Nothing worth someone giving their life over. I wasn't worth what they'd done to Marcie, and I wasn't worth whatever he planned on doing to tho poor unfortunate soul Paul chose.

The young woman Paul grabbed from the mass of people might have once resembled me in the loosest definition possible. Most of her hair was long and brown, like mine, and through the purpling bruises and disturbing gaping hole where her nose should have been, I could see that her skin tone might have once been a golden olive, like mine. I committed her appearance to my memory, guilt swimming in my gut for her sacrifice. Taller than me, with pus filled lesions covering one arm and chunks of muscle ripped from her other. Her blue eyes, like everyone else's, were dead and showed no hint of fear even though she struggled against Paul's ironclad grip. I slammed my own eyes shut, memorizing every detail about the young woman I could in a private show of grateful reverence.

Paul and Shilling, with surgical gloves reaching their elbows and white masks covering the bottom halves of their faces, took the woman by her arms and dragged her fighting form from the room. Paul glanced back once, a victorious gleam shining in his eyes, just before they left, leaving the rest of us to stew in a stale silence as we listened to the two men chuckle at their victim's pained struggle. My heart ached for her, but I didn't know what I should do. They'd protected me of their own free will. Would her sacrifice be in vain if I stepped out and let Shilling take me instead?

What was I supposed to do? What was the right thing to do?

What would John have done?

After the fateful sound of the other steel door leading to Shilling's operating room slamming shut, the other residents shifted from their man made wall and began their journey, sliding numbed blue feet toward the doorway, out of my room. I waited, frustrated tears coating my eyes, but I refused to let them fall. Remorse for letting them take the young woman slammed into me, weighing me down. At the same time, Power stood resolute behind the stone wall, convinced I'd done the right thing.

I wasn't so sure anymore.

Leaving Marcie, who'd slept through the whole ordeal like a rock, I stumbled to my freezing feet and made my way to the hall, arms crossed tightly over my chest in a completely useless attempt to retain some warmth. Goosebumps rose under my shivering fingers, though I couldn't tell if they shivered from the cold or the fear I valiantly was trying to swallow down. Either way, my stiffened joints protested the movements, aching with the cold chill that emanated from the entire thirteenth floor.

Residents moved, as if they didn't quite know how to walk, around the hallway and various rooms without aim or purpose. How many pill bottles had been dedicated to the victims of this floor, to keep them submissive and unable to function well enough to fight back? Shilling was a monster of the lowest, most awful form. It was a fact I already knew, but the people around me, who didn't even resemble people anymore, set the notion in stone.

I slipped through the masses, noting that the closer I got to the operating room, the fewer residents I ran into. Until, within the telling darkness surrounding the ominous door, I stood alone, arms wrapped around my upper body as the shivers intensified. Alternating, wild, shrill screams alternated with pleading whimpers coming from the woman inside the room drifted through even the heavy metal door, making my stomach twist into uncomfortable knots. But, I had to know. I had to see what that woman had chosen to endure in order to give me a chance to live.

The pads of my toes ached with the sharp frostiness of the damp floor as I leaned up onto my tiptoes. My fingers latched onto the space beneath the tiny rectangular window and I peered in, praying I wouldn't see anything as horrible as I knew I would.

Red.

The knots in my stomach churned and pumped. The woman's jaw opened much farther than I thought the human jawbone could, pouring another agonized scream out of it's depths. Her eyes stretched open wide, bulging with mind blowing terror, as her hands, restrained in thick, red stained, leather straps formed fists so tight her knuckles protruded inched outward.

Shilling and Paul stood at her side, Paul tightening the restraints on her wrists, chest, legs, and feet as Shilling stood hunched over her thigh, what looked like a rusted scalpel in his hand, digging around with it in her leg. The thigh he hovered over was nothing more than ground meat anymore, large, twisted chunks of meaty flesh ground together, spilling over the opened skin alongside much more blood than I though possible to come from a human body.

Shilling turned to Paul, pointing to a thick red cord in the midst of all the wrecked, mutilated muscle of the injury. I squinted at the two men, actively ignoring the gory sight that made me feel absolutely sick. Shilling's face mask twitched and shifted as he spoke words I couldn't hear to Paul, still indicating toward the large vessel.

Femoral artery, Power supplied. He's left it in tact. She won't die any time soon as long as he doesn't sever it.

A deep, disturbed shudder ran down my spine. My hand shot up to cover my mouth as I dry heaved toward the floor, forehead pressed against the freezing cold metal door.

That poor woman. All because of me. My fault. Her agony was my fault. It should have been me on the operating table. They'd been looking for me, and took her as a punishment.

Shut up and calm down. There's nothing you can do about it. They chose to take that chance and protect you. Don't you figure there's a reason for that? You're not meant to be in there, so stop your ridiculous pity party and get yourself together!

Ah, there she was. My always faithful voice of reason and encouragement. My hands formed frustrated fists that I grounded into my cheeks, punishing myself for the pain of the woman in that room.

Swallowing, I tugged a pieces of my hair to snap myself out of it and stood straight again. Breathing rapidly and lightheaded with all the chaos engulfing my whirling mind, I leaned up again and braved a peek back into the room.

Two pairs of eyes that encompassed absolute evil and inhumanity stared back at me.

A startled shriek shot from my lips and I jumped back, clamping my hands over my mouth. Shilling and Paul abandoned the tortured woman on the operating table and stalked for the door separating me from them. Their gaits and the horrible glints in their eyes matched, casting an even eerier light on their movements, and I found myself trembling as I stood still, like a fool while the disgusting duo advanced closer and closer.

Run, idiot!

Chapter 35

My body kick started itself the moment it heard the screeching sound of metal grinding on metal again.

Run, run, run, run, run! Power screamed, clawing at the stone wall, nails digging into the surface and leaving her fingers bloody in her attempt to jump in the pilot's seat since my own mind had apparently left the building. I shook my head, knocking the fear and shock loose long enough to start pumping my legs in a desperate flee from my tormentors. My feet slapped against the chilled tiles, but the blood rushing in my ears, pounding like a drum, drowned out the sound.

Chancing a glance behind me proved to be my biggest mistake. Shilling, in his older age, was rather far behind me, but Paul was the athletic sort, it seemed. He closed the distance between us much quicker than I felt strictly comfortable with, so I pulled from every shred of endurance and stamina I'd stored up over the years and kicked my panic driven legs into overdrive.

"Kate!"

Marcie dove from the room we'd slept in, throwing herself at Paul and knocking him to the ground in a bundled heap of limbs and cries that rolled into the opposite wall. The thud that vibrated the walls from their collision caused my steps to falter, fighting with myself over whether I should go back for her or not. I couldn't just let her-

Don't even think about it, you stupid imbecile! If I have to say it again, I swear I will have you slitting your own pathetic little throat! RUN!

Maybe it was her tone, so like Robbie's that I was used to following the orders of, even though he never verbally abused me as Power did. Either way, I shut down any conflicting emotions and fell into that submissive state where all I could do was follow instruction to a T. My emotions detached themselves from my logical thought, giving way for the Kate that thrived in the environment where someone else was in control. Power knew what to do. Power was confident and level headed. Power was logical. Sane lacked all of that, and so, even if she wasn't in the pilot's seat, Power possessed all control over whatever choices I made until the situation ended.

Kate was useless. Pathetic. Stupid.

Power was none of those things, and everything that Kate needed.

Nurses' station. It's the only chance we have, even if it is a really stupid idea to trap ourselves.

My body obeyed on command, and hurled itself over the counter, taking a quick peek back to see if either of the monsters behind me could see where I'd gone. Lucky me, they both tangled and wrestled with Marcie, who revealed herself to be quite a bit scrappier than she'd ever given away. She thrashed and kicked and bit as if she'd grown up a heathen on the streets. I found myself immensely proud of her, even as my heart pounded in fear for her life.

Hurry up!

I dashed beneath the counter, yanking open the door to my secret hiding spot and slid inside, my breaths coming out in visible white puffs as I pulled the scrap of fabric I'd tied to the handle, sealing me inside the dark, dank cabinet. I inhaled, only to fill my lungs with the musty odor of rot and mold. My lungs itched, begging me to allow them to cough up the vile air, but I refused, even as tears dotted the corners of my eyes.

For several minutes, with eyes sealed shut as I muttered prayers for help under my breath, the blackness consumed my world and for that little while, nothing outside existed. The silence separating me from the rest of what was happening on the thirteenth floor allowed me a brief, pretend reprieve. My frantic mind began its gradual descent into a more calm, level headed state. My thoughts shifted into neat little compartments, organizing themselves into easily pluckable places. I could see everything clearly, as if I'd set every aspect of the situation out on a table for inspection. Puzzle pieces fit together, plans formed in impressive clarity, and my body calmed the panic threatening to take over.

I opened my eyes, letting out a peaceful, cleansing breath.

The cabinet door ripped from its hinges, flying across the nurses' station and crashing against the far wall.

A hand reached down, flailing to grab for anything. I waved my arms out, slapping his away on instinct, and allowing him the close proximity to latch onto my wrist by proxy. He yanked, and a flurry of swear words leapt from my lips as red hot pain seared up my arm, the joint in my shoulder a hotbed for pain and unbridled agony. I knew that feeling, by experience. The very distinct pain of bone being jerked from its socket couldn't be mistaken for anything else, and as a cry of frustration left my lips, I cursed myself for constantly making these stupid decisions. Was it instinct to swat at the hand trying to reach me, or just stupidity? Or, was my sense of instinct stupid to begin with?

I fell, hurtled out of my brief hiding spot, onto the floor. Soggy old paperwork provided a pathetic cushion for my body, and despite the horror of the situation and the anguishing pain in my shoulder, I still found myself wrinkling my nose at the thought of coming in contact with the disgusting piles of refuse.

Pop it back in place! Pop it back in, Sane! We don't have time for you to be a goody toe shoes!

Paul stepped closer to me, towering over me and casting his dark, malevolent shadow over me as the glint in his eye sparkled in delight at our positions. That same filthy, gross trash I'd wrinkled my nose at slipped and slided under my hand as I used it to push myself back upright. Without giving myself enough time to be scared of the pain or what Paul might do to me in the next few seconds, I pulled my knees up to my chest and laced my fingers around them, thumbs facing up.

Good. Good. Robbie taught you how to do this, Sane. You can do this. Just hurry up!

I kept one eye on the leering Paul, who must have felt like a god from his point of view, looking at what seemed to be me cowering in fear. As his delusional smile brightened with every second that he relished the situation, I pulled back against me knees, feeling the muscles and tendons grind against each other, stretching to make room for the joint to relocate back into place. I recognized the shocks of sharp pain that warned me not to go any farther, but I didn't have time to play nice with it. I had to survive.

Paul leaned down just as the joint slid back into place. Bright, colorful starbursts danced across my vision as the pain temporarily took over, and I groaned, clenching my teeth as I endured it until it faded enough for me to see straight again. Just as that pain receded, though, another round exploded in my jaw. I knew the sensation well. How could I be a stranger to the punches that I'd endured for years on end under Jensen and Sons? A sick, depraved sense of nostalgia washed over me as the blows rained down on me before I could come to my senses.

You're absolutely useless! I hate you, Sane! I hate you! Stand up and fight if you want to live! Power prowled all over the entirety of the space she lived in behind the stone wall, gripping at the roots of her hair with white knuckled fists as she screamed at me and my stupefied state. Her stilettos rang out sharp clicking sounds against the ground she paced, sounding more like gunshots than the heels of shoes.

I whimpered once, gaining nothing more than a furious, rage filled glare from her for my weakness. Didn't she know I'd have let her out if she'd been strong enough yet? Her recovery from her stunt in Shilling's office and the gymnasium before that still wasn't complete enough for her to take over, but God and all His angels knew I'd have thrust her to the forefront myself if it's have been possible. Why was she so angry with me?!

It was that righteous anger bubbling in my stomach that thrusted me into action, finally. I wish I could say I began dodging punches, while throwing some back of my own, but I'd never been a fighter. Power dominated that area, while I inhabited the more peaceful, subtle kind of life. Instead, I shoved my arms out, catching Paul's starched white collar, and twisted my fist into it until my knuckles dug into his throat, and by proxy, his windpipe.

The moment he realized I'd snapped out of my paralyzed stupor with that move, though, he bore down on me, straddling my flailing legs and moving the target of his own fists from my face to my stomach. It only took one solid hit to knock my breath out and release my grip on his collar and throat. My stomach seized up against the attack, clenching the muscles there in a poor attempt to protect myself.

Don't stop moving! Keep going!

Desperate, I muscled past the pain and shoved my hands to the sides of his face, pressing my thumbs directly into his eye sockets with as much force as I could muster under the circumstances. Blood spurted from behind my thumbnails on both sides, spraying my face and neck with the crimson liquid I'd become so familiar with over the course of my life. Deep down, I knew being literally showered in someone else's blood should have bothered me, but another detached presence in my head stomped those thoughts down, demanding my physical survival as priority over my mental or moral survival.

Paul screamed, not the angry growl of a man with pride at stake, but a shrill wail so distorted and panicked that no one could have mistaken the level of misery he was in. His hands gripped my wrists, knocking away, but the damage was done. More blood poured in dark trails from the inside corners of his eye, dripping in rapid succession from his jaw to my dress, drenching me in yet another disgusting substance. He continue to scream, pawing at his face in a frenzy of hysterics that fueled his anger toward me. With a savage roar, he lashed out, throwing a blind punch in my direction and catching me in the arm I'd only relocated back into its socket minutes before.

I cried out again, blood pounding in my ears so loud I could hear nothing else.

No! Wait! Power said, raising her head and perking her ear up, lights dancing in her eyes. Lights that looked an awful lot like hope. That's not your pulse! That's the door! Someone's trying to get onto the thirteenth floor!

I opened my eyes, bracing myself for another wild punch. Paul roared, the only word I could think of to describe the awful sound coming from his throat, and pulled his fist back to swing at me again, his other arm pressed against his injured eyes.

But, behind him, my shocked gaze focused on the twenty or so dead expressions attached to horrifically mangled bodies, all staring at him. Hunger lit up portions of their faces as he wailed as if I'd dismembered him. A single one of the men or women he'd helped deform was a thousand times stronger than he could ever be, I realized as I took in individual corruption of what had once been smooth, human flesh. None of them made a sound as they closed in, digitless hands outreached, eager to make contact with their tormentor on their own terms.

My focus swung back to Paul just as his fist flew toward my unguarded face, on a collision course with my already bruised nose.

This is going to hurt.

The blow never came. The quick slapping sound of skin meeting skin made it to my ears, but no pain or force accompanied it. Heavy, excited breathing grew in volume all around, a depraved symphony of charged tension. My eyes, wide with appropriate fear, swung to the spot the sound came from. Paul had thrown the punch, but his fist, still clenched but trembling now, hung encased by another hand that gripped his knuckles tightly, jagged yellow nails digging into the skin and drawing even more blood. I followed the line of the hand all the way up to its owner, unable to steady my own quick, shallow breaths.

The scarred man who bit the nurse glared down at Paul with such fiery hatred that I winced, flinching back away from him. Paul sputtered, confused as he struggled to clear the blood from his vision to see what was keeping him from his mission of bludgeoning me, possibly to death.

"Let me go, you ugly, worthless nothing!" he snapped when he realized who held him back. He attempted to hide the surprise inside his dictator command, but failed miserably. As all the other residents looked on with unchanging, empty faces, the scarred man's lips twitched the smallest bit in an upward movement.

It was all the others needed. They closed in, filling the nurses' station, spilling out into the hallway, as their arms wrapped around Paul, tugging him off me. Countless hands grabbed at the panicking, screaming man, dragging his helpless frame as a swarm. The scarred man stood still as they disappeared with Paul into one of the doorless rooms. One last, shriller, more hysterical cry came from the room, followed by a loud crack, then silence.

The scarred man's grin widened, as if he knew exactly what had happened. He held out a hand to help me up, his pupils dilated and watery.

Power watched, her wariness floating into my subconscious like a heavy fog. But, she verbalized no protests, so I placed my hand in his clammy one. He pulled me to stand, watching as I bent over the counter and wheezed, pressing my forehead against the dingy, cracking laminate. Everywhere that Paul had hit felt a thousand times worse than I remembered being beaten felt. Maybe I'd forgotten over time, even though it was so familiar.

I rolled my head to stare at the scarred man as my stomach screamed in agony. "What did you mean when you said it?" I asked, my tongue thick in my dry mouth. God, I was so thirsty.

The man's mouth never opened and he gave no hints that he planned on answering my question. Instead, his intense stare bored into mine, taking in what had to be a harrowed, filthy and fragile sight.

Another bang on the door to the stairwell had me jerking back in surprise, but the scarred man simply looked over his shoulder at the door as it shook against the frame. Was it a rescuer? Or was it another staff member eager to torture more innocents?

Without so much as another glance my way, he turned and walked, silent, away from me and into the room his fellow ward mates had taken Paul.

Chapter 36

The door rattled against the frame, sending a violent metal grinding sound onto the entire floor that sliced into my eardrums like alarm bells, screaming at me to get moving, get going, get doing. Groaning with the combined weight of all my aching muscles and bones, I pushed myself away from the counter and stood, swaying in my dizziness for a moment. Gathering my bearings with a deep, trembling breath, I blinked hard a couple times, breathing out the pain of every bruise and sucking clean air back into my lungs to replace it.

Marcie.

Forcing air through pursed lips, I straightened my back and ignored the pain in order to walk away from the nurses' station in search of my friend.

Where's Shilling?

My feet padded against the tile floor at a quicker pace at Power's very valid concern. I prayed I wouldn't find them together, with Marcie in another horrible position because she martyred herself for me. Again.

Adrenaline, in a strange twist of normalcy, built slowly in my veins as my legs pumped in time with my growing panic. What started as an uncertain stumbling walk transformed, in a dozen shifting steps, into a near hysterical sprint. My arms reached out in wild circles and I tripped several times, crashing into door frames to inspect every room for any sign of Marcie or Shilling. Each empty room weighted down the lead in my stomach more and more, until I came to the room the residents had dragged Paul.

His body laid in the middle of the crowd of inmates, crumpled and broken. His head faced the wrong way, the skin of his neck twisted in a macabre velvet curtain of wrung folds. And, as much as it sickened me to admit, I took great pleasure in the shocked and terrified expression on his post mortem face. His dead eyes stared out to nothing, while his mouth, where so many insults and cruel taunts had spewed from, remained jacked wide open in a silent scream.

With a shudder that encompassed my whole body, I turned from the only occupied room, even though the occupants only stared blankly as they stood like demented mannequins all over the space, and continued my mission.

I found Marcie in the room we had slept in the past two days. The moment her platinum hair appeared as I rounded the corner to peer in, my panic dissolved into dust particles that drifted away in an explosion of relief. My shoulders sagged and I propelled myself into the room, reaching for her.

She didn't see me coming. Her left side faced me, showcasing the oozing gash in her cheek and the angry redness surrounding the stitches holding her eyelid to her bottom lash line. Her gnarled, twisted fingers shielded her face as she jumped backward with a whimper, stumbling back over her feet and landing hard on her bottom. Still ingrained with the posh decorum of a high society aristocrat, she rushed to pull and tug her skirt to cover any indecent bits that her position might have exposed.

My gaze swung to the other side of the room to see what had her so afraid, though, in some way, I already knew.

Shilling lunged at her, a rounded hook of wood with a glistening long blade connecting the two ends of the piece wielded in his grip, held high above her head. Marcie screamed, cowering into the corner in an upright fetal position. The blade in Shilling's hand had the chance to slice a single lock of her hair from her head before my body collided with his, saving her the exact same way she'd rescued me only minutes before.

I swung, bumblebees zinging through my veins, under the glory of the Big Top. Air collided with my body with more and more force the faster my trapeze sailed through the air. Without hesitation, my body dropped to hang upside down, eliciting a generously positive reaction from the audience. Hands clapped and voices cheered from the wooden stands. Awed gasps reverberated through the tent, bouncing off the walls to sneak into my ear like little secretive whispers. The scent of the chalk layered on my hands floated toward my nostrils, and I breathed it in deeply, savoring the familiar aroma.

The crowd continued to cheer as I flipped and moved from one trick to another, sliding into each position with the ease and grace of a heavily seasoned performer. The actions felt fluid and came without hesitant pause, as it did to many of my coworkers. I imagined myself as a beautiful black snake, slithering around and through the swinging trapeze bar, playing with the many stunts

I carried in my arsenal as if they were nothing more than child's play.

This was where I had confidence. This was where Sane melded with Power into a fantastic oneness of satisfied, cocaine high wholeness. Fear couldn't touch me up here. Timidness was a word I could scoff at. This was where I was the star. I was on top.

I was alpha.

I blinked, and the crowds disappeared, throwing my movements slightly off with surprise at the change in scenery. The brilliant sunshine yellow and crimson red of the Big Top had vanished, replaced by the cool depths of blue and grey my private circus cave inhabited. The noises of the excitable crowd mellowed into a medley of water and stone rushing to meet at the small waterfall behind me. My cocaine high sensations faded, making way for a calm satisfaction that turned the corners of my lips up. Not a blinding performance smile anymore. No, now my lips curved with sincerity instead of showmanship.

I sighed in contentment, continuing on with my performance. Neither setting held more satisfaction in my soul than the other, but I couldn't deny how much the performance high consumed me and fulfilled the emptiness inside. The same emptiness that Power liked to exploit to make me afraid. I would have none of that here, and she enjoyed the performance too much to even attempt anything.

My body danced through the air, sometimes barely holding onto the trapeze bar. Wind rushed to meet my face, cooling down the thick sheen of sweat accumulating there. For the first time in a long while, I experienced pure, uncut happiness. My soul forgot all about Rosenton Home for the Criminally Insane. People like

Shilling and Paul no longer existed. I'd never experienced the horrors of the thirteenth floor.

But, I'd also never met John.

Or Esther. Or Ed. Or Lottie, or Marcie, or even George.

My eyes snapped open. The trapeze swing hung deadly still in the middle of my cave. I hung upside down, from my knees. My fingers flexed and cracked with the unease crawling its way up my spine. The air, which had been so filled with life and addiction, tasted stale on my tongue. Stifling, even, as beads of sweat dripped from my forehead to splash in the cool dirt below.

The audience sat, crammed so tight their knees touched, on the old wooden stands. They seemed unaware that they had somehow materialized inside an inner chamber of a cavern, without the glitz and sparkle of the Jensen and Sons Big Top. Every single pair of eyes seared my skin with its unwavering gaze, their attention successfully trapped on my frozen air sculpture hanging from the wooden bar. The low light coming from the few torches John had left on our last excursion casted shadows across each audience member's face, creating an eerie scene all around me.

I wriggled a bit, making my knees more comfortable against the bar. The crowd erupted, screaming my name and jumping to their feet while slamming their hands together in excited claps.

And then… Then, I couldn't do it anymore.

One stocking clad leg, with a still perfectly pointed foot, rose from the wooden bar and I curled it to my chest. The pressure on my other knee was agonizing, but it would only last another second.

I pulled my other leg from the bar and plummeted to the earth.

I landed so hard the air ejected from my lungs in a painful burst. An undignified growl of frustration shot from Shilling's mouth as he also landed on the disgusting floor beside me. The strange blade, that I recognized vaguely as a heavily used, but extremely sharp bone saw, clattered across the room before coming to rest at Marcie's feet.

Marcie whimpered, kicking the weapon away with her toes. Power cursed her for being so stupid, and for once, I agreed with her harsh judgment. If Marcie would have simply picked the bone saw up and either used it on Shilling or handed it to me, I had no doubts the situation would have been rectified in a single instant.

She'll be nothing more than a liability here. Tell her to run!

"Run, Marce!" I cried, scrambling to my feet as Shilling did the same. His eyes were bright with the very insanity he'd made a career of banishing, and the glee that danced across his face at my arrival let me know that one of us would die before this was over. One of us, whoever was stronger, would leave this room, while the other stayed here to decompose and rot amongst the other breathing mannequins roaming the floor.

What I told him was true, Sane. I do own him. It will be hard, but I will come out the victor here.

To have such confidence might have helped me, but that had always been my downfall. Too timid. Too hesitant. Too quiet. Too mousy. But, with her... with Power, I had a fighting chance.

That's right. Use me. Be the selfish brat you are, and use me when it suits you, she taunted, her grin wide and mocking. Maybe you've been spending too much time around George. Only giving me freedom when it suits you.

But she wasn't real, I told myself. How could I be a bad person if I caged someone who wasn't even sentient? Much less someone who enjoying the feel of blood running through her fingers, produced by the glint of her own knife.

And yet you're feeling guilty. Do people normally feel guilty for the wrongs they've committed toward the imaginary?

Was she imaginary? My mind rewound to the day before, when Marcie had looked straight through her. If no one else could see her, she had to be imaginary. A figment of my imagination!

Or just invisible. Use your brain, you peon. I'm as real as you are, just unfortunate enough to be stuck in your weak mental state.

The thoughts in my head raced around and around as I tried to make sense of it all. The time for a moral debate on my mental wellbeing and Power's questionable existence certainly could've come at a better time, I thought, as Shilling pounced from the corner of my eye.

I lunged for him as he ran at me. Marcie remained frozen in her spot, watching the two of us assault each other with wide, terrified eyes flicking back and forth between us and the banging and violent shaking of the exit door down the hall.

My palms met his starched white doctor's coat with force that surprised me, considering how little faith I held in my abilities to defend myself. Lord knew I could take a beating; I'd had enough practice with that. But, could I dish one out, if it meant the safety of my friend?

However, as much as the force behind my attack exceeded my expectations, I still had no experience in fighting back. Shilling used the momentum I'd created in throwing myself into knocking him down like a practiced brawler, shocking for a man who seemed to be much more of a studious type. His fingers wrapped around my wrists in a vice grip and he spun me around, slamming me into the opposite wall.

As soon as his hands left mine, I began throwing punch after punch into his chest, leaving no room for a spare second of hesitation.

Hit his face, moron!

Power's advice came too late. Shilling caught my fists in his hands with ease and slammed my body back into the wall, over and over again until my vision blackened and air had to fight to fill my aching lungs. I'd never been a crier or a shouter during a beating, but as the doctor's hot, angry breath crashed against my face and neck with every excruciating impact I made with the unforgiving wall behind me, I found myself grunting and whimpering like a scared child.

"You think you can leave me?!" he screamed, spittle spraying across my face. Another slam into the wall just as my vision began to return blacked it out again. "After everything I've done for you?! Just because you're pregnant?! I'll kill him and I'll kill you, too before I let you leave me!"

He's lost it! He's not even talking to you anymore. Fight back! Fight back, you stupid, useless girl!

But, what could I do? With no breath in my lungs and no sight, I couldn't even find my way past the pain and panic to form a coherent thought, much less create orders for my brain to send to my flailing limbs. Even less so when the pressure of his thick, large hands compressed around my throat, cutting off any chance of oxygen meeting my starving airway. I felt my windpipe crush under the weight of his palms, sending waves of hysteria to overwhelm every corner of rational thought still left in my mind.

I kicked out at him, desperate to have him release me from his grip, but the rage encompassing him prevented him from feeling any of it. My own hands rose to grip his, and I pried at his hands with everything I had left. I would not be the one to rot here! I wouldn't die so easily!

Let me out!

Power rushed me, shoving at any weak bindings I had left to try to restrain her. She ripped at the cords and ropes, ripping cage doors from their hinges in her frenzy to take over me. But what could she do? Even if she took control, my body was still the same as if I'd been in control. Still too weak, physically, to fight Shilling's attack. And, I did not want to die as her. I wouldn't, couldn't, die as Power.

So, as I struggled to kick out at and throw my own weak punches at Shilling, I threw up as many obstacles as I could to trap Power below the surface of control. With every passing second, willpower and strength bled out of my pores, weakening my defenses to both enemies. Consciousness seeped out, taking my very essence with it, until I had no choice but to give in. Power screamed and screeched at me, threatening me with torture beyond even what Shilling seemed capable of. Her beautiful face contorted into something horrible and furious as she cursed me and called me every name in the book. I barely heard her as Shilling's hands tightened, accelerating the path to my death. My end.

I floated, the pressure building in my bulging eyes. Nothing held onto me any more as my limbs went numb first, followed by a road of numbness that traveled all over the rest of me until I felt nothing whatsoever. My legs stopped kicking. My arms hung at my side, as if I'd become nothing more than a rag doll. As the last shred of my precious consciousness fled, my head lolled to the side and Power, spitting in her rage, shoved me into the depths of my mind, behind the wall. Neither of us sat in the driver's seat as we both hung, suspended, in that strange limbo below the surface.

My body gave out as we fought, and my death closed in.

I had lost.

CHAPTER 37

I - the not sentient me - fell back inside the recesses of my static filled mind, crashing onto the floor in a cloud of old dust. Pain should have shot up the back of my head as it bounced off the concrete floor the wall stood on, but I felt nothing aside from the slight pressure of the impact. Even as my head bounced a couple more times, I only felt the motion itself, and none of the pain that should have been there.

Fogged blackness stretched on as far as the eye could see in every direction, the only other objects in sight being the wall, which I was still fortunate enough to be on the free side of, and an old winged back chair with stuffing pouring from the various rips throughout the mauve fabric. A small circle of clear space surrounded me before being overtaken by the thick and heavy fog that obscured everything else.

Was I to spend my death here? Would this be my penance? To remain in the place I trapped my insane alter ego for the rest of eternity?

A distant screaming caught my slowly returning attention. The shrill sound grew in volume until another shape broke through the blackness, flying at me with such speed that it was left impossible for me to dodge. It collided with my already disconcerted body, and I grunted out of habit rather than pain as we careened, rolling in a mass of limbs and hair, several feet away from my original landing spot.

"Useless whore!" the other form screeched, the name calling alerting me to it's identity. Power. Her palm came down against my cheek, whipping my head to the side as she straddled my waist to continue her assault. The sting swelled across my face, and I wondered if I'd ever stop being beat. A small, slightly insane, smile lifted my lips as I realized I was literally hitting myself now.

"Is it funny?! I'll kill you before he ever has the chance! I won't die because of someone as worthless and stupid as you!" Fingers, with nails digging into my tender scalp, wrenched at my hair, yanking and pulling handfuls from the root. Why was it I could feel that pain and not the pain from before?

At first, no will to stop her resided in my apathetic form. But within seconds, in a moment of pure, avenging glory, my mind changed. How dare she? What right did Power have to want my body? By all childish rights, I had been owner to my body and mind first, and she was nothing more than an unwelcome intruder. She had tricked me, hurt me, used me, tormented me for years on end. I was in this demented place because of her! And I had laid down and taken it, without question, without any kind of fight back. I'd let her control me, manipulate me for far too long, and her reign as the domineering boss deserved to come to an end. Even if I died, she would not take me down as easily as my abusers before.

The heel of my hand caught her in the temple, sending her face reeling to the side. She fell off me, stumbling to her feet and shaking her head, as if dislodging the pain. It took only a few seconds for her to regain her bearing, and in that time I stood to my own feet, eager to stare her down and show her I wouldn't be so easily mistreated anymore.

A sneer grew across her furious face. "So, now the mouse wants to fight back? What will you do, Saney? Nibble me to death? Feel so sorry for yourself I let you go? Play the victim so well I feel pity for you? Or maybe you'll just whine so much about your poor, pathetic life that I leave before I get bored to death."

"Shut up! I am so sick of you and your intrusion of my life! No more, Power! You're done!" I yelled, stalking toward her, stopping only when I stood mere centimeters from her face. "Go die in a ditch, you heartless wench!"

She threw her head back, exposing the ivory skin of her elongated neck, and laughed. "You choose one heck of a time to stand up for yourself, sweetheart! What do you have to lose now? Shoot, what could you possibly have to gain by picking a fight with me now, of all times? You really are as stupid as you look." She reached toward her face with her manicured hands, flicking tears of laughter from the corners of her eyes with such a graceful, dainty motion that I found myself momentarily jealous of her ability to look so regal and cool, even in this situation.

"If my body dies now, I want to at least be the only one left standing in it." The sneer accenting my cruel words created a smirk on her lips, while something feral and excited flashed across her narrowed eyes.

"I suppose," she replied, taking a single step back, the heel of her stiletto clicking against the concrete, "we have a score to settle, then, don't we?"

I don't know if the horror I felt showed in my face, but I know by the satisfaction in her haughty chin raise that she saw the nervous clenching of my fists as she stretched taller, to impossible heights. Her legs stretched farther and farther, for what seemed like miles, matching the way her arms did the same, though her torso and head remained unchanged. Her limbs, whether by illusion compared to her size or reality, looked far too thin in proportion to her overall gargantuan size, almost like the legs of an insect.

My head tilted back to watch her grow, and I struggled to hide the very real fear bubbling up from my racing heart. Skin previously in tact on her cheeks stretched and split by fleshy strings, each one snapping the wider she opened her scarlet painted lips. That familiar ear to ear grin finalized itself across her face, and as I took a shaking step back to get a better view of her fifteen - no twenty - foot high stature, she reared forward, landing on all four of her elongated limbs, directly over top me.

I threw my hands over my head in an effort to keep her from crushing me, but it seemed she didn't want to do that anyway, as she stopped herself from coming down as low as she could have. I spun around, searching wildly for a way to fight or run or something other than just wait for her to annihilate me.

Sick cracking sounds, like snapping pretzels, echoed from all four sides. I flinched away from each, only to trip closer to the next. Power giggled, and I watched as the joints in her lengthened, thin elbows snapped with terrifying quickness in the opposite direction, forming a sinister cage around me.

I struggled to breathe. How could I fight her? Was this what she was capable of? What chance in hell did I have against this... this monster?

"I can smell your hopelessness, Sane. Ready to throw yourself down and sob it out now? Isn't that your go-to solution?" she hissed, licking her lips and smearing the lipstick all over. She paused, then laughed, glaring at me, her face upside down from her position above me, looking at me beneath her belly. "No, I take that back. Your default solution is to run, isn't it? So, do it, Sane. I do love a good chase. Go! Run!"

My every instinct screamed at me to obey. Obey and survive. Muscles in my legs twitched, ready to race away and never look back. Even my arms tensed to ready themselves for the pumping motion I'd normally use to run.

I planted my feet, terrified but determined to fight. For once in my life, I had to fight, and prove that it was her who was useless. I didn't need her! I could take care of myself, and her help was no longer welcome.

"I won't!" I cried, voice breaking with fear. Her teeth sparkled despite the lack of light, and she twisted her upper torso 360 degrees to look at me upright. The thrilled elation masking her features glowed, and she skittered closer to me, the palms of her hands padding across the floor until she hung only a few feet from me.

"So you will stay and fight for your right to live, then? What a pleasant surprise!" she cheered. I glowered up at her enthused face, hanging only just above. "Let's begin, shall we?!"

Her lower torso spun to match up with her upper body as she flung her legs up into the air in a flip that ended with her facing me on all fours. She looked like a giant Daddy Long Legs, towering above me. I remembered playing with them as a child, finding them in the corners of my room.

"They're harmless", Robbie had told me the first night I'd spent with Jensen and Sons. Back when we shared a trailer as the only two children employed. I'd only been six when his father had adopted me, and he nine, but his father hadn't wanted me to sleep alone or be under the care of any of the other performers. They were untrustworthy folk, I imagined, thinking of the brutalities their successors had dealt me.

"Look! They don't bite, and you can pick them right up!" he'd exclaimed, grabbing one of the spider's long spindly legs and pulling it from under my bed. I'd cried out, waving my hands in front of me, begging him to put it away or, better yet, kill it.

"Kate, it's fine! They can't bite at all, you know. They just kinda munch on dead things they find, really. They won't hurt you. I'd never let them stay in the cabin if they could hurt you." He'd held the spider in his hand, keeping it closer to his body than mine. I'd peeked from between my fingers, eyeing the terrifying arachnid with suspicious hesitance.

"But, it's still a spider, Robbie! Spiders bite and make webs and do all sorts of scary spider things!" I'd cried, backing up on the bed against the wall, as far away from him and his little pet as possible.

"Well, these don't do any of those things. Maybe they're not really spiders. Bruno calls them harvestmen, but that sounds stupid to me. They're Daddy Long Legs, and they're nice. Look! Look, he's crawling up my arm, Kate! See? He's nice! He just wants a place to stay safe, is all!"

I'd peeked between my fingers again at the dubious duo, the boy and his spider. Indeed, my new brother was letting the insect step its way up his forearm with graceful, long strides. Robbie had smiled at the bug, flicking his grey gaze from me to it and back again several times through his messy black hair, checking my reaction. I remembered reaching out, then, with a single pointed finger toward them, deciding to trust my new brother. He'd nodded at me in encouragement, something he'd do millions of times over in the coming years, and brought his arm closer to me, slowly, so I wouldn't be spooked.

"Just grab one of his legs and pick him up for a second. He won't hurt you. He's friendly, I swear."

I'd barely felt the tiny leg between my fingers, even as a child. But, I'd plucked the Daddy Long Legs from his arm all the same, and I'd held it up in the air from that one leg, letting it dangle in front of my face for closer inspection for a few moments. I'd only just become comfortable with that when one of the spider's free legs twitched in intent to move. I'd shrieked and thrown the bug across the room, sobbing in fear. Robbie had just smiled at me, telling me how well I'd done to face my fear and touch the spider, much less grab it and pick it up. He'd made me feel as if what I saw as my failure was a great accomplishment, and that had made my little girl heart feel much better. It'd given me what little confidence I had over the years.

I looked up at Power, layering the image of that Daddy Long Legs over her, picturing the similarities in my mind. I dug deep, reaching for that confidence Robbie had fostered in me, hoping it would grow into something great. This was my chance to show that. I was more than my fears. I could be Kate the Great all the time. I could hold that courage I harnessed on the trapeze in the rest of my life. I could be whole. I could lose all need for Power.

Her gaping mouth opened fully until only the base of her skull kept the top of her head from falling off the bottom half. An ear splitting, shiver inducing scream sounded off from her throat. I slammed my hands over my ears and shuffled backward a few steps in a fruitless attempt to escape the horrifying noise. Her head snapped back to it's natural position and she grinned at me, flicking her tongue across her sharp teeth.

"Come and get it, Sane," she taunted, hunkering low in a stance that prepared her for a frontal assault. Before I could react, she pounced, crashing into me and knocking me back to the ground. We rolled, nails scratching and fingers pinching, in a chaotic mess. Girlish hair yanking soon gave way to raging blows that rivaled anything I'd ever felt before, but the sound of Power's gasps of pain and her visible winces made my own contusions worth it. Where had this sudden burst of strength come from? To be the one hurting Power... I felt on top of the world, in a strange and foreign way.

Limbs flew as we fought, desperate to destroy each other in order to be the last one standing. To prove our worthiness to claim ownership of my body. I wrapped my arm around her neck, pulling her into a headlock, and tightening it as much as I could. One of her lengthened arms slithered around my waist and jabbed into my stomach with razor sharp nails. I felt the sharp stab only a second before warm sticky blood darkened my shredded dress. In return, I shoved my foot down onto the palm of her other arm, balancing all my weight into my heel and crushing her hand.

We continued on, doing everything we could to hurt each other, for several more minutes. Power continued to yell obscenities at me, calling me more and more creatively offensive names with every passing moment. Her clear shock at my ability to fight her back fueled her own attempts to subdue me, which, consequently, fueled my determination to subdue her.

Blood poured from her nose where I'd punched her, and I reared back to repeat the motion. She took the moment to circle her arm around me again and plant her hand on my throat, digging her fingers into the skin. Her nails pierced the skin and I wailed as she pressed her fingers further and further in, until the digits had buried themselves knuckle deep into the flesh of my throat.

Pain! So much pain!

The pain channeled itself into a purposeful rage, and my own arm changed course to mimic her movements. Before I knew what had truly happened, I felt the rubbery texture of her own skin giving way to the thick blood coursing through the veins in her neck. Her pulse vibrated beneath my palm, revealing her panic even as she held onto her attempts at a poker face.

"I'll rip your throat out," she gargled, crimson liquid trickling down either side of her natural lips.

"I'll return the favor," I wheezed, choking against my crushed windpipe.

We glared at each other, caught in a timeless stalemate of certain death. Her fingers flexed experimentally within my flesh, and I did the same back to her as a reminder that I held her fate in just as precarious position as she held mine. Her eyes narrowed, and more blood overflowed over her bottom lip, like a dark waterfall.

And then, knowing we'd both lost and deciding, with one mind, that each of us had to have the last word, our fingers tightened in each other's flesh and we moved at the same time, yanking back with the innards of each other's throats in our hands. The disgusting innards slid through my fingers, slipping down to drop in sickening globs to the concrete below. I watched in horror as the remains of my own neck did the same through Power's hand. Our eyes met, something accepting yet defiant lurking between us.

We ripped each other's throats out, and collapsed, chest to chest, to the floor.

Chapter 38

It surprised me when my swollen eyes actually opened, greeted by the rather depressing, grungy sight of the dilapidated ceiling. Black mold spread across several cracked tiles, bringing out my inner prissiness as I screwed my face up in disgust, first thing. Oxygen flooded my starved lungs in the next second, and my chest inflated greedily, sucking in as much air as I could. My neck hurt, bolts of aching pain shooting through the delicate skin there. For a moment, I wondered if Power had somehow ripped my throat out in physical form also, but the memories of Shilling's hands around my neck resolved my inner concerns about that.

The violent banging sound coming from the exit door seemed more frantic than before, accompanied by the rattling of loose screws and jarring echoes of each impact. The sound nearly went unnoticed by my ears, it'd been going on for so long.

My head flopped to the side, my blurred vision clearing more bit by bit, until everything slid mainly into focus. The shining black blobs a few feet away from my face connected to a taller column blob of white. I blinked hard, forcing clarity in my sights. The blobs sharpened, revealing polished black shoes and a long white doctor's coat.

Shilling. How could I have forgotten that I hadn't won the last round? Of course, I hadn't killed him. I'd been weak and unsure of myself. A new sense of confidence surged through my veins, leaving no room for the usual timidness and uncertainty I always seemed to find myself dwelling in. My eyes flicked up, taking note that he no longer faced me. Garbled, unclear words poured from his lips as he threatened Marcie, who cowered in the corner while screaming her lungs out. He had no idea I was alive still.

A slow smile spread over my chapped lips.

My senses returned to me, hazy at first but sharpening quickly, as I rose to my feet. Marcie's lone eye darted to me, wide and terrified. I lifted my pointer finger to my lips, pressing it there and shaping my lips to form the universal, "shhh" sign. Her alert stare returned to Shilling, who laughed at her quakes and whimpers. I imagined his blood pouring through my fingers, a single fatal slice to his jugular. A pleased moan caught in my throat, only stopped by the knowledge that I had to keep my silent advantage secret.

Despite the situation, I took a moment to assess the strange sensations coursing through my body. Where I'd always felt weak and flighty before, only a sense of determination and duty remained, driving me with a defiant force that settled foreign to my very soul. My bones seemed heavier, anchoring my willpower down to a solid desire to complete my mission, my purpose.

"Kill them all," the scarred man had said. While I still struggled to fully comprehend what "all" encompassed, a strong instinct making itself at home in my body screamed at me, not to obey necessarily, but that his words had been right.

My brow furrowed as I fought to understand the new way my body and mind seemed to be acting. To obey and endure, my motto, my way of life, seemed so unbelievably wrong now in the midst of what replaced that tried and decidedly untrue aphorism. A newly formed intuition led me, whispering in my ear to observe and act. Make my own decisions, and rely on myself. Trust myself, like I did on the trapeze or the tightrope. I needed no safety nets to perform, and I needed no safety net to live.

"You'll die here," Shilling hissed, stalking toward Marcie, the bone saw gripped tight in his hand. "Your corpse will be here forever, and when your snob of a mother asks about you, we'll just tell her you and your new friend Kate sneaked away, never to be seen again after your mysterious escape. You see her dead body?" he continued, gesturing back at me without turning to see me. Marcie glanced up into my unwavering eyes, searching for reassurance and safety through her uncertainty. "Your's will be just like it, in this room forever."

Something glinted off the blood soaked blade in his hand, the smalled refraction of light. But, from what? My eyes narrowed as I made a quick search of the walls and ground, trying to find what could have possibly retained its shine in this dank place.

There.

I honed in on the jagged shard of relatively clean glass. The window, I mused, looking back up at the only source of glass I knew of on the entire floor. The cool breeze easing into the room confirmed my suspicions. Somewhere in the tussle between Marcie and Shilling, the window had been shattered. My chapped lips split, stinging, and bled a little as they spread into a satisfied smirk.

Marcie's lone frightened eye popped back and forth between me and the doctor, not knowing what to do or how to save herself. Was that what I looked like in my own insecurities? Was that why Marcie and I had bonded? Because, deep down, we were both clueless and terrified to act of our own volition? No wonder Power had been infinitely frustrated by me, unless we were soaring through the air under the Big Top. In the few short moments I took to examine the area directly around her alone, my mind gathered up at least three ways for her to at least try to save herself, yet she either failed to see them or was too scared to act on them.

Again, I caught my friend's eye and lifted my pointer finger to my mouth, maintaining that eye contact as I stooped to grasp the vaguely triangular shard of grimy glass.

"You'll be okay," I mouthed to her, unfolding myself back to my full height, the sharp edges cutting the flesh of my hand and allowing bright red blood to escape and drip from my fingers. It seemed my body was bound and determined to bleed in some way, as if it felt a need to add more gore to the already gruesome thirteenth floor so I'd fit in somewhat.

Perhaps out of habit, I waited for Power to give me the go-ahead to attack while Shilling continued to taunt Marcie, not catching on to her obvious split attention in his glory and pride filled dialogue. But, her voice never rose up from the depths of my mind, and when I closed my eyes and reached back into the recesses, I found nothing. No wall. No chair. No Power. Her presence, which I could normally pinpoint somewhere inside myself, simply did not exist. I searched her out, digging deep inside my head, checking every crevice and corner.

Nothing.

Had I succeeded? Had I truly gotten rid of her? She'd ripped my throat from me at the same time I had hers.

Was that to blame for my newfound confidence? Had I-? Had we-?

I shook the inner monologue from my head, focusing on the real and now. I had all the time in the world to figure it out later. For now, I just had to survive, and that meant taking down Shilling in any way I could. Not by running, but by fighting.

I took a silent step closer to him, shooting a warning look to Marcie as I raised the jagged shard high above my head, ready to plunge it into his throat and make our escape. My arms thrusted down, ready to all but lob his still gloating head off.

It was the eardrum shattering, metal on metal, crash from down the hall that startled me, making me flinch mid-swing and miss Shilling entirely. The screeching sound echoed all the way down the hall, inflicting obnoxious pain straight through my ears.

Shilling spun around, his face a picture of rage and his body tensed likewise, only for it all to halt for a split second when his eyes landed on me. His eyebrows shot nearly into his hairline, where beads of sweat pooled, ready to drip down his purpling face. The three of us stood at a shocked and confused, paralyzed state for several seconds before I shook out of it first. I no longer had the element of surprise, but I would not lose my chance for me and Marcie to escape Rosenton once and for all. The blood coated glass in my hands reflected in his eyeglasses, casting an eerily rose tinted glow across them, as I lifted my arms to swing at him again.

Footsteps fell heavy outside the room, their paces frantic and halting, as if looking through other rooms. The owners of the feet yelled at each other, or maybe out to the thirteenth floor in general, but I couldn't understand the words through my determination to end all the horrors of this godforsaken institute once and for all. My peripherals disappeared, granting me tunnel vision and the conviction to finish the job.

"Kate! Where are you?!" That voice, I recognized instantly. Shilling's head swiveled from the weapon in my hand to the doorway, searching for the owner of the voice, no doubt thinking it was his lucky break. I threw him a meaningful sneer before whirling around, hiding the glass blade in the folds of my threadbare skirt, and sidestepping diagonally to put space between us and keep him in my returning peripheral sights at the same time. The last thing I needed was to give him the opportunity to use his own blade on me from behind. I was no longer that stupid. If only Power could see me now. Assuming my suspicions were correct, anyway.

It was John who appeared in the barrier free doorway first, but it was the polished silver pistol in his hand, aimed at Shilling within a half a second of his arrival, that held my attention.

A gun.

A gun. Where on God's green earth had John gotten a gun in this place? My breath hitched and the bloodied glass shard dropped from my hand, clattering to the floor and skidding a foot or two away. Fear coiled around my chest like a boa constrictor. I didn't know myself to be afraid of guns, but then again, I'd never actually knowingly been so close to one. Guns were powerful, much more so than a puny knife or switchblade. Robbie had kept a gun in his trailer for years, just in case, but I'd never seen it. It was as if a whole new level had been introduced into this sick game. Despite my new fear, though, I sighed in relief at the fact that the gun was being used on my side of the fight, and not Shilling's.

George followed up behind John, taking in the scene with a cool indifference, as if it were just part of whatever nonexistent job he had. If anything, the slight tilt at the corner of his lips and the easy way he leaned against the doorway led me to believe he found the situation amusing. He looked over the room quickly, taking in all the details, and if I knew him at all, he was likely coming up with his own plan aside from whatever one he and John had concocted to get up here.

A strangled sob erupted out from behind me, jerking my attention away from my rescuers and back to my mangled friend, still cowering on the floor like an abused, broken china doll. That single moment, which also grabbed John and George's focus, proved to be just enough time for the power play in the room to flip for the worse. So quickly that I felt utterly dumbfounded for a moment as everyone made their reactionary movements, the room burst into a flurry of activity. Then, as fast as it had happened, it froze. Everyone except me had moved in some way, and, as if my body was stuck on a delayed setting, I was the only one who dared move after everyone else froze. My aching, yet numb, feet twisted slowly, turning my body as I studied the new situation we'd found ourselves in.

Marcie stood ramrod stiff, fingers on both of her hands twitching and making panicky fists. Tears ran down her face, clear and salty on one side and ruby red on the other. One of Shilling's thick arms wound its way across the top of her forehead, pressing it back against his chest and exposing her porcelain throat to the bone saw he held up to that fragile skin with his other white knuckled and trembling hand.

"Don't you dare," I snapped, the fury simmering in my stomach making me nauseous. No, not fury. That word sat awkward on my tongue. Maybe it was fear? But, I'd never felt this way about fear before. Fear was debilitating, wasn't it? I couldn't be this calm, not when I was scared. It simply wasn't how my very essence worked.

My surprise took a voluntary back seat, making way for my attention to be cast on George's lithe form receding back into the shadows, skulking the perimeter of the room until he came to a stop in the corner closest to Shilling and Marcie. The corner she'd stooped in only moments before, prior to the power exchange. I looked to John, receiving an almost motionless nod of his head, letting me in on the rather haphazard plan. I brought my attention back to the doctor before the fuming psychopath could catch on.

"Where is Paul?" Shilling demanded, hugging Marcie's stiff body closer to his chest, the blade of his weapon barely grazing her neck. A thin stream of blood dripped down, revealing exactly how sharp the blade was. He could end her life in half a second if we didn't play by his rules, at least for now.

I glanced back at John, wondering if he'd seen Paul's corpse already. I doubted very much that the other residents had been lucid enough to dispose of the body. He looked away, answering my question. Did he think I'd done that to him? I'd snapped his neck with my bare hands? Surely he knew the likelihood of that was slim to none.

After all, I seemed to prefer slitting to snapping.

"Where?!" Shilling yelled. A thick sweaty sheen coated his face, leaving his gold framed glasses to slip down his nose. He didn't bother to readjust them. Marcie whimpered again in his grip, muttering pleas and prayers as she shook, doing her best to angle her head away from the bone saw.

"I don't know," I lied, straightening my shoulders, taking control of the spiraling situation before it got worse. His face flashed a dark crimson, furthering his anger.

"Tell me where my son is or I'll lob her head off and play baseball with it! What have you done with him?!"

The distant odor of smoke wafting into my flared nostrils nearly made me miss what he'd said, and when the realization settled in, I blinked stupidly.

Son?

Shilling's face transformed, swelling and darkening into a deep plum color as we failed to provide him with an answer. The only answer we had meant certain death for Marcie, where his ignorance of his son's death gave us a chance, even if hopelessly small.

He laughed then, shaking his head, as if scolding himself. "Like a herd of violent lunatics would care about another person! How stupid of me!"

I always thought that the bad guy in stories would give some warning before acting on his intentions. In books, they always seem to give ample time for the hero to reverse the situation at the climax, rescuing the damsel and leaving the villain as a loser, with nothing to show for his intricate evil plans. There was always some sort of big speech, where the bad guy told the good guy about how he'd never win, and that speech was always the deciding factor.

I realized, as Marcie's decapitated head dropped to the ground in front of her body, that those speeches were made when the villain thought he'd won. He was full of pride and glory, never thinking he could lose anything. Maybe our biggest mistake was letting him believe, for a second, that his son, his equally insane son, was lost.

I dropped to my knees, mouth gaping at the horror in front of me.

An impossibly loud pop exploded, echoing in the room and leaving me temporarily deafened with its volume.

Marcie's headless body fell to its knees, in an almost identical mirror image of what I'd done only a nanosecond before. It slopped to the side, useless and lifeless, landing in a heap on top of her detached head. From beneath her own bosom, Marcie's face stared out at me, her face filled with the instant terror of recognizing her own death. Platinum, ratty hair spilled from under her torso, tangling in her twitching fingers until those, too, stopped moving.

The ringing in my ears faded, leaving room to hear the horrific screams tearing themselves from my throat. The sound of anguish. Of disbelief. Of hysteria. My throat went raw as each scream of denial ripped from my esophagus, and they only paused when every last molecule of air had been banished from my lungs, and I had to inhale another searing breath to start the screams all over again.

I had failed.

Chapter 39

My screams echoed off the walls, intensifying until they all melted into one horrifying, never ending cry that sounded as through it were bleeding, seeping from the pores of the walls themselves. Shilling's body crashed to the ground beside Marcie's, a single circle of fresh blood bubbling at his temple, where the bullet from George's gun had exploded into his skull.

My arms wrapped around my middle, squeezing my stomach as if causing myself pain would erase what had been done. Erase the empty, yet hopeless, eyes in Marcie's detached head from looking at me from under her own body. When that didn't work, my fingers wound themselves in my hair, tangling in the strands and yanking at the roots as every pain filled scream left my throat more and more raw. My body rocked, unable to cope. Unable to breathe.

I failed. I didn't save her. She was dead. I'd let her life end in terror, in fear, when all she deserved was to find peace and happiness. What had I done? What had I become?

The word, "no" parted my lips, leaping from my tongue out into the open air over and over between guttural screams of denial.

The world around me shattered, cracking and falling apart in great chunks, which whirled around me like a chaotic cyclone before stopping and dropping to my feet. Only for me to look up, hoping to see I'd imagined it all, and see her body, her head, laying there again, looking at me with such utter despair and disappointment that the whole thing started over again. The shattering, the tornado, the stillness, and the realization, forever on loop behind my eyes.

Two pairs of rough hands clasped around my arms, jerking me to my feet. My knees refused to cooperate, and I found myself hunched over, being carried between John and George, my arms stretched out across John's left shoulder and George's right one as the arm attached to each of those shoulders supported my waist. Both men's necks felt slick with sweat, and when my head lolled to the side, landing on the hollow between John's neck and chest, the sharp, acrid odor of smoke choked my lungs.

"Go. We can calm her down outside. Just go!" George snapped, forcing the three of us forward, toward the door they had somehow broken down. My body jerked in the direction they moved, John's hot breath colliding with my greasy hair and sending it flying every few seconds. The two men hauled me out, but something in me snapped to attention as we crossed the threshold to the stairwell. I panicked, twisting in their grips until I faced the thirteenth floor again.

"We can't leave them! We can't leave her!" I cried, shoving myself past them. My foot barely touched the grimy floor before they restrained me again, pressing forward until we reached the first set of stairs. Black fog rose from the lower levels, alarming my already panicked brain.

"What's going on? We have to free them! We have to let everyone know they can escape now! We can't leave them there to die!"

John shoved me against the far wall, holding me hostage as I screamed and protested.

"We can't do anything for them, Kate," he whispered, his face so close our noses brushed. Sadness, such deep sadness, emanated from his searching eyes that I stopped struggling, and tears cascaded from my eyes in thick waterfalls down my cheeks. "None of them will survive out there. No one will help them, or believe them. Didn't you see the emptiness in their eyes? It's been over for them for a long time. They're not human anymore, and we don't have time to get them all out. The building is about to collapse."

"But, Marcie-"

George pulled John back, glaring at me from beside him. "Marcie is dead. Her body is of no importance anymore. What do you expect to do? Bring her decapitated head to her mother for a proper burial? Don't be stupid."

I shook my head, squeezing my eyes shut as I sobbed. "No! No, we have to try! We have to... We have to..."

"What, Kate?!" George yelled, shoving John aside to take his place in front of me. "We have to what?! They're all dead and have been for a long time, and unless you cut the crap and get your act together, we will be too, and it will be your fault for keeping us here with your idiotic hero complex!" His spittle sprayed across my face, mixing with the tears. Rage like a roaring fire glowed in his eyes, his fingers bruising my shoulders where he gripped them, as if to prove his point.

"He's right. We need to leave before we're trapped. We have to go, now," John added, prying George away, his voice much softer and plying. An elaborate, unplanned game of good cop, bad cop, I supposed. Either way, it worked. Either sensing my submission or simply taking advantage of my pause in fighting against them, they pulled me away from the wall and began hauling me and my useless, trembling legs to the staircase again.

What started as uncomfortable, bad smelling gray fog quickly transformed into unbreathable, eye burning, hot, pitch black walls of opaque smoke the closer we got to the ground floor. John tugged off his shirt halfway down and held it to my mouth, a desperate attempt to keep me breathing, even if he didn't. Heat, impossibly scorching heat, singed my skin, fueling our rush to get out of the building.

It wasn't until we rushed through the door to the bottom floor that I saw the actual fire. Tongues of fluorescent orange and yellow flames licked at the walls, peeling the paint, melting the cheap furnishings, and engulfing the structural beams of the building. I stopped in my tracks, even as if felt as though daggers were digging themselves into my stinging eyes, and took in the scene. Giant, gaping holes littered the ground floor ceiling, the fire eating away at everything it touched. Beams crashed to the ground, forcing me back to the very real, very important reality.

John and George guided me through the inferno. The sharp, threatening cracks and pops of the flames taunted my ears, dancing in and out of my limited vision. We hunched low, already desperate for any single molecule of oxygen for our burning lungs. White hot embers scalded the exposed flesh around my arms and legs, and I was instantly grateful that the two men had thought to carry me through, instead of exposing my bare feet to the furnace-hot floor. I watched as black flakes of scorched material landed on John's bare arms, searing into the tanned skin. He kept moving as if he didn't even feel the pus filled blisters forming.

It seemed like the once short pathway from the stairwell door to the giant double doors at the entrance took centuries to get to. As soon as we crashed through the threshold to the fresh, clear outside world, though, my lungs exploded with the clean air. Coughs wracked all three of our chests, and the three of us forced ourselves to keep going, only allowing ourselves to collapse at the end of the winding dirt driveway. In all my time at Rosenton, I'd never stepped foot from the front doors onto the front lawn and driveway. The fact that something so close was so unfamiliar made me feel like I'd stepped into a whole new world. I was an alien to this new planet.

"You got her!" The Mexican accent told me of Esther's presence, even though my eyes were in far too much pain to see anything past the desperate watering of my tear ducts in an effort to clear the smoke residue from them. Two thin arms wrapped around me, pulling me up off the ground. "Thank God! Oh, thank God!" she cried, before uttering more exclamations in Spanish that I couldn't possibly follow.

I wheezed, my lungs still aching for the clean night air, and Esther released me, stepping back.

"Where's Marcie?" Lottie asked, somewhere to my right. My throat ached for water, begging past the sharp agony the strangulation, raw screams, and smoke inhalation had gifted me.

"Dead," George replied, his own voice thick with smoky pain. Even so, he managed to sound just as cold and unaffected as usual.

Silence permeated the air after that, whether as a silent tribute to our deceased friend or because they truly had nothing to say, I didn't know. After a while, when the pain in my lungs receded from pure agony to just bearable, I broke the quietness.

"Ed?" I rasped, barely able to vocalize that one simple syllable.

No one answered me for a moment, just long enough for me to wonder if they understood what I'd asked through the rough quality of my voice.

"He's enjoying himself, once last time," George replied, struggling to form each and every word.

"He locked all the doors from the stairwell except the thirteenth floor and our floor before the fire. No one will get out, except us," Lottie elaborated, a sad lilt to her tone that instantly filled my stomach with yet another pit of dread.

"No..." I breathed, letting more tears fall, dripping onto the light dirt to make tiny darkened circles of mud. How could we lose two? Just to save me? How many people would have to die so I survived? How many people that I cared about would be killed so brutally?

"Robbie said he'll be here with the car by ten. It's nine-forty-five, now," Esther said, changing the subject. I'd have to wait to properly mourn my friends. Waves of heat warmed our backs as Rosenton burned. Screams of the other patients filled my ears, making me cry out in frustration. Why?! Why couldn't they have been released, too? I dropped back to my knees, slamming my hands over my ears, while I sobbed for the souls inside. Was it possible that I was beginning to hate my friends? The people who'd been my everything for nearly a year? How could they just abandon all those people? Never give them a chance? Why did no one deserve life to them?

John's sweating hand found mine, clasping his fingers between my knuckles and pulling them to his lips to plant tiny, consoling kisses on them. I allowed the action, but couldn't bring myself to look at him.

"They couldn't be saved, Kate," he whispered, and the sorrow in his voice let me know he at least hated it as much as I did. "Shilling had taken everything from them. They were dead inside already. He made sure of it. Remember how he broke them all? How he made sure they could never function without him? Just walking zombies, only a scalpel away from becoming just like the ones on the thirteenth floor. This was a mercy to them."

His words, meant to be comforting, weren't. I wasn't entirely convinced those on the thirteenth floor couldn't be saved. I glanced up, through painfully blurred eyes, at the thirteenth floor. Flames crawled from the windows, climbing higher and higher.

Kill them all.

My breath caught in my throat, and I began hacking again, wheezing for air between coughs. John rubbed my back, leaning his head against my collarbone, obviously exhausted.

Kill them all.

This was what the scarred man had meant. He knew. How did he know? Was that even possible? Had his state of constant torture given him some kind of near death prophetic powers? Or...

My eyes drifted over to George. I couldn't see, but I felt his gaze land on me. Had he known the scarred man? Had he told them of their plan, somehow?

Kill them all. Mercy killing. Dead inside already. Empty shells.

The scarred man had known, and he'd been at peace with it, even advocated it. The world spun around me. That instinct, the new instinct that had taken hold of my body and mind, affirmed it. I could never know this was the best thing or even an okay thing, and I'd never be at peace with so many deaths on my hands, but something... Seeing the confidence, the go-ahead in the scarred man's command. It took that jagged, broken glass edge that shredded my heart to pieces off.

Shilling had told me that Ward F was the only ward whose residents had any hope the very first time we'd met. And only days before, he'd told me, again, that our ward was different. We were aware. Was that the deciding factor? The stone that tipped the balance in our favor? I sniffled, wiping my sooty hand across my nose as the sobs continued. I'd never know for sure. I'd never have peace over what had happened tonight.

"Robbie has a place for us. It's an old, abandoned mining town. We can start over, and forget all of this," Lottie piped up as the screams coming from the burning building began to fade. It seemed George was rubbing off on her, considering her lack of care for the people still dying inside the building. "That box of chocolates, the one you went crazy over, it had the details and a couple keys on a piece of paper under a false bottom. John found it just before he met with Robbie. He knew you wouldn't have been so worked up over nothing. You should have seen him ripping that box apart, Kate."

I'm sure if it'd have been under different circumstances, when my life hadn't cost hundred of people theirs, I would have felt relieved or eager to begin anew. I would have smiled, or began chattering about plans for our new life of freedom and hope. But, I couldn't sync that elated feeling with the awful guilt and depression over the people dying, burning to death, inside Rosenton.

As a pitch black car rolled toward us from the secluded road ahead, I stared at Rosenton Home for the Criminally Insane and wept, praying their souls would at least rest in peace, even if their bodies couldn't.

I wished so desperately to say I breathed a sigh of relief that it was all finally over. Reality, though, was far different than my wishes. Tires crunched the few small rocks closer to us. Robbie hopped out of the car before it even stopped moving and engulfed me in an embrace so tight my rips popped and shifted. Wet, fat tears rolled down his face, landing on my shoulder as he expressed his thankfulness. Before long, John joined the hug, adding more tears, that he'd never admit to creating, to my tattered dress. Esther came next, followed shortly by Lottie. George waited much longer, but in the end joined the massive cluster of sobbing, wailing bodies, if only to act as the sole dry pair of eyes in the group.

We disentangled only to file into the sleek car, squeezing into the seats. I paused, the last to remain outside the car. Was this real? Had all of it actually happened? Would I really have to hold on to this for the rest of my life?

Rosenton caught my eye again. Power was gone, another body to add the to casualties of this place, leaving this strange sense of wholeness in my chest that hadn't been there before. As the screams died out completely, signaling the end of all life inside the hell house asylum, that new instinct nudged at my guilt, reminding me of the way Power would push me into things with her snippy reprimands.

I felt no peace over what had happened, but instinct told me it'd been the only way out. The only way for my friends to survive. The only way for no one to ever be committed to Rosenton ever again. The only way for Shilling to never hurt another soul.

That was as close to peace as I knew I'd ever get.

I slid down into the front passenger seat and closed the door. Robbie asked me something, but I couldn't make out the words. I only heard my own silent prayers for the unfortunate inmates that never had a chance.

Epilogue

Bacon sizzled on the stove, the hot grease popping and hitting my knuckles in tiny specks. I stirred the scrambled eggs in the skillet on the opposite burner, grinning to myself while I hummed along to the new song on the radio. Heavy boots stepped along the wooden floor behind me. Floors that had taken four months of the two years since Rosenton had burned to the ground to repair and make sturdy. Luckily, the old mining town Robbie had secured for the five of us was several states away and had only been recently abandoned due to emptied mines. According to him, the workers had been so convinced that the mines would produce for decades that they'd built lives for their families by them, only for the shafts to run dry in a few short years, forcing the families to uproot and move where money could be made again. We'd only had to make minor repairs to most of the houses, but electricity and running water and gas had been a tricky affair to orchestrate. They'd required falsified documents that hid us from anything to do with the Rosenton fire.

Those documents were what John and I had used to marry, only a couple months after our escape. I suppose going through something as harrowing as what we'd seen at Rosenton really put how short life was into perspective, and we wasted no time dancing around what we already knew we wanted. We even had our first date the day after the courthouse wedding, and we hadn't looked back since.

George and Lottie had remained close. Too close for my liking, but Lottie was a stubborn girl who still believed with all her heart that George hung the moon and stars. He preferred it that way, and manipulated her with a scary excellence into all but worshipping him. I suspected he'd twisted her mind and abused it so much that she truly thought she couldn't live without him, but our position in life was already so precarious that none of us dared to rock the barely floating boat. Instead, Esther, John. and I came to the unspoken agreement that we'd leave them be unless he hurt her or she became unhappy. So far, neither had happened. Lottie seemed content to be his shadow, his pet, and to give all of herself for him. It broke my heart, but I was too chicken to talk to her about it. Something I knew I'd regret in my later years, but just couldn't seem to make myself act on it. I rationalized it by telling myself he'd helped her beat anorexia, and that she was a young girl still, only sixteen to his eighteen, and she would see him for what he was in time, and then we could support any decision she made from there.

I hadn't heard a peep from Power, nor felt or seen her presence since that fateful day either. I'd come to a strange, unexplainable understanding, though, that somehow my defiance and willingness to kill her had somehow melted her essence into mine. I'd gone over the logistics in my head too many times to count, laying awake at night, trying to figure out exactly what had happened to her, to me. The Hyde to my Jekyl had disappeared, but had she really? I couldn't express the sensation to John, though God knew I tried, but the fact was that I could actually feel all the things I hadn't felt before. Things like confidence, defiance, and fearlessness, which had only manifested through Power or performance before, finally appeared within my own mental capabilities. Even better, the pieces of Old Kate, the timidness, kindness, and cautiousness, seemed to balance our the intensity of those newer emotions, and vice versa. I was made whole, without even knowing I wasn't whole before.

"Smells good," John said, leaning on the counter on the other side of the hot stove. He smiled at me, drumming his fingers against the cream tiles. They'd originally been white, but both of us had decided we'd seen enough white interiors to last ten lifetimes, and had promptly changed them out.

"That's because it is good," I said, shooting my own grin back at him. He leaned down and pecked my cheek just as the sound of tiny, barefoot feet padded their way into the kitchen. John walked over, picking our son up and hoisting the babbling one year old onto his hip. A wet, slobbery hand plopped itself on John's forehead, making him screw up his face in disgust.

"That's pretty gross, there, son," he said, swiping at the drool slimed across his head and wiping it back on the boy's bib. Anthony giggled and squirmed to be let down.

"What do you want for lunch?" I asked, scooping out a small portion of eggs onto a saucer for Anthony. John came up beside me, filling a plate for each of us as I picked the toddler up and secured him in his high chair.

"Whatever you feel like making is fine with me," he replied, waiting for me to sit at the table before taking his own place. His impeccable manners were ingrained to his very soul, it seemed, and it made him all the more endearing to me.

We ate our breakfast in a peaceful silence, the morning birds chirping outside the window above the sink. Anthony mimicked the sounds, making both John and I chuckle a few times. Later, after John rinsed his dish, kissed the two of us on the forehead, and headed out to work the back garden before it got too hot, I washed the remaining dishes and began the process of tidying up the bedrooms. Anthony followed close behind, dragging a wooden wheeled horse on a rope lead, chattering up a storm as I worked. I pretended to converse with him, throwing in the occasional shocked face just for the giggles it solicited from my son.

The shrill ringing of the phone interrupted my progress. I froze, unsure what the sound was for a moment. We never received calls, only made them. It could only have been a wrong number, I decided, and ignored the foreign sounding noise. Anthony tugged on my pant leg, whining with that certain tint of worry toddlers often used when they needed reassurance against the unfamiliar. I picked him up and kissed him, explaining the phone, and what the ringing meant.

It calmed him until it began ringing again, just a few short minutes after it had stopped. This time, he cried, fat tears welling in his brown eyes as he held his arms up for me to hold him again. I hoisted him up and made my way to the living room, where the telephone vibrated with the obnoxious ringing noise. I picked it up mid-ring, cradling it between my shoulder and ear while readjusting Anthony on my hip.

"Hello?" I greeted, unable to hide the wary note in my voice.

Static filled the line for a second before, "Kate?"

My spine straightened, and I felt every ounce of resolve in my body surge forward, ready to defend the life we'd made.

"Who is this?" I demanded.

"It's Robbie." My body sagged with relief first, then straightened again in surprise.

"Robbie! Where have you been? I haven't heard from you in over a year!" My legs gave way, letting me sink into the couch, placing Anthony on the floor to play as I grasped the receiver tightly in both hands, desperate to hear my brother's voice.

"I'm so sorry," he started, sighing. "I know I should have contacted you sooner, but I was sorting things out. Things you need to know about now."

My heart raced in my chest, pounding against my ribcage. "What? What do you mean?"

A crinkling noise resounded from his end, making me think he was likely changing position in a chair or something similar. "Never mind for now. How are you? I've missed you."

"Fine, Robbie. Everything is great. You have a nephew, and I think I'm going to have another. I'll find out soon. Life is as perfect as it can get. Please tell me whatever you're going to say isn't going to ruin that." The words spilled out in a clumsy rush. I was too eager to get the pleasantries out of the way and find out what he called for. What had made him reappear after vanishing without a way to contact him so long ago.

"I'm an uncle?" he asked, the awe shining in his voice. I could visualize the grin on his face, and it eased my anxiety a little bit. "That's great. I guess I should let you know you're an aunt, too, huh?"

"That's fantastic! Is that why you left?" I pried, teetering between excitement of the news and frustration that he hadn't gotten to the point yet.

"No, no. That-that just happened in a whirlwind, really. Do you remember the receptionist? Ellie? We've been married for a while now. Just shortly after you and John, actually."

"You couldn't call and tell me?" I couldn't help the snippy tone. As happy as I felt to hear from him, I couldn't help but want to smack him for letting me worry he was dead on the street somewhere for so long.

"I'm sorry. I should have. I've just been knee deep in some other things. That's what I needed to talk to you about, though. Just listen to me before speaking, okay?"

My lips pursed and I nodded before realizing he couldn't see me. "Alright," I replied, squeezing my free hand into a tight fist. He inhaled over the line, as if he was nervous and wanted to get it all out in one breath.

"We're brother and sister, Kate."

"I know that," I couldn't help but interject.

"Hush, now. I mean it. Don't say anything until I'm done, or I'll never get it all out."

"Okay, okay. Go."

"We're not adopted brother and sister. We're blood related. Well, halfway, at least. My dad was your dad, too. I've always known. He told me before he died. But, I didn't know if it was the craziness his mind had after the accident talking, or if he was telling the truth. So, I didn't say anything until I had proof. I found that proof last week. Both our birth certificates. Pictures of him and a woman who looks almost identical to you. A woman I barely remember from when I was a kid. Documents where he searched you out for years before finding you at that orphanage. I don't know what happened, but you're a blood Jensen. Or, you were, anyway, before you became a Kingwood." Robbie chuckled at his poor joke, but I found I couldn't breathe.

"How?" I breathed, unable to raise my voice above a disbelieving whisper. My son toddled around the couch, shrieking in joy in the background as he banged around on something I couldn't find myself to be concerned about.

"I don't know. I don't know what happened, or why you got put up for adoption, or even what happened to your mom. I just knew I couldn't let anything happen to you in that place."

I swallowed, remembering the letter from my mother I'd found years before. Her name was Evelyn, and she had spoke straight out about knowing she'd be dead before ever meeting me. Pieces began to fall into their slots, forming a puzzle that slowly revealed the bigger picture. Robbie was the older brother she talked about. Robbie had told me once that his mother had died in childbirth. Had his father married my mother, then? What had happened afterward that had left her incarcerated, though? Would I ever know?

"That's why you felt so bad. That's why you forgave me so easily," I whispered, struggling to keep track of all the new information whizzing around my head.

"Sort of. I meant it when I said I should have been on top of all those things happening to you as your ringmaster. I should have never been in the dark. I'll never forgive myself for that. Even more so when I knew you were really my sister and I'd sworn to my dad - our dad - that I'd always protect you."

"You know my actions were not your fault, Robbie. It was-"

"We'll never agree on that, Kate. Let's drop it. Anyway, I have other news, too..."

My eyes squeezed shut, and my chest ached, unsure if I could take any more surprises in one day. "What?" I asked, preparing myself for the worst.

Robbie paused, and I got the distinct impression that he was gathering the courage to speak again, as if whatever he said next was even more important than the revelation about our family's secrets. I sucked in my breath and held it, unashamedly terrified of whatever he would say next.

"I've bought all the equipment from Jensen and Sons back. I'm the heir, but I can't ever be a ringmaster again. You're the next in line. Jensen and Sons is yours. You're the new ringmaster."

www.ingramcontent.com/pod-product-compliance
Lightning Source LLC
Chambersburg PA
CBHW060753210726
48292CB00013B/70

* 9 7 8 1 9 3 0 1 1 2 7 4 2 *